GW00708373

American Rebel

JOSS GIBSON

ALTO PICO

First published in Great Britain 2012
by Alto Pico
Copyright © Joss Gibson 2012
This book is copyrighted under the Berne Convention
No reproduction in any form without prior permission
All rights reserved

American Rebel is a work of fiction, pure and simple. Although inspired by real events and real lives, this is a work of imagination and as such makes no claim to historical or objective truth, nor is any infringement of the rights of individuals, living or dead, intended in any way. See Author's Note for more information.

ISBN-13: 978-0-9573388-0-7

Rights enquiries for all media should be directed to the publishers Alto Pico
www.altopico.com

For background to the story, including photographs, illustrations and authentic FBI reports from the time, visit
www.americanrebelonline.com

Author's blog
jossgibson.blogspot.co.uk

Twitter
@jossauthor

The Production Team

Illustrator	Jeremy Jones
Editorial Consultant	Julia Mannfolk
Cover Design	Igor Boskov
Legal Advisor	Daniel N. Steven
Copy Editor	Sarah Cheeseman
Online Designer	Alex Jollands
Spanish Editor	Nick Kyte

For Pamela and Madeleine,

and for

Megan and Leah

ACKNOWLEDGEMENTS

When American Rebel first began to take shape twenty-five years ago, the idea was born of pure serendipity. I love secondhand books and bookshops. One day, I stumbled across William Morgan's name in a book called *Cuba: An American Tragedy* by Robert Scheer and Maurice Zeitlin, published in 1964 by Penguin. There was only a paragraph or so about Morgan, but with tantalizing hints of an intriguing story. I was hooked.

With little in the way of hard facts to go on, I wrote a screenplay based on Morgan's rise and fall, told from the point of view of an invented journalist named Calvin Towne. Granada Films picked up the screenplay and Leigh Jackson came on board as co-writer. For a few months, we raced to meet editorial deadlines, only for the project to be dropped when Sydney Pollack's *Havana*, starring Robert Redford, failed to ignite audiences at the box office.

For some years, the story sat on the back burner. When circumstances allowed a concentrated period of writing, I found myself drawn once again to the tale of Morgan's spectacular rise and tragic fall, finding in the story a series of contradictions and conundrums, a poignancy, the seeds of a comic book adventure, a moral tale, even a certain mythic quality. It was a fascinating mix, but still I struggled to shape a narrative that would satisfy my desire to do more than tell a simple tale of derring-do, to dramatize the facts. I wanted more.

New files from the CIA and FBI became publicly and easily accessible, not least because so many years had passed. Eyewitness accounts and news stories emerged, adding color and background to the bare facts, and the jigsaw was suddenly more than just blue sky pieces that all looked the same. Latinamericanstudies.org provided a superb visual resource and well-documented archive of news material and internal US government communications. An article in the online Havana Journal by Christopher Goodwin, entitled *La Revolucion's William Morgan, Eloy Gutierrez Menoyo and the Second Front*', originally published in the London Times, presented the story in vivid terms. And Hank Alberelli's wonderfully dramatic account published as *William Morgan: Patriot or Traitor?* both tantalized and inspired.

Naturally, I continued to locate and devour any books that might even have a mention of Morgan: Che Guevara's *Reminiscences*, Lyman B. Kirkpatrick's *The Real CIA*. There was *Tocayo* by Antonio Navarro, Fidel Casto's *Memoir of Che*, Armando Valladares' searing account of his time in prison, *Against All Hope*, Victor Marchetti and John D. Marks' *The CIA and the Cult of Intelligence*, Fabian Escalante's *The Cuba Project*, Paul D. Bethel's *The Losers*, to name but a few. Morgan, if he figured at all, was still little more than a footnote, but then as Churchill had it, history tends to be written by the victors.

As I started to construct the story, I found Ray Brennan's *Castro, Cuba and Justice*, published by Doubleday in 1959. There was no mention of Morgan, but there was a sharp mind and a fine writing style, and the dust jacket photograph of a hard-bitten journalist that would help me model Ray Halliwell, my fictional journalist. My thanks are due also to the Chicago Sun Times for employing both Rays.

The more I worked on the structure—taking many elements from the old screenplay, not least my journalist Calvin Towne—the more I felt certain that only a combination of fact and fiction could reflect both the simplicity of the story—a hero's rise and fall—and the complex politics of the time, especially for new generations of readers not born when the revolution took place. Michael Colin's poignant 2004 documentary *Lost in the Shadows* helped to characterize those complexities. In the same film, a clip of Morgan live on camera, being interviewed by Klete Roberts for CBS News, presented a perfect parallel of how Morgan and Halliwell might interact. Aran Shetterly's masterful account of Morgan's life and times in *The Americano*,

Algonquin Books, 2007, proved the most valuable single source. Shetterly's work was a brilliant synthesis of story and background in documentary form. He'd done his homework and showed a passionate commitment to his subject. He even went so far as to suggest tantalizing theories regarding Morgan's demise.

Jay Mallin and Robert K. Brown's Merc *American Soldiers of Fortune*, a slim but ruthlessly efficient and exciting book, gave the whole of the second chapter over to Morgan's story. A fabulous piece of journalism, the authors presented what they knew with confidence and what they didn't know with wonderfully creative suggestion. I owe them both a great deal in terms of both story and style.

I reviewed all the material, shuffled the scene cards, sat glued to newsreels and replayed *Soy Cuba*, the Soviet-produced film of 1964, packed with devastating imagery and energy, as I wondered—where next.

I read the The Miami Herald feature stories on the battle Morgan's widow was fighting in 2007 to have Morgan's US citizenship restored. The judicial battle put the last pieces in place. I knew I had the beginnings of a story that would stand on two legs. Now I had a way to travel back in time with Ray and María, even as Morgan came forward to meet us. The next four years were spent writing that story, always conscious of my obligation to my sources, to those who lived through events described here and to those who are related to the characters in this book and protective of their memory.

This story relies on real people, many of whom are still alive. I have shamelessly used both their names and their identities as they crossed paths with Morgan and occasionally placed them where they were not to meet the needs of the story. I hope they will forgive me the liberty of doing so.

To those people, living and dead, who were there, including the brave people of Cuba, and all those dragooned by me to play their parts in bringing this story to life; to the journalists, the writers and the publications that have been of such inestimable help, I owe an enormous debt of gratitude. Thank you.

Last but not least, I would like to acknowledge the unfailing, generous and loving support of my partner, Anni. Whatever merits American Rebel may have are to her credit. Naturally, all errors and omissions are entirely the fault of the author, myself.

Joss Gibson 2012

PART ONE

For it's so clear that in order to begin to live in the present we must first redeem the past, and that can only be done by suffering, by strenuous, uninterrupted labor.

— Anton Chekhov, The Cherry Orchard

1

The ice storm raging a mile below the plane offered María Jensen the last chance of a reprieve. Flight 377 had been circling high above Chicago's O'Hare International Airport for almost an hour and María, like the other passengers, was sure they would have to divert. But just as she began to relax, the 'fasten seat belts' sign flicked on and the captain announced a window in the weather.

The plane began its descent into the thick clouds, dropping through air pockets as if bumping down stairs. María's fingers whitened as she gripped the armrests. Passengers in adjoining seats—seeing the prim, olive-skinned woman mouthing the words to a prayer—might have assumed a fear of flying. But it was not flying that scared María. Even with advancing years, she was seldom, if ever, morbid.

She was still holding on, though not as tightly, as they taxied to the terminal, and didn't finally let go until the plane stopped at the gate.

The airport bus took her to the city center where she caught a cab to the one-star Ohio House Motel. She made the driver wait while she checked in and deposited her overnight bag. María was proud of the bag, equipped with wheels and an extendable handle, yet just small enough to qualify as carry-on. New when she had started the legal proceedings, now—six months on—it was beginning to scuff at the corners.

Half an hour later, when the cab reached Michigan Avenue, she paid the driver out of her green leather purse, pulling the folded notes one by one from the change pocket, hesitating over the tip and finally settling on a dollar. The driver didn't seem impressed. He certainly didn't thank her.

As she stepped onto the sidewalk, the air wasn't quite as cold as she had expected, though she felt the skin on her face and hands tighten, adjusting from the stifling heater in the cab. Looking up and down the broad street, María noticed the gaudy Christmas baubles hanging in the bare branches of spindly black trees. She had to crane her neck to take in the thirty-story buildings in glass and steel that lined most of Madison.

It was almost four-thirty, and the light was already fading. Rain was falling and not quite freezing, steady and remorseless, turning the mounds of snow to slush. María was dressed not for the weather, but for the occasion. She wore a gray wool coat with a faux fur collar of a lighter gray that was far from waterproof and already damp. Salt and grit crunched beneath her best black heels. She pulled the flyer from her pocket and unfolded it awkwardly under the open umbrella.

The flyer advertised a book signing. The author's name, in block letters even bigger than the title, was Ray Halliwell. The picture, head and shoulders only, showed a shock of white hair, the handsome face tanned and lined. And yet, the man in the photograph was not the man she remembered. Except the eyes. The eyes were familiar. She felt her stomach churn, but there was no turning back and, with the plane's delay, time was short.

Flyer in one hand and umbrella in the other, María crossed on green at East Chicago and headed north on Michigan, just as the cab driver had instructed, making her way toward the big-chain bookshop.

2

August 1957, one a.m., half a mile off the north coast of Cuba, near the Bay of Matanzas.

William Morgan sat in the companionway to the boat's cabin, reading a Marvel Boy comic by the light of a torch and drinking steadily from a bottle of Matusalem rum. From somewhere below, a barely audible Buddy Holly tune came over the tinny transistor radio.

Without looking up from the dog-eared comic, Morgan groped for the bottle and took another swig. The rum was sickly and warm, but it would have to do until they got back to Miami and ice-cold beer. The day had been hot, mid-nineties. The long evening had hardly cooled the air at all and the night had brought no wind, not a breath.

A drip of sweat from one eyebrow hit the comic like a breaking egg. It landed on a panel showing Marvel Boy smashing his way into a nest of bad guys, liberating the serum that will save the world from a deadly virus. Morgan's mind somehow connected the drop of sweat soaking into the page with the serum, but only briefly—that kind of thinking was not his style. He turned the page.

Behind him, a haphazard pile of heavy-duty wooden crates littered the cockpit floor. There were ten boxes in all. Morgan didn't know exactly what was in them, but he could guess: Garands, ex-army MIIs, a few Thompson subs and maybe a couple of Stens—though, not being American, Stens were harder to come by. Some of the arms were working models from shady dealers on the mainland, but many were bought from more-or-less regular surplus outlets as harmless decomms intended for collectors. There was always someone willing to replace the firing pin and do a bit of machining for the right price.

Ammunition was trickier. When his three years in the Army penitentiary at Chillicothe were up and they finally cut him loose, Morgan had started as a buyer for Bartone's operation. He found out pretty quick just how hard it was to source live ammunition at all, let alone precise calibers for specific guns. This consignment, like the others he'd delivered over the past two years, would need someone skilled enough to make ramp-and-throat modifications to barrels, magazines and chambers to handle the ammunition available without jamming. But none of that was his problem—Morgan was just paid to deliver.

At the stern of the boat, Jack Turner scanned the beach and the line of palms beyond for any sign of movement.

"What exactly am I looking for?" he said over his shoulder, trying for a casual tone but missing.

Morgan had warned the younger man he'd be jumpy the first time out. He turned to see Jack gripping the guardrail as he craned forward, his foot tapping like a metronome on the teak deck. The twelve-hour trip had been hard going, what with Jack crashing around the boat, dropping things and asking dumb questions. And the nerves were only getting worse.

"You'll know when you see it," said Morgan.

"Is it always like this—the waiting?"

When Morgan was slow to answer, Jack's foot started tapping again.

"Relax," Morgan said. "Count the money. It passes the time. Here—"

Holding the rum bottle up, Morgan waggled it from side to side, keeping his nose in the comic.

"I'm good," Jack replied, as if he'd downed some already.

Morgan smiled to himself. Yeah, right.

He turned a page of the comic to see Marvel Boy let loose a deadly shower of atomic radiance from his special wristbands, but something—maybe a dull head from the booze—made him lose interest. He threw the comic onto the chart table, and pulling his bulky frame upright, he groaned and yawned, tilting his head beneath the low roof of the cabin. He flicked the radio off, then the torch, and took the three stairs to the cockpit in one. Clearing the overhang, he stretched to his full six-feet-four and walked aft to join Jack at the stern.

"What have you got?" said Morgan.

The sea was black and oily with a faint, reluctant swell, and he could just make out the flat yellow-gray strand that seemed to hold the tree line suspended above the horizon. The only sound was the occasional slap of water against the stern.

"Just the beach," said Jack.

"You smell something?" Morgan said.

Jack must have caught a whiff of smoke because his foot stopped tapping, and as he peered into the darkness, he seemed to pick out a light he hadn't noticed before.

"What is it?" Jack asked, but Morgan said nothing.

As they watched, the light seemed to dip and rise and dip again. And then it broke into two. Dark shapes were forming beneath the lights, morphing in front of their eyes. The outline of a small boat began to emerge, no longer than a skiff but narrower, more like a canoe. Then there were two, then three, then four. From beyond the random lapping of the sea against the boat came a new sound, rhythmic and human: paddles breaking the water's surface.

"Boats!" Jack hissed. "Coming this way. Are these our guys?"

All at once, the moon arched out from behind the clouds, and blue-white light swept across the water, revealing a line of four boats snaking toward them like some kind of religious procession. Men in white smocks and straw hats, their faces greasy and tanned, swaying kerosene lanterns on poles above their heads, their paddles rising and falling as if to a coxswain's chant only they could hear.

"Jesus—" Jack murmured. "Don't look much like rebels, do they?"

3

Ray Halliwell was dressed immaculately in a powder-blue suit that might have looked garish on another man. Using a display table as a desk, he was signing copies of his book for a queue of twenty or more fans while a camera team set up nearby. The shelves behind him were decked with more copies of the book, and there were posters on the walls with the same photo as on the flyer. Behind his picture—with tasteless vulgarity in Ray's opinion—were cutout images of some of America's more famous postwar enemies, from the Vietcong to al-Qaeda.

Two young PR people—a rail-thin man and a short woman wearing trendy red-rimmed glasses—buzzed nervously around the desk and the people in line, trying to hit the schedule and keep things moving.

Ray handed back a signed copy to the next in line. The skinny PR man checked his notes and crouched to whisper in Ray's ear, somehow managing to draw attention to himself while appearing to be discreet.

"PBS is pretty much there, and I know they're on a deadline. Call it five minutes, Mr. Halliwell?"

"Okay," Ray said under his breath, "but give me those five, will you?" He paused for the irritation in his voice to register.

A glimmer of understanding and the thin man backed off, suddenly interested in his file of notes. Ray turned to the next reader in line, a man about his own age.

"Hi, how are you?"

"Just fine, thank you," the man replied. "Would you mind signing to Jimmy? He's my nephew—out in Afghanistan right now."

"Of course. And tell Jimmy to come back safe. From me."

"I will, sir. Thank you."

The man took the book from Ray's hand and held it a moment. There were things he might have said written there in his eyes, but confidence failed and he moved to one side.

A twelve year old with gel-spiked blonde hair was next in line. He didn't look like someone who spent a lot of time on foreign policy, but the young sometimes caught you by surprise, especially as the years rolled on.

"This for you, son?"

"For my dad. It's Christmas."

"Yeah, I noticed," Ray said, with a wry smile. "Dad got a name?"

The boy paused in thought, then, looking pleased with himself, said, "Yeah. Mr. Daniel Atkins."

"Okay if I write 'Dan'?"

"I guess," the boy said.

Ray handed the book back. "I hope he enjoys it."

"I don't know," said the boy, "but it's cool I got it signed by somebody."

The thin man was back.

"Mr. Halliwell?"

Ray turned and glared at him as the next in line—a woman who looked to be in her sixties perhaps, and more than a little nervous—handed him a copy of his book. She was wearing a gray wool coat.

"We should go, sir, really."

Ray said to the thin man, "Wait."

He opened the copy in front of him and glanced up at her.

"Sorry. Anyone in particular I should write here?"

Gathering herself, she said in clipped tones, "My name is María."

"Okay, María." He scribbled the inscription and handed the book to her.

"*Gracias*," she said.

For a moment, he was confused. No, bewildered. But he couldn't say why.

"Sir," said the thin man, "we have to—"

"For the love of *God!*" Ray snapped. "I hear you, okay?"

The thin man recoiled, folding his arms one over the other at the affront, crushing the sheaf of papers in his hand. Ray stared hard at him for a moment and then turned back to the waiting line.

The woman in the gray coat was gone. He craned to look around the queue, then stood up and stepped out from behind the desk. The thin man breathed a sigh of relief and gestured in the direction of the camera crew.

"Thank you, sir. This way."

But Ray was heading for the street.

4

There were two men in each boat. As they pulled alongside, one or other of the men—sometimes both—stood up, swaying comfortably with the swell, gripping on to the foot of the guardrail.

The small boats were so low in the water that only the men's faces were visible above the deck, peering up at the big boat. They said little to Morgan or Jack, merely nodding or grunting as they took hold of the first crates, but their eyes darted this way and that, taking in the boat and the gringos. When they spoke, they talked quietly to each other in a harsh, rapid-fire Spanish, swallowing the final consonants as if finishing a sentence took too much effort.

Ten minutes later, three of the boats were already on their way to shore and the fourth was waiting alongside. Morgan and Jack lifted the last of the crates from the cockpit deck to the gunwale. The crate was heavier than the others, and Jack staggered, then lost his hold, letting go and jumping back to avoid getting his toes crushed. The crate hit the deck at an angle, popping the lid with a splintering sound, and two ancient Italian carbines clattered onto the teak, the excelsior packing curling around them like dry seaweed.

"Pick up," Morgan said, his voice taut from the effort of holding the weight.

Jack stuffed the rifles back into the crate one at a time. He appeared excited by the feel of the guns in his hand.

"Come on. The lid—"

Jack positioned the lid, with the nails protruding, and banged it down with the heel of his hand.

"Lift," said Morgan.

The men in the small boat slowed the heavy crate's descent until it lay between them like an undersized coffin. And then, without a word, they pushed off.

As the small boat came about, one of the men looked up to Morgan and Jack and raised his paddle in salute.

"*Gracias, Señores*," he said. "*Cuba libre.*"

"*De nada*," Morgan replied.

Jack said to Morgan, "You ever wonder why these guys are doing it?"

"We have guns, and they're willing to pay for them."

"I mean, what are they fighting for?"

"We're done. Let's go home," Morgan said. He kicked at the loose straw on the deck as he reached for the stern anchor chain.

The moon had disappeared from view, and the little boats were dissolving once more into the sea.

"Hey, Bill?"

"What?"

"Thanks. For getting me in, I mean. Thelma's already spent the money, but this is going to change everything for us, with the baby and all—"

Morgan let the chain slide and stood up straight, as if suddenly attentive to Jack's words. But it was something else. The sound was distant—beyond the bay, for sure. It could be anything, and he wanted to be wrong, but he'd heard this sound before. Jumping up onto the gunwale, one hand on the cabin roof to steady himself, he scanned the horizon.

"Mr. Bartone only gave me a shot 'cause of you," Jack said. "I mean, I'd still be totting a hod, and you know what working construction pays."

Morgan was looking north, toward the open sea, toward the Florida Keys, ninety long miles away. Jack was still talking.

"Lousy forty bucks a—"

"Shut up!"

Jack stopped dead. He looked up at Morgan, bewildered. He too, must have heard the low *thum-thum* of powerful marine engines, only he could have had no idea what the sound meant.

Morgan knew. He knew well before the silent, bright flash of the 40mm cannon briefly lit up the horizon. Before the magnesium dashes of tracer fire scored the night sky overhead, hitting the water close to the boats and sending plumes of spray into the air like decorative fountains. A PT boat, war vintage, once fitted with torpedo tubes for close attack on larger vessels, but now stripped back and loaned or given to the Cubans as surplus to requirement; mahogany-planked hull, 1,800 horsepower gasoline Packard engines. The sound they made was unmistakable—like no other boat. More like an aircraft.

The second cannon salvo followed moments later, and again the flashes were soundless for a couple of seconds. Morgan followed the line of tracer to see rounds cut through one of the small boats like cheese wire. The smallest box of all—the one with the grenades—must have caught, because just as the boat began to crumple, it exploded in a bright orange ball. The shock wave thumped into Morgan's chest. He saw a body pirouette through the air and land awkwardly in the black sea, like a flubbed splash dive. Two of the other boats were awash, and there was burning debris on the water. Someone was howling in pain.

Morgan noticed headlights bouncing through the palms toward the beach beyond the burning boats. Jeeps or trucks of some kind. Military, police. It didn't matter.

"Shit," he said softly.

Jack was standing there gawping like a kid at a fireworks display.

"Get the anchor up—now!" Morgan shouted to Jack.

He lunged for the wheel and the ignition, knocking Jack to one side. He turned the key, engaged the forward anchor winch with his right hand and at the same time, pressed his thumb to the starter button, willing the engines to catch.

Instead, the motor whirred and died. The searchlight strobed over them as the eighty-foot patrol boat raced straight for their position. Morgan steadied himself. He checked the gear lever. *Neutral . . . full choke . . . glow plugs ready*

. . . He pressed the starter button again and once more the motor whirred and moaned, but didn't fire. He swore, then prayed briefly and took a deep breath. The clanking of the forward winch finally stopped. He pressed the button a third time. The engine and the whole boat vibrated as the crankshaft turned, forcing the pistons to life. Blue diesel smoke came coughing from the exhausts.

Morgan felt a surge of hope—until he looked around to see Jack, frozen and staring at the oncoming craft, with the stern anchor still down. He shouted again, though he knew it was already too late. They would never outrun a PT, even an old one. A boat like that could hit forty knots. He had ridden them in Japan, easing the monotony of eighteen months' peacekeeping duty after the war. Hell, he had even tried waterskiing behind one—until the shore patrol caught them.

At three hundred yards, the PT boat slowed and came off the plane, its bows dipping and the stern rising in response. As it rocked and steadied in the water, they heard the bullhorn crackle and hum. Then a booming, distorted voice with a thick Cuban accent.

"Cut your engines and prepare to be boarded. You are under arrest!"

Morgan's mind was working fast but coming up with nothing. He would leave the engine running, that much he knew. What happened next was anyone's guess. The PT boat was closer now and he squinted under the dazzling searchlight at the dark figures lining the deck, each with a gun trained on them. He raised his hands and faced the light, glancing around to make sure Jack was following suit.

He wasn't. Instead, he'd decided to haul in the anchor chain, now that it was way too late to help. He even appeared relaxed, as if they really had just gotten in a good day of fishing and were heading for port and the nearest bar.

"Leave it!" Morgan barked.

But Jack didn't seem to hear. Instead, he kept at it, hand over hand, yarding up the wet chain and letting the slack clank onto the deck.

"Jack! Leave it!" Morgan shouted.

But still Jack carried on.

The bullhorn squawked again. "Put up your hands! Do not move!"

There was nothing Morgan could do. He stood with his arms still raised, wedging himself tight against the port side of the cockpit as the wash hit them. Adjusting his features to those of a man both surprised and innocent, he shouted to the patrol boat.

"Okay, guys, okay, relax. *Pesca!* You know, fishing!"

It was a vain hope, but just maybe, if they stuck to the story no matter what, there was a chance. The Cubans might not believe the fishing cover, but the guns were gone and they would have to prove otherwise. It was worth a shot.

The PT boat's engines kicked into reverse, straining at the water and churning the surface to bubbling eddies and whirlpools. Morgan rehearsed the line: *norteamericanos, vacaciones,* just my buddy and me. Rented the boat in Miami. Thought we'd do a little fishing, see the sights, live aboard, you know?

He made a silent wish before glancing at Jack, hoping fervently he had come to his senses.

What he saw made him blanch. There was Jack, one hand on the wet chain, the other on the anchor, bracing with his knee on the padded cockpit seat, clutching the dripping steel in the crook of his right arm, left hand on the long shank.

Even from across the cockpit, with the anchor held like that and the look of excitement on Jack's face, first impressions would say it was a weapon. From the patrol boat, there was no doubt.

5

Ray pushed at the heavy glass door of the bookshop and all at once, he was out. He was instantly aware of the rain, then the chill. Offices were beginning to empty, and the sidewalks were a moving sea of umbrellas as people made their way home in the early evening dark.

His eyes slowly adjusted to the gloom and he scanned the sidewalk left and right, avoiding the brightly lit shop windows and concentrating on the people moving past in quick, short steps, attempting to keep their footing on the slush and grit.

He looked for a woman alone, but then just about everyone was alone in the crowd—moving fast, collars up, heads down.

And then—*it had to be her.* Even at this distance he was pretty sure. She was putting up her umbrella as the white "WALK" sign blinked, hurrying across East Chicago Avenue.

Dodging other pedestrians, Ray squinted against the cold needles of rain and made it to the intersection, but the traffic was already moving and the line waiting to cross was static, two or three deep. He could wait with them and try to keep her in sight, or go. He decided to go, ignoring the red "WAIT" letters. Horns blared, but he reached the other side with only one near miss. The disapproving looks of those waiting formed a defensive line against him. He pushed past them, politely but firmly. Then he was running as fast as his seventy-year-old legs would go.

But he could no longer see her. He stopped, his hair wet now, his suit shoulders darkening as the rain soaked into the material. Suddenly, he was angry. He should have waited and watched, and now he'd lost her.

Think. Where could she have gone in the space of a few seconds? It took a moment for him to register the coffee shop two doors down, just twenty yards from where he'd last seen her. He walked over and tried to peer through the shop window, which was bleary with condensation. A woman stood waiting at the counter, her coat roughly the right color and length. She wore a hat and held a folded umbrella.

He went in and eased past the first few tables, and realized at once that it wasn't the woman from the bookstore. Then he saw her in the corner, near the dripping window, taking off her coat and sitting down at a small round table. A copy of his book lay beside her coffee cup.

Ray let the door close and brushed back his sopping hair. He walked toward her and felt his senses come suddenly alive, noticing everything about her: the careful, precise way she stirred her coffee, the way she sat upright in the chair, her back straight.

As he reached the table, her eyes came up to meet his. Ray slowly eased himself into the chair opposite, their faces close now. She put her coffee spoon down in the saucer under the cup. Even amid the hubbub of customers and the gurgle of the latte machine, the sound of the spoon on china was crisp and clear. Neither said a word.

6

For a long time after the event, Morgan would wonder that the reaction from the patrol boat hadn't been a good deal more decisive. If he had been in the *guardia*'s place, looking at the excited gringo swinging around at him like that, his finger would have gone to the trigger for sure. He might even have made the shot.

As it happened, only one young man on the PT boat felt the same way. Perhaps fear kept the others from reacting. They certainly looked scared to Morgan, trying to cover him and Jack, and keep their footing as the boat rocked from side to side. And given the uneven motion of both boats, the chances of the only round fired hitting Jack in the chest at fifty yards were remote at best.

When the shot came, it was Jack who looked most astonished. The bullet must have passed straight through, between the ribs and missing the sternum, because he was still standing, still holding the anchor, even as the sound of the shot died away and a small patch of blood began to seep into his pale shirt. Only when one knee buckled slightly did he take half a step back to sit on the cockpit bench, anchor in his lap, mouth open. He didn't even blink—just looked somehow disappointed.

Morgan reacted on instinct. He dived for cover, stretching for the throttle lever and yanking it down from neutral to full ahead, practically snapping it off. The engines revved high and loud, but instead of surging forward, the fishing boat twisted and kicked to the left, forcing its bow up and ramming the exposed hull of the PT boat. The mahogany planks splintered as the soldiers on deck pitched sideways. One went over the side and thudded off the cockpit roof directly above Morgan's head before sliding into the sea.

Morgan made a grab for the wheel, spinning it to starboard, just enough to pull his craft back off the patrol boat and scrape along its hull. The screech of wood and fiberglass clawing at each other was like fingernails on a blackboard.

And then they were free. With the rudder set straight, the fishing boat suddenly ripped away, props gripping the water.

Keeping his head down as they put twenty yards, then fifty, then a hundred between them and the Cubans, Morgan at last allowed himself one look back at the patrol boat. It hadn't budged, and he wondered if he had holed it below the waterline. It hadn't even come about to give chase. The searchlight was flailing around and even found them once or twice, but by veering a few degrees to port, then starboard, he lost it easily.

Steering for the open sea, he checked on Jack, now slumped on the bench, still cradling the anchor in his arms. Eyes wide open.

As the sun rose, its warmth began to burn off the sea mist lingering in clumps over the ocean. It would be hot again today, but there was a chill in the air that made Morgan shiver. A mile or so from the Keys, the flat, calm water was listless and gloopy under the boat as it drifted, engines off.

Jack's body was laid out precariously on the gunwale, arms tucked neatly to his chest, looking like a proper corpse prepared for burial. The blood had soaked his shirt from shoulder to waist. A big orange gas cylinder full of liquid propane, which Morgan had dragged up from the galley, was tied around Jack's waist with a thick rope.

Morgan held the Matusalem rum bottle in one hand, studying the image of a bird in flight. He couldn't be sure if the bird was a swift or a swallow, or a creature that existed only in the artist's mind. A moment later, he hurled the bottle as far as he could into the mist and didn't hear it hit the water.

He mumbled the opening to the Lord's Prayer because that was all that came to mind, then put one hand on the cylinder and one under Jack's shoulder, and shoved.

Body and gas cylinder splashed into the clear blue water together. But when Morgan looked over the side, he saw the cylinder heading downwards with a sense of purpose where Jack seemed to hover for a moment, arms outstretched. Morgan suddenly noticed that the eyes were open. And yet he had closed them for sure. Maybe the force of hitting the water had pried them open again.

Then the rope became taut, the weight of the gas cylinder gave the body a sudden downward yank and a few bubbles emerged from the mouth, like Jack was trying to speak. The vacant stare and the arms held wide gave him the appearance of someone reaching out, or falling in slow motion from a great height.

Moments later, the body vanished in the deep water. Inches beneath the sea's surface, tiny translucent fish darted this way and that, as if looking for something lost.

7

Ray had always found it difficult to sleep with the window closed, even in the depths of winter. But Sally felt the cold. She had her back to him as he tossed and turned, waking from time to time, then sliding back into fitful dreams. The bad nights were rare, usually brought on by the stress of a speaking engagement or a fight in the press—but tonight was definitely one of the bad ones. The appearance of a ghost will do that to you.

Like a guilty man, he'd rehearsed what he would say to Sally on the way home, staring vacantly at the city lights beyond the murky window of the commuter train. The fact that he would be leaving right in the middle of Christmas, and with the family staying, was not good and she would be righteously upset. But María had asked for his help and he had agreed to do what he could, even if that meant deserting the family and taking an early flight to Washington the next morning. He was sorry, but he had no choice. It was not as if this was the first time he'd put a cause before personal concerns. That was who Ray Halliwell *was*—or so he said to himself.

When it came to it, he presented his decision as a fait accompli, leaving no room for debate. Sally maintained a dignified silence for the rest of the evening, ministering to the family and reading a story to her grandson. By the time they got to bed, talk between them had ceased altogether.

The dull glow of a winter dawn, liquid behind the curtains, convinced Ray that any chance of sleep was gone. Heaving himself awkwardly onto one elbow, he pushed back the covers and willed his legs to move over the bed edge until his feet found the bedside rug. Elbows on knees, he sat for a moment, allowing his blood pressure to equalize. Then he stood up and shuffled across the warm wood floor to the en suite bathroom. Once a novel luxury to them, the en suite was now a necessity since both were up once or twice during the night. They were getting absurdly old, he thought as he found the light switch—no doubt about it.

Ray was examining his face in the mirror when he saw Sally's reflection appear beside his own. She paused in the open doorway. She was fixing the cord of her gown.

"I'll make tea," she said, without looking at him.

Ray breakfasted alone in his den. He wanted time to look for the photographs, hidden beneath the accumulated detritus of almost fifty years. Creating order in the realm of physical things was not his strength, and though he often beat himself up about it, nothing changed and the clutter quietly grew around him. He even toyed with the notion that piling one thing on top of another created a logical sequence every bit as efficient as hours of filing might achieve—if only things would stay put.

After an hour's rummaging, destroying any implied chronology without a second thought, Ray was sitting at his desk with several black-and-white prints laid out around him. Files and discarded papers littered the floor. He picked up the first photograph and pushed his spectacles farther up his nose. A young man poking his head around a doorjamb, looking like a Marx Brothers still of Chico, innocent and surprised, smiling for the camera. Inside the room, a man and a woman to one side of him, turning toward the photographer. Ray smiled, remembering the moment.

The next snapshot, taken from a low angle, as if the subjects were ten or twenty feet up a mountain slope, showed a group of ten men against a jungle background, most of them crouching, one or two standing, all armed.

A figure at the back of the group, wearing a German helmet from World War Two, aimed a bolt-action rifle off to camera right. Beneath the rifle muzzle were four men, all smiling or laughing, wearing bush hats with the crown pushed back the way one might with a baseball cap. In the center Ray picked out Morgan. He was wearing a beret and some sort of hunting jacket. To his right were three men in ragged uniforms.

Ray picked up the next photo, this one in a dusty frame, the glass cracked across the top left corner. Ray turned the frame over and picked at the metal staples holding the cardboard backing in place. He struggled to pull the cardboard from the frame. Frustrated, he pushed at the glass, and all at once, it gave way. He didn't notice the cut on his forefinger made by a sharp glass edge.

This one showed three figures: a woman flanked by two men. Morgan was laughing; Ray just looked tense. María, as always, seemed implacable, serene.

He hardly recognized his younger self, thin and gaunt, but he remembered the moment. Menoyo had taken the picture at Morgan's insistence and despite Ray's objections.

He wiped the heel of his hand across the picture to clear the dust and left a faint smear of red. Only then did he realize he was bleeding.

Ray dressed in front of Sally's full-length mirror. He opted for a dark suit and a subdued tie with a white button-down shirt, the kind he had favored all his life. Sally said the shirt was considered 'preppy' these days, but he had only a vague sense of what the term implied, and cared even less.

Across the bedroom, the TV was on, showing images from the conflict in Afghanistan. He'd turned the TV on out of habit, not intending to listen or watch, but, like journalists the world over, afraid he might miss a breaking story without it. When he did watch, he found the punchy, shallow delivery difficult to take. He preferred what he saw as the more considered, in-depth reporting of times gone by, only dimly aware that he was slipping into the fogyism that comes with age.

Ray straightened his tie for the third time and reached for the briefcase sitting open on the dresser. The photograph of Morgan, María and himself was now clean of blood, and he slid it into one of the lid pockets before closing the case. He checked his watch. Eleven o'clock; the cab was due.

The widescreen TV in the living room was on as he walked down the broad staircase to the hallway—a football commentator recounting the gripping details of the last quarter. His son Phil and his grandson Spencer were sitting on the couch, glued to the game. Phil's fortieth birthday had passed a year ago, and Ray still had trouble believing that his son was now approaching middle age, with less hair than he himself had, and a bigger paunch. They joked about it in the office, where Phil looked after the day-to-day running and managed things when Ray was on a speaking tour or hawking a new book.

Phil came out to help him on with his coat. Sally was in the kitchen with her back to them, dealing with the dishes in the sink and fixing lunch at the island.

"All set?" said Phil.

"Yeah," Ray replied, adjusting his coat. He set his overnight bag on the floor and the briefcase on the hall table, together with his house keys. He opened the case, took out a sheet of paper and handed it to Phil.

"What's this?" his son asked.

"A list. As many names as I can think of from those days. A lot will be dead by now. I want you to find out who, if anyone, is still kicking."

"Okay."

"See if you can get phone numbers, that sort of thing. You can use the Internet, right, and Google?"

"Your knowledge of technology astounds me, Dad," he replied dryly.

"There's a priority order to the list. The guy at the top is crucial. We haven't much time."

"Okay, I'll start now. You remember how to pick up your e-mails remotely?"

"Remotely, yes."

"Or call me."

Phil looked toward the kitchen and back to his father. From the street, a short toot of a car horn announced the waiting cab.

"I'll talk to her."

"It's okay, son. You guys just have a good time while I'm gone."

"We will."

"Couple of days, no more," Ray said. "I've got the cell phone, much as I hate the damn thing."

"Good," said Phil. "Use it. It won't bite. I'll get Spence."

"No, leave him to the game. And say 'bye to Anni for me?"

"She's at the store, picking up the ham. I'll tell her."

Phil opened the front door and led the way, carrying his father's bag. The cab was parked on the street beyond the drive, engine running, exhaust fumes condensing in the freezing air.

For a moment, Ray hesitated and thought about going to her, kissing her or at least calling goodbye from the step. But he didn't do any of these things. He and Sally knew they felt differently about this trip in a way unlike all the times past when he'd put his own life before family. There was no point in pretending otherwise.

He followed his son outside into dazzling sunlight reflecting on the snow-covered lawn, and closed the door gently behind him.

8

Naturally, given the way things had turned out, Bartone was mad as hell with Morgan. He ordered him to lie low, wait for things to cool off. A couple of weeks, he said, no more. If anyone asked questions, play dumb. When the time was right, he'd get a call, but until then, best stay out of the light.

Morgan too, was mad—but at himself. He needed to talk to Thelma. He had to explain what had happened, and how. She would be going crazy. Bartone had said it was a dumbass idea and that under no circumstances should he go near the girl. When Morgan started shouting, two of the guys were on him in a flash, and he took a couple of solid gut punches before he remembered his manners. Bartone threatened at first, then abruptly changed tack and promised to make sure Thelma had what she needed. Money was not an issue, he said. Morgan should trust him, go back to his apartment and lie low.

"Understand?" Bartone had said, nodding to his goons to let go of Morgan's arms.

*

There would be someone watching him, that much he knew. Morgan kinked the blinds to check the street out front and straightaway saw the guy sitting in a tan Ford parked across the street.

He recognized the watcher as Carl, part-time doorman at the Eden Roc Hotel and one of Bartone's gofers. Carl was not exactly covert, smoking and tapping the bodywork in time to the radio. Morgan released the blind and went out into the hall, closing the door to his apartment behind him. At the back of the building, he opened the window and eased out onto the fire escape. After walking two blocks to make sure he wasn't being followed, he took a cab to Thelma's.

*

As soon as she saw him, she crumpled—before he even said a word.

He gently eased her back inside the apartment, closed the door with his foot and held her tight as she sobbed and beat on his chest. And when she finally collapsed on the sofa, Morgan covered her with a blanket and sat by her, stroking her head. He poured her a drink and then quietly told her how. He made only a few minor adjustments to the truth, telling her Jack had died instantly and gone over the side when the bullet hit him. But that was just to save her from unnecessary nightmares. In the evening, he scrambled eggs for them both, but she didn't touch a thing. All night he sat by her bed, watching her sleep and wake repeatedly, crying dry tears and taking deep, heavy breaths.

Before he left in the morning, he made a call to her closest girlfriend—a girl called Karen—and talked her into calling in sick in order to spend the day with Thelma. When she arrived at the apartment, Morgan put some money on the sideboard, went back to his place and slept. Carl and the tan Ford were gone.

Over the days that followed, he saw Thelma whenever he could get away from his watchers. Time and again, he told her it was unlikely Jack's body would ever be recovered, and explained that going to the authorities either here or in Cuba would only bring a storm of trouble down on their heads. His analogy became pointedly ironic when Hurricane Audrey swept up the Gulf of Mexico in June and made a devastating landfall in Texas and Louisiana. On her way past the Keys, Audrey whipped the seas into a fury, somehow bringing what was left of Jack's bloated body to the surface, where it was spotted from a pleasure boat and reported to the coastguard.

In the investigation that followed, Thelma rushed to tell the cops everything she knew. She was mad with grief and furious at Morgan, at Bartone, the Cubans—everyone—and she named names. Bartone was hauled over the coals, but talked his way out of any direct involvement. After twelve hours in the can, they had to let him go. When he got back to the shipping office in the dockside warehouse he used as cover for his operations, he ranted and threatened, and vowed to make somebody pay. As a first step, he called his two best enforcers together and outlined his vision for Morgan.

But they were too late. Twenty-four hours before Bartone's men broke down the door to Morgan's apartment, he'd taken a bus over Seven Mile Bridge, then walked and hitched until there was no more road. He found a cheap hotel in Saddlebunch Harbor and spent his days lying on the single bed, drinking milk and watching the ceiling fan go round and round. He wondered about his chances of getting to Bartone before his goons came for him in the Keys. If he was going down, he wanted to go down fighting.

But the more he worked on a plan, the less sense it all made. This wasn't about Bartone or Thelma—or even Jack. This was about twenty-eight years on the planet, with nothing to show but a catalogue of failure. No wonder his parents had pretty much given up on him. They were churchgoers. They lived in a good neighborhood in Cleveland and were heartbroken when their son turned out to be an embarrassment to them and a danger to himself. They knew nothing about his life in Miami, of course. It had been enough to watch him grow into manhood with a police rap sheet, two knife wounds and a dishonorable discharge. After the army and his time in the pen, they'd gotten him a job with the Monsignor as a church caretaker. It wasn't much, but it was steady work, a breathing space. He'd lasted a month before deciding to hit the road. His father had driven past as he stood by the highway with his thumb out, and hadn't even recognized him.

They never said so, but Morgan was sure they would have been happier had he given his life for his country. At least then they would have a flag and a medal cabinet, and could hold their heads up in public. If he had the courage, he thought as walked down the beach toward town, he would save Bartone's goons a trip and do the job himself.

He saw the poster as he came out of the store carrying a quart of milk and eating cheese puffs. There was no cinema for miles around, but Saddlebunch Town Hall was holding a screening of *Shane*, starring Alan Ladd, that night. Morgan, and maybe twenty other people of all ages, sat on hard metal folding chairs. The sound was crackly, and the projector kept overheating so that they had to pause occasionally to let it cool off.

When the movie was over, he came out of the hot, sticky hall into the night air and walked to the beach nearby. He sat cross-legged on the sand, looking out over the black water of the ocean. And suddenly, he knew exactly where he was going—and why.

9

It would be another year until the new underground Capitol Visitor Center was officially open, with an entrance to its subterranean world some distance from the building proper.

Extension Room E1.036 had the lingering smell of fresh paint, and a hint of dust in the dry air. It was little bigger than a community college classroom, and the blond-veneered desks and black leatherette chairs looked as if they had never been used; quite possible, since this whole underground complex was still being completed. A man in coveralls was working at the back of the room, using a wrench on something hidden in a wall panel.

Everett Capaldi, María's lawyer, screwed up his nose and squinted over his aviator-style glasses. He was forty-seven years old, with receding hair, and came across as a bit solemn on first meeting. He had worked steadily up the tree of his conservative midsize practice in Cleveland, where he also sat on the board of the port authority. Becoming a lawyer was entirely natural to such a sober personality. Perhaps for this reason, he was both assiduous and happy in his work. Never more so than when an apparently ordinary woman like María walked into his offices with an extraordinary case—one with the reach to bring him here, to the epicenter of American legal and political power.

"María," he said. "Good morning."

Capaldi needed no introduction to realize that the man with her was Ray Halliwell. After all, the trip to Chicago and a personal appeal so late in the day had been largely his idea. All through the preparation he'd done on the case, Ray Halliwell's name had come up in one context or another. But each time he'd suggested trying to bring the renowned author and campaigner onside, María had found a reason to resist. In the weeks leading up to the Senate committee hearing, Capaldi had become even more convinced that no matter how heartfelt María's own testimony might be, the case still depended too heavily on her word, and her version of events. María fought him, right up to the eleventh hour when he'd put the flyer in front of her and stated—with uncharacteristic bluntness—that Halliwell's testimony would make the difference between winning and losing.

Naturally, Capaldi had been curious as to why his client had shown such reluctance to approach a man she'd often mentioned as a friend, and the journalist who had first brought Morgan international recognition. Now this man was standing in front of him, Capaldi was even more intrigued.

"Everett," said María, "this is Ray Halliwell. Ray, my lawyer, Everett Capaldi."

"I'm very glad to see you, sir," said Capaldi. "María's spoken a lot about you."

"And you," said Ray.

"I wish we'd gotten more preparation time with you, sir," said Capaldi. "Please, sit."

"I agree," Ray replied, "but I think I understand what you need from me. I'll do my best."

As they took their places at the witness table, a door opened and the committee members came into the room, each carrying similar buff files. Leading the way, and chairing the committee, was Senator Chris Hawkes, a Maryland Democrat newly elected in 2004. Capaldi had done his homework on Hawkes, a man who was still tipped for great things but who had apparently struggled to build a power base during his three years in office. As an African-American, he was no doubt accustomed to punching his way through. But he seemed to have mistaken life on the hill for a meritocracy. The truth was that being smarter than the old guard was a real handicap, especially if you let it show. More recently—so Capaldi's sources said—Hawkes had taken his knocks and learned to play by the rules, do his time, work the committees and jump on the chores nobody else wanted.

Chores like this case, lost in the mists of time and potentially embarrassing, with no discernible upside. Hawkes was, by all accounts, a decent man, but Capaldi had to assume the unspoken brief was straightforward: run a quick-and-dirty damage-control exercise, take the brownie points, move on.

Then there was Marjorie Wallace, a Southerner and a Republican, who outranked Hawkes with eight consecutive years in office. Strictly speaking, she should have been chair, but as a safe pair of hands and with marching orders to assess Hawkes' performance, she preferred coach.

The third member of the committee was Chad Dyer, a senior official with Immigration, a man who knew the rules inside out and would ride shotgun for the decision makers.

"Mr. Capaldi?" said Hawkes as the committee took their seats, indicating that the lawyer should approach.

Capaldi went to the bench and listened carefully to Senator Hawkes, nodding from time to time. When he came back to the witness table, he leaned over to María and Ray.

"They want to talk to Ray first," he said without explaining further. "It's okay."

As Capaldi sat, Senator Hawkes was calling to the back of the room.

"Sir? Excuse me?" He was addressing the workman with the wrench. "Could we have this room now?"

The man looked surprised, as if it hadn't occurred to him that he might be in the way, but he didn't argue. Collecting his tools, he made his way to the door with barely a glance at those gathered for the hearing.

When the man had gone, Hawkes tapped the microphone and opened the proceedings.

"Ladies and gentlemen, let's get started. I'm sure this is unnecessary, but may I please remind all here to switch off their cell phones?"

Nobody moved, except Ray.

"*Damn*," he muttered under his breath, patting his pockets in search of the cell phone Phil had asked him to carry.

When he finally found it, he pressed a couple of buttons, but to no avail. María took the phone from him and turned it off.

"Thank you," whispered Ray.

Senator Hawkes cleared his throat. "Let the record show the time and date as December 20, 2007, nine-ten a.m. The case before us, one William Alexander Morgan, deceased, US citizenship revoked September 9, 1960, on the grounds that this individual was a combatant in a foreign national army, thereby contravening the United States statutes prohibiting such action. This appeal to review is brought by Mrs. María Jensen of Cleveland, Ohio, represented here by counsel Mr. Capaldi. This committee is now in session."

Hawkes didn't have a gavel to bang down and had to settle instead for shuffling the papers in front of him.

"We note the presence of Mr. Ray Halliwell at the witness table. Sir, your reputation is well known to us. Before we proceed, this committee would like to establish your interest in this case, and the capacity in which you appear here."

Ray had expected the question, though perhaps not straight off the bat, and had his answer ready.

"As a witness, Senator, at the request of Mrs. Jensen and counsel."

Hawkes shifted his attention to Capaldi. "Counsel, you will be aware that prior notification of witness testimony is required by this committee and by due process?"

"Yes, sir, Senator," said Capaldi. "It was extremely unlikely that Mr. Halliwell would be able to appear here today, for a number of reasons, not least work commitments. This situation only resolved itself in the last twenty-four hours. Time constraints prevented a formal notification with our written submission. My apologies."

"Counsel, let me speak candidly. This committee has no desire to see this case become a public issue, even in the hands of a respected author and public voice such as Mr. Halliwell."

Ray interrupted.

"Sir? Senator, may I speak? I am here for one reason and one reason only. I *knew* William Morgan. I have a firsthand account to offer the committee, which is entirely relevant to this case. There is no other motive, certainly no public agenda. I am here as a private citizen to support Mrs. Jensen's appeal, that is all."

The committee room was silent. The recorder looked up from her machine and waited.

"A moment," Hawkes said, turning to his colleagues. He covered the microphone with his hand.

The committee began to confer. Capaldi was looking nervously from Hawkes to Ray and back again. He had seen Ray's presence as an advantage, heavyweight support for the case. Now—before they even got started—it was in danger of becoming a liability.

"Everett? Water?" María's voice was calm and quiet.

With his mind working frantically on the next play, he looked surprised to see her next to him, as if he had forgotten she was there.

"Thanks," he said.

She poured him a glass from the pitcher. Capaldi watched as María turned next to Ray, fascinated by the relationship between his client and the man he'd only ever seen on television.

"Water?" María said, keeping her voice low.

"You were always oil on troubled water, " Ray replied, his face breaking into a broad smile.

María frowned. "What?"

"No, nothing," Ray whispered, still smiling. He took a sip.

"What?" she said again.

Capaldi pretended to study his papers, but he was alert to every beat and straining to hear every inflection between the two people next to him. Still, he could make no sense of the signs.

Ray said, "It's good to see you, that's all."

"I never did get your jokes," María said.

"I know," said Ray.

Like brother and sister?

He was still studying them out of the corner of his eye when Senator Hawkes took his hand from the microphone and spoke.

"Very well, Mr. Halliwell. We would like to establish the nature of the connection between you and William Morgan before proceeding further. Counsel?"

Capaldi leaned forward to his own microphone.

"By all means, Senator."

There was no other response, and Capaldi knew it.

"Mr. Halliwell?" said Hawkes. "Please proceed."

Ray took a sip from his water and cleared his throat.

"I first met William Morgan toward the end of 1957. At that time, I was a reporter for the *Chicago Sun-Times*, special subject Cuba. I made regular trips there in that capacity. In fact, I was there more than I was home in Chicago—"

PART TWO

10

At twenty-six years old, Ray felt at least ten years older that morning in late September 1957. He had a window seat aboard the Pan Am Lockheed Constellation en route to Havana's José Martí Airport.

He was still smarting from a row with his boss, Jim Sturry, deputy editor of the *Sun-Times*, responsible for foreign news coverage. When Ray got the call to return to Chicago for a meeting, he'd known right away something was up. But he hadn't expected to have to justify covering Cuba at all.

"Look we said we'd give it a couple of months," Sturry said before Ray had even taken his seat at the board table, "well, time's up. The readers aren't reading, Ray—not according to marketing. You're writing about the mob down in Havana, but we got the same guys here. Trafficante, Lansky, Luciano, whoever. Readers care about the bad guys in their neighborhood, in this city. Nobody cares where they take their vacations."

Ray had argued his case, but Sturry had just shrugged and chewed on his pipe as he surveyed the Chicago skyline from the fifth floor. "You're wrong, Jim," Ray told him. "People care. People want to know what's going on. That's where the dope on the streets is coming from. That's where the money gets laundered and the wise guys pick up more than just their tans."

"It's all too far away, Ray. We need something closer to home, stories for the ordinary Joe."

Ray tried again, this time citing the resistance building up in the Sierra and the cities, but Sturry waved the argument away. "Bunch of students and the disaffected. Batista's got an army, courtesy of the US government, and I feel for them, really I do. The guy's a monkey. But he's their monkey, not ours. I want you to think about coming back to crime."

"You want to replace me?" Ray had said, bewildered and beginning to get angry.

"No," Sturry had said, "we'll let the wires handle Cuba until something happens—if something happens. I just want you where you can do some good, rattle a few cages, you know—like you do. Think about it."

Ray had thought about it. He'd gone back to the crummy two-room apartment he rented downtown, opened a bottle and paced the floor, glass in hand, swearing abuse at Sturry and making up his quitting speech.

But there was no one to hear him and all of a sudden he felt tired, worn out with the job, the shitty apartment and fighting the odds. He'd always thought the job would take him to the heart of things, to where the action was and to the place where he could make a difference, however small. But he hadn't reckoned with the dead weight of management, reader numbers, ad revenue and the rest. He hadn't reckoned with his own fading enthusiasm for the role of outsider, sticking a toe in and taking it out again with a two para story doomed to be buried on an inside page.

"Mr. Halliwell?" The stewardess handed him another sour mash and discreetly took away his empty glass.

"On the rocks, sir."

She was smiling, almost pouting. Her nails were painted a rose-pink. Even with his mind still churning, Ray noticed the curve of her ass inside the tight aqua skirt and suddenly realized he remembered her from a layover some months ago. Jean. Or Jane—one of the two. He smiled at her and muttered a 'hey, how are you', before turning back to look out on the ocean below.

Sturry had given him another three months back on the island—only because Ray had made it clear he'd quit without the concession. In return, he'd had Ray promise that if nothing changed in the coming weeks, he'd take the crime desk again.

Ever since he'd had the conversation, Ray had felt low and irritable. Mooching the bars downtown in his few remaining days stateside hadn't helped. He'd become introspective and for him at least, examining your own navel was a kind of weakness. Nevertheless, he found himself analyzing his own life, and not much caring for the results.

There was some *thing*, some vital piece of the jigsaw missing. He'd always wanted to be a journalist, right from the time he was in high school and he came to realize he could make a living doing what he loved best—writing, talking, engaging with others. Sure, he had a kind of life in Cuba, sending regular wires, drinking, hanging with the wolf pack—and there was always Pam. He had a kind of life back in Chicago, mainly centred around the paper and downtown bars. The Billy Goat Tavern was his favorite watering hole on Fridays. The guys from the *Tribune,* archrivals of the *Sun-Times* boys, thought they owned the place, and it was fun to mix it up with them over drinks. There were more tourists these days, curious to meet the owner, Billy Sianis, infamous for putting a curse on the Cubs. They had asked him to leave a World Series game and take his goat with him because it was upsetting other fans. Big mistake—the Cubs hadn't won since. But still there were pieces missing. A lot of his old buddies were married and settled by now. They owned houses and cars and quite a few had already produced kids, those little miracles of life that as far as Ray could see, were perfectly designed to eat you alive and destroy any chance of independent thought. Whenever he went to supper with guys like that—and it was rare he'd put himself through it—he felt like he was eating meatloaf with aliens. But still, the niggles remained. Maybe life was passing him by in some way, maybe—

A passenger sitting across the aisle chose that moment to lean over.

"You're Ray Halliwell, aren't you? *Chicago Sun-Times,* am I right?"

Ray was in no mood for chitchat. "Good health," he said, holding his glass up, and turned to look out the window at the blue Caribbean glittering below.

"I know your work," said the man, his broad belly straining at the loud Hawaiian shirt.

"Nice to know someone's reading," said Ray, taking a long slug from his glass.

Undaunted, the man said, "I run a hotel down at Cienfuegos. The Plaza?"

Ray groaned inside. He was pretty sure he knew where this was going.

"Did you know that every time you mention rebels and all that good stuff, our bookings go down? Did you know that?"

Many responses came to mind, all with a common theme.

"No, sir, I didn't. But that sounds like a story to me. Thanks for the tip."

The man turned to his companion, softly muttering profanities. Ray waggled his empty glass at the stewardess.

"How 'bout another here, Jean?"

Her smile faded as she took the glass and refilled it. She held the glass a little too high for him to reach.

"It's Joan," she said.

*

Six or seven rows back, the man in the crumpled white suit and two-tone shoes reading a Captain America comic book was, unlike Ray, in the best of spirits.

"Bam! Bam!"

A boy, maybe nine years old, on the opposite side of the airplane aisle was pointing his index finger directly at Morgan and about to let go another round.

"Randy, stop it!" said the woman in the next seat—presumably the boy's mother. "I'm sorry," she said to Morgan with a strained smile. She grabbed the boy's wrist and forced him to lower his hand. "And stay still!"

"Hey, buddy?" Morgan said to the boy.

The boy stopped fidgeting and gave him a suspicious glare.

"Here you go," he said, handing over the comic book.

"Say thank you, Randy," said the kid's mom, but Randy kept his head down.

"Thank you," she said to Morgan. "You're very kind."

"My pleasure, ma'am," he replied, twisting to see her better. "It's a long flight for a little guy."

11

Pan Am's load control supervisor at José Martí Airport was under pressure to make a decision. Attached to the passenger manifest were two telexes that, taken together, made no sense. The first warned that a VIP aboard Flight 291 from Miami, by the name of Lyman B. Kirkpatrick, would be met airside by a US Embassy car and should be extended every courtesy, including being allowed to depart the airplane first.

The second telex told of a disabled passenger, traveling in a party of two, who required assistance. Normal procedure meant allowing other passengers to leave the aircraft ahead of the disabled person, to save any unnecessary delay. But the name on the second telex was also Lyman B. Kirkpatrick.

The most likely explanation was a clerical error. But when the supervisor had spoken to the New York office, he couldn't get a straight answer. Now he could see the silvery Constellation, its sleek lines reminiscent of a flying fish, taxiing from the runway onto the apron. The black limousine with diplomatic plates was already parked and waiting at the gate.

The supervisor elected to do what anyone might do in his position: play it safe. So, as the plane came to a stop, the passengers heard an announcement from the captain.

"Ladies and gentlemen, I would ask you kindly to keep in your seats at this time and wait to retrieve your belongings until instructed to do so by the cabin staff. This will just take a moment. Thank you for your cooperation."

Ray looked around to see one of the stewardesses—not Joan—helping a man in a black suit, flat-top and black-rimmed glasses to undo the seat belt buckle. At the same time she was holding the man's arm as he struggled to stand. In the confined space, things were not going well, and the man appeared to be stuck halfway out of his seat with the stewardess struggling under his weight. Ray was about to offer help, when a man in a white suit and gaudy two-tone shoes appeared beside the stewardess.

"Ma'am?" he said with a polite smile. He turned to the man in black. "Put your arm around my neck, sir."

Ray watched as together, they began to crab their way down the aisle toward the front exit. The door was already open, and Ray could feel the hot tropical air wafting into the cabin. He watched them go. Another announcement from the captain thanked the passengers for their patience and asked them to begin disembarking.

Ray rose quickly from his aisle seat, mostly to avoid the Cienfuegos hotelier, who was still glaring daggers in his direction. Moments later, he stepped out into the heat and the bright sun to see a US Embassy black limo with fender flags waiting on the tarmac. The unlikely pair—white suit and black suit—were just negotiating the last of the steps. Ray followed them down. He saw the man in the white suit join the snaking line of passengers on their walk to the terminal building.

Hovering uncertainly by the limo was a familiar face: John Dempsey. "Embassy press attaché" was the transparent cover for Dempsey's real job as the CIA deskman in Havana. Dempsey's nervousness and the mere fact that he was here in person suggested to Ray that the stricken VIP was probably down from the Agency's headquarters in Langley, Virginia.

"John," Ray said as he passed Dempsey, "I see the brass are in town. Anything I should know?"

"Not a thing, Ray," said Dempsey, wiping his brow and climbing into the limo's front seat. "See you tonight."

Outside the terminal, Ray caught a cab. The driver used his horn and some fine expletives to force his way through the jam outside the building. Soon, they were skirting the airport perimeter fence toward the main highway.

Ray opened his briefcase and picked out the invitation card for the evening reception at the US Embassy. Hosted by the American Telephone Company in the presence of the Cuban president himself, General Fulgencio Batista, it was exactly the kind of event Ray normally avoided. But he was curious about the Langley guy, and he should catch up on things with the wolf pack anyhow. Not to mention Pam. He put the invitation on the seat next to him, noting with distaste the gold-embossed instructions for black tie. Nevertheless, he would be there.

He was leafing through the rest of his papers when he happened to look up and see a figure walking at the side of the road, toward the city: white suit, two-tone shoes, battered leather suitcase.

No one in his right mind, thought Ray, would set out deliberately to walk fifteen miles to the city—not with both the temperature and the humidity at ninety and a fierce midday sun baking the ground beneath your feet.

As the cab drew level with the walking figure, Ray couldn't help but turn and stare. The man's face was damp with sweat, though his expression appeared relaxed, even tranquil, and from what Ray could tell, the guy was whistling as he walked. Ray sat back in his seat and returned to his papers, but then on impulse, he said to the driver, *"Pare aquí."*

They pulled over fifty yards ahead. Ray looked back to see the man approaching the open door of the cab, neither speeding nor slowing his pace. Just as it seemed he might walk on by, the man stopped abruptly and bent down to peer inside at Ray in the back seat.

"How you doing?" he asked, as if someone else might also be needing his assistance today.

"Need a ride?" Ray said.

The man thought about it. "That's a kind offer, sir. Thank you."

He squeezed his big frame into the cab. Ray slid sideways to make room. The man settled his suitcase carefully on his knees and then realized he was sitting on something. He reached down and, with some effort, pulled out the crumpled Embassy invitation.

"Sorry," he said, handing the card to Ray.

"It's not important," Ray replied, unable to hide his amusement. "And I mean that."

As the cab began to pull away, the man offered Ray his hand.

"William Morgan," he said with old-fashioned formality.

"Ray Halliwell," Ray said, oddly charmed by this man who managed to defy the usual pigeonholes, yet exuded a certain sense of caricature.

"I'm grateful, Mr. Halliwell. Little warm out there today."

Ray nodded but said nothing for fear politeness would prompt the strained, banal chatter strangers in confined spaces feel obliged to inflict on each other. But he needn't have worried. This Midwesterner, William Morgan, seemed quite content to remain silent, paying close attention to the passing scenery and tapping lightly on the lid of his suitcase. Ray was relieved, but also surprised, even a little peeved, realizing he might end the ride without a clue beyond what he could observe about the man. He studied the suitcase. There was a name tag with nothing written there and several distinctive stickers, oddly enough, all for destinations within Florida—theme parks, that sort of thing.

"You travel light," he said to Morgan.

Morgan took a second to reply, but when he did, he turned to make full eye contact and smiled broadly.

"Yes, sir, you might say that."

To Ray's surprise, Morgan went back to looking out the side window. He was tapping the suitcase again and whistling *'As the Caissons Go Rolling Along'* faintly through his teeth. Ray recognized the tune.

"Military man?" Ray asked.

Morgan stopped whistling and turned to Ray. He appeared to be coming back from a world of his own, and the delay was a little unnerving. In the end, rather than offer a direct answer, he posed a question.

"May I ask you something, sir?"

"Sure," said Ray, guarded but still curious.

"You wouldn't be the same Ray Halliwell who writes for the *Chicago Sun-Times*, would you?"

Ray's heart sank. Maybe this guy too, owned a hotel or a bar. He should have just kept his mouth shut.

"That's me."

Morgan beamed with pleasure. "Well, sir, this is an honor. I've been doing a lot of reading about the island and to my mind, well, you tell it like it is. Now here we are, meeting on my first day in Cuba. What are the chances?"

Ray waited for the follow-up observations, but Morgan just went back to whistling and tapping.

"And you, Mr. Morgan. If you don't mind my asking, what's your story?"

"As of now, sir?" Morgan's expression was more guarded. "Right now, I'm not sure I have one. But watch this space—isn't that what you guys say?"

"Yes, it is," said Ray.

Morgan's easy, all-weather smile was back.

"That's what I heard."

Half an hour later, the cab turned off the Malecón coast road, which marked the city's northern limit, and took a right onto Cuba Tacón, coming to a halt in the bustling backstreets of Old Havana. Morgan got out and then leaned in to say his goodbyes.

"I appreciate the ride, Mr. Halliwell."

"The Bodeguita's right down the street," said Ray. "You can't miss it. If you've got time to kill, you might want to walk the way we came, along the seafront. They say you'll see all of Havana at the Malecón Seawall."

"I might just do that. Thanks. It was good to meet you."

"Likewise, Mr. Morgan. Good luck."

Ray could see Morgan in the wing mirror as the cab pulled away. They'd hardly spoken the rest of the trip, and all Ray had managed to glean was that Morgan was in Havana for the first time meeting friends, and would stay a day or two at most. Though relieved not to have been forced to keep a conversation going, Ray felt a little deflated at discovering so little of interest about the man. Maybe there was nothing *to* discover.

He checked his watch. Jamie had taken over his apartment for the duration of his trip to the States, and was still there so Ray would stay a couple of nights at the Riviera and to hell with expenses. If the hotel could freshen up his creased tux, he'd get in a swim and an hour's shut-eye before this evening's reception. It was going to be a long day.

12

Ray didn't get his afternoon nap, but he got the swim, and the hotel had done a good job on the tux, making him look better than he felt. He was only ten minutes late. He strolled across the US Embassy compound toward the reception.

By day, the Embassy building was a faceless box of concrete and glass, seven stories high. But lit up against the night sky, it seemed both more festive and less austere. Situated in Vedado, northwest of Old Havana and close to the sea, many of the pricier hotels were nearby, including the brand new Hilton, due to open in a couple of months.

Two marines in full dress uniform stood to attention as each guest arrived. Ray handed the crumpled invitation to a keen young man at the reception desk.

"Thank you, sir. Right along the corridor and—"

"Why, Mr. Halliwell—"

Ray saw the long, slender fingers first as she slipped her arm into his, but the purr was unmistakable. Pam Pettifer had used all her feline grace to appear as if from nowhere. She allowed Ray to kiss her on both cheeks but didn't kiss him in return, lest she muss her perfectly painted lips.

They went into the ballroom and stood on the fringe of the fifty or so guests, all in evening dress and black tie. Right away, Ray picked out John Dempsey and, in a wheelchair beside him, the man Morgan had carried off the airplane that afternoon. Two Cuban army officers were standing with them, smiling and listening attentively.

"Is he Langley?" said Ray.

"Lyman B. Kirkpatrick," said Pam. "Assistant Director, no less. He seems okay."

"What's he doing here?"

"I can't tell you that." She lifted her chin in mock indignation.

"Of course you can," Ray said, not looking at her.

"They're calling it a 'review.' Truth is, they're worried the ticking clock in Cuba is set, but they don't know when the alarm's going off."

"And the wheelchair?"

Pam was suddenly conspiratorial. She liked gossip, particularly if it carried a hint of the tragic. "Polio, apparently. Not so long ago. Contracted on an exotic foreign posting somewhere in Indo-China; that's what I heard."

Ray took a flute of champagne from a passing waiter without bothering to hand one to Pam. She wouldn't touch a drop until she was off duty later in the evening.

"Well, the wolf pack awaits," she said, releasing his arm.

Ray took a slurp of champagne. "God help me."

"Call me?" she purred as she started back for the lobby.

"Naturally."

*

Less than a mile away from the Embassy, nineteen-year-old Alejandro Merrero was leaning against the driver's side of an Edsel sedan as dusk became full night. Parked on the median strip of the busy Avenida de los Presidentes, the car was jacked up with the spare leaning against the rear bumper. Either side of the median, cars and cabs and buses were honking and switching lanes to no advantage in the slow crawl of traffic. Car fumes and the humid night air made the avenue feel more like a clogged tunnel than a broad thoroughfare.

Alejandro could hear Hector moving about underneath the car. Although they were both attending the university, they had known each other only by sight until two weeks ago, when the *Directorio Revolucionario* had put them together for this job. Hector was supposed to be the leader and supposed to know what he was doing, but Alejandro was worried. It all seemed to be taking so long. What was he *doing* under there? Alejandro lit a cigarette and inhaled deeply. He scanned the lines of cars, uniformly gray-black under the yellow streetlights.

Hector was struggling to push a cast-iron manhole cover aside. The words *Electricidad cubano*, in raised lettering, formed a banner across the middle of the cover. In the confined space under the car, even with a pry bar and heaving with both hands, it was very slow going. Grunting and gasping, he scrabbled to turn himself around. He braced his shoulders against the back wheel of the Edsel, cursing by turns the oily chassis and the hot exhaust pipe. When he was in position, he used both feet to shove the cover with all his might, and this time it moved a few inches, scouring the concrete as it slid away. It was enough.

Alejandro heard the scrape of metal on tarmac and a hissed, "*Okay!*" from Hector. He reached into the trunk of the car and pulled out a battered brown leather suitcase, all the while scanning the horizon for any sign he was being observed. He put the suitcase on the ground next to the car and squatted down, close to Hector's position. He opened the lid and eased the contents out, taking care not to snag any of the wires. The dynamite sticks were wrapped with black electrical tape. Hector's outstretched hands, greasy and blackened, were waiting. Alejandro handed him the device like a newborn baby.

Alejandro craned lower to watch. His accomplice set the alarm fifteen minutes ahead, as they had agreed—more than enough time to be blocks away when the thing went off. Hector began to lower the device down toward the bundle of electric wires he could just make out in the murky shaft. Relieved, Alejandro stood up to check the surroundings once more, heart still pounding.

He did not immediately register the distinctive white hood of the patrol car two lanes away. At night and under the street lights, it looked more like a cab than a police cruiser. When he realized his mistake, a wave of panic pulsed in his stomach. He took two rapid drags on his cigarette as he watched the patrol car move into the far lane.

When one of the officers looked over in his direction, Alejandro rolled the spare wheel to the trunk of the Edsel, as if to put it away. As he lifted the wheel, he took one more furtive glance at the police vehicle. It was still moving.

"*¡Rápido! ¡Ven!*" he barked, hoping Hector could hear him.

He could see a leg poking out from under the car, and he tapped it with his foot to get some reaction. Alejandro peered over the trunk lid to check that the patrol car was still moving away. He was horrified to see it signaling left and crossing the stream of cars to make a U-turn at the next intersection.

"*Mierda*," he said, the panic rising. He kicked harder at Hector's leg and yelled as loud as he dared, pleading with his friend to get out from under the car.

"*¡Sal! Ahorita!*"

Hector reacted quickly this time. He crawled backward, catching his collar on an exhaust clamp, cursing as the material held him fast and then ripped. Alejandro pulled frantically on his jacket and helped him stand. Hector cleared the car, stood up and brushed himself down.

The two policemen had parked the patrol car and were walking toward them.

*

"Ray the Rottweiler!" said Gerry Gordon, the first of the wolf pack to see his approach.

Gordie's pink face betrayed his discomfort at having stuffed himself into a tux that no longer accommodated his corpulent frame—if indeed it ever had. He was standing next to Amelia Frankenheim, who was smoking a thin cigar with practiced ease. Ray was always happy to see her, but tonight it would be at the expense of putting up with Gordie, Norman Williams, the grand old bore of the American press corps, and the young pretender to his throne, John Fitzwalter.

"Miss us, Ray?" Gordie said, the flesh of his neck rippling. He chuckled at his own wit.

"Nah, Gordie, not even a little," Ray said, his eyes elsewhere. "Amelia, you look stunning."

Amelia appreciated compliments, especially from guys like Ray who didn't feel themselves excused from common courtesy by the inconvenient reality of her preference for women.

"I do, don't I?" she said. "How was the snow?"

"Deep." He lifted his glass a few inches. "Gentlemen—"

"Ray," said Williams, his inflection suggesting he had only just noticed Ray's arrival. "I read your piece. Very moving. A little sensational, perhaps?"

Asshole. Perhaps it was the British-style irony that Williams tried to affect. Whatever it was, it succeeded in annoying Ray every time.

"You think? She'd been tortured. Skull caved in. A *grandmother*, for Christ's sake!"

"The police said—"

Ray didn't let Fitzwalter finish. He had seen this double act before and had no patience for it. "Who's kidding who here?" he said. "The police did it, and you know it. You just didn't write it."

Fitzwalter did nothing to hide the loathing on his face.

"No, but you did, and once your mind's made up, why confuse it with facts?"

"Up yours, John."

For a moment, no one spoke, not even Gordie. It was John Dempsey, at the podium, who broke the awkward silence.

"Ladies and gentlemen, good evening. May I introduce our honored guests tonight—both men you know well. President Fulgencio Batista." He waited a few moments for the applause to die away. He went on, "And the president of American Telephone, Mr. Henry Williams."

Batista's oiled hair was swept straight back from the protruding brow and hooded eyes. He was wearing a white dress uniform with gold epaulets, gold braid and the usual array of medals on his left breast.

"I need some air," Ray muttered.

Amelia found him on the broad balcony a few minutes later. The speeches were still going on, and Ray was leaning on his elbows and staring out at the city lights as she came over and stood beside him.

"Got a cigarette?" she said, stubbing out her cigar butt in a palm planter. "I hate these things."

Ray pulled a pack of Chesterfields from his pocket and shook one out.

"Thank you, kind sir," she murmured.

He lit hers and another for himself.

Ray cranked his neck from side to side, attempting to relieve the neck strain threatening to become a headache.

"If you're going to tell me to lighten up, forget it."

"I didn't say a word," Amelia said, blowing smoke, "though, as it happens, I believe you'll find our job is to write about the world, not change it single-handed."

"Roll over, is that it?"

She stared at him. Hard.

"That's not it, Ray. I don't see myself like that. I'm sorry if you do."

"You know I don't."

"I don't want to patronize you, Ray, but you leave me no choice. You're the new kid on the block. And I'm glad you're here, really—I am. It brightens my day and makes me remember why I'm here, too. But that righteous anger you feel? That outrage? You think I didn't have that right here on my sleeve when I got to Cuba? Hell, even *Gordie* had it— though, in his case, in big letters on a T-shirt. You think because the great Ray Halliwell feels things so deeply, the rest of us don't?"

"I didn't say that."

"Yes, you did. You may not have meant to, but you did. I like you, Ray. I'm not even offended that you think I'm just doing it by numbers."

"Amelia, give me a break. I'm sorry already."

She took a slow drag on her cigarette.

"We're witnesses to a civil war. It's not personal, Ray. It just feels that way sometimes."

*

Alejandro gripped the roof gutter of the Edsel, arms outstretched and legs spreadeagled. Next to him, one of the cops was patting Hector down for weapons. The other policeman leafed methodically through their identity cards, flicking one page after another. They were in no hurry at all.

Alejandro checked his watch, squinting at the hands in the gloomy light. A couple of minutes, maybe three or four. He stared hard at Hector, willing him to look up.

Finally, Hector turned. Alejandro twisted his arm so Hector could see the watch on his wrist. Around them, the cops and the traffic moved in slow motion. Both knew what they had to do.

Then, like a jump cut in a film, they were running, the cacophony of car horns, revving engines and voices vanishing from their awareness. For a few seconds, neither of them heard any sound but their own pounding hearts.

Alejandro felt the wind in his face. For the first few yards, he was all tension, but as he ran and ran, he felt suddenly alive, exultant, immune. He twisted around, as if to share the moment with his friend, just in time to hear the shot and see Hector crumple to the ground. Alejandro wanted to stop and he wanted to keep on running. In his panic, he tripped and fell, the rough gravel gouging his cheek and temple. He started to crawl and felt a desperate urge to throw up. They would shoot *him* now, he was sure of it.

He turned to see the silhouettes of the policemen aiming their guns—just as a geyser of orange flame erupted beneath the Edsel, throwing the car into the thick night air like a cheap toy. A wall of heat knocked him down. He blinked and gasped for air. He wanted to sleep, but knew he had to get up. He looked for the policemen, but they had vanished, and as his hearing returned, he realized that all around him people were screaming and shouting. He could hear sirens in the distance. The car was burning. He could see Hector lying on the ground; he hadn't moved. And suddenly Alejandro noticed himself whimpering, tears tipping from his eyes. He began to shake violently. He pushed himself to his knees and then to his feet. He staggered and steadied himself—and then, once again, began to run for his life.

*

"What in God's name was that!" said Amelia.

The pulse of light in the night sky had been followed almost immediately by a dull thud. Then the lights went out. Amelia heard the exclamations and subdued cries from the party and a voice appealing for calm.

"Ladies and gentlemen," said the microphoned voice, "we have an emergency generator. Please just stay where you are and we'll have the lights back on in a couple of minutes."

"And I was having such a lovely evening," said Amelia. She took a drag on her cigarette and turned to Ray, intending to share the moment. But she was alone on the balcony.

*

The mangled Edsel was still smoking when a breathless Ray reached the Avenida de los Presidentes. The traffic was gridlocked, and drivers were standing outside their vehicles, chatting and smoking to pass the time. A fire truck, an ambulance and two patrol cars were parked on the median strip, near the site of the explosion. It seemed as though half the police in Havana had turned out.

"*Prensa*," said Ray as he ducked under the cordon tape, but a policeman, shirtsleeves folded back to reveal thick arms, grabbed him by the shoulder of his tux and twisted him away. Ray put the card in front of the man's face as he struggled to get free.

"*Chicago Sun-Times—¡Mire! ¡Léalo!*"

Only when a police captain who recognized Ray nodded his approval did the cop reluctantly let go.

Ray walked away from the cop with the air of a matador—chin up. He could see Jamie, the flash on his camera going off every few seconds, his shoulder-length hair instantly recognizable. He was photographing a body.

"What's happening?" he said.

"Hiya, Ray. Well, we got this guy—" He nodded at the corpse. "And a whole bunch of body parts, and a burning car."

"Yeah, that I see. Tell me, who called you?"

"Nobody. I was just walking around, you know."

"Walking around? That's what you do in the evenings?"

"Yeah, sometimes."

"Quite a social life, Jamie."

"Beats dressing up like a penguin."

"You're a real comic. So?"

"So, three dead. Two cops and this guy. Caught in the act—that's how it looks. Then *boom*. They found a couple of identity cards over there, near the car. Students at the university."

"So we're one short, right? Where's number four?"

"Walked away, I guess."

"You got the car?"

"Yeah, plus I got gruesome and not so gruesome. Take your pick."

"Thanks, Jamie. What would I do without you?"

"Take your own, I guess, or use an agency?"

"I was being rhetorical."

"Uh-huh."

Ray walked toward the burned-out car. The flames had been extinguished, but he circled the still-smoking shell warily anyway. He didn't know what he was looking for, but without a notebook, he'd need to recall whatever details he could find for the story.

It was then that he saw the suitcase. At first he didn't place it. He couldn't think why he should have any recollection of an old leather suitcase, now lying open and empty at the scene of a bomb blast. Checking the police were not watching him, he closed the lid, stood the case upright and wondered about the owner, the man with no story.

13

The Bodeguita del Medio was standing room only, and even then you'd have to fight for the right. The power outage must have hit the old town because candles were the only light source, not just on the tables, but all along the crowded bar.

Ray was pushing his way through groups of hip young people, mostly Cuban, all with drinks in their hands, shouting back and forth to each other in a desperate effort to be heard above the general din.

"Ray! Over here!" Gordie was calling to him from a table near the door, a table he was sharing with Amelia. Gordie got to his feet, still calling to him. "Hey, buddy! Come on."

Ray went right on by.

"I don't think he saw me," he said, leaning to yell in Amelia's ear.

"He saw you," she said.

"What?"

"Never mind," she yelled.

Ray hadn't really expected to find Morgan, but there he was at the end of the bar. He was sitting on a barstool methodically chewing nuts from a bowl. He looked completely at ease, oblivious to the riotous crowd around him and apparently all alone.

Moments later, Ray was beside him at the bar. If Morgan was surprised to see him, he didn't show it.

"Hey, Mr. Halliwell," he said.

"*Mojito!*" Ray shouted to the barman, who was already pouring two bottles of white rum into four or five long glasses stuffed with mint leaves and lime.

The barman gave the slightest nod of his head and added two more frosted glasses to the line.

"You got to try a mojito," said Ray. "They're famous for them here."

Morgan raised his hand to the barman. "Just a Coke, buddy."

"Come on, Morgan. You want a taste of the real Cuba, don't you?"

"I don't drink alcohol, sir."

"You *don't*? Well, you're just full of surprises. Might be a good time to start, you think? Say, what happened to your suitcase?"

"What?" Morgan seemed genuinely confused by the question.

"Your suitcase. The one you had this morning in the cab—you know the one."

Morgan's quizzical expression darkened and the smile vanished.

"What exactly can I do for you, Mr. Halliwell?"

"What about the truth? How would that be?" said Ray, eyes fixed on the Midwesterner. He raised his glass. "Here's to the man with no story," he said. "That's you, isn't it?"

Morgan didn't respond. Instead, he leaned back on his stool, waved his arm and spoke to someone standing directly behind them.

"Hey, *hola*."

Ray turned to see two young women who stood out even in the beautiful Bodeguita crowd. The blonde was wearing an elegant white dress, cut low and square at the neck, with a single strand of pearls at her throat. The brunette, a bit taller than her companion, with dark coffee skin, wore shimmering black sequins. Standing side by side, they had a stunning effect, like mirror images, or a negative and positive of the same photograph. It was with an effort that Ray turned his attention back to Morgan.

"Hey, you hearing me at all?"

Morgan stood up. Ray was suddenly aware of the Midwesterner towering over him. This was the first time they had stood side by side, and Morgan was a good six inches taller. The two girls stood flanking Morgan like sentinels. For some reason, Ray was reminded of a boxer about to go into the ring.

"I'd like to talk to you, Mr. Halliwell, I really would," said Morgan. The voice was calm and barely raised, despite the din in the bar. "But right now I have to go. Thanks for the drink. We'll meet again, sir, I'm sure of it."

Morgan turned away to follow the two girls, not toward the bar's front entrance, but to the service door.

"Get out of Cuba," Ray called after him, but Morgan probably didn't hear him over the noise.

As the service door closed behind Morgan and the two girls, Ray looked round to see three policemen pushing their way from the front entrance into the crowded bar.

14

"Mr. Halliwell," said Senator Hawkes, "did you have any idea where Mr. Morgan went after you spoke with him in the bar?"

"No, sir, not then. He was clearly involved with one of the organizations fighting the regime, but I had no idea which one or what his intentions were."

"And the contacts, these two young women he left with?"

"María Ramírez—now Mrs. María Jensen. And Blanquita—" Ray hesitated. The surname had gone missing over the years.

"Pérez," said María, "Blanquita Pérez. She was my friend—my best friend. It was my job to meet William that night, and Blanquita came with me. It looked better."

"I see. You say this kind of activity was your job, Mrs. Jensen. Can you elaborate?"

"I was a student then, at the university, but I was also a member of the revolutionary movement. Mainly, I carried messages from one part of the organization to another. Sometimes I helped people to find a safe location in the city. Or to go to the mountains."

"You personally took Mr. Morgan to the mountains?"

"No. Not this time. I took him to a safe house. Later he went to the mountains—with others."

"This was in order to join the forces of Fidel Castro?" said Senator Wallace.

"No, ma'am," said María, "we were completely separate from Fidel. I was part of the *Directorio Revolucionario*. I joined at the university. Although we were based in the city, the decision had been made to form a new guerrilla group in the mountains. Fidel had opened the first guerrilla front in the

Sierra Maestra. We became the Second Front of the Escambray."

Senator Marjorie Wallace shuffled in her seat and leaned toward her microphone.

"Mrs. Jensen, it was nevertheless Mr. Morgan's intention to join this group and to fight as a combatant, is that correct?"

"To fight? Yes. William fought with us. *For* us. For a free Cuba."

Capaldi had watched Senator Wallace closely as María was speaking. He didn't have to be a lawyer to see she was already ticking boxes. If the central question was whether Morgan had forfeited his citizenship because he'd been a combatant in a foreign army, the senator seemed to believe she was more than halfway to proving the case for. He cleared his throat and waded in.

"Just to be clear, Senator, the Second Front of the Escambray was one of several rebel groups fighting against the Cuban National Army and the dictator Fulgencio Batista. It was by no means a regular army unit itself, but rather a group of students, farmers and professionals from the cities—especially at that time. Hence William Morgan's role in training these men and women in guerrilla warfare."

"Yes, thank you, counsel," Hawkes said. He checked his watch. "Let's take a break for coffee and reconvene here at eleven o'clock. Recorder, a thirty-minute recess, please. Could you arrange for the refreshments now? Thank you all very much."

Senator Hawkes stood first, and the three-member committee left the room as one.

Refreshments must have been standing by, because the main door opened and a man came in, pushing a trolley with a thermos of coffee and a neat tray of cookies.

They gathered around the trolley and helped themselves, alone now in the committee room. Capaldi unscrewed the thermos lid. The aroma of coffee was reassuring and welcome. No one spoke much, each of them mentally going over the past hour and a half. Ray handed the first cup to María.

"You okay?"

She nodded and sipped the hot drink appreciatively, holding the mug with both hands.

"Is the room really cold?" she said. "Or is it me?"

"It's cold."

Ray turned to Capaldi

"I was talking with María before we started," Ray said, leaving his back to María. "I've got my office working on tracking down a couple of people—"

As the two men huddled in earnest conversation, like coaches at the first-quarter break, María helped herself to sugar, one spoon and then another. Even after more than twenty years in America, she preferred her coffee sweet, the sweeter the better. They were, of course, rude and unthinking to exclude her this way, but she felt no urge to join in their talk of strategy and tactics.

She wandered toward an alcove in the wall, where a window might have been if they'd been above ground. Instead, there was just an air vent. Perched on the narrow sill above the vent, the weak stream of warm air helped to shut out the cold room and everything in it. María held the warm coffee cup to her chest, closed her eyes and counted backward from a hundred, trying to calm herself.

At eighty-eight, she stumbled and stopped. Morgan was laughing, his chest heaving as he gulped for breath. She had his arms pinned to the bed under her knees and was tickling him gently, tracing his ribs with her nails. He could have thrown her off using one hand if he chose, but then, they were both naked, so why would he? Morgan was bearded, but that couldn't have been so—the timings were wrong.

María opened her eyes to see Capaldi and Ray still talking. She sipped at the coffee and set her mind back to the task. She made good progress to sixty-four, using the same inner chant she had used a thousand times in prison. There, she'd learned to isolate her mind, to retire from the roaches that scuttled over legs and arms, from the echoing wails of those whose minds had snapped.

Long periods in solitary confinement—once for more than six months as punishment for resistance to the prison regime—had been the worst, leaving her with a gnawing hunger for wind and rain and sun. She remembered the rain especially and the relief it brought, changing the color of the mud in the courtyard from tan to puce. By gripping the bars on the high window and heaving herself up, she could feel the cool wetness on her face and just see the sodden ground before dropping back to the concrete floor, weak and exhausted. Sometimes she would let herself cry then, knowing she was alone, thinking of the children.

Again she forced herself to count. At fifty-five, she thought of the torn old prison bible she'd smuggled into solitary, and her favorite story, Job's patient acceptance of his own trials. She had tried to emulate his example. But even he might have been at a loss to deal with what she found when she was finally released.

María's house had been confiscated by the regime and she had spent her first night of freedom at her parents' home in Santa Clara where her daughters were then living. Her youngest daughter ordered her mother to sleep in the hall, calling her a traitor to Cuba. A few weeks later, the twelve year old had attacked María, pulling at her hair and clothes. A short time after, her elder daughter had grabbed a pair of scissors and tried to stab her.

María sought the advice of a priest who told her to find work and a new place to live in order to give her daughters time to adjust. Nuns in Havana offered her a room and board in their convent. In return, María helped to care for the sick, those who had found their own refuge there. She also knitted sweaters for sixty-five dollars a month and returned to Santa Clara whenever she could to give the money to her ailing parents for the care of her daughters.

Little by little, the strategy had begun to reap benefits, though nothing happened overnight.

In September 1978 Castro announced that any former prisoners who wanted to leave Cuba could do so with their families. For María, it was a dream come true and, with the help of a loan from her sister, now living in New York, she began to make the necessary arrangements to fly to America, with her parents, her children and their new spouses.

There was just one hitch. María's case was deemed by the authorities to be 'special.' Her family would be allowed to leave, but María would not. On the night of October 27, 1979 she watched their plane take off for Miami. The next day, she visited the cemetery at Colon where William was buried and sat by his grave and cried.

It was not until July 1980 that the bureaucracy relented and María was allowed to join those waiting at Mariel on the Cuban coast for boats that would take thousands of 'undesirables' to Florida. The final count had one hundred and twenty-five thousand Cubans arriving in Florida on one thousand seven hundred boats. Twenty-seven migrants died on the journey, including fourteen on one overloaded boat.

She forced herself to count again. At forty-three, she heard her name.

"María?" said Capaldi. She looked up to see the two men already sitting at the witness table. "Ready?"

María stood up from the sill and opened the palm of one hand to a last breath of warm air from the vent.

"Yes."

The committee filed back into the room and took their seats. The recorder was already waiting at her machine.

"Senator Hawkes?" said Capaldi.

"Counsel?"

"Senator, forgive me, but is there any way we could do something about the temperature in here? It seems a little chilly. I don't know if you agree?"

Hawkes glanced at Senator Wallace for confirmation, as if a woman would be sensitive to such issues where a man like himself would not. He was embarrassed when she batted it right back to him with just a look.

"I'll see what can be done, Counsel, thank you. Recorder, would you mind alerting those responsible? Thank you."

The recorder picked up a phone and, covering the mouthpiece with one hand, spoke briefly, then nodded to Hawkes.

"Okay," said Hawkes, "let's get started. Mr. Halliwell, we'd like to continue with your testimony. Counsel?"

Hawkes looked at Capaldi for approval, even though they both understood the gesture was merely a formality.

The senator turned to Ray. "After Morgan left the bar that night, can you tell us, when was the next occasion you had contact with him?"

"It was two or even three months later, Senator. Late February or March as I recall. I imagined he'd left the country. That would have been the sensible thing to do."

"You met with him?"

"No, not then. I received a note. It was in an envelope addressed to me, but delivered by hand and titled 'Why Am I Here.' I remember the punctuation was a little haphazard and it was badly typed, but his signature was on the bottom. The note had been pushed under the door of my apartment—"

15

"Why—am—I—here," Pam said. "I don't get it."

She was lying on the bed, examining her slender legs and reading in a distracted way from Morgan's note. She swept a hand from smoothly shaved calf to thigh, in search of any imperfection.

"If you don't know—" Ray said.

"Funny man," Pam said. She didn't like the offhand way he'd made the quip without even bothering to look at her. She used to think his casual sarcasm sexy, even sophisticated, but not anymore. Too often these days it felt personal.

Ray was standing at the window with his back to her, wearing white boxers, toweling his wet hair and scanning the street below. Whoever had delivered the note was no doubt long gone, but he wanted to be sure. He caught a glimpse of a woman crossing the street—a blonde. But she disappeared down a side street before he could be sure of his intuition. Besides, Pam was still talking.

"I mean, it should read, 'Why am I here?'—question mark. Or 'Why *I* am *here*'—statement."

"So you going to fail him in English, one-o-one?"

"I'm just saying—tenth grade, no more."

She found something on her thigh that caught her attention.

"Fourth floor are pissed, I know that," she added, almost to herself.

Ray turned, suddenly interested. "What do you mean?"

"I mean, the guy's got a file. William Morgan? I'm sure it's the same guy. I pulled it a few days ago for John."

Ray came over and sat beside her on the bed. He studied her for a moment and then ran his hand slowly up her outstretched leg.

"You're tickling," she said as the goose bumps rose on her skin, though she did nothing to pull away.

"Am I?"

"Stop."

"So?"

"So what?" said Pam. She let the note slip to the bed.

"*So*, can you get me sight of the file?"

Pam sat up on her elbows.

"Ray Halliwell. You wouldn't be using my weakness for the older man, would you? Just to get a story?"

"What did you say?" he said in mock surprise.

"You heard me."

Ray smiled. He moved his hand to trace a butterfly line up her silky flank.

"Working with spooks is making you unusually suspicious, young lady."

"Oh, really?"

"Yeah—really."

Pam knew her part well and pouted as if she'd been scolded.

"And if I'm a good girl?"

*

A couple of days later, Ray was sitting at the kitchen table in Jamie's darkened apartment with Morgan's file open in front of him, spot-lit by an anglepoise light that squeaked each time he moved its flexible neck. The folder was stamped "EYES ONLY" in red letters, as were some of the documents, especially those relating to FBI or CIA surveillance.

The blinds were closed. Across the room Jamie had set up his tripod, with the camera pointing down at the floor. He was crouching to position a five-by-seven head-and-shoulders shot of Morgan that could have been an enlargement from a passport original or, more likely, a police mugshot. Either way, Morgan was unsmiling, with a direct stare carrying more than a hint of menace. Jamie made a final check through the viewfinder and pushed the plunger on the shutter release cable. The flash popped and whined as the batteries recharged the unit for the next shot.

"That's that," Jamie said, picking up the photo of Morgan from the floor. "What else you got?"

Ray's attention was flitting back and forth between the file and the note from Morgan that had been pushed under his door. It took a moment for him to process Jamie's request.

"What?"

"This one's pretty unusable," said Jamie. He wandered over to the table and handed it back to Ray. "The guy looks psycho. Got anything better?"

Ray leafed through to the back of the file. He found another shot of Morgan, in full dress uniform, probably upon graduating from boot camp. "This is the one."

Jamie studied the shot. "This I can use. I'll crop it like so, okay?"

But Ray didn't hear him. A candid picture of two young women sitting in a café together, taken with a very long lens, had caught his eye. The brunette was checking her makeup in a vanity mirror. The blonde was glancing away from her companion and into the middle distance. Ray recalled his fleeting impression of her from that night at the Bodeguita, when she and her friend had appeared so confident and self-assured, even cocky. This young woman was different, with a hint of melancholy beyond her years.

"Here," he said, holding the photograph out to Jamie. "This one, too. Can you give me a single of this girl?"

"Cute," Jamie observed as he went back to the tripod. "Very cute."

Ray shuffled the papers into a neat pile and began to read again from the beginning of the file, cross-referencing what he saw there with Morgan's note. He turned over the dry five-page summary and stopped at the first police charge sheet—a poor copy of the original and barely legible. It cited

Morgan on a felony charge for attempted robbery with violence following what seemed to be a bungled attempt to hold up a convenience store. He had been picked up for the offense a week later and positively identified, but denied any involvement. A month later, the charges had been dropped for no obvious reason that Ray could see. Perhaps Morgan's being just sixteen at the time had something to do with it. The report cited his parents' offer to provide police with a surety on their son's behalf.

Ray turned to the first paragraph of Morgan's note and read.

"Only a hundred miles from Miami, men must fight and die for freedom in a country ruled by a dictator, supported and supplied with arms by the United States. I cannot say I have always been a good citizen, but being here, I can appreciate the way of life that is ours from birth. Here men fight and die for the simple freedom that we as Americans take for granted."

The flash on Jamie's camera popped somewhere behind Ray, but he hardly noticed. Putting the man in the letter together with the man in the file was taking a real effort of mind. He flipped a couple more sheets of police files: one a misdemeanor involving public drunkenness and trespass, the other a petty theft charge with a guilty verdict, recorded on a separate court charge sheet. He got to the digest of Morgan's military record. The man had signed up on his eighteenth birthday and been kicked out with a dishonorable discharge five years later. In between, he had racked up a remarkable list of crimes, from brawling to assaulting an officer, to going AWOL on two occasions, and even arson. Three of his five years in the service had been spent behind bars, where his record was little better: refusing to work, fighting and spending a good deal of his time in solitary. The psychiatrist's examination spoke of a man with "sociopathic tendencies, a loner with a relatively high IQ and no discernible ambitions to better his situation, despite a solid middle-class family environment."

Ray turned back to the note and read on.

"Here the impossible happens every day. Where a boy of nineteen can march for twelve hours with a broken foot without complaint. Where a cigarette is smoked by ten men. Where men do without water so others may drink, where they march twenty miles on a cup of powdered milk, carrying a rifle, ammunition and a fifty-pound pack. Men untrained in the ways of war, who meet and defeat the Cuban army at every turn."

If this was indeed the same person detailed in the military record, Ray had no way to account for the transformation. He double-checked the signature dated a week ago, and wondered if Morgan had really composed the letter. Sure, it had some convincing grammatical errors that made a neat fit with the renegade in the file, but those could also be the result of poor translation.

Ray conjured a picture of the man he had sat beside in the cab and, later, at the Bodeguita. Reticence, Midwestern manners and homespun common sense characterized the guy tapping his battered suitcase and whistling the US Army anthem. But at the Bodeguita, Ray had glimpsed another facet to Morgan. Goading him about the suitcase, he'd seen something more dangerous and unpredictable in the man's character. It showed itself for only a moment before the mask was back in place.

Jamie was standing beside him as he turned the page to read an FBI report with photographs attached.

"Hey, isn't that Bartone?" said Jamie. "What's your man doing with a mob boss?"

"What's he *doing*?" said Ray, as if the answer were obvious.

Jamie looked blank.

"Putting us and this godforsaken island on the front page, my friend—*that's* what he's doing."

Jamie studied the surveillance photo again for clues, but all he could see was Bartone and Morgan, with two others, standing together outside a warehouse. Ray took the photo from his hand and put it back in the file.

"Think about the big picture, Jamie. And give me a headline."

Jamie thought about it. "Flat tire comes to Cuba?"

"*What?* What's that? Flat tire?"

"You know, like 'bozo'—or 'oilcan' maybe?"

"Exactly what language are you speaking, Jamie?"

"American."

"And that says it all."

"The guy's a hood, right?"

"Wrong, Jamie. The guy had, shall we say, a checkered past leading him to clash with the law. A loner who—"

"Got kicked out of the army, you said."

"Who had trouble dealing with authority figures—a natural-born rebel without a cause."

"Like the movie."

"Now we're getting somewhere. A rebel who came to Cuba and found—?"

"Paradise? Just kidding."

"A cause, Jamie. He found a cause."

Jamie's expression brightened. "Spiffy. Can I get a byline on this one?"

16

Amelia Frankenheim lowered her copy of the *Chicago Sun-Times* to see Ray making his way across the dining room toward her table.

The doors to the terrace of the Havana Yacht Club were thrown open, and the contrast of solid walls and tall, widely spaced windows sliced the large room into chunks of light and shade. White-jacketed waiters glided between the busy tables, serving salads from silver trays and pouring white wine from sweating bottles. The hum of conversation was low but lively, the atmosphere intimate. Havana society came here to see and be seen, but only at lunchtime. Mornings and afternoons, the club reverted once again to the province of those acquainted with sailing and the sea.

"Sorry," Ray said as he slumped unceremoniously into the chair opposite Amelia.

"My time is yours—especially now."

"Come on, Amelia, when have I ever been punctual?"

"Don't be so defensive. I'm serious. You're boss." Her finger tapped the folded copy of the *Sun-Times*, showing Morgan's photograph above the crease. "I hear this got syndication."

Ray's smile was coy. "Jealous?"

"Yes," she said, drawling the word in a way that implied some reservation. "Naturally. But also curious. No direct quotes? You *have* actually met this guy, right?"

"Sure. Twice, actually. Don't worry, there's more to come."

"Like whether the guy is for real?"

"Exactly. Did you order yet?"

"No, but as it seems you're about to stand me up on top of being late, I think I'll do just that."

Amelia was looking over Ray's shoulder and watching John Dempsey wind his way between the tables. He was giving a wave or a word here and there, but proceeding toward them with a definite sense of purpose. Ray followed Amelia's look and then slowly sank down in his chair and buried his nose in the menu. She enjoyed his discomfort.

"What did you expect? Try to be nice."

A moment later, Dempsey was standing beside them.

"Amelia," he said by way of a greeting.

"John." Amelia had a knack for imitating others. For Dempsey, she laced her impersonation with gentle mockery.

"Ray," he said, regaining some composure, "could you give us a minute?" He looked across the room toward a corner table, where Lyman Kirkpatrick sat with his wheelchair pushed tight under the white tablecloth, as if trapped.

Ray closed the menu and stood up.

"This won't take long, Amelia," said Dempsey.

"Take him away, Officer," she said, getting yet another flutter of uncertainty out of Dempsey. Amelia watched them all the way to the table and the waiting Kirkpatrick. She saw Ray shake hands perfunctorily with Kirkpatrick. It was only when the waiter appeared beside her that she returned to the menu.

"What's good today?" she said in perfectly accented Spanish.

Kirkpatrick studied Ray through his black-rimmed glasses with unnerving attention, but appeared in no great hurry to say anything. He was perfectly still, and when he did finally speak, Ray couldn't help but feel as though he were sitting in front of the school principal.

"I appreciate your time, Mr. Halliwell, and I'll come straight to the point. As you know, we have a file on William Morgan."

Ray flinched in spite of himself. He looked at Dempsey.

"Come on, Ray," Dempsey said. "We pay her salary for Christ's sake. It's a two-way street."

If Kirkpatrick enjoyed making Ray squirm, he didn't show it. Dempsey, on the other hand, was fidgeting like a retriever at his master's side, anticipating the kill. It was only with an effort of will that Ray managed to confine his reaction to a shake of the head.

"We're assuming you will have further contact with Morgan, especially given his new high profile, courtesy of your paper. It's our understanding you may be planning a trip to the Escambray. For which you'll need a pass."

Ray let Kirkpatrick's words hang in the air. They had him by the short hairs, but there was no reason to make their lives easier by giving anything away before he had time to work out the angles. These guys had sanctioned the story, that much was clear. But why?

"Be that as it may," Kirkpatrick went on with steady confidence, "I'm sure you'll appreciate that Morgan may feel a little exposed, given the Cuban authorities' reaction to your piece—as, indeed, you yourself may. We can help with that situation."

And with that, Ray was back in the game. Now that he knew what they wanted from him, he was ready to make his move.

"Mr. Kirkpatrick, you're offering what exactly? Protection?"

"That's not what I said."

"But it is what you meant, isn't it? And let me guess, in return, all you guys would ask is access to a little information here and there, placing a story perhaps, giving US interests—as perceived by you, of course—a fair crack. Am I on the right lines?"

Now Kirkpatrick was silent.

"And Morgan. You cut him the same deal for the inside story on life in the mountains, troop strengths, armaments, strategy, political affiliations, maybe even leverage if the rebels keep making headway—as it seems they will—against this corrupt, murderous regime, which, I'm sure I don't need to remind you, has been actively supported by the Agency for years. Hedging your bets, Mr. Kirkpatrick? You guys don't like to be on the losing side, do you? And tell me, is there some sanction you have in mind if you can't get your groceries here? My press card? *Persona non grata* and a plane ride to Miami?" Ray leaned forward with both elbows on the table. "Try it."

"You're overreacting."

"Am I?"

"We're not asking you to endorse the message, just to pass it on."

"Listen, you let the file slip because you knew about the note and you knew I'd do the story anyway. You were hoping the stuff in it would help discredit Morgan, and when it didn't, you got yourselves a new angle, with me as the messenger boy."

Ray slowly pushed his chair back and stood up.

"Thank you, gentlemen. There was a question mark in my mind about Morgan, but no longer—not unless you guys are a whole lot cleverer than you're looking about now. And frankly, that's a risk I'm willing to take. Say hi to Pam for me, John. You may pay *her* salary, but you don't pay mine."

Ray took a step away from the table, then turned back.

"By the way, if you're out on the water, take it easy. Wind's against the tide, and you know what that means."

Ray walked away and Kirkpatrick glared at Dempsey as if he should explain.

Dempsey shrugged. "How should I know? I'm not a sailor."

Amelia didn't look up as Ray approached, but she could sense the mood. He took his seat opposite her and flicked open the menu.

She gave him a minute before she said, "How do you feel about shellfish?"

"I feel good," he replied, loosening his tie. "Very good."

17

Ray stood to one side of the lobby entrance, protected from the already hot sun by the hotel portico. His portable Smith Corona typewriter, in its battered black case, sat next to his knapsack on the ground. He was wearing a sleeveless khaki bush jacket bought specially for the trip, with more pockets than he needed, too new and well pressed to be worn casually. Together with the sturdy boots, purchased at the same shop two days before, the ensemble made him feel rather more conspicuous than he would have wished.

Saturday was the Hotel Capri's changeover day, and at two p.m. the driveway was chaotic with coaches and cabs jostling for position like jammed bumper cars. Bag-laden trolleys steered by impatient porters were weaving between the vehicles. The guests, both new and departing, huddled like nervous sheep corralled by the comings and goings in all directions.

Ray had thought carefully about the rendezvous. The photos in Morgan's file were a clear indication that María was subject to regular surveillance, which was why he had chosen the Saturday changeover as his departure time. The crowds and the confusion could only help them slip away.

As far as Kirkpatrick and Dempsey were concerned, the Agency had little reason to interfere with Ray and his plans at this stage, unless purely out of spite. Better to let him reach Morgan, establish contact and revisit the proposal thereafter. Whether the Cuban authorities felt the same way was another matter, and it was the police, in whatever guise, that Ray was watching for as he waited.

Tracking María down had been straightforward. From the copied photograph and the details in the file, it was a simple case of checking the university records on the pretext of writing a piece about students most likely to succeed. The university's administration office was flattered by the request and offered the information freely. Persuading her had proved much more tricky, and it was only after Ray had met with and gotten a green light from the hierarchy of the *Directorio Revolucionario*—the student revolutionary group of which she was a part—that she'd finally contacted Ray to arrange a time and a place. Still, she made it patently clear that she considered his 'special request' for her to act as his guide—because she'd met Morgan, however briefly—was at best irrelevant and at worst irrational. María would be working under orders.

"Hey, buddy!" Gerry Gordon bellowed. He came down the lobby steps and dropped his bag on the ground. The big man was sweating and a little breathless, with the damp stub of a cigar clamped between his teeth. "You on the one o'clock? Let's grab a cab together."

"No, Gordie, I'm not."

Gordon fished a hotel matchbook from his top pocket and pulled a match to light the butt. Ray noticed the sweat rings on his shirt, under the arms and where his barrel chest pushed against the fabric.

"You're not *what?*" Gordon said. He tried and failed to light the cigar butt, apparently having forgotten his own question.

"I'm not on the one o'clock flight."

"You got a bag," he said, as if this fact alone offered clear proof to the contrary. "And boots?" he added with a quizzical tone.

"That's right, Gordie, I'm wearing boots."

With a new match and three or four energetic puffs, Gordon finally got the stub to light, producing clouds of blue smoke.

He beamed with satisfaction. "So?"

"So what?" said Ray, taking a couple of steps to escape the haze of smoke and Gordon's pink inquisitive face.

"So where you going?" Gordon said to his back.

Ray ignored the question. A few cars back in the queue, he spied a dull green station wagon matching the description María had given him. Ray didn't recognize the young man driving, but he was certain the woman wearing sunglasses in the back seat was María. When the station wagon found a slot and stopped, she stepped out and waved.

Gordon, whose journalistic instincts were considerably sharper than his boorish manner might suggest, quickly made the connection with María. As Ray hastily grabbed his knapsack and typewriter, Gordie gave a low wolf whistle.

"Okay, say no more, *amigo*."

Ray stopped dead. He wanted to knock some of that tiresome locker-room banter out of his churlish fellow reporter, but there was too little time, and too much at stake, to waste on a buffoon like Gordie. He took a breath.

"Forget it," he said.

"I will, buddy," said Gordie, watching Ray head toward the station wagon. "Didn't see a thing—my eyes are dim! Hey, see you next week, okay?"

"*Hola*," said the young driver, taking Ray's bag and typewriter and putting them in the trunk. "I am Alejandro," he added.

"How you doing?" said Ray.

Ray slid into the back seat of the car beside María and pulled the door closed.

"Hi," he said to María, "everything okay?"

Forty minutes later, the station wagon had cleared Havana's southern suburbs and was on the main road to Santa Cruz del Norte and Matanzas. They would head east along the coast and then southeast across the island, toward Cienfuegos.

Ray's shirt back was sticking to the red vinyl seat. He had already discarded the bush jacket and was wearing dark glasses against the sun's glare and the hot, dusty wind buffeting through the open windows. For the first few miles he'd tried making conversation with María, but she was clearly in no mood to talk. As soon as she was certain they were not being followed, she'd closed her eyes and now appeared to be sleeping. Alejandro was mostly concentrating on the road, though he couldn't resist checking out the *yanqui* reporter in the rearview mirror and trying a few words in excited Spanish. Ray pretended not to understand.

The road was narrow and badly potholed. The tarmac cut through flat russet fields of bare earth, ready for sowing with corn or rice, and deep-green grass pastures with a lone grazing cow or a tired-looking donkey tethered to a post here and there. The air smelled of coffee and dung and woodsmoke as they passed roadside farms and *bohíos*, the simple palm-thatched huts of the *campesinos* who worked the land.

But it was the clouds that caught Ray's eye. Streaks of black stratus—soon to spread and build, bringing the regular afternoon rains of the tropics—crept stealthily around the knees of the white cumulonimbus like circling sharks.

Ray looked at María and saw that she was still sleeping. As the car passed a line of royal palms, planted with military precision by the roadside, the sun strobed across her face. Her blonde hair was ruffling and twisting in the wind. Her arms were folded like a defiant child's, and her dress lay crimped over her tanned legs.

A pothole banged him back into the now.

"*¡Perdón!*" Alejandro yelled.

Ray could see the young driver's grin reflected in the rearview mirror and wondered if the apology was genuine. María opened her eyes for a moment, checked the landscape and promptly closed them again without a word.

Ray shuffled and stretched his legs as well as he could manage, leaning forward to pull the sticky shirt away from the skin of his back. The hot wind dried the damp material quickly but did little to cool him. He settled back against the warm vinyl, already longing for a good shower and the crisp, dry cool of an air-conditioned room.

18

For twenty miles they skirted the foothills of the Escambray Mountains. With the setting sun behind the car, the shadows slowly climbed the steep slopes, leaving the orange peaks lit like a row of church candles, before extinguishing them one by one.

As the last glowing mountain top winked out, they were approaching a checkpoint, manned by both soldiers and police. Idling in the roadway behind two other cars they sat under arc lights while, fifty yards ahead, a half-dozen soldiers stood at the makeshift barrier, checking documents, passengers and the trunks of cars. Ray had come armed with a letter from a sugar mill owner in Cienfuegos, inviting him to see the mill and talk about the island's number one product for a piece he was writing on the economy. He would never meet the man or write the article, but it provided a reason for being here.

The soldiers waved the first car through and Alejandro inched the station wagon forward, drumming his fingers nervously on the steering wheel.

María turned to Ray. "Give me your passport."

Ray did as he was told and she handed his passport and her identity card forward to Alejandro.

"*Cálmate*," she said to Alejandro, with a clear tone of command rather than concern.

"*Bien*," he replied, without much conviction. But he stopped his furious drumming.

A moment later, the car in front was through the barrier and it was their turn. Two soldiers were waiting for them, each with a gun slung over his shoulder. The headlight beams illuminated them from the waist up, leaving only their faces shadowed beneath their cap bills.

Without warning, María slid over to Ray, took his arm and put it around her neck, letting her head come to rest on his chest. He had suggested before the trip that she might pass herself off as his translator, but now it seemed she had something else in mind. The awareness of her body close to his, though a little unnerving, was certainly no hardship, even under the circumstances.

"*Sus papeles*," said the first soldier as he leaned down by Alejandro's window, shining his flashlight around inside the car and into Ray's eyes, momentarily blinding him.

The second soldier was walking slowly along Ray's side of the car, also shining his light on the occupants, but keeping his distance and with one hand on the grip of the Thompson. María snuggled a little closer and kept her eyes closed, feigning sleep.

The first soldier examined their papers, paying particular attention to Ray's passport and the letter from the sugar mill. Ray listened to Alejandro and the soldier discussing him.

"*El Americano es tan feo que tiene que pagar para estar con ella.*"

Ray just about got the gist of it. Alejandro seemed to be telling the soldier that the American was so—he was pretty sure he had the word right—*ugly* that he had to pay the woman sitting next to him for her company.

The soldier gave the papers another cursory glance and handed them back.

"*Ah, los yanquis, nada más que dinero y nada de cerebro,*" said the soldier, stepping back and signaling to raise the gate. "*¡Adelante! ¡Pasen!*"

All money and no thinking, or was it mind? No, brains—

As they pulled away, María slid back to her side of the car. Ray began to bristle at the idea that neither María nor Alejandro had brought him into the story before they hit the checkpoint. Alejandro's fingers were once again drumming, now in relief, and he was whistling as he drove slowly under the barrier and weaved between parked jeeps and a troop truck.

"Eh, Alejandro," said Ray. "*Entonces, ¿soy feo?*" *I'm ugly am I?* He saw Alejandro's eyes dart to the rearview mirror in surprise.

"You have Spanish?" said Alejandro, turning to look excitedly at Ray. "I have some English!" A sudden bend in the road surprised him, and he had to swerve a little as one wheel strayed over the narrow shoulder.

"*Bueno,*" said Ray. "Then watch the road."

Even María smiled. Ray turned to her next.

"I thought we agreed you were my translator."

She said, "It seems you don't need one."

They stopped twice during the night, first for gas at a one-pump station where they had to wake the owner from his bed, and later to meet the call of nature and, if possible, grab an hour's sleep. Ray offered to drive, but María said it would look odd if they were stopped. Alejandro said he preferred to drive anyway because he was too excited to sleep.

It was during that second stop, as María dozed, stretched out on the back seat, that Ray and Alejandro stood together some distance from the car and smoked cigarettes. *Alejandro.* It was a common enough name, but a faint bell was ringing in Ray's mind.

"So why are you on this trip, my friend?" said Ray.

"*¿Que?*" said Alejandro.

The language barrier was still up. Ray moved his hands to an imaginary steering wheel. "Why? Why do you go?"

"Ah!" said the young man. "I go to the mountains. To fight."

"Are you a fighter?"

"*Estudiante.* But I learn. Maybe with *el Americano*, yes?"

"What do you know of this man, Morgan?"

"He is good man. Strong man. Please, you can take photograph of me with him, like this?"

Alejandro put his arm around Ray's shoulders to demonstrate.

"Yeah, okay," said Ray, a little embarrassed, "I can do that. But why now? Why go now to fight?"

Alejandro withdrew his arm, much to Ray's relief. The young man dragged on his cigarette and stubbed the butt out on the ground.

"I must go," he said. "Havana is finish for me."

Ray looked directly at him. *The identity card*, he thought. *Alejandro*.

"You're the one that got away, aren't you?"

Again, Alejandro struggled to understand.

Keeping his voice low, Ray pursed his lips to make a schoolboy imitation of an explosion.

It was Alejandro's turn to look embarrassed. "You know?"

"Yeah, I know."

Alejandro said nothing.

"Don't worry," said Ray, "I can keep a secret."

Ray looked back to the station wagon.

"You know each other? From university?"

"Some. Little."

"What do you know?"

"She is leader. With the *Directorio*, you understand?"

Ray nodded and waited for more. It wasn't fair to the kid, but he waited anyway.

"You say—*secret?*" said Alejandro.

"Yeah. I never reveal my sources."

Alejandro didn't understand the words, but he got the drift. All at once, he was conspiratorial.

"*El Americano?* She say to me, her heart go boom, boom. *¿Entiende usted?*"

At first light, they were less than twenty miles from Cienfuegos and traveling between tall stands of golden cane on either side of the road. It was the time of the *zafra*, or cane-cutting season. Occasionally they passed a group of *campesinos* dressed in ragged shorts and T-shirts. The men wore broad straw hats and carried their machete-like cane knives tucked into belts, slapping at their sides with each step. Many were walking to the fields; some traveled in open trucks, herded together like livestock. Some were already at work. As the car sped past, the zing of the metal blades slashing through the woody stems of the cane sounded like the ricochet of bullets.

To the north of the road, the four-thousand-foot mountains of the Escambray, now backlit by the rising sun, cast long shadows over the plain. Although not as tall as the Sierra Maestra to the east, where Castro and the July 26 forces had their bases, the Escambray seemed all the more imposing because they rose straight up from the flatland with no ramp of foothills to diminish the effect.

The battered green station wagon slowed as it labored up a winding road above Cienfuegos on the road to Ranchuelo. Movement on the side of the road drew Ray's attention: four black vultures flapping upward to the bleached top branches of a long-dead cottonwood, probably disturbed by the station wagon's approach. From a lower limb, the body of a young man dangled from the noose around its neck, the head lolling unnaturally to one side. The face was smashed and bloody, and around a bare bicep was the black and red armband of the July 26 Movement. A cardboard sign slung around the neck bore, in crude painted lettering that had dripped and run, the single word "*Traidor.*"

"Stop! Alejandro! Hold up!" said Ray.

Alejandro did as he was told, and Ray was out of the car in an instant, scrabbling in the knapsack for his camera.

María got out too, and slumped over the car roof. Ray pulled out the small Leica he had borrowed from Jamie. He checked the film winder and began snapping pictures, first from a distance and then nearer, until he was standing directly in front of the body. He could hear the hum of the flies and caught the sweetish, almost lemony smell of death. He forced himself to look up at the face. The tongue was bulging like a sausage from the blood-encrusted mouth. He was so morbidly engaged with the horror in front of him that the scream from behind came like a heart attack.

"*¡¡Para ya! ¡Para ya!*" she wailed. "*¡Basta!*"

Ray turned to see María shivering with rage, eyes ablaze.

"What?" he said, heart pounding and angry now. "What the hell is it?"

"Get in the car!" she cried. "Now!" She got in, slamming the door hard behind her, and began shouting at Alejandro, for what Ray could only imagine.

The next moment, Alejandro had gunned the engine, backed up and pulled onto the highway. Ray started to wonder whether they might leave him standing there. But the car screeched to a halt beside him, raising a haze of dust.

He opened the door and got in beside María.

Her body was rigid, her jaw clenched. She wouldn't meet his gaze. Ray had no idea of the connection between María and the body hanging from the dead snag—only that there was one.

19

Hotel La Unión faced directly onto Calle 31, a dead-straight street in the strict grid pattern characteristic of old town colonial Cienfuegos. Alejandro parked directly outside the main entrance of the severe pastel-blue exterior with its large floor-to-ceiling windows shuttered against the sun. A doorman hovered but didn't approach, perhaps uncertain of the provenance implied by the dusty green station wagon.

"This is your hotel," said María. "You will be contacted tonight. Expect a man by the name of Tomás. He will offer you a tour of the harbor. You can remember?"

"Yeah, I can remember," Ray said.

There'd been no more conversation after the boy in the tree. Even Alejandro had been silent for the half hour it took them to reach the heart of the city, but now, as they sat with the engine running, his fingers were once again drumming on the steering wheel.

"*Alejandro*," María said to him, "*las bolsas.*"

Alejandro opened the driver's door and left it open. He went to the rear of the station wagon to retrieve Ray's bags and typewriter in its case. Ray took his chance.

"María—"

She was waiting for him.

"His name was Eduardo. *Is* Eduardo. Eduardo García. He was seventeen years old and he loved baseball. He *lived* for baseball. Write that in your newspaper."

Ray studied her. He understood about the boy, but this seemed personal.

"Have I *done* something?"

"You've done nothing."

Far from offering absolution, she made the words sound like an accusation.

"Look, it was ugly, and taking pictures like that? That's my—"

"Your job?"

"Yes."

"I understand, Mr. Halliwell."

"Ray. Please, call me Ray."

She studied him closely. "Why?"

"Why? Because we're here together, because—"

"Because it's your job to get along with people."

"If you want to put it that way."

"Like the woman from the Embassy?"

Now Ray was silent.

"I delivered Morgan's note to your apartment."

So, it had been her that day.

"You're judging me?"

"Not for the reasons you imagine, Mr. Halliwell."

"Then what is it?"

"This woman works with the CIA, no?"

"What? And you think I do?"

"You were also seen at the Yacht Club."

"I don't believe this—"

Ray opened his own door and was halfway out of the car when he turned back to her.

"You're upset, I know that, and I'm sorry about your friend. You're also way out of line. Thanks for the company."

Alejandro was standing on the sidewalk with Ray's bags. He looked sheepish, as if he'd overheard the words. He couldn't have missed the tone.

Ray took his bags.

"Thanks, kid. I guess I'll see you later."

"Tonight we go together," Alejandro said.

"Yeah."

"It is okay," Alejandro added, though whether he was talking about the next day or about what had just passed between Ray and María was not clear.

"*Hasta luego*," Ray said. And with that, he walked up the steps to the hotel entrance and the waiting doorman.

Ray paced in his hotel room and smoked his second cigarette, lit with the butt of the first. It was an indulgence, but he had two sealed cartons of two hundred apiece in his knapsack—Winstons and Chesterfields—to give to Morgan and his comrades. He'd been told cigarettes were always in short supply. It occurred to Ray that Morgan had probably taken cigarettes on his journey too, perhaps leaving from this same hotel, maybe even this very room.

The austere façade of the Hotel La Union hid a sumptuous courtyard where—with the benefit of rest—Ray had managed to regain his composure and put the fracas with María in perspective. She was young, exhausted by the road trip and disturbed by what they'd seen. Besides, who really knew which side someone was on in this war—or why?

He was sorry things had ended as they did, not least because this young woman had something that intrigued him. By turns distant, even cold, then passionate in the extreme, María had left him with a hunger for more. It took nerve to have a dig at him like that and although way, way out of line, he liked that she could confront him. Another young woman detailed to accompany a so-called VIP on a lengthy overnight journey might have treated the *yanqui* reporter with deference. Which was *not* to forgive the CIA thing. That still smarted.

He was pacing again now, trying to turn his mind to work. He'd done a rough draft of a story based on the trip so far, themed by the idea that he was retracing Morgan's own journey to the mountains, trying to put himself in the Midwesterner's two-tone shoes. But the piece was forced and now lay scrunched in a ball in the wastebasket next to the dresser. He went to the window and looked out on the city's nightscape, wondering how much longer he'd have to wait for the man called Tomás.

When the knock at his door finally came, it was so soft Ray opened it half expecting to find no one there. Instead, he found María.

Without waiting to be invited in, she brushed past him, carrying a knapsack like his own. He had the distinct impression that her hair brushed his face as she passed him in the doorway.

"Are you ready?" she said.

"Hello to you too," Ray said to her back.

To his surprise, she dropped her bag by the made-up bed and pulled the coverlet down as if she were about to get in. Then she tugged and rumpled the pillows and sheets.

Ray closed the door and looked on with hands in pockets.

"The maid will be pissed," he said.

"What?"

"Nothing. A joke."

"They should believe you slept here," she said.

"Of course," he replied. "Shouldn't you be on your way to Havana by now?"

"A change of plan."

"So why the change?"

"Tomás was arrested this afternoon. We have to assume they know you are here and they know why."

"So? I'm an American reporter—or a CIA agent, depending on your point of view. Either way, what can they do?"

"You will be deported, after questioning by the secret police. They will want to know who helped you."

"So I won't tell them."

María stopped and stared.

"Oh yes, you will. Eventually you will. Everyone does. Even Americans, Mr. Halliwell. We should go, now, before it is too late. There is a curfew and we must be careful."

"Where?"

"A safe house, close."

"I still don't get why *you're* here?"

"Because the police have also been to my mother's house in Havana."

Something stupid, something very like, *'I'm sorry'* came out of his mouth, but she wasn't listening anyway. He was still struggling for the right words when María picked up his knapsack and handed it to him.

"*Vaya*," she said.

They took the stairs to the ground floor, passed the door leading to the lobby and walked quickly down a corridor marked '*Servicios*' toward the hotel laundry.

The laundry was deserted, but the up-and-over metal door to the loading dock was open and a truck was backed up to it, ready to be loaded with wicker hampers stuffed with bundles of white sheets and tablecloths.

María edged past the truck and jumped down from the dock. Ray followed on. Across the service road, they picked their way through stunted palms and hook-thorned clumps of bougainvillea toward a low picket fence marking the perimeter of the hotel grounds. The narrow streets of the old town beyond were eerily deserted under a few weak street lights.

"Wait," said María.

Ray could see nothing, but catching the sound of a car engine, he checked left and right for any sign of the approaching vehicle.

María pulled on his sleeve and crouched down behind the fence. The police car, lights off, purred toward them at no more than ten miles an hour before turning off down a side street. Moments later, the road was once again deathly quiet.

They stepped over the low fence, crossed the road and walked quickly up the narrow street opposite, hugging the uneven walls of the old houses, using doorways to stop and listen. They came to an alleyway too narrow for cars, with overhanging balconies draped with wash. Ducking into the shadows to catch their breath before going on, Ray was suddenly aware of light spilling through slat shutters, the sound of muffled voices, kitchen pots and a whining child, hinting at the life within.

They traversed the next block without incident, giving the street lights a wide berth, until they came to an unremarkable wooden door, old and dry with brittle flakes of blue-green paint, indistinguishable from a hundred other doors in the area.

María knocked. The door opened almost instantly and an old woman, who looked to be in her eighties, ushered them in. She bolted the door behind them and Ray noticed the woman held something heavy in her left hand, which she quickly tucked in her apron. From a shelf she picked up a burning candle, stuck with melted wax to a cracked yellow saucer, and held it up to see their faces. After a moment, she snorted and began to shuffle away down the dim hall toward the dark interior of the house. Ray could smell fried onions.

"Her name is Pilar," said María as they followed on. "Both her son and grandson are *desaparecidos*. Disappeared. For three years."

A smoking oil lamp lighted the kitchen. On the stove, a pan of onions, green peppers, garlic, oregano and bay leaf was sweating deliciously in oil. Ray was hungry. He was tempted to comment on the wonderful aroma and searched his mind for the right words in Spanish. It was then he saw the old woman retrieve the heavy object she'd tucked away at the door and realized it was an ancient revolver she was holding in her liver-spotted hand.

The old woman opened a box on one of the high shelves above the cooker. She got out a stained rag and wrapped it around the heavy gun before putting it back in the box.

"*Vengan*," the old woman said.

She picked up the candle and led them out of the kitchen, through a low doorway and down some rickety stairs to the basement. In the gloom, Ray picked out a few boxes, a chair and two old army cots set out side by side on the earthen floor. On one wall a mirror was propped on a shelf above a wide metal dish with a jug of water beside it. There were two old towels draped over the bowl. Ray could only just stand upright between the dusty wooden joists supporting the floor above.

The old woman said she would bring food. She put the candle on a wooden box. Then she turned and clambered back up the stairs and they were alone in the murky basement.

María busied herself hanging a spare blanket from one of the beams, trying to make a kind of screen between them. She dragged one of the cots until it was hidden from Ray's view by the hanging blanket.

He put his bags down and sat on the other cot, almost falling backwards on the sagging canvas. A minute later, Pilar reappeared holding a plate of rice and black beans covered with the spicy onions and pepper, a dish known as '*sofritos.*' Ray struggled to get up from the canvas cot. Careful to duck the low beams, he took the plate from the old woman, thanking her in Spanish.

"*De nada,*" said Pilar. She waited a moment, apparently to see Ray take his first forkful of the food.

"*Bueno. Gracias, señora,*" he said, chewing the piping hot dish with his mouth open.

The old woman seemed satisfied and, with a nod of her head, she turned and went.

Ray took the plate to one of the wooden boxes and sat. He could only see María's feet moving around beneath the blanket. He ate the food quickly and with gusto, watching every small movement from behind the screen and trying to guess the rest.

"I never expected to eat so well on this trip," he said, cleaning his plate.

María didn't reply. He wondered if she'd heard him. He waited before trying again.

"Cigarette?" he said, shaking one from the pack. He craned sideways and was surprised to suddenly catch a glimpse of her in the mirror. She didn't see him. He noticed her hair was wet. He sat up straight, embarrassed to have caught her unawares.

"No, thank you," said María's disembodied voice.

Ray lit his own. The damn blanket hanging there was beginning to annoy him.

"María?"

"What?"

"Can we talk?"

"What about?"

Ray took a long drag.

"I wanted—to apologize. Which is not something I do that often. I was rough on you and I'm sorry."

He could hear the sound of splashing water, but no response.

"Did you hear me?"

Again, nothing. Maybe she had her head wrapped in a towel.

He craned sideways, aware he was intruding, but unable to resist. What he saw shocked him. María had a pair of scissors and was shearing off swaths of her long, damp hair above the neckline. He sat upright, taken aback. He heard the scissors make another cut, then another. Then, without thinking, he was on his feet, pulling at the hanging blanket. He must have pulled too hard because it fell to the floor and all at once, they were standing face-to-face, just a few feet apart. What was left of María's hair was an unruly mess of short clumps. She looked terrible.

Ray took a step toward her, not sure what he was doing or why. He ducked too late and cracked his head on the low beam.

"*Shit! Goddamn!*"

He dabbed at his head and found blood.

"You okay?" María said.

"No! I'm not okay as it happens—"

She was watching him closely.

"Let me look."

"*No!*"

He caught her eye and noticed she was barely suppressing laughter.

"I could have broken my skull!"

María let her laughter go.

"*What?* What's so funny?"

"Nothing."

"Then why are you laughing?"

"I don't know."

"It's not funny," he said.

"No, you're right," María said, 'it's not funny, not at all."

Ray dabbed again at his head. Again he found blood.

"Look!" he said, showing her the result.

"That's bad," she said, "very bad."

"You're not much better!" he said.

And all at once, they were both laughing.

20

When Alejandro came for them at first light, they'd gotten only a few hours' rest. They'd talked for a while, then gone to their cots. The hanging blanket stayed where it had fallen on the earth floor.

They drove through backstreets to the city perimeter and retraced their route into the city for a few miles until they were in open country. Eventually, they turned off down a dirt track running between tall stands of cane, like walls to either side. Half a mile into the fields, the dirt track came to an abrupt end where the cane gave way to coffee plantations.

Alejandro let his two passengers out and then reversed into the cane stands at the edge of the field until the station wagon was surrounded on three sides, visible only from the fourth—or the air. Using a cane knife, he cut some of the tallest cane stalks and laid them over the car until it was almost completely covered. Ray was helping him camouflage the car when he noticed that María was no longer with them. He looked around but couldn't see her anywhere. When he asked, Alejandro told him not to worry, that she would be back.

A couple of minutes later, María appeared with a man wearing the usual straw hat of the *campesino*, torn shirt and ragged shorts. He didn't smile or greet them in any way.

"This is our guide," said María. "Let's go."

Two hours later, they were already a thousand feet up the steep slopes of the Escambray. On these higher slopes of the mountains there was little sign of cultivation, and instead, prickly marabou brush covered the land around them. A few thorny acacias and palms dotted the steep slopes, and they had passed one or two huge ceiba trees with their distinctive green trunks and thick branches draped with all kinds of epiphytes. Along with the sticky heat, they had to contend with biting flies and relentless mosquitoes.

Ray said, "How do you know Morgan's not CIA?"

"I don't."

María was ahead of him on the trail.

"Well, there you go."

"But he's not."

"You don't know anything about him," Ray said.

"I know he fights with us," she replied. "That's enough."

He was several yards behind her, slipping on wet roots and loose rocks and sweating profusely, struggling to keep up and puffing air through pursed lips like a steam engine.

"Why?" he said, shifting the case with the heavy Smith Corona typewriter from one hand to the other and cursing the marketing people who had sold the beast as 'portable.'

"*Why?*"

Ray stopped walking, put the case down and rested his hands on his hips, breathing deeply.

"Yeah—why? He's an American. This is Cuba."

"I noticed. You're an American, Mr. Halliwell," she said. "What are *you* doing here?"

"It's Ray,'" he said.

"Okay, *Ray*," she said as she started up the trail again. "Maybe you should save your strength for walking."

*

A thousand feet below them, a small man with bright, restless eyes made his way to the main road and managed to flag down a passing army truck carrying supplies to Cienfuegos. The driver of the truck reported the hidden car to his sergeant, who, in turn, alerted his captain, a man named Fernández García. Soldiers were soon swarming over the station wagon.

As his men ripped the interior apart, Fernández García was using his field glasses to scan the mountains for any sign of movement. Fernández García had been born into a wealthy family, originally from Castile. His job in the army—hunting rebels—aligned nicely with his sporting interests. The thought of finding those who had abandoned the car gave him the rush of excitement he always felt before the hunt.

He knew those who had left the car would be making their way into the Escambray and along a trail he knew well, toward the rebel camp. Moreover, he knew that by traveling by truck two miles down the main road and using another dirt track available only to the military, he could intercept anyone on the trail within an hour.

*

As Ray plodded on in the sticky, buggy heat, behind him Alejandro was happily murdering a popular song.

"*¡Alejandro!*"

María was glaring down at them from a dozen yards up the trail.

"*¿Que?*" said Alejandro, apparently unsure of his crime. He let María walk on before turning to Ray. "She's the crazy one, no?" he said, and then banging his hand against his chest, he added, "Boom, boom!" and grinned at Ray.

Ray pulled a pack of cigarettes from the top pocket of his now sweat-soaked bush jacket.

"You have a cigarette for me?" said Alejandro.

*

From his position on the lower slopes, Fernández García trained his field glasses on two figures standing together. He knew at once that he was looking at his quarry.

He panned right and glimpsed two more figures, intermittently visible as they moved through the marabou and stunted palms edging the trail. The straw hat on the man in front indicated a campesino, no doubt a guide. As for the others, he couldn't be sure, but he couldn't wait to find out.

His platoon, young conscripts in ill-fitting uniforms, lounged or sat on the ground.

"*¡Despiertense!*" he growled.

Watching them scramble to their feet and form a line of sorts, he would have exchanged them all for two good hunting dogs. Fernández García had long since given up trying to motivate men such as these with words or the thrill of the chase. Instead, he relied on fear and a certain talent for melodramatic gesture. One man in particular, a peasant draftee, was slow to stand. His name was Ochoa. It was not the first time he'd been insolent with a look, or dragged his heels under orders. Drawing his Colt pistol from the leather holster at his hip, Fernández García flicked off the safety and racked the slide to chamber the first round. His men had witnessed these kinds of theatrics before, but they never failed to impress. They knew their captain was not the kind to make idle threats.

Now that he had their full attention, he stared hard at each man in turn. He walked the line and stopped at Ochoa, whose head was bowed despite being ordered to stand to attention.

Fernández García put the barrel of the loaded pistol in the soft tissue under the peasant's chin and slowly pushed, bringing Ochoa's head up until their eyes met. Then he pushed further, forcing Ochoa to stand on tiptoes, the barrel sticking so far into his gullet that the soldier was gasping for air. Fernández García held him there before lowering the pistol and releasing the man.

Then he turned his back on his men, almost willing them to make a move. No one did.

With a shout for them to move out, he set off towards the waiting truck, breaking into double time.

The platoon, relieved that their captain had not shot any of them, set off after him, rifles clattering against their web gear. They had to trot to keep up. Ochoa spat on the ground and made a quiet vow to himself.

*

María waited for Ray and Alejandro to catch up. The guide had indicated they had another two hours to go before they were safely in rebel territory, somewhere near the Nuevo Mundo camp deep in the mountains. But at least her mood seemed to be improving.

"Ray?" she said. "You okay?"

"Yeah. The cans are chafing, that's all."

They each had a dozen cans of sweetened condensed milk in their rucksacks. Even Ray had accepted his portion of the cans, taken from a cardboard box in the car before they set out. María had explained that the sticky white gloop was a staple for the rebels. Robust, durable and easy to transport—unless you had several in a rucksack on your back—condensed milk in cans was doled out a sip at a time on long marches across the mountains and deep patrols into enemy territory.

"Here," said María. She took the weight of the rucksack in her hands as Ray released the straps and put it on the ground.

He bent down to adjust the cans, conscious of her watching him and annoyed with himself for being such a crybaby. Alejandro and the guide were a hundred yards in front of them on the trail.

"How's your head?" she said with a smile.

Before Ray could respond, they heard a shout.

"¡Corre!" Run!

They looked up to see Alejandro heading at full tilt toward them along the line of the ridge.

"¡Soldados!"

Ray and María froze. They heard more shouts and a gunshot. Then, without warning, Alejandro fell face-first to the ground.

The sight left Ray too stunned to move. He waited for Alejandro to jump up, to begin screaming and running again. He waited, but nothing happened. María had already dived for cover off the trail. He should follow. But he knew he had to retrieve the typewriter in its case first.

María shouted, "Leave it!"

She was already hidden from sight, beckoning him to follow. Ray grabbed at the case. Then he was running, crouching low, directly behind María, weaving their way deeper into the dense marabou at the edge of the trail, as fast as they could go.

21

Standing over the body and watching his men fan out into the marabou, Captain Fernández García calculated with practised ease the remaining hours of daylight, his chances of finding the three who had got away, and the possibility of a counterattack from the rebels. The campesino guide they would not catch, of course. He was on his way back to the fields, where others would vouch that he had been at work all day. Informers would deal with him sooner or later.

Fernández García studied the dust-covered face of the young man at his feet. This was a city boy, probably a student. Even though the bullet had shattered a piece of skull the size of a small saucer, leaving a messy crater just above the right ear, he could see what was left of the brilliantined pompadour typical of young urbanites. The tight-legged jeans and sneakers were enough to confirm his suspicions that this was yet another susceptible romantic, a would-be hero drawn to the cause by propaganda, false promises and wild imaginings. And Captain Fernández García had every reason to believe that the youth's companions, cowering somewhere in the bush nearby, were much like him.

In fact, the past six months had seen the trickle of disgruntled students and workers and professionals from the cities become a river of potential new rebels, and encounters like this were not at all unusual. In the early days, there was generally little bloodshed and a distinctly amateur feel to the cat-and-mouse game, but as the human flow to the rebel cause grew, the army generals had encouraged patrols to make examples of those who dared to try to reach the mountains. An unwritten order gave officers like Captain Fernández García the authority to shoot first and ask questions later, which suited him perfectly. He felt no more personal animosity toward Alejandro or his companions than toward the ducks and doves he shot in the mangrove swamps, or the ibex and wild boar he had hunted as a boy with his father in the mountains of Spain, but he used the same instincts and, sometimes, the same strategies.

He blew two short blasts on his whistle. "*¡Vamos!*"

The conscripts, relieved to be recalled so soon, gave up the search and made their way back through the marabou to the trail. Captain Fernández García ordered his sergeant to form the men into a column for the march back to barracks, and the sergeant did as he was told. It would not be long before their quarry believed themselves safe and came out of hiding. The tactic had worked before, and it would work again.

*

María had heard the captain call his men back, but she waited until she was sure the soldiers were retreating.

At last, she whispered, "They're going."

Ray started to move, but she pulled him back.

"Wait."

"Alejandro," said Ray. "We have to get to him."

She shook her head. "There's nothing we can do. We have to stay here until we're sure."

"You said they're leaving."

"Maybe, maybe not. We will see."

Ray was breathing hard. "Goddamn it, they shot him in the *back*. That's murder. They can't get away with this."

"Sshhh!" she hissed. "Just wait—"

"But if they know we're here, why are they going?"

"Maybe they don't know. Now, you *must* be quiet."

After the sounds of the soldiers had faded, they heard nothing but the breeze and the cicadas. They waited and listened for the longest half hour of Ray's life, until finally María began to lead the way back toward the trail. Crouching low, they crept through the thorny marabou, scratched and gouged at every turn. But when they reached the trail, the only sign of Alejandro's body was a patch of dried blood staining the bare earth.

"Shit," Ray said softly. "Shit, shit, *shit*!"

María made the sign of the cross and touched her fingers to her lips. She stared at the ground.

Taking the cue, Ray stood with her in silence. There was nothing to say that would make any difference, and nothing to do but start walking. And yet neither of them stirred. Leaving this moment and this place felt suddenly like leaving a graveside. There needed to be a final act, a handful of dirt or the closing of a prayer book, but there was no preacher, no service to conclude and no mortal remains but the dark stain in the dirt.

As they stood side by side in the shadow of the high peaks, dusk was coming quickly. The low bark of the first tree frogs of the evening was beginning to augment the drone of the cicadas. They had maybe an hour until dark. He waited until she looked at him.

"We go up, right?"

Only half an hour later, the gathering gloom was beginning to throw the distant lights of Cienfuegos and the coastal strip into sharp relief against the dark blank of the ocean. Without their local guide, neither Ray nor María had any real idea where they were or where they were heading, beyond the general notion that going uphill made sense. And they may well have carried on for another half hour if the trail had not abruptly switched back to run sharply downhill.

"What do you think?" said Ray. "Did we miss a turn somewhere?"

"Maybe. I don't think so. It's hard to see."

"Well, it might head back up again on the other side of that slope," said Ray, pointing into the distance, "but we won't know till we get there."

"And it will be dark by then."

"We'll do better in daylight." When María didn't object, he said, "And I'm thinking maybe we should get off the trail."

Her smile, albeit forced, caught him by surprise.

"What?" he said.

She shook her head. "No, nothing. I'm happy you're here. That's all."

Ray realized she was offering a kind of compliment and for a moment, he was embarrassed. He was also pleased.

"I wish I could say me too," he said.

*

Captain Fernández García's irritation was growing by the minute. The whole point of retreating down the trail with the body had been to draw the fugitives out of hiding. Doubling back to create a controlled ambush where the trail dipped downward for a time was a strategy he had used before to good effect in this very spot. The quarry would be tired, their guard down and the chances of taking them alive much better than if he tried to flush them out of the marabou.

So where *were* they? It was almost dark, and even allowing for their trepidation and unfamiliarity with the trail, the two young men—for so he believed Ray and María to be— should have stumbled into the trap by now. Fernández García now had to consider the possibility that they were still cowering in the marabou, cold, frightened and waiting for daylight.

He could, of course, wait them out. Sooner or later they would have to show themselves. But in the meantime, he and his men would be exposed to counterattack, and without the numbers to defend themselves against a rebel force of any size. Another officer might have walked away, content to have killed one potential new recruit and shown the others what they would be up against if they persisted in their folly. But the captain liked to win, and besides, he had a duty to fulfill. Interrogators always needed fresh sources of information about the networks of rebel contacts and safe houses, and as much as he despised them for their crude methods, it was part of his job to feed the machine. He had often reflected on the irony that the most ruthless and enthusiastic torturers he dealt with were often unlettered peasants—members of the very class the rebels were fighting to liberate. But Fernández García had as little as possible to do with such men. That side of the work disgusted him and bore little relation to the noble art of the hunt.

He gave the order. The recruits emerged from their ambush positions and spread out to make a broad sweep either side of the trail with night coming on. They understood that their captain's plan had failed. They also understood that their captain's patrician sense of duty was an immutable force, futile and even dangerous to resist.

*

Ray was sitting on the bare ground of the small clearing, his back against a stunted almond tree that had somehow taken root and survived far from the plantations on the lower slopes. He had first watch. María was curled up beside him on the ground.

Slapping at the whine of yet another mosquito hovering by his ear, he tried not to think about the ants, scorpions and centipedes that were surely about. It was one thing to step over or on them while hiking, quite another to sit down with them in the dark. But surely bugs had to sleep too, thought Ray, and the creepy sensations were likely just his imagination. Besides, he rather liked his new role as woodsman and protector and didn't want to blow it by flinching and waking María—not without good cause. It was then that he caught the sound of something large moving through the undergrowth.

His first reaction was to tell himself he was hearing things. But when the sound came again and María abruptly sat up, he knew it was real.

"What was that?" she whispered.

"No idea," he whispered back.

They listened again, both of them rigid, staring into the bushes across the eight-foot clearing. There was just enough starlight to discern shapes and movement.

María jerked her head in the opposite direction, indicating they should try to hide. And very slowly, as quietly as they could move, they began to edge around to either side of the almond tree, sliding on their backsides to find cover behind the thick trunk and low branches.

By the time the scuffling and scraping sound came again, Ray and María were mostly hidden from view. It was becoming clear the sounds were not human but animal. No doubt it was that rather comforting thought which left them so shocked by what they heard next.

The voice was that of a young man speaking softly so as not to be heard.

"*Su sólo un jutia.*" *It's just a tree rat.*

"*No tan fuerte,*" came the urgent reply. *Not so loud.*

They had only a partial view of the clearing, just enough to see something the size of a large cat dart toward them, stop suddenly to stare at the two strange creatures crouching there and then veer away, keeping low to the ground until it vanished into the relative safety of the brush.

For a moment, Ray stopped breathing. He didn't blink or move a muscle as the figure of a man holding a weapon materialized from the mass of dark shapes and undergrowth on the far side of the clearing. But his mind was racing. How the man could see anything in this gloom Ray had no clue. Watching the soldier reach into his pocket and pull out what was presumably a cigarette, he found himself oddly annoyed by the guy's casual attitude. Surely he knew better than to light up and give away his position. But that appeared to be precisely what the young man was about to do. The soldier crouched on his haunches, holding his rifle butt down, and cupped his hands.

Ray waited for the rasp of the flint and the flare of light, but it never came. Instead, he saw, from the corner of his eye, the flash of a gun muzzle and heard the staccato of automatic gunfire. He watched the soldier slump peacefully to the ground, without so much as a whimper, still clutching his rifle as if it were precious to him.

Suddenly, the noise of gunfire and clamoring voices was everywhere. Ray too, was making a noise as he and María hugged the ground and each other—the sort of high moaning that one might make on a rollercoaster without realizing it.

The din began to subside into intermittent bursts, farther away now. Ray and María were still locked together, their faces pressed to the dirt under the almond tree, when they heard a voice calling to them from a few feet away.

"Guys? You okay?"

Ray sat up and peered through the low branches to see a figure crouching at the clearing's edge. The metallic ting of another lighter lid opening and the rasp of the striker revealed this time a chiaroscuro portrait of a bearded, sweaty Morgan.

"Mr. Halliwell, I presume," Morgan said with a grin. He held the lighter higher and studied María.

"Say, what happened to your hair, *muchacho?*"

*

At almost the same moment, some forty yards from the almond tree and hidden from sight by a thicket of marabou, Captain Fernández García lay dying.

The bullet had passed through his windpipe and severed the carotid artery. He couldn't speak, but it occurred to him as he stared up at the stars that the shooter had been remarkably accurate, even merciful—in keeping with the finest traditions of the ibex hunt. The single-shot kill, as taught to him by his father in the Spanish Pyrenees, was not simply a way of preserving the trophy's skin intact; it was also a fitting tribute to a noble adversary, an act imbued with a sense of honor.

Putting aside the workaday explanation for his death he knew would figure in the official paperwork and even in the records of the rebels themselves, *el capitán* Fernández García allowed himself a final indulgence. He chose to think of himself as an ibex, and of Ochoa, the peasant soldier from his own platoon, who had shot with such calculated efficiency, as a true hunter.

22

A thin shaft of early morning sun edged across Ray's face as he slept, warming his skin and creating a delicious sense of luxury. The canvas cot felt so comfortable it took him some time to remember where he was, and more time still to command his limbs to move and his eyes to open.

There'd been no opportunity the night before to take in the detail. Now, he could make out a palm-thatch roof, porous walls of rush matting and latticed panels of woven palm speckled with light. Rough-cut planks framed the open door and window. There was a faint smell of woodsmoke in the air, and he could hear voices in the distance.

He sat up awkwardly on the edge of the camp bed, his muscles stiff and aching, and leaned forward to peer out through the doorway at the bright day beyond. From what he could see, the ground was sandy and bare of vegetation but ringed in the distance by tall palms and thick undergrowth—a green wall surrounding the patch of reddish earth.

Ray eased himself up from the low bed and stretched as he stood. He went to the open doorway and stepped out.

As his eyes adjusted to the brightness, he could just make out two or three *bohíos* at the margins of the open area, tucked neatly under the canopy of the trees and camouflaged as if they too, had grown right up out of the ground. In one corner of the clearing, an open-sided *bohío* appeared to serve as a chow station. A huge iron cooking pot hung over a smoking fire while a man stirred the contents with a wooden paddle and suddenly, Ray was hungry.

"Mr. Halliwell!"

The shout snapped him out of the reverie. He looked across the compound to see Morgan waving.

Ray returned his wave. Morgan walked toward him, grinning.

"Welcome to Nuevo Mundo. You sure know how to sleep, sir. It's almost eleven."

"Yeah, well, busy night, you know," Ray said. He shook hands. "And please, just Ray."

"Fine, Ray it is," Morgan said. "There's a meeting about to start, and some folks here would like to meet you. Come on and say hi, and then we'll leave them to it."

"Right now?"

"Sure. Why not?"

"I'd like a shower first."

"That's funny. Come on."

Ray followed Morgan fifty yards to the shade of an open-sided *bohío*. They ducked under the palm canopy to find several men gathered around the map table.

Morgan directed his attention to a wiry man with a thin beard and black-rimmed glasses.

"Ray, I'd like you to meet Comandante Eloy Gutiérrez Menoyo, leader of the Second Front of the Escambray—*el Gallego* to us. Gallego, this here is Mr. Ray Halliwell of the *Chicago Sun-Times* newspaper."

"Mr. Halliwell. Welcome."

Next, he introduced a tall, handsome man with a full beard and a peculiar stillness about him.

"Comandante Jesús Carreras, Black Berets column commander."

Ray shook his hand and studied his eyes for a brief moment, but gleaned nothing more about the man.

"Capitán Montiel, my right-hand man, Mr. Ray Halliwell."

Montiel offered a polite, "Welcome."

"Edel and I," said Morgan, "well, let's just say I wouldn't willingly go into a firefight without him."

"Brothers," Montiel said with simple grace.

Five more men were gathered in the *bohío*, all wearing green fatigues and sporting beards.

"Comandante Artola, Capitán Lorenzo, Dr. Armando Fleites, Capitán Redondo in the fine cowboy hat. And Max

Lesnik, based in Havana, chief of propaganda. Max is visiting, too. Isn't that right, Max?"

Lesnik ignored Morgan and, fixing Ray in his sights, said, "Perhaps we can talk more afterward, just to set the ground rules."

There was no chance to follow up on Lesnik's comment but Ray stored the name. Some of the men—whose names he would have to learn to remember over time—were already gathering around the table. A well-worn map was pinned to the surface, its corners ripped and stained. Others were perching where they could, on packing crates or leaning against the roof posts. Morgan led Ray away from the meeting and back into the bright sunshine.

"Don't let Max worry you," Morgan said to Ray as they walked together. "Underneath it all, he's okay."

"Max doesn't worry me," said Ray.

"Good. Gallego asked me to fill you in on the nature of the meeting, but leave them alone to do the business. You okay with that?"

"Sure, but aren't you missing out?"

"I gave my two cents already."

"So what's it about?"

"Che Guevara is marching this way from the Sierra with two hundred men, under orders from Fidel."

"Which means?"

"It means an alliance between the July 26 Movement and the Second Front, the better to fight Batista. Or else it means the communists want control here—depends on your point of view."

"But you don't like Guevara?"

"Never met the guy, but I don't trust him—and that's worse."

"Because he's a communist?"

Morgan stopped and thrust his hands in his pockets, kicking at the dirt with one boot. Ray waited for him to respond.

"You could say that, and you'd be right," said Morgan, "but it's a good deal more than that, too. Way I see it? You've got a guy in charge like Batista, who thinks he's untouchable. The communists—the guys running Russia, North Korea, and China right now? I think they're the same as Batista. They don't count the cost, because they don't have to. There's always a cost, especially if you want to live free."

"And that means you won't work with communists?"

"We'll work with them if we have to, but not *for* them."

"And how do you draw the line?" said Ray.

Morgan grinned. "That's what the meeting's about right now. So, how about the guided tour?"

"Don't you have to get back?"

"Like I said, Gallego's already got my two cents. Come on, I'll show you around."

Morgan strode off toward the far side of the compound.

"Let's start with the hospital—you'll be amazed at what these guys do up here with not much."

As he followed Morgan, Ray noticed, a little distance from the open area, in the shade of the palms, four men with shovels and the unmistakable outline of two growing piles of dirt building beside two freshly dug graves.

"They brought him in this morning," Morgan said. "Alejandro—was that his name?"

Ray nodded.

"It's a damn shame. I'm sorry."

"Me too," said Ray. "He wanted me to take a picture of him when we got here, with you."

For a moment, they were silent. Then Morgan spoke.

"There'll be a service, a few words."

"There's two graves," Ray said.

Morgan nodded. "Yeah. The army usually takes their own, especially when it's an officer. At first, I couldn't understand why he'd been left. Then, from where we found him and from the wound, I say he'd been shot by one of his own waiting for him on the trail."

"One of his own men shot him?"
"Wouldn't be the first time."

It was past ten o'clock when Ray finished the piece he was working on and pulled the single sheet of paper from the typewriter to look it over.

He had called it 'Two Graves,' but he didn't for a moment expect the copy-editor in Chicago to go along with the title.

Ray silently read through the conclusion to the story.

The young man from Havana who came to the mountains so full of hope and expectation, an engagement ring on his finger and a family waiting for him in the city, never met the man whose orders resulted in his death. The older man, wearing the uniform of an army captain, would no doubt be surprised to find himself side by side in death with this would-be rebel, his enemy, their graves like those of a father and son in a family plot.

The simple service, conducted by a rebel padre who visits the camp once or twice a week, often for this very purpose, was over in less than five minutes. The words were Christian, taken directly from the Bible, but there were no flowers and no tears among the mourners. They've seen sights like this all too often in the months of fighting.

I stood with María, my contact and companion on the journey to the mountains. Three or four of the comandantes, including the American, William Morgan, and the leader of the Second Front, Eloy Gutiérrez Menoyo, attended the ceremony. When the service ended, it was business as usual at the Nuevo Mundo camp. As we walked away, I could see another rebel patrol heading out in single file to meet the enemy.

As he finished scanning the copy by the dim light of a smoking oil lamp, Ray felt suddenly despondent. The flimsy sheet of paper with smudges where the ribbon had stuck, containing fifteen hundred words for a young man he'd liked, a young man with his whole life ahead seemed inadequate and mean in memoriam.

He tucked the sheets of paper under the typewriter roller and groaned. He stretched his stiff back, promising himself he would revisit the thing tomorrow, when he'd slept.

He stepped outside into the night air pulsing with the loud thrum of the cicadas and the low racket of the tree frogs—sounds already so familiar to him that they registered only when he took the time to listen. He needed to get good and drunk, preferably in a bar, ideally the Bodeguita or the Floridita. But the Second Front ran a strictly dry operation and the nearest bar was twenty miles back down the mountain. He lit a cigarette. The cigarette tasted good, though it reminded him of all the pleasures he was missing.

He knew María was quartered with two other women in their own *bohío* near the hospital building. They'd hardly seen each other since arriving at the camp. Just briefly at the rather perfunctory service. A few minutes later, Ray found himself standing outside María's quarters, debating whether to call her name. Before he could decide, one of María's roommates emerged from the *bohío*, a towel over her shoulder and a precious communal bar of soap in her hand.

"*Hola*," Ray said, more surprised to see her than she was to see him.

The woman smiled, put her hands on her hips and waited as if expecting the usual *piropo*—the sometimes poetic, often downright lascivious compliment that a red-blooded Cuban male was likely to offer any beautiful woman he encountered.

"María?" Ray said, returning the smile a little uncertainly.

If the woman was disappointed, she had the grace to hide it by looking back into the *bohío* and calling out, "*¿Dónde está, María?*"

The woman turned back to Ray. "She is walking, that way." She pointed in the direction of a narrow path leading away from the camp.

"*Gracias.*"

"*De nada*," she replied, performing an elaborate courtesy that raised giggles from inside the hut.

Ray followed the woman's directions away from the camp and into the darkness. He was alive to every sound or movement. He was excited at the prospect of being with her out here. In lieu of a bar and ice-cold drinks, alone together on top of a mountain, the air so much cooler than on the plain and the stars out, was some compensation.

A hundred yards or so down the dark path at the edge of a steep escarpment, the tree cover gave way to a broad, open vista. Here, at the greater altitude of Nuevo Mundo, the combination of a star-filled black sky, still burnished a deep crimson at the horizon, and the cluster of lights that was Cienfuegos seemed two-dimensional, like a painted backdrop, too perfect to be real.

Ray could just make out the standing figure and the steep drop that marked the end of the path. His heart was racing a little. He was just thirty yards away when he realized she was not alone.

"Here you go," said a man's voice. "Guava. And ripe too. Try it."

The voice belonged to Morgan.

23

Ray was frantically shoving notebook, pens, camera and spare rolls of film into his knapsack as the rebel columns formed for departure on patrol. He'd overslept and missed breakfast, having spent too many wakeful hours wallowing in his own thoughts, brushing away bugs and trying to get comfortable on the cot.

"¡Tigres de selva!" came the shout from the parade ground outside Ray's bohío. "¡En filas!"

Morgan's booming voice calling the men to attention was unmistakable and Ray heard what sounded like a hundred boots hit the dirt as one in response. He stepped outside to see two columns of men standing completely still, their weapons held at forty-five degrees in front of their chests, ready for inspection.

Morgan, wearing a beret low on his forehead, British-style, was walking the line nearest to Ray—a total of maybe twenty men. Jesús Carreras was walking the other. Ray retrieved his camera from the knapsack and began to frame a shot. He set the speed ring at one twenty-five for average daylight, just as Jamie had advised, put the camera to his eye, pressed and heard the mechanical click of the shutter. The column was already on the move. He would have to catch Morgan quickly.

He waved and called, "Hey!"

"Not a chance," said Morgan as Ray approached.

"Every courtesy—that's what the boss said."

"Okay, not a chance, *sir.*"

"That's funny," Ray said. "You know what else is funny?" He was looking toward Menoyo and Lesnik standing together outside the command post.

Morgan followed his look to see Menoyo smiling and waving, apparently at Ray.

"Tell me," said Morgan.

"It wasn't even my idea," said Ray. "Comandante Menoyo believes I should see a real patrol in action. I agreed. So what do you say?"

Morgan murmured to Ray, "I say you're a devious son of a bitch."

"Shall we go?" said Ray. "Don't want to keep the men waiting."

An hour and a half later, Morgan's Tigers of the Jungle column were walking a trail a thousand feet below the Nuevo Mundo camp, skirting strips of cultivated coffee and tobacco, careful to keep cover under a canopy of trees.

Ray was near the head of the column trudging alongside Captain Roger Redondo, who was beginning to get on his nerves. Despite his rank, Redondo was just nineteen years old and somewhere along the line he'd clearly fallen in love with America. He wore his cowboy hat slung on his back, held by a lanyard, and imitation aviator glasses with showy yellow lenses on his nose.

"Five times I was in America, three times in Miami, one time in New York and one time in Dallas, Texas. That's where I got the Stetson," said Redondo, pulling on the lanyard to retrieve the white cowboy hat. "Twenty-seven bucks I paid. That's good, huh? This is the real thing, not some cheap tourist shit, you know?"

"It's a fine hat," said Ray, wiping sweat from his brow and wishing he could get away. He'd tried slowing down and speeding up, but Redondo kept pace no matter what—and even waited for him if he stopped.

"So you don't speak Spanish?" Redondo asked, and then carried on as if the question merely rhetorical. "That's a pain, eh? When you are in Cuba, a reporter, and you can't speak to the cats you meet—"

"I get by," said Ray. He tried quickening his pace in another vain attempt to escape.

"William told me I translate for you, to make sure you understand. That's cool with me, man. You have a question, you ask me."

"I'll be sure to do that," said Ray.

As if in answer to Ray's prayers, the drone of a light aircraft in the distance made Redondo fall quiet and look up at the sky. Morgan and his men were suddenly bristling.

"*¡Avión! ¡Ocúltense, ahorita!*"

Morgan shouted the order to take cover and unceremoniously grabbed Ray by the jacket, pulling him toward the dense brush beside the trail. The whole column began to melt away as the plane approached from the north.

"What is it?" said Ray, peering up at the sky.

"Twin prop spotter, though last time I said that it turned out to be a crop-duster, which got a laugh. Army recon. The air force has jets."

The light plane flew steadily toward their position. They heard the change in the engine's pitch as it passed high overhead and banked right, tracing the line of the foothills. A minute later it had all but vanished to the west, and the column was reforming on the trail. Ray was left sitting, scribbling in his notebook.

"Come on," said Morgan, "I want you to meet the neighbors."

Ray got to his feet.

"Neighbors?"

"The man of the house is called Bermúdez. He and his family farm coffee here."

"A good cup of coffee I could handle."

"Maybe," Morgan said with a sly smile, "maybe not. What they grow, they sell. It's the only way to scratch a living up here."

Morgan, Ray and Redondo shook hands with Señor Bermúdez and his wife outside the crudest of *bohíos*, ragged palm thatch thinly covering not just the roof but the walls too.

Ray noticed straight away that Señor Bermúdez was bruised and cut around the face. He'd either taken a bad fall or been on the receiving end of a beating. His lip was split and there was grazing around his jawbone and the left eye. The farmer and his wife ushered the three men inside.

The floor of the hut was bare earth, compacted over the years. A metal coffee pot was perched precariously on the charcoaled wood of a fire giving off only the faintest wisp of smoke. The place gave the impression of cleanliness and order, not least because there was so little in the way of material possessions: two makeshift beds of rough straw with well-worn blankets thrown over, a small table low to the ground and a corner dedicated to a shrine for the Virgin. There was a rosary and a cheap greenish-white plastic statue, eight or nine inches high, that glowed disturbingly in the gloom as if it might be brightly luminous at night. Ray had seen similar things in the street markets and tourist stalls of Havana.

They sat cross-legged on the floor. Señor Bermúdez's wife poured what looked, and even smelled, a lot like coffee into two dented aluminum mugs. Redondo politely refused, offering a long explanation apparently connected to pains in his stomach. But it didn't take Ray long to realize the real reason when he noticed the host and his wife remained empty-handed. There were only two mugs in the house.

Ray could not refuse, but his first sip of the brown liquid made him wince. He was pretty sure there was probably some coffee in the mix, though the bitter taste was more akin to what Ray imagined might be acorns or some other kind of nut.

"*Bien, gracias*," said Morgan taking a long sip from his own mug. He paused a moment before asking the farmer to tell him about the army's visit.

The farmer began to reply in tones so soft and with an accent so guttural that Ray was soon struggling to make sense of his words.

"He says soldiers came yesterday," Redondo translated.

Señor Bermúdez told them the soldiers had asked questions and helped themselves to rice and coffee before heading east. He'd told the officer he could not afford to give them rice or coffee, but the army had taken what they wanted anyway, leaving almost nothing.

Ray saw that Señor Bermúdez was fighting back tears. For once, Redondo had enough sense to remain quiet. When his wife reached over to lay her hand on his, Ray could sense the farmer's rage and shame.

The army officer had asked repeatedly about rebels in the area and did not believe Señor Bermúdez when he told them he'd seen nobody but his fellow farmers. It was then that they'd beaten him.

When he finished speaking, Señor Bermúdez stared at the open fire, poking at the embers with a twig. For a long while, no one said anything.

Eventually, Morgan reached into his pocket and pulled out some coins.

"*Por el café y el arroz.*"

He held out five pesos, offering to pay for what the army had taken. But Señor Bermúdez put his hands up to refuse the money.

"*El ejército debería pagar, no usted,*" said Señor Bermúdez.

"He says the army, not we, should pay for what they took," Redondo whispered to Ray.

"*El ejército pagará. Confíe en mí,*" said Morgan.

"He says—"

"I got it," said Ray. "The army will pay, right?"

"Right!" Redondo said brightly. "Too right."

Morgan held out the coins again, more insistently this time, and Señor Bermúdez accepted them.

The rain started a little after four o'clock that afternoon. Morgan had called an early halt to the patrol so they could set up camp. The first heavy drops fell as they were still putting up tarpaulins, tying them with rope and thick string to the branches of trees. Minutes later, they were in the middle of a downpour of surprising intensity. Those that could huddle under the tarps did so. Soon, the run-off from the dry earth was creating rivers of muddy water channeling through the makeshift camp, forcing those who'd made their pitch in the wrong place to move.

For fear of generating smoke where there should be none, Morgan ordered no fires to be built even as the rain eased. There would be no hot food and no dry clothes, at least until the next day. The men had to make do with a couple of cans of condensed milk passed from one to another as an evening meal. Ray took a sip of the sweet, sticky liquid and passed the can on.

As dusk turned the dark skies darker still, Ray was using the last of the light to write in his notebook, recording the meeting with Señor Bermúdez in physical detail: the hut, the bruised face, the simple shrine. But he was distracted. Each time he looked up, he found Ramirito—a shy seventeen year old—staring right at him and smiling encouragingly. When Ray did not smile back, the young man's confidence faded and he pretended to busy himself with wiping the moisture from his rifle.

Finally, the light fast disappearing and the pages damp and beginning to stick together, Ray closed the notebook and put it away in his knapsack, retrieving a pack of cigarettes at the same time.

Ramirito was still watching his every move.

"*¿Cigarrillo?*" said Ray, offering the pack.

Ramirito beamed with shy anticipation.

"*Gracias, señor, gracias, muchas gracias.*"

Ramirito leaned over to Ray for a light and cupped his hands to hide the flame. He sucked deep and long, holding the smoke in his lungs before slowly exhaling. He took one more drag and looked admiringly at the cigarette before turning to his comrades and softly calling a name.

"*Fredo!*"

Another boy, about the same age as Ramirito, scampered from his own tarp toward them and took the offered cigarette, carefully shielding it from the rain. Ray watched as he went back to the group, took a drag and then passed it on.

"Thank you, mister," said Ramirito.

As he started to edge back to his own place Ray called to him. Ramirito turned around to see Ray about to throw the pack.

"Here," said Ray, "for you."

The young rebel wanted to refuse, but Ray threw the pack anyway. Ramirito caught it with both hands.

24

The column began to stir before first light. Ray was pretty sure he hadn't slept a wink. Every bone in his body ached from the cold. His wet clothes had only partly dried, and his knees, hips and shoulders were bruised from lying on the hard ground. The skies had cleared during the night, and with the weather coming from the north, the temperature had fallen sharply. Despite his body's protests, Ray managed to get to his feet and tried gingerly to stretch hoping to recover some movement in his stiff limbs. Then he stumbled toward the deeper undergrowth in order to pee in private.

Morgan was waiting for him when he got back.

"Hey, buddy, how'd you sleep?"

"Didn't," said Ray, checking the camera lens for moisture and wiping at it with his sleeve. "But thanks for asking."

Morgan laughed. "I tried to tell you."

"Yeah, yeah. Look, can we talk about this over breakfast?"

"Sure," said Morgan. "Let's see, coffee and toast, and would you like the egg poached? I'll get right on it."

Morgan walked away, still chuckling. Even Ramirito was grinning sheepishly. Ray stuffed the rolled-up shirt that had been his pillow into the damp knapsack and craned his stiff neck.

"Maybe a little bacon?" Morgan called over his shoulder.

"Go to hell."

Two hours later, the world seemed a very different place—even to Ray—and even without a fried breakfast. The sun had come up in a pristine blue sky, and clothes had miraculously dried as the column tramped along a level trail. Best of all, a foraging party had come across wild sugar apples and guavas to accompany the condensed milk ration.

Ray had torn into the fruit, gorging himself, much to the amusement of Morgan and his men.

The plan was to make their way to the village of Nuevo Mundo, namesake of the rebel camp, and catch up on any news of the army column that had stopped at the Bermúdez farm. The village, having suffered more than once from the army's brutal attentions, was sympathetic to the rebel cause, but Morgan would still approach with caution.

As it turned out, his instincts were spot on. The first clue was the point man, coming back at a dead run when they were still half a mile from the village. Gasping for breath, he told of a heavy army presence, including two trucks and a jeep, and up to a hundred men. Morgan led his column quickly and quietly off the trail, skirting the strip fields of coffee and sugar around the village and keeping to the thicker cover of jungle scrub and trees.

They were just a few hundred yards from the nearest village house. Morgan used only signs to direct the men. They crouched low and moved as silently as possible through the undergrowth. Ray was sticking close to Morgan, crawling the last few yards on his belly to reach a small ridge just high enough for them to see—and be seen. Before they got there, they could hear distant screams and shouts and occasional gunshots. What they saw when they were able to survey the scene moments later, was worse still.

The twenty or so *bohíos* were situated around a dusty square with a stone well at its heart, capped by a simple corrugated metal roof. Some buildings were already on fire, and others were being torched. Several of the villagers were lined up by the well, kneeling with their hands on their heads, guns trained on them. A burly sergeant walked among them, shouting and pistol-whipping men and women at random.

Redondo tried to stand, but Morgan grabbed him and yanked him back down.

"*¡No! ¡Quédese!*" Morgan hissed.

Morgan pulled out a battered pair of field glasses and trained them on the scene. Even without binoculars, it was quickly clear to Ray that the sergeant was not getting the answers he wanted. He watched the distant dumb show in horror as the man kicked one of the kneeling women, knocking her sideways into the person next to her, who fell in turn against the man by her side, until three or four of the kneeling figures were lying like fallen dominoes on the ground. A pig, loosed from its pen, ran squealing across the square, only for one of the soldiers to level his machine gun and riddle the animal with a burst of fire. It lay quivering in the dust, legs kicking madly as it tried to stand, until another burst stilled it.

"Jesus Christ!" said Ray under his breath. "Can't you do something?"

Morgan was silent, scanning the village and counting to himself. He handed the field glasses to Ray.

"He's the one. The sergeant. He's the one."

Ray panned about to locate the sergeant, just a distant lump without the glasses. He couldn't find him, but he saw two soldiers drag an old man from one of the *bohíos*. The old boy looked to be in his seventies. The soldiers held him by his arms. Then the sergeant reappeared. In big close-up, Ray could see him swig from a bottle, then put his face close to the old man's.

The old man appeared to be smiling and nodding assent. When the soldiers released his arms, the old man tried to embrace the burly sergeant, only to get a backhand across the face. The blow did nothing to prevent the old man picking himself up off the ground and making another attempt to hold the sergeant in his arms.

The sergeant turned and vanished from view. A moment later, he was back, one arm raised. The glint of sunlight on metal dazzled Ray for an instant, and it was a millisecond before his brain registered the knife in the sergeant's hand. The sergeant grabbed a handful of the old man's unkempt hair. Ray saw the knife blade sawing at the man's face, slicing across the mouth from ear to ear.

25

With a stick, Morgan scratched a crude map in the dirt, showing the only road leading to the village and the terrain around it. Ray had to wait for the details until they were trudging in silence toward the chosen site for the ambush.

"With seventeen men and no heavy weapons or mines to block exits from the kill zone, we could end up looking pretty stupid," Morgan explained to Ray, "hence the location."

"Which is?"

"There's a culvert. Floodwaters in the rainy season undercut the road, so there's a makeshift wooden bridge. A grenade or two in the right place should be enough to weaken it, but it'll take the weight of a vehicle to bring it down. Which is why the timing matters. If we get it right, that should close the front door."

Morgan stopped walking and turned to Ray.

"You're with Montiel, away from the action. Like glue, you hear? I'm serious. No photos, no heroics. Clear?"

"Clear."

A mile and a half from the village, Morgan's men began to scout their positions at the ambush site. Near the bridge, Morgan deployed his men bearing rifles on high ground, back from the road but with good elevation. To the front of the kill zone, the closed end of the V, he put the maximum firepower—four men with submachine guns—much closer to the road.

Ray stayed out of the way, watching the preparations with a new admiration for Morgan's cool competence. Morgan repeated the same words to all his men: *"No el sargento, ¿entiendes?"* There was no argument. The sergeant would come later.

Morgan himself set the booby trap. Carefully, almost lovingly, he wedged the Mills grenades between two of the bridge's wooden supports, having removed the pins and secured the levers, each wedged with a stone. A piece of string tied to two of the stones led twenty yards down the dry culvert to a point where a man could hide. A single tug should dislodge the stones and release the levers, detonating the four-second fuses. Redondo got the job of pulling the string.

Montiel and Ray scrambled up the slope to a rocky outcrop overlooking the bridge and the road to it. Although seventy yards away from the action, they had a grandstand view and good cover. Montiel pointed out the line of retreat if things went against them, and briefed Ray on keeping low and following his orders.

"You are my job," he said to Ray in all seriousness. "Please—"

And then they waited, each man with his own ritual to pass the minutes: weapon checks, a prayer silently mouthed, a piece of gum chewed hard, nervous confirmation of sight lines and the next man on either side, a crucifix kissed and tucked away, spare magazines counted and arranged within easy reach on dry vegetation, a little shuffle to avoid a cramp.

After twenty minutes, nothing. Ray strained to spot Morgan, but he couldn't see anyone from the column. It was as if they had never been there. As if the stretch of road and the brush on either side were deserted. Only Montiel's low murmur made the situation real.

"Down, please," said the young man.

Ray did as he was told, more for Montiel's peace of mind than his own. Suddenly, the young rebel's eyes opened wide and he was grinning. He put a hand to his ear, encouraging Ray to listen, and his eyes scanned the trees around them, searching for the source. Ray's ear was tuned for the engine of a truck or a jeep, and he had heard nothing of the sort. But as he watched Montiel's face for clues, he heard it.

"*Toco-toco-tocoro-tocoro.*"

"See? See?" whispered Montiel, pointing with one finger to the canopy of the trees on the other side of the road.

Ray could see nothing but green leaves and the sun-bleached branches of dead trees. The distinctive call came again, and this time Ray allowed the sound to direct his eyes. There was the bird: a trogon, ten inches from beak to tail, still as a rock, but surprisingly obvious now that he'd found it. The red, white and blue plumage precisely matched the colors of the Cuban national flag.

He was turning to tell Montiel he'd seen the bird when the first truck appeared. The driver shifted gears and double-clutched to slow for the bridge ahead. The column of troops marched in ragged formation behind, then the jeep and the other truck.

The bridge was narrow, just wide enough for the two-and-a-half-ton GMC canvas-backed truck to edge over the wooden structure in low gear. The driver was leaning from his side window, looking down to adjust his line, when the first grenade exploded. Despite its weight, the truck rose on its axles. The bridge structure remained intact—but only for an instant.

A beat later, another explosion. The truck shuddered and creaked, and in slow motion started to nose-dive into the culvert. The ruptured fuel tank ignited in a bright ball of flame, engulfing the cab and the unfortunate driver. Before the smoke had even begun to clear, the shooting began. Soldiers poured from the back of the burning truck right into the line of fire. Even from Ray's position, seventy feet away, the thunderous rattle of small arms hurt the ears. More grenades whomped into the road, sending dirt flying. Panicked soldiers ran into each other as they tried to find a refuge from the crisscrossing fields of fire. But there was no place to hide. Some just sat where they fell, stunned and helpless, waiting for the inevitable. One or two found cover and tried to return fire, only to be picked off by Morgan's riflemen.

Black smoke drifted over the road, making it hard to see what was going on farther back from the bridge, but Ray knew it could only be more of the same. He heard shouts and saw one or two rebels emerging from cover, rage or excitement usurping caution, and saw one of them slump back to vanish in the marabou. A stray bullet, probably a ricochet, zinged close to Ray and Montiel, and both ducked behind the rock.

Little by little the rate of firing slowed, the automatic bursts growing more sporadic, the rifle shots now with time to echo clearly before dying away. And then, as quickly as it had begun, it was over. The hurt and dying could still be heard, and the smoke still drifted lazily over the road. But the thing was done.

Taking Montiel's lead, Ray stood up to look down on the chaos. Some of the rebels were already walking among their victims, kicking weapons away, prodding at corpses and the wounded. He heard a pistol shot—a mercy kill, he supposed.

And then, on the far side of the burning truck, there was movement. Gasping for breath, the burly sergeant was crawling on his hands and knees. From where Ray stood, it seemed that he had every intention of making his escape on all fours. He must have known he would never make it, but the instinct to survive drove him on.

The sergeant was whimpering now, talking to himself and looking nervously from side to side, aware of the rebels around him. He quickened his speed, but on hands and knees it made little difference. The boots kept pace on either side and behind him. Tears rolling down his cheeks, he finally slumped onto his backside and began to drag himself backward in the dirt, begging and staring from one impassive rebel to the next.

The rebels fired almost as one. The sergeant was still talking as he jerked and fell sideways, eyes wide and full of fear. He was dead before he hit the ground.

Ray's body had tensed and shuddered in rhythm with the gunfire. Now that it was over, he was frozen where he stood. His eyes were open but he was thinking nothing. His throat was parched and dry, his ears ringing. But the smells lingered; hot metal, cordite, sweat, clogging dust, iron-sweet blood, and urine. Ray trapped a rising wave of nausea at the back of his throat and held it there for a few seconds, until he could hold it no longer.

Afterwards, he held himself against a tree and spat phlegm and gasped for breath. He heard Morgan's voice echoing through the still air.

"Somos los soldados del Segundo Frente del Escambray! Váyase a casa a sus familias."

We are the soldiers of the Second Front of the Escambray. Go back to your homes. Take your wounded, he added. *Leave your weapons. Don't come back!*

26

Even in the darkness, Ray could see that jagged cracks and fissures had appeared in the crusted surface of Alejandro's grave, eerily suggestive of pressure from below pushing upward. Exactly the same effect was apparent on the grave of the army captain buried beside Alejandro and on all the other graves—except one.

The most recent burial had been that same morning. The young man was called Pedro López-Famosa, and it was he whom Ray had seen shot during the ambush. Pedro had not died immediately from the bullet, which had passed through his intestines. Even when the fighting was over, he was still perfectly lucid, angry at himself and, despite excruciating pain, railing against the enemy soldiers and his bad luck. But he couldn't walk, and for much of the way back to the camp they had had to carry him. The trail had soon become too narrow and steep for the improvised stretcher, and so for the last couple of miles Morgan and others had carried him on their backs. At first, the boy held on tight, but as time went by fever weakened him and he could no longer hold on. Morgan, who made the last leg to the camp, had gripped him by the wrists.

Peritonitis killed Pedro overnight, despite Dr. Armando Fleites' efforts to clean the wound and fight the infection.

Ray lit another cigarette, and for a moment the flame from his lighter made him night blind. He had thought he was alone, but then he heard something.

"Who's there?"

"Hey, buddy." The voice was unmistakable.

"Morgan?"

"You smoking that on your own?"

It seemed that Morgan had been crouching unseen at Pedro's grave, just a few yards away. In three long strides, he stepped over the mounds of the two graves separating them and was standing next to Ray. As he arrived, he helped himself to Ray's cigarette.

"Pedro didn't make it," said Morgan suddenly, as if he were talking to no one in particular.

Ray wasn't sure whether Morgan expected a reply or was just thinking out loud.

"I heard. I'm sorry."

"Yeah, well, me too, but I'm still mad at him. I was just telling him so."

"Why?"

"Because he forgot everything I taught him."

"Maybe he was just unlucky."

"Maybe he was. Or maybe I didn't do my job right—there's the black bat."

"Black bat? How's that?"

"That's what I call the fella that doesn't let you sleep. Son of a bitch."

"What about the sergeant? That keep you awake, too?"

Ray hadn't intended the question to be provocative, but that was how it sounded.

"You do what you have to. It's bullshit, but there it is."

It was Ray's turn to hold the cigarette out.

"In five months," said Morgan, "guys under my command? Seventeen dead, including Pedro here. Thirty-two wounded, of which eleven will never return to active duty. From a total of thirteen engagements."

"I saw another group come in today," said Ray. "They looked like students, young guys fresh out of school, factory workers, God knows."

"They start basic tomorrow." Morgan paused, then added, "You should come see. Then we'll have our talk. But I still think there's not much to say."

He turned and started to go without saying goodnight.

"The man with no story," said Ray when he'd gone a few yards.

"Something like that. G'night."

As Morgan walked away, Ray could hear him whistling *'As the Caissons Go Rolling Along,'* until the pulsing chorus of cicadas and tree frogs and crickets and katydids finally smothered the tune. Ray shivered, even though the night was warm and his skin was greasy with sweat. He slapped at a mosquito whining close to his ear. He missed, but caught his ear with a stinging smack.

"*Shit*," he muttered, but there was no one to hear.

27

The new recruit had shown a degree of arrogance in volunteering to be Morgan's first opponent in the wrestling, and had paid the price. The takedown was so swift and effortless that from where Ray stood, it looked as if the young man had performed some kind of acrobatic trick with little more than a helping hand from the American.

Ray snapped a picture of the training session. He had woken with a feeling of nausea and a red rash on his side was getting itchy in the heat, but he felt a little better now that he was up and about.

The young man on the ground was rolling over onto his knees and wheezing. Morgan pulled him to his feet, whispered a few words of encouragement that made the boy nod and smile, and sent him back to join the line.

"*Tú*," said Morgan. "*Ven acá.*"

He was looking at a pale-skinned boy a head taller than his fellows. This one had a patrician bearing: chin up, a certain hauteur in the eyes. Ray wondered if Morgan had picked him for that very reason.

The young man pushed back his hair, checked his audience with a leisurely nod and sauntered toward Morgan, stopping a couple of yards away and dropping into what looked like a practiced crouch. Morgan pulled the sheath knife from his belt. Holding it by the blade, he tossed it to his volunteer, who caught it easily in his right hand. Then Morgan turned his back and said over his shoulder, "*Ven.*"

The young man hesitated. The line of recruits grew very still and Ray took the photograph: Morgan in the foreground, calm but attentive, the young man preparing to attack from the rear.

The young patrician crept forward, then lunged from high and right. Morgan spun right, hammering the right arm above the elbow, opening his hand and sliding down to the wrist, his left palm now on the upper arm. Stepping forward, he brought his attacker facedown in the dirt. Still holding the knife hand, he put his boot on the shoulder blade, ready to break the wrist and dislocate both elbow and shoulder.

Some of the recruits in line let out a whoop of excitement; others winced at the fate of their friend and seemed to contemplate their own turn to come.

"Mr. Halliwell," said a quiet voice at Ray's shoulder.

Ray turned to find Max Lesnik beside him.

"Enjoying the show?"

"Yes, actually."

"Comandante Menoyo has a little time. I thought maybe now the two of you could talk, as you requested."

Comandante Eloy Gutiérrez Menoyo, '*el gallego*,' was waiting in the command post where Ray had met him a few days before. They were alone except for Lesnik, who seemed to be planning to stay, and a young man, presumably a secretary, sitting behind a desk piled high with paperwork.

"Please sit," said Menoyo.

"Thank you."

"Everything is well?" Menoyo enquired.

"Very good indeed, thank you," said Ray, "you read the first piece?"

"Of course. I was impressed."

"I'm glad. Me too. Your guys are getting the copy to Havana with terrific speed. I don't know how, but I'm grateful."

Menoyo took the compliment with a shy nod of the head. "So, you have questions for me now?"

"Yes sir," said Ray.

"May I see them?" Lesnik said without warning.

Ray felt himself bristle, though he said only, "I don't have them written down."

"Perhaps we could run through them first—make a list maybe," said Lesnik.

Ray was silent. He looked from Menoyo to Lesnik and back, then said, "Gentlemen, it's very kind of you to give me this time, but I don't conduct interviews with preapproved questions."

Lesnik appeared bemused. Then he frowned and said, "You have to understand, Mr. Halliwell, you are the first journalist to come here and to be afforded this access to the Second Front—and to Comandante Menoyo especially."

"Yeah, I get that, Mr. Lesnik. And we both know how much you need the publicity. But there's another thing."

"And that is?"

"You're responsible for propaganda, is that right?"

"Communications," Lesnik replied.

"Communications, then," said Ray. "The point is, nothing I write is subject to prior scrutiny or approval."

"You can't expect us to allow—"

"Yeah. You see, sir, right there's the problem. I *do* expect. I expect you to let me do my job with complete independence."

"Not possible, Mr. Halliwell. These are difficult times. Much is at stake, and we have to be very careful about the messages we send out, here in Cuba and with your readers in America."

"That's your privilege, Mr. Lesnik—as long as you're talking about press releases or taking an ad. I'm not running messages, sir, not for the Second Front or anyone else. That's not what I do."

"Should I remind you again about the privilege of your situation here? This is exclusive access."

"Maybe I should remind *you* of the privilege of having me here. The public knows about the July 26 Movement. They're reading about Fidel, Raúl and Guevara, but who knows about the Second Front?"

"Gentlemen," said Menoyo. "Max. Mr. Halliwell."

The Second Front chief spoke without raising his voice above the conversational, yet he wielded sufficient authority to silence two men unaccustomed to being silenced. Ray wondered how he managed it. Physically, Menoyo was slight, with narrow shoulders and long, thin arms. He stooped in the way tall people sometimes do, as if to accommodate those closer to the ground. He was just twenty-five years old.

"Max?" said Menoyo, in one word managing to convey his wish to speak with Ray alone.

Lesnik cast a sideways glance in Ray's direction, and for a moment it seemed that he might object. Then he stood, closed the file he had open on his knee and tucked it under his arm. He saluted his commanding officer. And with that, he pushed his chair back and walked out.

"Max is okay," Menoyo said when Lesnik had gone. "In the city, it's not just propaganda. He is a leader, you understand?"

"Yeah," said Ray.

"So, we begin." Menoyo called to the youth at the desk. "*Miguel, por favor.*" Turning back to Ray, he said, "To translate. If we need. Now please, begin."

Half an hour later, they had covered the preliminaries and had begun to touch on Menoyo's personal background. From time to time, when the language became difficult for either of them, Miguel stepped in, but on the whole, the two men managed to understand each other well.

Menoyo, it turned out, like many other Cubans, had come from another land. The youngest of six children, he had come to Cuba as a teenager with his family—or what remained of it—following the ravages of the Spanish Civil War. His father, Carlos, was a doctor and a left-leaning Social Democrat who eventually became a major in the medical corps of the Republican army, fighting Franco. When the Republicans lost the war, the doctor paid the price for being on the wrong side and was barred from practicing medicine. Menoyo's elder brother, José Antonio, had been killed in the battle of Majadahonda near Madrid, after volunteering to fight the Franquistas when he was just sixteen. The second eldest, another Carlos, fought with the

Free French in World War Two, and it was he who first emigrated to Cuba, eventually managing to bring his family to the island to join him.

When Batista came to power in the 1952 coup d'état, Carlos got involved in organizing against the dictator, following the family tradition of resistance to tyranny. He was shot dead in the abortive attack on the presidential palace in 1957. Menoyo had been called to identify his brother's corpse, laid out on the cold marble floors of the palace alongside forty other young people killed that day.

"Some of the attackers escaped, if I remember right," said Ray.

"Yes, but they were betrayed and murdered by the police."

"The Humboldt Seven Massacre?"

"Yes."

"You know who was behind the betrayal?"

"Yes. The palace attack was a failure, but it was enough to frighten the Communist Party. It was the party. They wanted to eliminate the competition. That meant the DRE."

"Is that why you don't allow communists in the Second Front?"

"Communists are permitted, but not if they come seeking converts. We are fighting for a free Cuba. We are fighting to end the dictatorship. We are not fighting to change the world, and we are not fighting for Moscow."

"What about Fidel?"

"He is a clever man. A leader."

"And a politician."

"Yes."

"Is he a communist?"

"You must ask him, not me."

"Do you have a problem fighting with him?"

"No. The purpose is clear. We must fight together to end Batista's rule. It is the only way."

"So Che Guevara's column will take control in the Escambray when he arrives?"

"No. Guevara will be an *ally* in the fight."

"How can you be sure?"

"Because that is the way it is. We will make sure."

Ray studied the slight man in front of him. There was something hard to read in Menoyo, something reticent, even private. More like a priest than a soldier.

"I want to ask you about Morgan,"

"Yes?"

"Your first impressions?"

Menoyo looked to Miguel for the sense of Ray's question, and Miguel explained.

"*Ah, bien*," said Menoyo. "*Extraño. Sorpresa.*"

"Strange," said Miguel. "A surprise."

"How?" said Ray.

"He was in a white suit, you know? *Rojo y gordo.*"

"Fat," said Miguel, "and red. From the sun."

"*Sí*," said Menoyo. "Some of the men worry he is CIA."

"And you?"

And then it happened. The man who never smiled, smiled. It was there and gone in the same instant, but it had definitely been there.

"No. I did not worry."

"Did he tell you why he had come?"

"He told me about his friend, yes."

"Turner, Jack Turner?"

"Yes. He said he could train the men to fight—with a knife, with their hands and with guns. He was useful. We needed a man like William then."

"And now?"

"We need him now, too. He is second in command. And he is *aplatanado*. You understand?"

Ray turned to Miguel.

"*Aplatanado*?" said Miguel. "In English, banana—"

"That's what I thought," said Ray. "Meaning?"

"A true Cuban," said Menoyo.

28

Ray waited all afternoon to interview Morgan, but he didn't show. And none of the other Second Front leaders seemed to be in evidence either. When he asked around, the answers were evasive; shoulders were shrugged and looks exchanged in a way that made him wonder what was going on.

He had been feeling out of sorts all day. Only bloody-mindedness was keeping him awake. Now, it was around ten in the evening and he was nursing a headache as he sat with Ramirito. They were watching a raucous domino game between four of the guys when he vaguely heard what sounded to Ray like a gunshot over the slamming of *fichas* on the wooden board and the shouts of foul play. No one else reacted, unless it was to show yet more enthusiasm for the game. Maybe it was just one of the rebels hunting for the nocturnal *jutia*, the large rat-like creatures that served as an important supplementary meat source for the camp.

Ray was still wondering whether his cot wasn't the best option when Morgan walked into the camp compound and straight past with scarcely a look, heading toward his quarters.

"Hey! Hold up," Ray called.

He was about to stand when Ramirito pulled him back by the arm.

"What?"

"*Quédate aquí*," said the young rebel. "*Stay.*"

Ray tried to read the look on the young man's face, but couldn't. He'd ask Morgan what this was all about.

Ray found him sitting on a wooden box in his *bohío*, head in hands, gun belt draped awkwardly over the side of the hammock. Wherever he'd been had taken its toll. His skin was pale, his eyes vacant. He looked shattered.

"Trouble?"

Morgan looked up.

"Ray—"

"I'm guessing now's not a good time."

Morgan seemed not to understand.

"For our talk?"

"No—yeah, yeah—tomorrow would be better."

Ray studied the big man, who seemed suddenly almost fragile. Morgan's head was bowed again, as if he'd fallen asleep where he sat. Ray went to leave. At the narrow doorway to the hut, he turned to see Morgan flopping down into the hammock.

"By the way, I don't know if it helps, but Gallego says you're a banana. Apparently, around here that's good."

The joke fell flat. Morgan's eyes were already closed.

It was too early for Ray to sleep and he hadn't seen María all evening. He walked to the *bohío* she shared with the two other women and hovered conspicuously outside until she emerged, arms folded over her chest.

Ray apologized for the late hour and they walked a little way to be alone.

"I'm just concerned, that's all," Ray said. "Something's going down, I don't know what, and Morgan looks like death. Perhaps you know what it is?"

"There's nothing to say."

"But you know?"

"Yes."

"Look, could we take a walk? To the viewpoint maybe?"

"Okay."

A group of four young men, including Ramirito, passed by, chattering away.

"Goodnight, sir," said Ramirito with deliberate exaggeration and a facetious salute to Ray, hamming it up for his friends.

They went on in silence for a while.

"Have you heard from home?" Ray asked.

María shook her head.

"Maybe when the courier returns."

"Perhaps."

When they reached the viewpoint, Ray offered María a cigarette and she accepted. He was more than conscious of the night he'd observed her in this same spot with Morgan just a few days before.

"You like him, don't you?" he said, almost thinking aloud.

"What do you mean?"

"Morgan. Alejandro told me."

"Told you what?"

"Boom, boom."

"What?"

"That's what Alejandro said."

The moment he'd said the words, Ray regretted saying anything at all. Mentioning Alejandro in that offhand way felt crass. And without meaning to, he'd given the impression he was making fun of her.

"I'm sorry, I shouldn't have said that. It was stupid and none of my business. Forgive me."

"I forgive you."

"I've been thinking a lot about Alejandro."

"Of course. Me too. But you're a reporter. You must have seen many things like this."

"I guess. I don't know, most of the dead people I've seen I didn't know or like. Maybe that's it."

"You need to rest."

Ray wiped at his brow and ran his hand round the back of his neck. He was sweating.

"It's still hot, isn't it? Even at night. Even in the mountains. I thought it would be cooler here."

"It *is* cooler. Much cooler. Are you sure you're okay?"

"I'm fine. Really."

They were quiet for a while, taking in the view. The coastal lights of Cienfuegos were flickering against the inky night sky, peppered with bright stars.

"You're not at all who I thought you were, Mr. Halliwell."

"It's—"

"Ray, I know."

"I think that's good on the whole."

"Yes, it's good. In answer to your question, yes, I like him."

"Who?"

She rose to the bait by putting her hands on her hips and throwing back her shoulders.

"Morgan?"

"Oh, him. I'd forgotten about him."

"He makes me laugh."

"Yeah?" said Ray. "So what about me? Don't I make you laugh?"

"Sometimes, yes."

"Oh, I see, it's the smack on the head thing again, right? You mean you laugh *at* me?"

"Sometimes," she replied. "But the jokes? No, I don't understand what you say."

"I could learn them in Spanish, just for you. How would that be?"

"You are a strange man."

"And you are a beautiful young woman."

María turned to look at him.

"You are flirting with me, Mr. Halliwell?"

"I'm trying, yes. I think here in Cuba it's considered rude not to, right?"

"Ah, that's why you do it? To be polite?"

"Not exactly."

She gave him a quizzical look. Ray wondered if she were encouraging him or making fun of his attentions.

"I like you, María. I'd like to get to know you better."

She moved away a little, back up the trail. Then she looked him in the eye. "I'd like it if we could be friends."

Ray let the stub of his cigarette fall to the ground and ground it underfoot. She waited for him. When he got to her, she slipped her arm into his for the walk back to the camp.

They arrived back at María's hut in silence, but it was a comfortable silence, perhaps for the first time between them. She turned to face him before going inside.

"You wanted to know why Morgan was as he was tonight. I will tell you—as a friend. There was an informer. A local man. Young. As young as Alejandro. A boy really. This evening there was a trial, led by Gallego and the comandantes. The boy was found guilty of passing information to the army. Information that cost lives. He was sentenced to be shot."

Ray knew what was coming, but still it hit him hard.

"It was William who carried out the execution."

29

The courier showed up from Havana with a copy of the *Sun-Times* weekend edition—specially flown in—featuring a spread devoted to Menoyo and the Second Front, and for a while, Ray was a celebrity among the rebels. Even Lesnik was happy with the outcome.

All and sundry pored over the article, passing it from hand to hand, and by the time it had done the rounds, the newspaper was torn and dog-eared. The courier had also brought some goodies, including a half-dozen Hershey bars, which were broken into tiny pieces and shared as far as they would stretch, and a welcome supply of American cigarettes.

There was a note from Jamie telling Ray his photographs were barely usable. He claimed that only by spending hours in the darkroom compensating for the work of an amateur, had he managed to work a miracle on Ray's behalf. In the same note, Jamie mentioned that Ray's editor in Chicago had phoned more than once and wanted to speak to him urgently.

Morgan had been away, busy with the new recruits, when the courier arrived. María too, was not at the camp. She had been sent for nurse training to a doctor sympathetic to the rebels, who maintained a small practice in a town twenty kilometers away. Left to his own devices, Ray had plenty of time to pick up gossip and stories from anyone he could persuade to sit and chat. Miguel was on loan to him for translation, and the two had become known as a double act. But as time passed, and having exhausted other options, he was looking forward to Morgan's return that afternoon and his solemn promise of time to talk.

They used a captured army jeep to reach the Second Front's radio station, makeshift forge and gun factory, all housed in and around the colonial farmhouse of a woman by the name of Señora Doña Rosa. She was waiting for them on the verandah of the house, hands resting on broad hips, face stern, as Morgan and Ray parked the jeep.

"This lady," Morgan had said to Ray on the drive up, "is our secret weapon. I'd back her against Batista any day."

Doña Rosa was in her seventies and had farmed coffee in the Escambray alone for twenty years, ever since her husband's untimely death, and together with him for many years before that. She took no prisoners, ran the place with military efficiency and did everything she could to hide her soft side.

"*Llega tarde*," she said, as the two men climbed the steps to the house. *You're late.*

"*Lo siento Doña Rosa*," said Morgan. "Mr. Ray Halliwell. From America."

She put out her hand and, for a moment, Ray wondered if he was expected to kiss it or shake it. He opted for the latter.

"You are welcome to my home, Mr. Halliwell," said Doña Rosa, "Please, come."

She led the way into a grand hallway with several doors leading off to either side. She turned to face them.

"You will join me for lunch." She made it sound like an order. Then, with a wave, she left them alone.

The radio station broadcast from one of the rooms under the call sign *Seis Feroces Barbudos*, or Six Ferocious Bearded Men as the English translation would have it. Morgan showed Ray the transmitter and let him take photographs of the announcer at work, reminding him to be sure nothing in the photographs would identify the location. Next, Morgan showed Ray what had been Doña Rosa's dining room. There were maps pinned to the walls as if the room were used for planning. But Ray noted too, the unusual arrangement of the large dining table and chairs, laid out in a fashion that could be interpreted as suitable for a court hearing.

"Is this where you held the trial?"

Morgan looked around and then fixed his gaze directly at Ray.

"Yeah. You know about that?"

"Yeah."

"So?" Morgan said. "You planning to write about it?"

"Is there a reason not to?"

Morgan seemed uncertain, the bluster gone. "I don't know. I think about my folks back home. How they'd see something like that, I mean reading it in a paper. I don't know."

The thought of Morgan as the son of a couple somewhere in the Midwest stopped Ray in his tracks. Morgan had *executed* a young man, and now he was suddenly concerned about how such a thing might look back in hometown America. Two very different worlds were connecting in a bizarre way through this man. Morgan's decision to come to Cuba and fight had them running parallel.

"Let's start with the backgtound. Can we sit?" Ray said.

"Sure."

They settled into their chairs and Ray took out his notebook and pen. "Okay," he said, "before we start, I need to tell you something."

"What?"

"I was asked to deliver a message to you. By our friends in the agency."

"Beware your friends."

"They are offering you protection in return for information. I said I'd pass it on. They made me the same offer."

"What did you say?"

"I told them to shove it up their asses."

Morgan grinned. "I'm with you."

"Okay. So I know about your friend, Jack Turner. That was all in the file—"

"What file?"

"Suffice to say the Embassy is keeping tabs on you."

"How did you get hold of it?"

"You don't want to know. So?"

"No. He's one of the reasons I came. But not the only one."

"What are the others?"

Ray waited.

"God, Ray, who knows?"

"What did you expect to find here?"

"I came with no real idea of what to expect. I just came for the fight. And there was nowhere else to go."

"Cleveland?"

"I thought you said you read the file."

"So you walk up a mountain and find what exactly?"

Morgan grinned and blew air through his lips.

"Ten, eleven, guys living off rat meat, sleeping out in the jungle, eaten alive by bugs, two or three rifles between them and the rest doing drill with sticks."

"Sounds alluring. But you stayed?"

"It was a long walk back."

"Come on, Morgan."

"They needed me. These guys weren't soldiers."

"And you were?"

"I'm not saying I was a good guy in the army, but something stuck. I had the training and I could pass it on. It was something."

"Okay, I see that," said Ray, "but is this really your fight?"

"It is now."

"You're an American. This is not your homeland."

"Not my homeland. My home. I feel at home."

"And when the fighting is over? What then?"

"The fight's not done yet."

"But when it is?"

"Who knows? I'll think about that when it happens. Maybe I'll breed tropical fish, that's what I loved to do as a kid. Are we done?"

"No, something's missing. Something about why. Come on, help me out."

"Like I said, there's nowhere else to go. I don't know what to say."

"Try."

Morgan blew air again.

"Okay—whatever about Jack, it didn't take me long to realize pretty much everyone up here had lost somebody. Brother, sister, mother, father, cousin, friend, whatever. The politics I didn't get, not then, maybe not now. But I got why they were here, and for the first time in my life it felt like I was useful, like I belonged. Does that make any sense?"

"Yes, it does."

"Okay. Good. So, are we done now?"

"Sure, for now. But don't think that's it."

"Give me a break. Come on, I want to introduce you to magic man."

The man in question turned out to be Captain Comacho, a veteran of the Spanish Civil War and, since then, a number of minor revolutions and upheavals throughout Latin America. Comacho, though getting on in years, was famous as an expert gunsmith.

Morgan was in his element and clearly in awe of Comacho's practical genius. Over the noise of the machine tools, Morgan demonstrated the weapons for Ray's benefit.

He claimed Camacho could turn a handful of spare parts into a working weapon in hours. The results may not have looked pretty, but they were generally effective. Camacho's signature weapon was known as the 'Cuban Winchester.' With interchangeable barrels, the weapon could handle a variety of ammunition from 9mm upwards. Comacho constructed the gun from the frame of a .45 Winchester lever action rifle, parts from an M-1 Garand and a variety of different pistol magazines, including the snail drum from a German Luger.

"This here's a beauty!" Morgan said, raising his voice to be heard. He pulled back on the lever action to show the empty chamber of the gun.

Ray was trying to hear, but suddenly, close to the heat of the forge, the sweats and headache he'd had the last few days was back.

"What do you think? Guy's a goddamn magician, right?"

Ray indicated he was going to go outside the hot shed.

"You okay?" said Morgan.

"I'll be fine. Just need some air."

Later, they sat down with Doña Rosa to a simple lunch at a table laid on the terrace, only partially shaded by the vine-covered arbor. They ate *boniatos fritos* made from sweet potato, followed by fresh fruit, and drank cool water and strong coffee. Ray had recovered a little, though he was still feverish. Doña Rosa noticed. She stood up from the table and, to Ray's surprise, put her hand on his forehead.

"*Tiene fiebre*," she said, looking at Morgan. *A fever.*

She returned to her chair.

"Drink," she said to Ray, "water. A lot of water. And rest."

"I'm fine," said Ray, "but I will. Thank you."

Doña Rosa was staring at him with concern and shaking her head.

"Don't worry," said Ray, "just a little too much sun—and a lack of mojitos."

30

Ray's mysterious symptoms had nothing to do with the weather or with his drinking habits. Instead, they would turn out to be the result of dengue fever. The disease, contracted from the daytime bite of the *Aedes* mosquito, very nearly prevented him getting the scoop on the first fateful meeting between William Morgan and Ernesto 'Che' Guevara.

He'd been doing his best to fight the achy and feverish feeling for three or four days now. But it was a losing battle.

The physical symptoms with his sight began the morning after their visit to Doña Rosa's house. The effect seemed to come and go with the slight fever he was running. It was really more often a blurring of the world around him than genuine double vision, but the effect was much the same. What he saw was the thing itself, whatever it was—a pen, the typewriter, the doorframe to his *bohío*—but with a ghostly shadow, thin and translucent, like a watermark, floating at a slight offset to the left or right. On occasion, the shadow circled the object with a slow, disorienting rhythm, until Ray blinked it away or willed it back into alignment.

Ignoring the warning signs, he put the cause down to fatigue. He hadn't slept at all well the past few days. He had tossed and turned and experienced cold sweats. The rash he had first noticed the morning of the hand-to-hand training had become increasingly itchy and had spread. But the new aspect of his condition, the thing that kept him awake most of the night, was the pain in his joints and limbs.

Finally, he saw the doctor and was told it was dengue. The doctor ordered him to bed and isolation in his *bohío*, where for two days Ray slipped in and out of consciousness. The headaches felt like axe blows. He had thrown up so often, nothing remained in his stomach but sticky bile. A bowl stayed at his bedside just in case.

For all the pain and discomfort Ray went through, there was, however, one major compensation: María. It was María who checked his temperature hourly, who forced him to drink as much water as he could take. And it was María who held his hand when the pain in his joints was so bad he doubled up and cried like a baby. She wiped his forehead, neck and chest with a cool, damp cloth when he was overheating, and wrapped him in blankets when he shivered with cold sweats that made him vibrate from head to toe.

The rash spread to his face and hands and even to the soles of his feet, showing as bright red and purple spots. It was this indicator that most worried Dr. Armando Fleites, because of its association with the more severe form of the disease: dengue hemorrhagic fever, in which the capillaries begin to leak, causing internal bleeding, and the liver enlarges. Hemorrhagic fever was most often lethal.

But as time went by, the doctor's fears subsided. Ray remained extremely weak from the effects of the disease and his inability to hold down food, but his vital signs were improving. Dr. Fleites had set up a saline drip to help prevent dehydration, but there was little else to do other than wait for the fever to recede.

By the third day, Ray was lucid and in less pain. María was by his side, and he managed a thin smile as she wiped his forehead with the cloth.

"Must be something I ate," he said.

She frowned and seemed puzzled.

"Joke," he said weakly, closing his eyes.

*

Ten kilometers away, at the very edge of what the Second Front called the free territory, Morgan and Jesús Carreras were sitting together on a rock overlooking a narrow valley. A thin trail snaked up to their position from below.

Carreras had the stub of a ragged cigar between his teeth. His long hair was pulled back in a ponytail beneath his beret.

He pulled a single match from the breast pocket of his shirt and struck it on the rock. Then he lit the stub and puffed hard until the tobacco caught. He took a drag and raised his chin, letting smoke flood from his nostrils.

"*¡Por Dios, Jesús!*" said Morgan, waving at the blue cloud surrounding them both.

"*¿Qué? ¿Cuál es su problema?*" Carreras replied with a grin. "*Yanqui*, go home!"

"Go home yourself, you goddamn cootie."

"What you say?" said Carreras. "What is this thing?"

"A cootie? It's a guy who looks like a girl sitting on a rock smoking a cigar."

Carreras didn't understand the words, but he got the tone. In reply, he offered Morgan a simple hand gesture, pinky and pointer fingers raised to make the horn.

"Me?" said Morgan, laughing. "That's you, my friend—you and your woman, if you could find one who'd say yes. Gimme that."

Morgan tried to grab the cigar from his friend's teeth, but Carreras parried, and the two started slapping at each other.

"Okay, okay," said Morgan, covering his head. "*¡Basta! ¡Perro loco!*"

At that moment, a very human-sounding birdcall interrupted their horseplay.

"*To-co-ro-ro! To-co-ro-ro!*"

Two hundred yards below them, Publio, a local boy and a good scout finally accepted into the Second Front when he had turned sixteen just two weeks before, was waving his rifle from side to side and gesturing at the trail behind him. The young boy looked breathless, but he had learned the hand signals he needed to tell Morgan the approaching column was within sight and up to two hundred men strong, confirming the intelligence they had received from other sources.

"*Están aquí,*" said Morgan. *They're here.*

He handed the field glasses to Carreras. "Try to be nice."

"*Naturalmente*," Carreras replied, a wicked grin betraying the lie to his words.

Morgan took up his position ten yards from Carreras, checking both sides of the valley before lying on his belly, Thompson at the ready, hidden from view by a clump of high grass.

Carreras continued to puff on his cigar stub. It was a couple of minutes before the column's point man emerge from the undergrowth. The man scanned the valley sides before taking a couple of tentative steps into the open.

Perhaps the blue smoke from the cigar wafting in the light breeze finally caught his attention, but whatever it was that alerted him to Carreras sitting nonchalantly on the rock, in full view of anyone approaching up the valley, the man dropped to the ground like a stone, fumbling to load his rifle.

"*Hola!*" Carreras shouted to him, his voice echoing and making the silence that followed all the more pregnant.

Still the man seemed confused about the best course of action. Finally, he elected to shout a warning to the approaching column, now barely fifty yards behind him on the trail. Seconds later, an officer emerged from cover, with several men following. The officer wore a beret. His hair was long and his beard thin and wispy, much like Menoyo's. But the body language was very different from Menoyo's. This man stood legs apart, hands on hips, gun holstered, staring up at the lone figure on the rock with all the assurance of a leader whose reputation preceded him.

"*¿Quién es usted, soldado?*" the officer shouted, scanning the terrain around. Carreras was still sitting, still puffing on the cigar, his Thompson submachine gun laid casually on his knees. He shouted back, "*Soy Jesús Carreras, Segundo Frente del Escambray. Y usted, ¿quién es?*"

The officer in the valley looked to his subordinate, as if for confirmation they were dealing with a madman or a fool. The man shrugged.

"Soy comandante Ernesto Guevara, con órdenes del mismo, Fidel Castro."

Carreras looked to his left and caught Morgan's eye. The American was grinning, too. Morgan raised his head to look down and saw Guevara's men bunching up behind their leader.

Lazily, Carreras stood up from the rock and stretched his limbs, cupping the Thompson under one arm and scratching at his neck with the other hand, as if the column's intrusion had woken him from a siesta.

"¿Contraseña?" Carreras shouted. He dropped the cigar butt to the ground and stubbed it out with his boot. *Password.*

Perhaps if Guevara had been a little slower to anger, he might have noticed there was some art to this pathetic excuse for a sentry. He shouted back that they had no password and needed no password, spitting the words with defiance and ordering Carreras to stand aside.

Carreras didn't budge. Instead, he shouted back an order to surrender. At first, Guevara said nothing. Then he called out in Spanish.

"Es una broma?" Is this a joke?

But there was no joke, and Carreras was no longer smiling.

Guevara never saw the signal that brought seventy camouflaged rebels to their feet, appearing—as if out of nowhere—on both flanks.

*

Even in the hospital hut and through the haze of his fever, Ray could hear the bitter row going on inside the *bohío* that served as Menoyo's command post. The whole camp could hear. But one voice in particular, with the strong Italianate lilt characteristic of Argentine Spanish, was dominating the debate.

Ray was alone. He lifted himself from the sweat-soaked sheets onto one elbow and craned to look out the hospital doorway. On the far side of the camp he could see more than a hundred men sitting on the ground together, some smoking and chatting, but most with their eyes fixed in the direction of the argument raging on the far side of the compound. He didn't recognize these men from his weeks at the camp, though many were wearing uniforms consistent with rebel forces, and his befuddled brain wondered how they came to be there.

Sitting up took him most of a minute, and still his head pounded. He felt faint. He gripped the edge of the cot and tried to steady himself. He reached for the trousers and shirt hanging from a nail by his bedside and fell back on the bed. He fumbled getting his feet in the trouser legs and also with the buttons on the shirt, his fingers feeling fat and unresponsive as he worked mightily at the simple task of dressing himself.

At the doorway, he held on to the wooden frame and let his eyes adjust to the bright sunlight outside. Inside the command post, he could just pick out Morgan and Carreras and Menoyo, with two or three others he did not know, one group apparently squared up to the other. But even from where he was, even ill, he recognized the Argentine. Having seen the photographs, he was certain the man doing most of the shouting and arm waving was Guevara. Ray suddenly knew he had a story, if only he could make it across the compound.

He plotted the staging posts he would need along the way. The first objective was to reach a trestle table sitting in the shade of the palms edging the camp. Several young men and women were gathered there watching a demonstration on stripping and cleaning a carbine rifle. He launched himself from the doorway in their direction.

Some of the students saw Ray staggering toward them, weaving left and right, and began to nudge each other as he approached. A few steps farther, almost skipping to keep his balance, he crashed against the table like a drunkard.

"*Perdón—perdóneme.*" He was already sweating from the ten yards he had covered, but determined to go on.

The next twenty yards felt like a marathon run in slow motion, with each step an effort of will. Eventually he made it, breathless and exhausted, to a huge royal palm near the command post. Now, unnoticed by those within, he could hear every word they were saying, or rather shouting, and see their faces. He could even hear Guevara's rasping asthmatic wheeze as he struggled for the breath to begin each new tirade.

Menoyo was telling Guevara who was in charge here— that much was clear—and Guevara didn't like what he was hearing.

Ray needed no translation for what happened next. Had he been closer, he would have noticed the blue veins in Guevara's neck pulsing and prominent. But what he did see, without any shadow of a doubt, was Guevara reaching for the pistol holstered at his belt. And what he heard, at precisely the same moment, was the authoritative metallic *shick-uck!* of the slide on a Colt 45 racking back. Morgan was standing with both hands held low in front of him. Almost hidden by his big hands was the gun, cocked and ready to fire.

Ray pushed himself off from the palm trunk and straightened up as best he could for the final few steps. Morgan and Guevara were eyeball to eyeball. Ray ducked under the palm-thatch roof in time to hear Guevara's stumbling English.

"I will remember you," he said.

Morgan smiled. "That's nice," he said.

Guevara turned to Carreras. "*Y usted, camarada.*"

This is my chance, Ray thought to himself. "Dr. Guevara, Ray Halliwell, *Chicago Sun-Times.*"

Everyone turned to stare. Ray was clinging to the door lintel, his face glistening with the effort of his journey across the camp. His double vision was back.

"I wonder," he said, "if you could spare me a few minutes—when you're done here, naturally."

It was Carreras who caught Ray by the arms as his knees gave way and he began to slide slowly down the doorpost to the ground.

31

Six weeks had passed since his brief encounter with Che Guevara. Ray was sitting up in bed in his private room—paid for by the *Sun-Times'* insurers—at Chicago's Memorial Hospital. He was still surprisingly weak from the virus, twenty-five pounds lighter and frustrated beyond belief.

The room was equipped with a television, a radio and a telephone. A broad cross-section of national newspapers and magazines was delivered to him in his room every morning, without fail. But getting any kind of clear picture of what was going on in Cuba was nevertheless impossible.

The CBS News at seven-fifteen, with Douglas Edwards in the hotseat, had yet again reported significant successes for the army, with newsreel of captured revolutionaries and a claimed body count that defied gravity. The US papers too, had a strong bias toward the Cuban government's version of events, not least because most international and American journalists had been confined to Havana under the emergency laws. As the rebels came down from the mountains and took the fight to the plains and cities, getting any kind of reliable information was almost impossible.

Batista's carefully managed propaganda admitted to battles around Santa Clara, Cienfuegos and Trinidad City in the immediate proximity of the Escambray, and more fighting near Santiago and Holguín in the East, close to the Sierra. But this version characterized the conflict as a desperate last stand by both the July 26 Movement rebels and the forces of the Second Front, hopelessly outnumbered and doomed to total annihilation.

The rebel version of the last four weeks of intensive fighting naturally enough took a very different line. Both *Radio Rebelde* in the Sierra and *Seis Feroces Barbudos* in the Escambray had been reporting significant successes, beginning with routs of the army forces encircling their mountain strongholds and going on to claim victories in securing major roads to nearby cities.

It was only thanks to one of Jamie's hobbies—besides photography and cameras—that Ray was managing to stay sane and, much to the astonishment of his editor, produce copy on the situation in Cuba from his hospital bed. As Ray sat surrounded by reams of discarded newspapers, typewriter balanced on his knees, Jamie was once again holed up in Ray's old apartment in Havana. This time, the photographer was doing something useful though, crouched in front of a short wave radio set, one side of his earphones pushed back on his head so he could hold the telephone to that ear.

"—I don't know, they're not saying," said Jamie.

Ray cradled the receiver to his neck and flicked through a copy of the *New York Times* as he spoke.

"Well, what *are* they saying?"

"I'm not sure, it's all, you know, Spanish man."

"It's their language, Jamie."

"Oh, ho-ho. I mean, it takes me a while to work out. Something about Santa Clara? Some kind of armored train—derailed I think. I don't know, maybe derailed. What's the Spanish for derailed?"

"Not a clue. What else?"

"Hold on. I'm going to try another frequency."

As Ray sighed and cradled the phone with his chin, Jamie was twisting the Bakelite dial slowly—he liked to think of it as the combination to a safe—and watching the red line on the Perspex indicator traverse upwards from 5,000kHz, through eight and nine. The hiss of interference rose and fell in tone as the dial turned, growing louder or softer, like a tuneless boatswain's whistle.

Ray could hear it all and felt himself growing increasingly, if quite unfairly, impatient.

"Come on, Jamie, before they cut us off again."

"Give me a break, Ray—and shut up a minute. This is a delicate operation and I can't hear with you—"

Jamie stopped midway.

"What?" said Ray. "What have you got?"

Ray listened hard. Even down the phone receiver he could hear the familiar sound of assembled voices singing Auld Lang Syne. Jamie was apparently humming along.

"It's that—"

"Yeah, I know what it is for Christ's sake."

"Happy New Year to you too, Ray. I could be at the Bodeguita, you know?"

"I know," said Ray. "I told you. I owe you."

"Big time."

It was quarter before midnight. Snow was falling outside the window to Ray's room, the white flakes luminous as the light from inside caught them for an instant. Ray looked up to see the door opening. He was sure it would be one of the nurses coming to hush him, even if it was New Year's Eve. But it wasn't a nurse. It was Jim Sturry.

Ray put his hand over the mouthpiece of the phone.

"Jim. What the hell are you doing here?"

"I hate parties. What can I tell you? Who's that?"

"I've got Jamie and his ham radio kit."

"And?"

"It's a mess."

"So what's new? Listen Ray, take a minute will you?"

"Something's going down Jim—"

"Take a minute, anyway."

"Okay, hold on." Ray uncovered the receiver and spoke quickly to Jamie. "Jamie, I've got someone here. Keep listening for me." He didn't hang up.

"What is it, Jim?" he said to Sturry, "You didn't come all this way to wish me a happy New Year, did you?"

"Maybe I did. But there's something else. How do you feel about becoming the next foreign editor of the *Sun-Times*?"

"Bingo!" said Jamie's tinny voice at the other end of the line. Both men heard him. Ray put the phone back to his ear and raised a hand to signal Sturry should wait.

"What have you got, Jamie?"

"I've got Camp Columbia's airbase comms. They're pretty excited about something. Security's at high alert."

Ray looked to Sturry who was lighting a cigarette, despite the hospital's regulations.

"Got anything to drink here?" said Sturry.

Ray hushed him. "And? Come on Jamie, talk to me!"

"Batista's just arrived at the airbase with his family!"

"What?" Ray said, staring at the earpiece as if there was something to see there.

"I don't know Ray, some kind of photo op on the tarmac, radio guys too. I'm trying to find a—"

"Jamie?"

"Yeah, I'm here—Jesus—I think he's getting set to blow the island!"

32

Senator Hawkes checked his watch and confirmed the time with the wall clock.

"I'm going to propose a recess for lunch and give us all about an hour. We'll pick this up again at two o'clock. Counsel?"

"Thank you, Senator, that's fine."

"I'm sure I don't need to remind witnesses and all those here present that these proceedings are held in-camera and must not be divulged or discussed in any way beyond these doors. This session is now suspended."

The three members of the committee began to gather their papers before leaving the chamber. The recorder wrote a final line on her machine before she too filed out of the side door, leaving Ray, María and Capaldi alone in the room.

"Everett?" Ray said, inviting a verdict on the proceedings so far.

"Good," said Capaldi. But the expression on his face seemed to tell a different story.

"What is it?" said Ray, as they stood up.

"Nothing, no. Let's talk about it over lunch."

"Okay," said Ray.

By the time they'd negotiated the long corridors leading to the Senate's underground cafeteria, Ray had managed—with María's assistance—to call his son Phil and talk to him.

As the three of them took their red plastic trays from the stack and joined the queue at the self-service counter, he was relaying Phil's information to Capaldi, checking María's reaction from time to time as he mentioned names she might recall.

"—Amelia was a buddy, but we lost touch some years ago," said Ray, reaching for a juice bottle from the chiller. "There were two or three other press contacts that might be useful—remember Gordie?—and Phil's working on those. No luck so far. But the good news is John Dempsey. What do you think?"

Capaldi was studying the labels on an array of plastic-wrapped sandwiches, his nose crinkling as he apparently strained to translate the literal descriptions of ingredients into an appetizing image in his mind.

"We tried. Several times in fact. Mr. Dempsey stonewalled."

A young woman with a sense of purpose about her chose that moment to interrupt.

"Mr. Halliwell? Joanne Simpson, *New York Times*. We met at the Carnegie Foreign Policy Conference?"

Ray took a moment to recognize her.

"Joanne. Hi," he said.

"I just read your book. Great, just great. Did you catch the review?"

"I did, thank you," said Ray.

"Do you have a few minutes, sir?" she said. "I'd love to do a follow-up profile. Maybe we could lunch together?"

"I can't, Joanne," said Ray, letting María pass him in the queue. The young woman studied María. The winning smile never left her lips. Ray began to move away from her and catch up with the lawyer.

"Everett?" he said, as Capaldi took a plate of feta salad covered in cling film and put it on his tray. He was talking over María now and struggling for the lawyer's attention.

"Maybe it's worth another try?"

"The personal touch?" said Capaldi.

Ray took a plate and put it on his own tray, wondering if Capaldi had meant to sound short.

They reached the cash register. "Let me get this," said Ray.

But Capaldi already had a bill in his hand. "I've got it."

Lawyer and client found a table across the room, whilst Ray paused to acknowledge two or three more acquaintances lunching that day. When he joined Capaldi and María, they had already begun eating. Capaldi was rolling pieces of feta to one side of the plate and gathering lumps of the white cheese like a little pile of bricks. Ray decided that no matter what Capaldi might feel about his suggestion, he was going to force the issue.

"Do you have any objection to my trying to reach Dempsey? Phil tells me he's right here in town, or at least a cab ride outside. A nursing home in Arlington. What have we got to lose?"

Capaldi looked up from the feta salad but said nothing. Ray turned to María.

"What do you think?"

She had both men's full attention now as they waited on a verdict.

"Perhaps you can persuade him," said María. "You are an important man now. Maybe he will listen to you. Everett?"

Capaldi sighed. "A written statement, whatever, could be invaluable."

"Great," Ray said, "I'll get back to Phil and see what we can arrange for later. There's an office upstairs where I might be able to use a proper phone. It's noisy in here and I hate these things," he added, waving the cell phone as he stood up from the table.

"You haven't eaten anything," said María.

"I'll take it with me."

When Ray was gone, Capaldi picked up a piece of feta with his fork and put it in his mouth. He winced at the salty flavor and the crumbly texture. He swallowed it quickly and looked over his glasses at María.

"What kind of cheese did you say this is?"

PART THREE

33

Sitting at the witness table, waiting on the committee's return, María was musing on what had brought her to this hearing so long after her life with Morgan was over.

There was no single event, no turning point, no crisis. In the early days, when America was new to her and the people so different from her, when she'd lived alone and had to fight for every last penny to keep going, she'd had no energy and no desire to rake over the past. Living from day to day was sufficient challenge.

But, over time, the past—far from receding—had become ever more present to her. It was she who had started this process, after a long and dedicated silence, without fully understanding why she was driven to act. It was she who had pursued the legal battle over several years, against the odds and against the vast majority of the professional advice she'd received along the way. It was her decision to take on the United States government and suggest—within the polite confines of legal argument, naturally—that the law as applied was an ass, and the government a spiteful, self-serving child, perfectly capable of holding a grudge for fifty years.

She'd been lucky to find Everett Capaldi, a hometown lawyer with no particular experience in the law as it applied to nationality issues, but with a dogged conviction that the law must apply to all equally, regardless of status, wealth or privilege. Other lawyers she'd approached—those advertising their skills and experience in the area—had sat back in their plush leather chairs and pushed the paperwork from side to side as they calculated the tiny fees she could afford, and the likely PR impact of defending a long-dead adventurer, forgotten by history, a man who fought with communists and was now safely returned to the obscurity from whence he came. Would the news media really see the winning of this case as a blow for freedom and democracy? Unlikely. Would the government really want to admit its culpability? Not a chance. Naturally, none of the lawyers she spoke with had said so in quite such plain language, but there it was nevertheless, expressed in blank looks, embarrassed smiles, unanswered e-mail enquiries and phone calls returned by office assistants.

Money would no doubt have helped open doors, but María did not have money. After escaping Cuba and coming to America, she'd settled in Cleveland close to Morgan's remaining family and her own daughters who were already in the country. The family had welcomed her and helped where they could as she worked to set up a new life, but still they had lives of their own and she'd spent many evenings and weekends alone, until some years after, she met George Jensen, a welder by trade, and slowly their friendship grew imperceptibly into love, and finally marriage. Throughout their courtship and in the years of living under one roof that immediately followed, she'd said very little about her past and nothing at all about her involvement with the revolution, nor had she given any details of her marriage to William Morgan.

George was not inclined to intrude on her privacy. It was enough for him to appreciate her for what she was, to know that his new wife had been married once before to an American from Cleveland and that she had two beautiful girls from that marriage, and now, grandchildren.

The decision to remain entirely silent about her past was harsh—harshest of all on María herself—but it was necessary, and so for a long time she never mentioned William's name to her wider family or to new friends. It was just easier that way.

But as the years rolled by, she found to her surprise that her mind more often drifted back in time, sometimes as she shopped or weeded the yard, or washed clothes or prepared the evening meal. When it happened, she would snap out of the daydream and realize she'd been away for quite a while.

She would scold herself and vow to keep her mind on her work, to live in the present, to think about her husband, children and grandchildren. But despite her best efforts, the reveries would return and with them, a niggling sense of unfinished business, of a responsibility undischarged, a story without an end.

And so, little by little, the wheels had started to turn. George had supported her with money, but more importantly with his patience and common sense and dry humor. Sitting at the witness table, she wondered what he was doing right now.

So deep in her own thoughts was she that María hardly noticed the return of the committee members. She stood mechanically with Capaldi. When they took their seats, she was relieved to see Ray scurrying in the side door and racing to take his seat beside her.

"I fell asleep," he whispered. They sat back at the table. "Damn, I hate being old."

She was glad to see him and grateful that his fluster helped bring her back from the far distant country that was the past.

After a few routine opening remarks, Senator Hawkes asked the first question.

"Am I correct in believing that you were married to William Morgan in the mountains of the Escambray?"

"Yes, Senator, that's correct," she said.

"Please continue."

María looked straight at Senator Wallace and sat straighter in her chair.

"We were in love, but there were strict rules governing the behavior of the Second Front with regard to relationships in a time of war, especially with the local communities, but also applying to us within the camp. Romance was forbidden unless it led to marriage. William and I spent a lot of time together. Soon, this was noticed and it was Menoyo who laid down the law."

"You were ordered to marry?" said Senator Hawkes.

"We were happy to go along with the rules. Very happy," said María.

Even the recorder looked up from her machine with something like a smile. But Senator Wallace, impatient as ever, was once again squirming in her seat.

"Mrs. Jensen, can we return to the dispute between Che Guevara's forces and the Second Front. How did that situation resolve? Am I right in assuming Guevara became the overall leader of a united force and that therefore William Morgan became a comandante in Fidel's forces?"

"No, ma'am. A working arrangement, an understanding, was reached to cooperate in a joint offensive against Batista's army, but the Second Front remained completely independent. Guevara didn't like it, but he had no choice."

"And the animosity described earlier between Morgan and Guevara? How did that play out in this new joint operation?"

"Menoyo could see the two of them would never be able to work together and so he made sure they fought on different fronts, far from each other. Menoyo and Guevara led the assault on Santa Clara. William led his own column toward Cienfuegos. The fighting was hard everywhere. For weeks we fought the army, leaving the mountains to take the war to them, to the cities. I thought the fighting would never end. Christmas came and went, but still the fighting continued. And then one day, I remember, it was early in the morning, just after dawn on New Year's Day. I was working in the field hospital behind our lines. William was leading his men against the garrison at Cumanayagua, a town on the road to Cienfuegos—"

34

Ramirito pulled his steel helmet, a relic of World War Two, down low over his eyes.

He squinted into the distance to see Morgan's command post, now just the shell of a building, its roof timbers exposed like the ribs of some dead beast. A hundred and fifty yards of cobbled street strewn with rubbish, bricks and at least two bodies lay between the low wall he was using as a sniper shelter and the command post. It was New Year's Day morning.

"*Shit!*" he growled, slumping down behind the wall and holding the Thompson across his knees.

Ramirito had learned a lot of English from being around Morgan. If he was going to die on this run, he wanted his last words to sound like the *yanqui* who had taught him to push out his chest and hide his fear. He peeked once more over the low wall to check the cover on his route, noting every doorway or upturned cart that might save him from getting shot.

"*Shit*," Ramirito said again.

Then he began to count—again, in English. "—*three, two*—" But before he got to "*one*," as if to get the jump on himself, he was up and sprinting.

He had twenty yards to go when he tripped and fell headlong, scraping his elbows on the cobblestones and letting his submachine gun clatter away in front of him. His helmet came off, bounced and wobbled on the street beside him. His hands hurt from breaking his fall, and it bothered him that he had let the precious Thompson hit the ground hard.

"Goddamn it, Ram, get your ass in here!"

He looked up to see Morgan leaning out from the command post and firing round after round from his Colt pistol in the enemy's general direction.

Crouching on all fours, Ramirito lunged for the submachine gun and scampered to the cover of the command post walls, where he sprawled in a heap on the floor. His helmet still lay in the road where it had fallen. He tried to slow his breathing. Morgan was back at the map table studying their latest positions with his captain, Edel Montiel.

"What you got, Ram?"

Ramirito spluttered his reply in Spanish. "Reinforcements. Cienfuegos Road. A hundred men."

Morgan said nothing. Instead, he traced a line on the map of the town, working out the best line of defense to prevent the reinforcements breaking through to the barracks.

Morgan was so engrossed in his thoughts that he was the last of the three to notice the gradual tapering off of the shooting around them. Only when it became eerily quiet did he look up and wonder what was happening. A few of his own men were still firing, but the army's guns had fallen strangely silent.

From to a gap in the wall, he looked down the street toward the barracks, but he could see no movement behind the smashed windows and no guns bristling from the roof or walls.

"What the hell is going on?" he wondered aloud. Then, cupping his hand, he shouted to his men to cease fire.

"*¡Alto el fuego! ¡Alto el fuego!*"

The shooting stopped. Smoke drifted from burning buildings nearby and he could hear distant voices, but nothing was stirring. The streets of the town had taken on a ghostly stillness.

All eyes were fixed on the double wooden doors, eight feet high, shutting off the barracks' courtyard from the town square. Though pocked and scarred from dozens of bullets and a nearby grenade explosion, they looked as solid as ever. Then, with a creaking sound that echoed in the silence, one of the doors cracked open, just wide enough to admit a long stick with a white handkerchief tied to the end.

It took some time for the door to open a little further. An officer and two of his men slid sideways out and took a few awkward steps into the naked arena of the square. Morgan—scanning the barracks for a trick—with Montiel and Ramirito following a little behind, stepped out from the command post and walked toward the army officer and his men. Morgan's mind was still racing to understand why this officer had chosen this particular moment to talk. The battle had reached a stalemate, but it was far from over, and if Morgan knew that reinforcements were close by, surely this man also knew.

There was now just ten yards between them. As if by an unspoken order, both parties stopped.

The officer, a short, rather plump young man, no more than twenty-five years old, gave a smart salute, the heels of his dusty knee-length black boots clicking together as he came to attention. Morgan returned the salute with a lazy action and tucked his thumbs in his belt.

"*Hable*," he said, clipping the word short. *Speak*.

The officer cleared his throat, raised his chin a little and began to talk, clearing his throat from time to time. Morgan had to concentrate to be sure he understood. It seemed the man was either asking for a ceasefire or—for no apparent reason—offering to surrender. Why? Something wasn't right, though Morgan was at a loss to know exactly what it was and how to respond. He decided to play the bluff.

"Unconditional surrender," he said in Spanish. "It's that or nothing."

The officer seemed to ponder this for a moment, then stood even more rigidly erect to demand Morgan's personal guarantee of reasonable treatment for his men, according to international convention.

Morgan gave his word.

The officer reached slowly for his pistol, unclipped the leather flap of the holster and, with all eyes on him, took it by the barrel and handed it to Morgan.

Morgan passed the handgun to Montiel without taking his eyes from the three men in front of him. The officer turned to the soldiers with him and spoke in such hushed tones that Morgan missed what he said. The soldier bearing the white flag began to wave it frantically from side to side and shouted toward the barracks. The heavy door opened a little wider, and one by one the soldiers emerged, laying their weapons on the ground. They formed a line, hands on their heads and fear in their eyes. Morgan was more puzzled than ever and still expecting a trick. This just didn't smell right.

Before he could ask anymore questions, the drone of an airplane floated through the air, growing louder by the second. Morgan looked up to see the silhouette of what might be a single-engine Sea Fury, designed by the British for use in World War Two.

At first, it seemed the plane might bypass the town. But as it came close enough for them all to see the distinctive black-and-white stripes painted on the trailing edge of each wing, the Sea Fury started to bank left, giving the pilot a bird's-eye view of Cumanayagua and leaving the men in the town square feeling suddenly very exposed.

Morgan was pretty sure it was not carrying a bomb load. The underside of the Sea Fury's belly as it banked showed clean lines against the bright blue sky. But the cannons could still cut a terrible swath through the center of town. Morgan swung around to the officer for some kind of explanation or reassurance, but he got nothing of the kind. The young man in the gaudy uniform looked suddenly very nervous. He had taken a few steps away, as if the idea of running for cover was pulling him back toward the barracks, and yet he must have known that movement in any direction would be construed as treachery. He began jabbering about his orders, trying to say they came from the highest authority and that this pilot must know, must have the same orders. But Morgan was no longer listening.

"Ramirito," said Morgan in a voice filled with quiet menace. "Your weapon."

Ramirito looked down at his precious submachine gun.

Morgan grabbed the gun from Ramirito's hands without taking his eyes from the plane.

"Take cover!" he shouted at the top of his lungs.

All around, soldiers and rebels drained away from the open square and hid themselves behind walls and cars. The Sea Fury's engines rose in pitch as it started to dive. Ramirito took a couple of steps away from Morgan, then ran for the command post.

Morgan squinted up at the plane. He imagined the pilot's view of the town and the big empty square with the barracks along the north side and the church to the west; a long boulevard of shuttered shops and drifting smoke that trailed away to the south.

As the Sea Fury took on mass and solidity, its wings dipping slightly left and right as the pilot corrected his line, Morgan thumped the magazine of the Thompson home to be sure it was fully engaged. He pulled back on the slide.

"*Hijo de puta*," Morgan raised the Thompson and locked the Sea Fury in the crude V-sight.

The pilot would not have seen Morgan yet, and even if he had, he would have no idea Morgan was aiming a weapon back at him. Besides, the idea of the wildly inaccurate submachine gun with an effective range of perhaps fifty yards was hardly a threat. In fact, it was laughable.

But Morgan was not quite as crazy as he looked. In the open square, a hundred yards across, the first cannon rounds to hit the ground would tell him exactly the line the plane was on. Then there should be just enough time to sidestep the line of fire and, as the Sea Fury passed directly overhead, to do some damage to its underbelly.

He could see the canopy and the outline of the pilot. He waited for the opening burst from the cannons. It never came. As the Sea Fury screamed directly overhead, its weakest point exposed and vulnerable, the blast of displaced air whipping up a storm of dust, Morgan's finger was pulling back instinctively on the trigger, taking up the play in the mechanism. But he didn't fire. Still keeping the Sea Fury in the V-sight, he turned to follow it as it climbed away and gave a farewell wing waggle.

Morgan lowered the Thompson and held it dangling at his side. His eyes were full of grit thrown up by the backwash from the plane's propeller. He blinked to clear his vision. As his eyes focused, he noticed there were hundreds of pieces of paper filling the air like enormous snowflakes.

He reached up to grab one of the pieces of paper floating around him in giddy circles. And there it was, in crude, badly mimeographed lettering.

Comrades, the war is over. The hated dictator has fled the country. Long live Free Cuba!

All around him, the revolutionaries were reading the same words. Some began shooting their guns in the air. Others were embracing or dancing. Ramirito was wheeling around in imitation of a plane and making obscene gestures to the sky. Several of the army soldiers had taken their hands from their heads. Some were weeping. But Morgan hadn't moved. He was still studying the leaflet, as if the words made no sense.

*

Outside the hospital, the whole column was lined up in jeeps and trucks, engines running. Wolf whistles, guns shot in the air, singing, hands clapping, shouts to get a move on, and Morgan holding María by the arms. She needed reassurance.

"Again," she said, "tell me again."

"It's over. Let's go," said Morgan. "You're riding with me."

The shouts and cajoling from the column seemed to rise in volume. María could hear her name and Morgan's.

"I still have work to do here," she said.

"It can wait," Morgan replied. "What you'll see today you'll only ever see once in a lifetime. It's everything we've worked for, everything these guys in the hospital have worked for. You owe it to them to be a witness. It's your duty. As your commanding officer—"

María hit him hard on the chest with both fists, and a whoop of excitement went up from the column, together with some less than respectful references to Morgan's ability to control his woman.

"Come on," he said to her, "please?"

All the way along the dusty roads to Cienfuegos, María clung tight to the dashboard of the jeep, bracing herself and the new life growing inside her against the potholes and dips in the road. She had yet to tell Morgan she was pregnant, but that could wait until they were alone together.

As the column entered the city down the broad Paseo del Prado, heading for the government buildings surrounding Parque José Martí, thousands of the city's inhabitants were already on the streets in wild celebration. Cars loaded to overflowing joined the rebel column for the cavalcade, passing by crowds ten or twenty deep lining every foot of the route. Flags and banners supporting the rebels and the revolution, kept for years despite the penalties for possession, were now unfurled from balconies and windows. Young and old alike openly wore the banned black-and-red armbands of the July 26 Movement. Cow horns and car horns blared against the background of drums beating and brass bands trumpeting the dawn of a new era for Cuba— and all this magically taking place on New Year's Day itself.

With people milling everywhere, the column slowed to a crawl. Cut flowers rained down on the jeeps. Euphoric young women were hugging and kissing the bearded *revolucionarios*—who were only too happy to respond. Even Morgan was shouting as he eased the lead jeep through the crowds.

"*Hola! Victoria! Libertad!*"

In reply, the crowds called back, "*El Americano, El Americano! Bienvenido!*"

180

35

Morgan and María walked into the lobby of the Hotel Capri in Havana to be met by an electrified wall of reporters, flashing cameras and television newsreel crews.

María felt queasy, most likely the result of morning sickness, but certainly not helped by the crazy scenes surrounding them. She looked for friendly faces and tried to stay calm in the midst of what seemed to be total chaos. *Barbudos*, *'the bearded ones'*, as all the rebels, whatever their affiliation, were now known—many carrying their weapons slung casually over their shoulders—mixed with a host of the famous and infamous. Some were dressed as if for a dinner party, even at midday, and all gathered for the media event of the year.

The relief was immense as she recognized Menoyo fighting his way toward them through the crowd. He was looking even thinner than she remembered, like a stick insect in an oversized, and newly pressed, uniform. María noticed too, that his wispy beard had been trimmed for the occasion.

"Hey, *Yanqui*!" said Menoyo as he hugged Morgan.

Morgan spoke softly, and in English. "How are things?"

Menoyo smiled and checked to see if anyone could hear them. When he replied, he too, spoke in English.

"Tricky," he said, "but that's for later. Come on, there's a room where you can clean up. I will show you."

Menoyo led the way through the packed lobby toward a broad corridor where the hotel's function rooms were situated. Far from the crowds thinning out, the confined space of the corridor was more jammed than the lobby.

Impromptu interviews seemed to be going on everywhere, and reporters with their notebooks open were scribbling and talking or nodding sagely as they started to write the history of the revolution on the hoof.

A portly man turned to see Morgan and reached out to shake hands. María assumed he too was a reporter.

"Who was that?" said María as they weaved in and out of yet more static bodies.

"Dominick Bartone."

"Is he a reporter?"

"No, he's Mafia."

María took a moment to understand what her husband meant.

"What's he doing here?"

"I don't know," said Morgan.

A busy little man, breathless and sweaty, interrupted them. Still some distance away, he was calling out repeatedly, "*Comandante Morgan! Comandante por favor!*"

Rafael Garriga, the Second Front's PR man, was already talking as he shook Morgan's hand, but gabbling so fast he was hard to comprehend.

"So, we have a press conference at five, but also a photo call. You will be needed for both, Comandante, if you please. And the party, dress informal—"

Menoyo raised both hands to signal enough.

"*Rafael!*" he pleaded. "*Más tarde, más tarde, por favor.*" *Later, please.*

María noticed Jesús Carreras was perched on the armrest of a sofa where the corridor opened out to the lush gardens beyond. He was smoking a cigar, his eyes fixed on the middle distance as he held court with a couple of entranced young women, like an Indian guru and his disciples.

"Hey, brother!" Morgan called out.

Carreras looked up, squinting into the dark corridor to see who had called him, as if shortsighted.

Carreras' expression exploded in a broad grin, the cigar still clamped between his teeth. Without a second thought for the girls he was leaving behind, he bounded toward Morgan. The two men locked in an embrace, each trying to lift the other from the ground or squeeze the life from their opponent. When finally they let go, Carreras took the cigar from his mouth and held the American's face roughly in his hands.

"So, you live yet, *yanqui?*"

"*Como ve, come vaca.*"

"I could eat you, *hijo de puta!*"

"Try and I'll shoot your balls off."

"What you say? *No habla español, eh, yanqui?*"

"Go back to your women; maybe for once you'll get lucky."

"I'm always lucky. Until I see you! Then *mierda!*"

The double doors to a conference suite, close to where they were standing, abruptly opened to disgorge a phalanx of photographers and reporters into the already packed corridor. In the middle of them—taller than anyone around by a head—barrel-chested and bearded, field cap over black-rimmed spectacles and searching eyes, talking incessantly, the Maximum Leader himself, like a queen bee surrounded by frantic attendants.

Moments later, Fidel was embracing Menoyo, subtly maneuvering the moment for the cameras, holding the pose just long enough to ensure the images would clearly show the fraternal relations between July 26 and the Second Front with, as it happened, Fidel towering over Menoyo.

"I want you to be the first to come and see me," he said. "We'll talk, okay? Come the day after tomorrow."

"*Sí Fidel,*" Menoyo replied, his expression colorless in contrast to the Maximum Leader's animated changes in tempo and mood.

And although the Maximum Leader lowered his voice for what he said next, María heard every word.

"This American adventurer, how much do we have to pay him to go home?"

"He's not an adventurer," she heard Menoyo reply, "he's a revolutionary like us."

Fidel squeezed Menoyo's shoulder and was already looking around for his next grandstanding opportunity. He said quietly, but audibly, "Even worse."

And then he was sweeping away, still talking and gesturing, the gaggle of attendants now trailing behind, elbowing each other and jockeying for position, camera lights flailing around the dark interior in the commotion.

"Okay?" Morgan said to María.

She didn't reply.

A quarter of an hour later, Morgan and María had signed in at the hastily erected trestle tables in the Nassau Room, where a line of hotel employees were busily allocating accommodation to members of the Second Front. Menoyo made sure the reception clerk would have the laundry service clean and press Morgan's uniform by five-thirty. When both María and Morgan found much to giggle at in their leader's womanly attention to detail, Menoyo gave them the finger and left them to conclude the paperwork alone.

Their room was on the fifth floor of the hotel. There was a balcony with a view of the ocean glittering in the early afternoon sun. When María opened the sliding glass door, the white net curtains billowed in the sea breeze. The double bed seemed to both of them to be enormous.

María took a step closer to examine the gift-wrapping around a tiny wicker basket lying on one of the pillows, but she didn't dare touch.

"What is it?" said Morgan.

María turned and smiled. "Chocolate, I think."

"Try it."

"Shall I?" said María.

She sauntered toward him, unwrapping the chocolate and biting into it. She put the other half in his mouth.

"*Yanqui*," she said, "is it over?"

"It's over, baby," said Morgan, putting his arms around her.

"The fighting? The killing?"

"All over."

María sighed. "Good. Because I have something to tell you—"

36

"Mr. Morgan! Comandante? Amelia Frankenheim, Baltimore Sun."

Amelia was standing and waving her notebook to get Morgan's attention. The press conference was full to overflowing with all chairs taken. Those who could not find a seat were lining the walls of the large Tortuga conference room. María was one of them, watching and listening from the back of the room.

The panel of Second Front leaders sat at a long table on a raised dais. Three or four microphones stood on the tabletop behind hastily prepared nameplates, illegible from any distance. Menoyo was centre stage with Morgan directly to his right; then Carreras and Dr. Armando Fleites. To his left, Max Lesnik, Comandante Artola, Capitán Montiel and Capitán Redondo.

Menoyo had opened the conference with a prepared statement paying tribute to fallen comrades and welcoming a new future for Cuba under President elect Manuel Urrutia, a former small-town judge handpicked by Fidel for his honesty and courage, and Prime Minister Cardona. As an independent and proud land that had cast off the shackles of a dictator, Menoyo said the process of building a fairer society was already underway, but with the vast majority of the work still ahead of them. Asked about his own role in the revolutionary government, Menoyo reiterated a point he'd made in all the interviews he'd been giving to the press: the Second Front was not a political organization, he said, but he looked forward to free elections and planned to take an active role in the democratic process. In the meantime, he said, he was willing to serve in any way he could and had every confidence in the President, the Prime Minister and the Commander of the Armed Forces, Fidel Castro, as they guided the country toward a fully restored democracy.

Reporters from *Prensa Libre*, *Excelsior* and the Catholic *Diario de la Marina* were given first bite at the apple and concentrated their questions on the political landscape as it lay ahead. The American press corps—including Amelia, Gerry Gordon, Norman Williams, the grandee John Fitzwalter and a host of Johnny-come-lately foreign news staffers—was naturally fascinated by Morgan, the Midwesterner turned revolutionary. Amelia was their point man.

"Should I call you comandante or mister?"

Morgan cleared his throat and leaned forward to the microphone.

"Just as you wish, ma'am," said Morgan, with his best western charm. "I got used to being called a lot of things in the mountains, including *el Gordo*—the fat guy."

A ripple of laughter encouraged Morgan a little further. "I guess the last year or so has fixed that problem."

The panel joined in the fun, Carreras trying to pinch an inch with others calling comments from the wings. María too, was laughing. Only when she heard her name whispered did she turn and react as if she'd seen a ghost.

"Did I miss much?" Ray said.

He looked worn and gaunt. His skin was pale and there were black rings around his eyes. It was clear the dengue fever had taken its toll. María threw her arms around him. Neither of them heard Amelia's next question to Morgan, asking if it was true he'd got married in the mountains.

"Yes, it is, ma'am," Morgan responded, "and I just found out today we have a baby on the way."

There was applause, even from the press corps, and a lot of backslapping from Morgan's comrades on the platform. Morgan had to raise his voice above the hubbub.

"That's my wife right over there at the back, in another man's arms."

No one in the audience was quite sure how to react, but all turned to look.

"Better late than never, Ray," said Morgan.

María's new status as a married woman had hit Ray like a hammer blow, but he forced a smile and a brittle recovery. He turned and waved to Morgan on the platform.

"Thank you, Comandante."

"Mind if we carry on?" said Morgan.

"You go right ahead."

At that moment, another latecomer to the conference squeezed through the door and took up a position at the back of the room. Heads turned—amongst them Ray and María—to see Guevara, arms folded, lean casually against the wall. A young man in uniform was with him, notebook in hand.

"Some people have called you an adventurer," Amelia called to Morgan. "How do you respond?"

Morgan took his time before replying. "When I went up into the mountains, it's fair to say I didn't have ideals. I could fight, I knew that, but I didn't truly understand what I was fighting for. When I came down from the mountains, I came down with ideals. These folk here beside me, they taught me a whole lot, and María, my wife, she taught me more than anyone, about the lives of the real people of Cuba, the farmers, factory workers, teachers, nurses. I hope I'm a changed man, at least in that respect."

Gordie was next with a question. "There's been some talk of book deals, even a movie. Can you tell us what your plans are now?"

"Sleep. And plenty of it. Beyond that, a little family time, good food, you know, clean sheets, that kind of thing."

Rafael Garriga stood and faced the assembled reporters, planning to wind things up, but before he could speak, Norman Williams was on his feet.

"Mr. Morgan, there are some people convinced this revolution is a red revolution, that the communists are behind it. What's your view?"

The room was suddenly quieter than it had been up until that point. María exchanged a glance with Ray and both of them were aware of Guevara just a few feet away. Menoyo whispered in Morgan's ear and the American nodded.

"Yeah, we've heard those rumors too. All I can tell you is this. We fought to make sure Cuba never again has to suffer a dictatorship, no matter what the color."

Williams wanted to press the case, not least because he always felt the need to show off in front of his mentor. He glanced at Fitzwalter, who was sitting impassively beside him almost as if he had preprogrammed his protégé.

"Dr. Castro claims the revolution is olive green. You've heard the expression, a melon revolution? You know, green on the outside, red in the middle?"

"Is that the same question, sir? I think I already answered that. Let me just add, I trust Fidel with my life."

37

The same evening, the Second Front hosted a huge and well-attended party around the rooftop pool on the twelfth floor of the Capri, a location gloriously open to the stars.

Far below, the streets of Havana were eerily quiet with scarce a vehicle moving unless to patrol the curfew. In contrast, the assembled crowd was in riotous spirits. There was music from a live band with brass, guitar and drums beating out the Cuban sound. An open bar was doing a roaring trade, with inevitable consequences. There were many more comrades *in* the pool, fully clothed and swigging from glasses and bottles, their arms around beautiful, wet young women, than left standing on dry land. Others were already fast asleep on the poolside sun loungers, exhausted but apparently deeply content.

Ray and María were dancing.

"And all these girls—" said María. "As if by magic they appear from no place."

"Nowhere, as if from nowhere," said Ray in his best schoolteacher's voice.

María put her tongue out at him. "Who cares?"

Ray shrugged. "I'm just saying, now you're married to an American and all."

María smiled but didn't reply. Instead she asked her own question. "Are you back in Cuba for good now?"

Ray thought for a moment. "They've offered me a job stateside. Foreign editor."

"But that's good news, no?" said María.

"I don't know," said Ray, "I really don't."

Conversation faltered. They were both relieved when Menoyo interrupted them.

"Please," he said, "I want you both to see this."

Menoyo was holding a metal waiter's tray with two tall glasses, frosted and beginning to trickle with condensation in the balmy night air.

"Two drinks on a tray?" said Ray.

Menoyo's expression did not alter from the serious. "Actually, my friend, yes. But not just any two drinks. You know what a *Sazerac* is?"

"I have to confess, I do not," said Ray, "but I have a feeling you're going to tell me."

"That feeling, Mr. Halliwell, is correct. Listen carefully, please. Take one old-fashioned glass, packed with ice. In a second, put a sugar cube and three dashes of Peychaud's Bitters. Add Rye whiskey—"

"You were a barman?" said Ray, interrupting.

Menoyo's expression remained calmly aloof, as if dealing with an imbecile.

"I *owned* a bar, *señor*. I still own the same bar, and if you are quiet, one day I will invite you. If not—"

María was laughing. Ray accepted his part with grace.

"My sincere apologies, Señor Menoyo. Please continue."

"Thank you. As I was saying, three dashes of Peychaud's Bitters and a good quality Rye whiskey. Now, returning to the first glass, you will recall, already cooled by the ice. Empty the ice and add Absinthe in a swirl to coat the sides of the glass. Pour in the mixture from the second glass and garnish with lemon peel. Here before you, you can see the result."

"Beautiful," said María.

Menoyo gave a little bow. "You are too kind. Now, I will take the Sazerac to my comrade—your husband, madam—and your friend, sir. Excuse me, please."

María and Ray watched him go, carrying the tray as if it were as precious and delicate as a bomb, his careful steps around the poolside only a little unstable.

Morgan was standing with the portly man they'd seen earlier in the hotel corridor. There was another man with them, not a Cuban, but another American by the look of him.

"I thought Bill was teetotal," said Ray.

"He is," said María.

"Well, I guess it's a special night."

Ray looked to her for a response, but he couldn't be sure she'd heard him.

After a moment, she said, "Ray, do you know those men with William?"

Even from the other side of the pool, Ray recognized Bartone straight away.

"One of them, yeah. What in God's name is he doing here? His name's Dominick Bartone, a mob boss."

"And the other?"

"No, I don't know him, but if he's with Bartone, he can't be good news."

Ray left the Capri around midnight and found the Wolf Pack at the Floridita, as arranged. He pecked Amelia on the cheek and slumped down beside her on the plush red sofa seat.

"I've heard of being fashionably late for a party" she said, "but for a revolution?"

"I was unavoidably delayed. Where is everyone?" said Ray.

"Norman's holding court at the bar, Fitzwalter's in tow. So no surprises there. Sir Hemingway is in his usual corner, acolytes all around, trying to break his record of eleven straight daiquiris, and Gordie's in the john—for some time now, actually—having tried to keep up with the great man. You look awful."

"Thanks."

"Drink?"

She took a sip of her own. Ray took the glass from her hand. He took a sip, made a face and handed it back.

"Glad you like it."

Amelia raised two fingers to a passing waiter and waggled her glass.

"Daiquiris then. Kill or cure."

Ray didn't argue.

"How long in the hospital?

"Seven excruciating weeks."

"So, this is a double celebration. Dengue and Batista. Both vanquished. It's almost like the two were connected in some way."

The waiter brought the drinks.

"What news from the home front?"

Ray took a long swig from his glass. He looked downcast.

"Is there a problem?"

"They've offered me foreign editor."

"My! Doesn't sound like a problem to me. So what are you doing here?"

"Trying to decide."

"Between what exactly?"

"It's a desk job, Amelia. I can't fly a desk."

"You could try. You already missed the main event. From here on, Cuba's going to be dull as dishwater."

"You think?"

"No, but there are more important things in life. Besides, you could hire me. I'll call you every day. Promise."

Ray put his arm around Amelia. Gordie appeared at the table, looking white.

"Oh, God!" he said. He sat down, holding his head in his hands.

"You okay, big man?" said Ray.

"No. I've just been sick as a dog."

"That's how the dengue started."

Gordie raised his head and stared at Ray, open-mouthed. "Are you serious?"

38

It was almost ten in the morning by the time Morgan, María and a ragtag line of hung-over comrades from the party located the house in the upmarket Miramar district of Havana.

Discreetly hidden down a long drive, the shuttered and deserted house on Avenue Seven-A and Sixty-sixth Street was, in reality, a mansion. Requisitioned by the Second Front with the approval of the revolutionary leadership, it had belonged to a property speculator and well-known *Batistiano*, Alberto Vadia, a man who had waited until the last moment to flee the country, reluctant to lose everything—bar his mobile fortune in cash and bonds. Vadia was now living in a hotel in Miami, waiting for what he believed would be a swift return when Castro's regime collapsed.

Morgan fumbled with the keys to the tune of impatient insults. The enormous front door finally yielded and swung open, the rush of daylight catching billions of dust particles swirling like smoke in its path. The place had probably been empty for no more than a matter of weeks, but already it had taken on the aspect of a haunted house, the interior seeming to shrink away from the intrusion of the living.

To describe what they found inside as sumptuous would be an understatement. They were standing in a vast double-height hall with a crystal chandelier as big as an upside-down Christmas tree. A grand central staircase with stone balustrades stretched up to a mezzanine gallery, wrapping around the hallway on three sides. To the left, double doors, left wide open, revealed a dining room that seemed to be as big as a tennis court, with one wall entirely comprised of a full-length mirror, accentuating the scale. A glass table stretched all the way into the gloom. To the right, another set of double doors led to a drawing room of equal dimensions, furnished with plush sofas and comfortable armchairs.

The men fanned out from the hallway, some murmuring their astonishment despite pounding heads and lack of sleep. Others flopped unceremoniously onto the furniture, closing their eyes and starting to snore almost instantly.

Morgan and María headed toward the back of the house. The kitchen, large enough to sit ten for breakfast and equipped with every convenience, boasted a walk-in refrigerator, still stacked with food. It was clear that when the owners had left, they left in a hurry. There was a utility area-cum-storage room for dry goods, and shelves laden with backup supplies of booze, including rum, gin and whiskey, four or five bottles deep.

"*Madre mía*," said María under her breath.

Morgan had thrown open the shutters of the floor-to-ceiling doors leading to the garden and was staring in disbelief at the enormous pool that lay beyond with its own bar, as impressive as any hotel.

María called to him. "William! Look at this!"

He was about to go toward the kitchen when he suddenly noticed a feature he'd walked straight by. Partitioning the kitchen and breakfast table from the drawing room was the grandest tropical fish tank he'd ever seen outside an aquarium.

Morgan was mesmerized. In effect, the tall glass sides of the tank acted as a transparent wall between the two spaces. He scanned the podium on which the tank sat and found a switch. He clicked it on and all at once, the tank lit up with green and purple effect lighting and the aerator began to bubble oxygen into the still and murky water. He assumed the neglected fish in the tank would be dead, having been left to fend for themselves for a couple of months. But he was wrong. As he stepped closer to the glass, his heart skipped a beat when he saw movement.

There were several dead fish floating on the surface, some quite large, their once vibrant tropical coloring fading to grays with the onset of decomposition. But whether because of the light or the movement of the water with the aerator, those still living were now suddenly animated and darting around as if woken from a deep sleep.

"María," said Morgan, "is there any food in there?"

"Enough to feed the whole camp for a week! What do you want?"

"Some bread or crackers, something like that."

"The bread will be stale, crackers I don't know. We'll cook something."

"It's not for me, it's for the fish."

"The fish?"

She'd had her head in cupboards and hadn't noticed the now illuminated fish tank. When she turned with an unopened packet of Jacob's Crackers in her hand, she couldn't believe her eyes.

"What are these people like?" she said. "How can they live like this? It's obscene."

"Gimme, gimme," said Morgan, leaning around the tank and holding out his hand for the crackers. María threw him the packet.

"Yeah, I know," he said between biting and spitting out bits of cellophane paper. "Amazing!"

"Don't you care? That people live like this and the rest must pay the price?"

"What? Of course I care," said Morgan, taking a handful of three or four crackers and scrunching them in his hand. "Look," he said, "I'm doing what I can to feed the hungry and redistribute the wealth."

"It's not funny," said María.

"Come see."

He sprinkled the crumbs on the water's surface, taking care to sweep the floating bodies out of the way. María stood on one side of the tank, Morgan on the other. Some of the fish could already smell the food and were rushing in all directions through the water in search of the source. The clever ones headed straight for the surface and began nibbling at the crumbs in frantic, tight-knit groups.

Neither Morgan nor María noticed the big fish that had been lying obscured by weed at the bottom of the tank, conserving energy perhaps, but now stirring and beginning to shake off the tiny stones in which it had partially buried itself. The fish, too big to register at first, altogether out of scale with the tank and the other fish living in it, burst suddenly from the camouflage of the plants and, with dreadful speed, accelerated toward the water's surface. There was just time for Morgan to notice the wide-open mouth before the leviathan engulfed the crumbs and the tiny fish feeding on them in one enormous gulp. It's head and dorsal fin broke the surface, sending shock waves through the water. The tail slashed to left and right and everything became opaque, muddy, devastated.

"Jesus!" said Morgan, taking a step back in shock. "Did you see that?"

María too, had recoiled from the tank and the still churning waters.

"What is it?"

"It's a goddamn monster, that's what it is," said Morgan.

39

The main channel was showing images of Fidel's triumphant arrival in Havana—some three weeks before—in preparation for his major television address to the nation. Thousands upon thousands of ordinary Cubans had gathered outside Camp Columbia, renamed Camp Libertad, to hear the words of the Maximum Leader.

María and Morgan were planning to spend the evening lying on the bed drinking cold beers and watching the whole thing on the small screen. Below them, in the living room, the *barbudos* were gathered, as if for a big game. They would watch events on the TV there, surrounded by the detritus of carry-out food snacks, empty bottles and cans. María regularly scolded them for the mess, but other than a few vague promises, nobody moved to fix things. She told Morgan it was like living with her brothers when they were teenagers.

The rally went crazy when *Il Maximo* appeared on stage. Even via the TV, the atmosphere was electric.

When he spoke, Fidel was masterful, an orator of consummate skill at the height of his powers and the absolute zenith of his popularity. Most of the crowd had never seen him in the flesh. Here was the legend come to life.

"The people are listening," he bellowed into the microphone. "The revolutionary combatants are listening!"

Morgan nudged María who was lying in the crook of his arm eating potato chips from the same big bag.

"That's us," he said, reaching for another beer, "and the animals downstairs. *Libertad!*" He raised his beer bottle to the black-and-white screen and took another handful of chips.

"And the army soldiers whose destiny is in our hands are listening!"

"You bet they are," Morgan replied.

María shushed him. "Quiet," she said, "you're supposed to be *listening*."

"I am," said Morgan, his mouth full. "Go ahead, turn up the sound."

María slid down the bed and cranked up the volume dial on the TV. She didn't come back to him, but sat at the end of the bed, hands between her knees, paying close attention to every word from Fidel.

"The first thing," Fidel went on, "we who have made this revolution must ask ourselves is, why did we make it?"

A catalogue of the crimes committed by Batista and his regime followed, delivered with all the drama of a courtroom indictment.

"You have to hand it to him," said Morgan, "the guy can hold a crowd."

"You don't find this all really strange?" said María over her shoulder to him. "Yesterday we were part of this revolution and today we're watching it on TV, like some kind of entertainment show."

"Now who's doing all the talking?" said Morgan.

María slapped his outstretched legs, but kept her eyes on the television.

"Who won the war?" the Maximum Leader asked the thousands gathered in front of him. He paused for dramatic effect before answering his own question. "The people! The people won the war!"

The cheers and waving arms he generated in the crowd was awesome and heartfelt.

"We are with you, Fidel," they shouted. "We are with you!"

Again he paused, touching the microphone from time to time as if about to speak and then changing his mind, teasing his audience. Then, as the chants subsided, he wagged his finger for a time before saying another word. This was theatre of the highest order.

"If some of us are hiding some ambition, are pushing for command," he said, a note of menace creeping into his voice, "this is not a noble proposition. The greatest crime that can be committed in Cuba today would be a crime against the peace. Anyone who threatens the tranquility and the happiness of millions of Cuban mothers is a criminal and a traitor!"

María was fidgeting and becoming increasingly tense. Her intuition told her where this was going. But when Fidel named the *Directorio Revolucionario*—the student movement of which she'd been a member—in the context of the enemy, she was stunned. Too stunned to say a word. Why, he asked, had they taken and kept weapons from abandoned army stores in the days following Batista's departure and before the arrival of the rebel forces?

"Arms for what?" the Maximum Leader sneered. "To fight against whom? To blackmail the President of the Republic? To threaten the government? To create organizations of gangsters?"

It was true the *Directorio* had taken arms from the arsenal of San Antonio de los Banõs, but only to keep the peace in Havana until a new government could take over. It was true they still held the weapons. But such a short time after Batista's flight from the island, María was incensed by Fidel's imputation of treason. To name the *Directorio* as an enemy of the revolution was a calumny of extraordinary proportions—and not just for her, but for all those who had fought bravely in the cities, in the Escambray and elsewhere, many of whom had given their lives in the process.

María was suddenly on her feet shouting back at the television image, "No! No!"

Morgan was shocked. He tried to console her, but she pushed him away. Fidel was just talking the talk, he said.

But he could not convince her.

40

There were five coaches lined up outside the newly opened Hilton, where many of the foreign press were staying. The lobby was full to overflowing. Ray was one of the late arrivals.

He scrabbled aboard the last of the coaches and found a seat saved for him by Amelia. Three hundred and fifty journalists from around the world had been flown in for the spectacle of a massive public trial. A certain Jesús Sosa Blanco, aged fifty-one, garrison commander in Holguin province under Batista, charged with fifty-six murder counts, was one of many to be arraigned in Havana's Sports Palace in front of an estimated fifteen thousand people. It was the last thing Ray needed this evening, but as the first of a rumored total of one thousand planned trials, it was a story he couldn't afford to miss.

"Well?" said Amelia. He squeezed in beside her.

Ray had told her over the phone that he'd made his mind up, but hadn't said which way.

"I'm taking the job."

For once, she said not a word. She put her hand on his and looked out of the coach window as they set off.

They got ringside seats, literally, as the trial was set to take place in a boxing ring. Jamie was there waiting. He'd already shot a roll when the head of the three-man panel— none of them judges or legally qualified—stood up at the microphone and addressed the crowd.

"Announcement!" he shouted. "This man is being tried for murder and robbery."

Fifteen thousand voices roared as one, hungry for more.

"And—he is an assassin!"

"Kill him, kill him, kill him!" the crowd chanted.

When the accused got his right of reply, he was impressively defiant.

"This is the Coliseum in Rome," he shouted back. "I met brave rebels in the mountains, not types like you here. All you do is talk."

Jamie lowered his camera and shook his head. He leaned over to Ray and spoke for them all when he said, "This is sick, man."

They shared a cab back to the old town together, but Ray refused a last drink and instead, decided to walk back to his apartment alone.

His route took him past the Capri. Making the decision had been cathartic and though he was shattered, the prospect of a quiet drink alone in the hotel bar seemed like a fitting way to celebrate the end of something and the beginning of something else—whatever that might turn out to be.

In the hotel bar, he ordered a Tom Collins and took it to the farthest and darkest booth. He wanted to be left alone to celebrate, commiserate—whatever. It was nearly three o'clock in the morning and there were not many people there, but one man caught Ray's attention immediately. Not the place, nor the time of day—or rather night—you expect to see a priest. He was wearing a dog collar, long cassock, the works. The sight was so bizarre Ray couldn't help but stare.

He noticed the priest didn't stop at the bar to order a drink, but appeared to be looking for someone. The priest came toward Ray and was almost at the table before he seemed to realize that whoever he was hoping to meet, it was not Ray. Close up, the priest's face was greasy, lined and unattractive, with a hooked nose and the sense that he might, at any moment, use the back of his sleeve to wipe it. Ray was relieved when he walked away.

He watched the priest's progress through the lounge and saw him sit with two others. Ray's curiosity was piqued even further. If he wasn't very much mistaken, the men in the booth were none other than Bartone and the man who'd been with him talking to Morgan at the party.

Bartone receiving absolution for his sins? Didn't seem likely somehow. Ray knew he had to get a closer look. He downed the rest of the Collins mix and picked a route that would take him on a sweeping line past their table and out to the lobby. He rehearsed what he might say as he walked the plush carpet and detoured around the potted palms.

Two guys, minders presumably, grew visibly restless watching him near their boss's table. Ray made a kind of half gesture to show his hands were empty, just in case they got the jitters, and made as if to walk on by. When he reached Bartone's table, he stopped dead.

"Excuse me?" he said.

Bartone and the priest looked up.

"Sorry to interrupt, especially at this late hour. Mr. Bartone, right? Ray Halliwell, *Chicago Sun-Times*."

Ray held out his hand but nobody moved, at least not at Bartone's table. One of the goons was on his way over.

"We don't know each other," Ray said to Bartone's companion.

"No, we don't," said the man, as if the conversation was over.

Ray turned back to Bartone.

"I just wondered—I'd like to get your views on the situation here in Cuba, run a little interview perhaps. Not now, obviously."

The goon was standing right behind Ray.

"Business interests, that kind of thing, old Cuba, new Cuba?"

Bartone still hadn't said a word. But he was watching Ray closely.

Ray turned to the priest. "You over from the States, sir?"

"Dominica," said the priest.

"Oh, is that right?"

"No interviews," said Bartone.

"Oh," said Ray, "pity. I'll say goodnight then. Have a good stay, Father."

As he walked away, Ray could feel the eyes burning into his back. But he was grinning to himself. He'd got the devil in him and he wondered if the priest had noticed.

He was still beaming with satisfaction when he hit the lobby and saw Morgan walking from the main entrance toward the bar.

41

María lay in bed, crumpled sheets thrown back and one hand under her head. She was staring out at the cloudless sky. It was just seven o'clock in the morning and Morgan was already dressed in his olive uniform, newly pressed by his own hand. He was adjusting the neat cravat around his neck in front of the mirror. On each of his epaulettes he wore the silver star of a comandante.

María pushed herself up onto her elbows. She felt a little wave of nausea ripple upwards from her tummy to her throat and steadied her breathing to let the feeling pass. At first, she'd been thrilled to feel the unmistakable signature of changes in her body. But lately, having to go so slowly at things each day frustrated her. There were so many things to do as they started their new life, not least making Los Pinos into some kind of home, however temporary.

"Very smart," she said, "for a *gringo*."

Morgan winked at her and laughed. He went over to the dressing table and picked up his holstered sidearm. María watched him buckle the belt around his waist, pushing the Colt down to sit lower on his hip, like a gunslinger. She felt a rush of anxiety she couldn't name or explain. Morgan bent down to check his face in the mirror and rubbed at his now clean-shaven chin. The skin where the hair had protected him from the sun was white. The contrast with his tanned cheeks and forehead retained the ghostly outline of the beard.

"How does it feel?" she asked.

"Strange. Very strange," he replied, "but I'll get used to it, I guess."

He came over to where she was lying and bent down to kiss her.

"Be careful," she said.

"Don't worry," he said.

And then he was gone, closing the door behind him. María let her head sink back down on the pillow and looked out of the window at the still empty sky.

*

Morgan had to pick his way gingerly through the sleeping comrades lying on the floor of the living room or stretched out on the furniture. Legs and arms were dangling this way and that. Some were cradling their weapons from force of habit. Others—mouths wide open—produced a cacophony of snoring, scratching and occasional farting.

He was tempted to wake them with a call to arms. But he resisted, heading instead for the kitchen where he found some sweet biscuits. He took a handful and made his way back through the minefield of sleeping bodies, putting whole biscuits in his mouth, stepping over Ramirito last of all. The boy was hugging a cushion.

As he closed the front door behind him, Menoyo was coming down the drive in a jeep, kicking up dust behind the vehicle and curving around the dry fountain to skid to a halt.

Morgan clambered into the passenger seat and offered Menoyo a biscuit from the pile in his hand.

"Breakfast?"

Menoyo ignored him and crunched the gear lever into first after several attempts.

"There's a clutch, you know that?" Morgan said.

"Screw you," said Menoyo between gritted teeth.

Finally, the jeep lurched forward, jerking both men back in their seats. Morgan was laughing as they took off down the drive.

"Yeah, cowboy!"

They were heading for Fidel's temporary headquarters at Camp Libertad. The streets of Havana were deserted save for young men with weapons, most wearing the black-and-red armbands of the July 26 Movement, guarding buildings or manning checkpoints. There were no buses or taxis, no people in queues waiting to go to work and virtually no shops open, bar the odd newsstand selling copies of the communist newspaper, *Revolución*.

"You saw the TV?" said Morgan.

"*Sí*, I saw it. With my father. He was mad as hell."

"María too. And you?"

"I don't know. With Fidel, I don't know. It's time you and my father met."

Menoyo's father, Carlos, was a militant social democrat, with a strong belief that neither communism nor capitalism could deliver a free and fair society. He argued, with great passion, that the answer lay in a balance between individual liberty and social responsibility.

"He believes Fidel is a dangerous man. Dangerous to Cuba and dangerous to us."

Morgan said nothing. He didn't want to contradict Menoyo's old man, but neither did he feel the same way about Fidel.

"Maybe on the way back?" said Menoyo.

"Sure, why not," Morgan replied.

Chaos reigned in the anteroom leading to Fidel's offices. *Barbudos* from the July 26 Movement lounged and smoked or chatted in small groups, and there were constant comings and goings between the offices and the anteroom—as far as they could tell from where they were sitting in the corridor beyond. The corridor was almost as busy as the anteroom, and they sat where they'd been told to wait, on hard chairs against the wall, self-conscious in their neatly pressed uniforms and cravats amongst the more slovenly and unbuttoned fighters. There was constant chatter, even shouting from time to time, going on all around them.

For almost two hours they sat side by side in the corridor. Finally, the same young woman in drab olive uniform who had shown them to their chairs reappeared, looking flustered. She checked her clipboard.

"There has been some confusion," she said in Spanish. "I'm sorry, you can see how things are. Follow me, please."

She led the way, not to the anteroom, but further down the corridor toward an open door with armed guards standing to either side. The guards moved to block their way as they approached.

"*Hay que entregar las armas*," said one of them.

The young woman spoke to Morgan in English. "You must surrender your weapon."

"Yeah, I know what he said, Miss. What I don't get is why. Everyone here has a weapon."

"Orders."

"Yeah? Whose orders?"

"Comandante Guevara."

"Yeah? Well, screw Comandante Guevara," said Morgan.

The door swung open at that moment to reveal Guevara himself, arm in a sling, cigar in mouth.

"Gentlemen, please," said Guevara.

He grinned at the guard still blocking the way.

"*No es importante*," he said.

The guard stood back and Menoyo and Morgan followed Guevara into the office—with their sidearms.

"I trust you can resist the urge to shoot me this time, Mr. Morgan?" Guevara said as he sat behind the desk. He indicated chairs for his visitors.

"It's Comandante, just like you," said Morgan.

"We have an appointment to see Fidel," said Menoyo.

"Fidel sends his apologies," said Guevara. "Urgent matters have called him away. But he asked me to convey his appreciation of all you have done for the revolution, you and the Escambray men and women. It is Fidel's fervent hope that we can work together to present a united front to the world and particularly, the world's press. I was at your briefing at the Capri. I had expected the public announcement of the dissolution of the Second Front."

Menoyo bristled. "May I ask why?"

"There can be no private armies in post-revolutionary Cuba, Comandante Menoyo. Surely you see that?"

"The Second Front of the Escambray is *not* a private army, any more than *Movimiento 26 de Julio*. The suggestion is an insult."

"No insult intended, Comandante, and I'm sure the new revolutionary army will find a role for you and your men— and of course you too, Comandante Morgan. Should you decide to stay in Cuba, naturally. Now, was there something specific you wanted to discuss with Fidel? Perhaps I can pass on a message?"

Menoyo stood up and Morgan followed suit. Guevara leaned back in his chair and chewed on his cigar.

Menoyo leaned on the desk with both hands, his eyes fixed on Guevara.

"I fought with you at Santa Clara. And I saw courage in you. But it was the kind of courage that led you to break your own arm in a foolish accident. The hot-blooded courage of a man who has yet to learn respect, for himself and for others. I will speak to Fidel—in person."

Menoyo walked out. Morgan lingered just long enough to make the slightest hammer action with his thumb as he pointed his finger at Guevara.

"See ya."

*

Carlos Gutiérrez Zabaleta, Menoyo's father, was trimming an overgrown bougainvillea in the tiny walled garden of the family's city home in Havana's Vedado district when Morgan and Menoyo arrived. Their debrief on the drive from Fidel's HQ had dissipated much of the seething anger both men felt at Guevara's arrogance, and they were in better spirits by the time they arrived.

"This is a great honor, sir," Morgan said when he was introduced to Carlos and his wife, Jacinta.

"No," said the old man, "the honor is mine. With your help, my son has come home, safe. A brother you had already from the mountains. Now you have a home in all our hearts. I will not call you 'son' until you permit me. But one day, I hope to earn that right."

They talked all afternoon, drinking first beer, then rum, and eating an endless stream of *tapas* dishes prepared by Jacinta. In time, they turned to more serious matters, like the abortive meeting with Fidel. By instinct, they kept their voices low.

"I have never asked for any office in government," said Menoyo.

Morgan said, "Eloy, they'll have to offer something."

Carlos was thoughtful. "They should," he said. "For the good of Cuba, for the sake of democracy, they should."

They were pretty drunk by the time they left at eleven. Menoyo insisted on showing Morgan the club he owned on the way home, but after ten minutes of trying keys in rusty locks and waking half the neighbors with the rattle of the metal shutters, Morgan was beginning to wonder if this was a good idea.

Finally, they were in. Menoyo tried the light switches but the electric was turned off at the mains, bills unpaid. He found some candles under the bar and conducted a quick tour for Morgan, talking plans to redecorate and the need to buy new furniture. Morgan said he and the boys would help.

They found a bottle under the bar and poured a last rum for the road.

"Eloy," said Morgan, "there's something I need to tell you."

"Here's to us," said Menoyo. "So?"

"You need to get that government appointment. But more than that, you need to want it."

"I have a bar to run."

"There's a country to run and you can't leave that to others. You know you can't. We both know."

"Sure I can."

"And see the revolution fail?"

"We won, William. We won the war. Batista's gone."

"He's two hundred miles away, Eloy, and already plotting his return."

"You and Batista talk regularly?" Menoyo said with mock surprise. "He told you that?"

"You might say that."

Morgan appeared—even through the haze of the booze—to be serious.

"Come on, William, it's late and I'm tired."

"You remember Bartone and the other guy, Nelson. The guys from the party?"

Menoyo said nothing.

"What if I told you they're offering me—us—a million dollars to assassinate Fidel?"

Menoyo was suddenly very sober. "I'd say you take your life in your hands, all of our lives. I'd say don't ever talk to them or see them again. And don't tell anyone about this—and I mean not anyone."

Morgan poured two more shots.

"Not even Fidel?"

"What are you, crazy? *Loco!*"

"Think about it, Eloy. Right now, Fidel relies on Guevara, his brother Raul and the other reds—for everything. We tell him about this. And we tell him we can bring these guys down. Result? Fidel knows who his true friends are. Eloy? You see—don't you?"

42

The press conference at the US Embassy to mark the official inauguration of the new ambassador, Philip Wilson Bonsal, was not the kind of event a reporter turns down—tedious as it was sure to be. Ray did his duty, along with the rest of the Wolf Pack and the dozens of foreign journalists lingering in the country, still mesmerized by the bright light of the revolution.

Bonsal had served as ambassador in both Columbia and Bolivia before coming to Cuba. Prior to that, he'd worked in business and, for a brief while in his youth, for AT&T in Cuba. With this experience behind him, he was considered something of a Latin expert. He was also thought of as a liberal, and certainly his opening remarks and his responses to the questions that followed were both carefully circumspect and optimistic of good relations between the two countries.

Ray sat with Amelia and Gordie, right behind Fitzwalter and Williams, who had together done their duty in asking all the right questions and, in the process, garnered as much attention to themselves as to the ambassador's responses. The conference closed and the assembled headed for the free drinks and canapés, lavish, but never plentiful at Havana Embassy do's. Ray was just putting his notebook away and wondering what on earth Jamie could have got for him from such a dull event, when Pam leaned over the back of the chair next to his.

"Hi, Ray," she said.

"Pam."

"How are you? I heard you were sick."

"All better now. Thanks."

He flipped the lid of his briefcase and clicked the catch home.

"I've got a new posting," she said. "Eastern Europe. Prague, probably."

Ray stood and turned to face her. She was as gorgeous as ever, maybe more so by virtue of the uncertainty in her eyes.

He smiled. "Good for you, Pam. I'll see you."

He walked over to join Amelia and Gordie at the table of canapés. He didn't look back.

Ray was back at his apartment by eleven. Except it was more like Jamie's apartment now. The photographer had started using the place while Ray was in hospital stateside, because the lease had come up on his own apartment. As a freelancer, he needed to cut costs whenever an opportunity arose. The *Sun-Times* had already paid the rent on Ray's until the year end, giving Jamie more than six months' money-saving grace.

What it meant in practice was that most of Ray's meager possessions were already packed up. Jamie had taken over the cupboards and storage space and turned the living area into a makeshift darkroom, with the window sealed against the light and a trestle table laden with chemical trays, timer clock and photographic enlarger. He'd even put a red bulb in the ceiling light fitting, directly above the sofa on which he slept. Ray had drawn the line at giving up his bed.

The light was on when Ray arrived home, though there was no sign of Jamie. Hanging by clothes pegs from a line strung across the room were drying prints of Ambassador Bonsal at the conference, every bit as dull as Ray had feared they might be. Whatever he decided to write about the event would be short and sweet, but he was too tired to think about that now.

He went to the kitchenette and spotted the note left sticking out of the coffee percolator. It was in Jamie's scrawled hand.

Take your pick of prints. No by-line needed. Mañana.
PS we're out of milk and coffee.

Ray poured himself a rum from the Havana Club bottle he'd bought to take on the plane. He could always get another. There was a tray of ice in the freeze box—which was rare—so he added two or three cubes to the warm golden liquid and churned the glass in his hand before taking a long gulp. He lit a cigarette and went to the window to look down on the street below.

He exhaled and stared at the cigarette. Then he sang the jingle out loud; "*Winston tastes good like a—dah, dah—cigarette should,*" but the moment he stopped, the apartment once again became oppressively silent and still.

He downed the rest of the drink, poured another and put the shower on to run hot. As he undressed, letting his clothes fall where they would, he finished the second glass and was just pouring the third when he heard a knock at the door. His first thought was Jamie, minus his key and with tales of a date that turned out to be not so hot after all. He wrapped a towel around himself and cursed the intrusion, just as he'd cursed being alone just minutes before.

"Jamie? Is that you?"

"It's me." He heard her familiar voice, faint beyond the door.

In days gone by, Pam might have been leaning against the door jamb, an overnight bag at her feet, her whole body playing Lauren Bacall from *To Have and Have Not*. Not tonight. Tonight, Pam stood away from the door, in the middle of the grubby corridor. There was no overnight bag, no hint of a smile and no clue in her eyes as to why she was there. She was holding a manila envelope low in front of her hips, like she was covering herself. She held out the envelope for him to take.

"What is it?" said Ray. He didn't reach out.

"A gift."

"From John? You should get him to do his own deliveries. And maybe during daylight hours."

"It's from me."

Ray eyed her suspiciously and then checked the corridor in either direction. Still he didn't invite her in. Finally, he took the envelope and began to tear at the sealed flap.

"I hear I'm not the only one going to a new posting," said Pam. "Congratulations."

Ray pulled a photograph halfway out of the envelope. He recognized Morgan straight away. He looked at Pam.

"What is this?"

"Like I said, a gift. I didn't want to say goodbye like that."

He pushed the photograph back into the envelope and let the door swing open.

"You'd better come in," he said.

Pam followed him into the room. The red light bulb was still on. Ray went to the kitchenette and neon light to examine the contents of the envelope more closely. Pam wandered around the living area.

"You got a new hobby?" she said.

"Jamie," said Ray, "he's taking over the apartment."

"Is he here now?"

"No—" Ray was studying a series of black-and-white photographs, mainly eight by five format, some ten by eight.

"Can I get a drink?" said Pam.

"On the side."

She found the Havana Club bottle and the ice melting in its tray. "You want one?"

Ray didn't reply. The long-lens shots showed Morgan with some others against a backdrop that appeared to be the Escambray Mountains, or a landscape very similar.

"What is this, Pam?"

"John thinks it's a landing strip. For planes."

"So, he *did* send you."

She handed him a drink.

"I swear. This is from me to you. John doesn't know I'm here and he doesn't know I spent an hour upstairs after the conference putting this stuff in an envelope. And he won't know after either, in case that's what you're thinking."

Ray was holding a typewritten report. He read enough to see the names Morgan, Menoyo, Bartone and Velazco, the Dominican priest, and to get the gist of some kind of conspiracy involving the Dominicans and the mob, sketchy but nevertheless incriminating. There were at least three documented meetings with a variety of the names in attendance, and speculation on the nature of those meetings that amounted to evidence of something significant going down.

"Pam, I really don't want to replay what happened before."

She downed her drink and headed for the door. Ray reached out and held her arm. She ripped away from him.

"Forget it. Just forget it, okay?"

"Wait up."

"Goodbye, Ray."

The door was half open by the time he got to her. He slammed it closed with the flat of his hand and stood close behind her, almost against her, his arms either side, trapping her.

"Let me go," she said. Her voice was small. She could feel his breath on her neck.

43

The postman called late in the day with yet another pile of fan mail for Morgan, some of it from grateful or adoring Cubans, but much of it from gung-ho Americans begging for an opportunity to be part of the revolution; young men who wanted to change the world—and their own somewhat humdrum lives—by joining the hero from Cleveland they'd read about in the US papers.

María put the letters with the others, those that had arrived the day before and the day before that. Then she went out to the garden and breathed in the cooler air of the late afternoon. She was glad to be home alone and glad she'd refused the repeated pleas to attend the official opening party at Menoyo's club. There had been so little chance to be quiet and alone over the past few weeks.

Menoyo and Morgan, with other members of the Second Front including María, had already made two long and exhausting trips back to the Escambray to begin the process of making good the promises made during the war.

The first trip lasted ten days, with eighty former fighters and others employed to make a comprehensive assessment of the most pressing needs: roads that would allow farmers to get their produce to market, rural schools to teach the children to read and write, and medical care in the form of nurses, doctors and rural hospitals. With these measures, particularly the medical care, they could begin to address the appalling and unnecessary suffering of the poorest people, victims of a whole range of diseases, from gut worms that would bore holes through the soles of a kid's feet, to malnutrition and leprosy.

The second trip heard the voices of the rural population expressed directly in a huge public meeting. The need for change was profound and María was passionate in her commitment. But she also needed time for herself, and today was the day she had chosen for a very private act.

All this was on her mind as she pushed the oil drum onto its end and walked back to the patio to get her olive-green uniform and the can of petrol she'd left there.

She gathered armfuls of brown leaves that were littering the grass and stuffed them into the oil drum. She snapped some dry branches she found on the ground, breaking them with her hands or over her knee, relishing the crisp crack of the wood, and putting them one by one on top of the leaves. Then, she unscrewed the metal cap on the red petrol tin with the blue-lettered Esso logo and poured a little petrol onto the leaves and twigs. She took a box of matches from her pocket, struck a match and tossed it into the drum. The sudden whomp of the flames caught her by surprise.

As the wood and leaves began to burn, she picked up the pants of her uniform and held them up. She noted the worn knees and the patch she'd sewn on the right hip to cover a tear when she'd caught the material on a nail.

Standing in the shadows of the garden, the sun sinking lower, she threw the pants into the drum as if disposing of something revolting. All at once, thick smoke began to emerge and for a moment, she wondered if the thing would burn or simply smolder and die. But then the flames caught again.

Her shirt was next. One epaulette was missing, the two button-down pockets open and creased. She held it out in front of her and then dropped it into the drum. As the smoke billowed, she stood back, shielding her eyes.

Ray was watching her from the patio of the house. When nobody had answered the door, he'd come around the side yard to see smoke rising from the far corner of the garden.

He was ranging through the oddest combination of emotions. There was the new job and the life to come. There was Pam and the life to be left behind. And then, there was María, with her blonde hair and straight shoulders, so pretty in a light summer dress, her hand raised against the billowing smoke. He'd fallen for her. In a way that was entirely new to him. A way he didn't yet understand, even now, even though it was all way too late anyhow.

She, in turn, had fallen in love with another man. She'd fought alongside that other man. She was carrying his baby, evidence of faith in him, in herself and in the future. María *inhabited* her life, lived it from the inside out, where Ray felt his own was little more than a wardrobe of disguises.

He was contemplating all this when María turned away from the fire and began walking toward the house, head down and arms folded, deep in thought. Ray's heart beat in time with each step she took toward him. But he didn't speak. There was nothing to say, as so often with María. Perhaps it was this wordless quality in her that he loved the most. She had almost reached the edge of the patio before she noticed him.

"Ray!" she said. "Jesus, you scared me!"

There was hardly a trace of physical change in the shape of her body, a little more roundness at the belly perhaps, but nothing to draw attention, except perhaps the way she'd instinctively wrapped her arms protectively around her middle.

"Nobody answered the door so I came around the side."

"But what are you doing just standing there? Why didn't you say something?"

Ray hesitated. "I don't know."

They sat together at the poolside on hardwood chairs, bleached gray by the sun, on the same side of a matching table that had also seen better days. The pool was only two-thirds full, the water coated with dry brown leaves over a dense, almost black layer of sodden mush, thick enough for frogs to sun themselves, dry-backed, with only their legs and undersides cooling in the slimy wetness.

Ray was talking about the show trial and the ongoing executions around the country, reported with gruesome pictures and lurid headlines in the Cuban press.

"I've stopped reading the papers. It's all too ugly," said María.

"I hear Prime Minister Cardona will resign in the next few days citing communist influence. Fidel is taking more power for himself."

"Fidel is running the country. That's what you're saying? But that's no surprise, Ray. It is very early days. When the elections come, things will be different."

"Maybe," he said, "we'll see. All I'm saying is, times are uncertain and it's vital to be careful about your enemies, and more especially your friends."

"Meaning?"

Ray took a breath and launched.

"Look, María I'm not trying to interfere, but well, I'm worried, that's all. Bill's been seen meeting with Bartone and a priest by the name of Velazco, who seems to represent Dominican interests. At the Capri and elsewhere. More than once. There are intelligence photographs. I've seen them."

María looked away from him, back toward the corner of the garden where the oil drum was still smoking. Her arms were folded tight across her chest.

She stood up from the table and looked down into the pool with its murky brown water and rotting leaves.

"Have you spoken to William about this?"

"No," said Ray, "not yet. That's why I'm here."

María turned to look him straight in the eye.

"To tell him you've been spying on him?"

"That's not fair. No. To tell him I'm concerned. Very concerned. If the Embassy spooks know about Bartone, if I know, it's a sure bet others do too. This is a dangerous game, María."

"It's not a game, Ray."

And all at once, Ray realized María was one of the players.

44

"María! Hey, *chica!*"

The voice was Morgan's, calling to his wife from the house. María was still standing close to Ray when Morgan appeared on the patio. The sounds of a party in progress followed him out, growing louder by the second.

"Ray!" Morgan shouted. "Where in God's name have you been, man?"

He was striding toward Ray, his eyes flitting between his friend and his wife. He was wearing his olive uniform with comandante stars, but with the collar unbuttoned.

"Around," said Ray, "you know how it is. Apparently, there's been some kind of revolution."

Morgan laughed. He held María in his arms.

"Hey, baby. You okay?" he said with tender concern. He looked over at Ray. "No excuse, man!"

"*Que pasa?*" said María.

"It looks like we're having a party, honey," said Morgan. "The boys felt the opening was not the same without you, so we took a vote. And here we are! And, I have a surprise for you. Guess who I found waiting at the door?"

"Who?"

"Come on," said Morgan to María. "No peeking!" He covered her eyes with his hands and turned back to Ray. "Ray! Back in two seconds. Don't go away this time, you hear?"

Someone had put on a record. People were beginning to spill out onto the patio. Some were already dancing, others carrying bottles of booze and plates of half-eaten food.

Ramirito was walking toward Ray, weighed down by a pile of logs in his arms that he was carrying toward the giant brick-built barbecue. Menoyo was trailing him with more wood, the two of them talking incessantly, apparently arguing.

"Hey, Ray!" said Ramirito, jerking his head in Menoyo's direction. "Listen to him! He knows it all, eh?"

Menoyo scowled. "*Idiota. Más tarde, Ray?*"

Ray waved them on. "Sure, go ahead, before you drop the lot."

Max Lesnik and Armando Fleites were each dumping a cardboard box on the bleached table by Ray. The boxes were brimming with cold bottled beers, frosted and dripping with condensation.

"Mr. Halliwell," said Lesnik, "how are you doing? Have a beer."

Ray shook hands with Dr. Fleites and took the freshly opened bottle from Lesnik.

"Thanks. I'm good. And you?"

"Busy. Very busy. But one must make time to relax, no?"

"Absolutely," said Ray. "Here's to you guys."

As they clinked their bottles together, piercing screams of delight made all three turn toward the house. María and Blanquita were holding each other and spinning in wild circles, laughing and jabbering together and finally crashing into Morgan, who caught them both in his arms. Blanquita's black hair and elegant, shapely body, shown to full advantage in a tight-fitting, knee-length red dress, was instantly familiar to Ray, but it took him a moment to place her. The Bodeguita Bar, over a year ago; the night he'd gone there to find Morgan. He'd only caught a brief glimpse of María's companion that night, but Blanquita was not the kind of girl you easily forget.

Standing a couple of yards distant from María and Blanquita, an older woman, short and wide, wearing a winter coat and holding a small suitcase, was watching the two young women with what might have been an expression of impatient disapproval.

"You remember Blanquita?" said Morgan as he returned to Ray and picked up a beer, flipping the top with the metal opener.

"How could I forget?" said Ray.

"That's her cousin, Rosa."

"The family resemblance is striking."

Morgan laughed. "This outfit needs a staff sergeant. I think we've got one. And I'm told she makes a mean hamburger."

"Bill," said Ray, "can we talk?"

"Sure," said Morgan, but as he spoke he was waving over a broad-shouldered man standing with a guy ten years younger. Both looked to be Americans, to Ray at least. "You gotta meet these guys."

Ray shook hands with them and Morgan did the introductions. "Gerry Hemming, Ray Halliwell, *Chicago Sun-Times*."

"Hi," said Hemming. He was stocky, unsmiling, with a thick neck and a suspicious look in his eye.

"You should write about this guy, Ray. He's a flyer, attached to the revolutionary air force now. Been dropping guns right through the fighting and dodging Batista's jets. What do you call yourself now, Gerry?"

"Technical advisor. Gives me plenty of latitude."

"And this here's Lee, Lee Evans, from near Cleveland, as it happens."

"How you doing, sir?" said the young man. He was in his early twenties, blonde and fresh-faced.

"Tell him what you're doing here, Lee," said Morgan.

Evans took a swig from his beer and raised his eyes to the sky. He was grinning broadly.

"Okay. Truth is, sir, I read your stories about Major Morgan here. Well, they just blew me away. So I wrote a letter. Never thought I'd hear anything, sending it via the post office in Havana and all. But here I am, thanks to you."

If Evans had expected Ray to be flattered, he was disappointed.

"That's how. Exactly *why* are you here, Lee?" said Ray.

It was Morgan who answered the question.

"Lee here's an advisor. Agriculture. Cotton in particular. Reckon we can get some cotton growing in the Escambray and the INRA's backing us. Lee knows all about cotton. Top expert, right, Lee?"

"Yes, sir! Grew up on the farm."

"Both these guys were in Korea. Right, fellas?"

The four of them chatted for a few minutes, but when the chance presented itself, Ray once again asked for a few minutes alone.

"Let's go down the garden," said Morgan. "It goes on forever. I heard the news. About the job I mean. Go Ray! Congrats man."

"Yeah, thanks to you I get retired early."

"That makes two of us. What can you do? Life moves on, right?"

"Maybe," said Ray. They walked a little way before either of them said more. It was Ray who broke the silence.

"So I hear frogs are on the menu?"

"You hear right. Aquaculture, it's the way of the future, man."

"And you're looking for investors. So María tells me."

"There's a whole lot of red tape—and money needed."

"Is Bartone an investor?"

Morgan stepped up into the gazebo. The wooden building was about ten feet across and hexagonal in shape, with low latticed walls. He took a pack of cigarettes from his breast pocket and jiggled a cigarette into his mouth before holding out the pack to Ray.

"Smoke?"

Ray shook his head at the offer, keeping his hands deep in his pockets and his eyes low.

"No, not Bartone," said Morgan. "The Ministry of Agriculture will put up the cash."

"So what's he doing here, Bill?" said Ray.

"What? Oh, same old. Trying to make friends and influence people."

"People like you?"

"I can handle Bartone."

"It's how it looks to others that worries me."

"You fret too much, Ray."

"I hope so."

"Look, you're a friend. Between us, Bartone's got a couple of old C-47 transport planes he wants to sell. He's looking for an introduction. The head of the air force is Pedro Díaz Lanz. He's a buddy of mine and he needs planes. Bartone and me? We've got a history. That's all."

"And guns?"

"Just the planes."

"What about Frank Nelson?"

Morgan said nothing for a moment.

"You know who Frank Nelson is, right?"

"Look, Ray, like I said, you're a friend, but this stuff's not for general consumption, you know that. When there's a story, I'll let you know."

"Don't patronize me, Bill. This isn't about a story. This is me looking out for you—and María. Nelson is a bagman. A fixer. He'd sell his own mother for the price of a drink. Amongst his regular employers—alongside the mob, of course—is the CIA. There are photographs of meetings, here in Havana and in the mountains."

Ray expected the information to shock. Instead, Morgan calmly took another drag on his cigarette. Ray was suddenly aware of a familiar expression on Morgan's face, the same dreamy, distant look he'd had that night in the Bodeguita a year before—the night Ray had tried to persuade him to get out of Cuba. Morgan was, once again, playing a hand. That much was certain.

"Sweet Jesus, Bill," said Ray. "Are you hearing me at all?"

Morgan grinned. "Remember the first time you said pretty much those same words to me?"

"I do."

"Things turned out okay, didn't they? Here's a promise," said Morgan. "Soon as I can, I'll give you a place to be and a time to be there. I can't guarantee an exclusive, but I give you my word, you'll have the inside track. You'll have access like nobody else."

Ray sighed a deep sigh. "I'm just trying to watch your back," he said, his tone quiet and deliberate.

"I get that, Ray. I do. And if anything ever happened to me, I know you'd be there for María. But I know what I'm doing—and why."

"Care to share the why? Just between us, naturally."

Despite being away from the other partygoers, Morgan kept his voice low.

"Because there's still a real chance this whole thing could go to shit. Everything we fought for, everything these guys have lived and breathed for years."

Ray swept a hand through his hair and started to pace around the gazebo in agitation. He still had some fight left. "So what are you, Superman? This isn't Gotham City you know, Bill, it's Havana, Cuba."

"That's Batman."

"Who gives a shit!" said Ray. "Give me that cigarette, now."

Morgan did as he was told.

"Goddamn it," said Ray, puffing hard to get it going, "these guys play hardball. They don't care who gets hurt, you know that." He took a long drag and waggled his finger at Morgan. "You got a family now, or almost—did I say congratulations by the way?"

"No."

"Well, congratulations. But let Fidel do his own fighting. What can you do?"

"Up in the Escambray, the reds are doing their thing right now, pushing propaganda down the throats of the campesinos. They're already starting to expropriate land owned by the campesinos in the name of the revolution, putting it under state control. The farmers, the little guys with a plot of coffee or cane or rice, they're getting nothing. In fact, they're losing the little they had."

"You can't go head-to-head with Guevara *or* Raul *or* the Communist Party, not now. You'll lose."

"But we can use their methods. Without ever declaring war."

"How's that?"

"We've been to see this guy at the US Embassy. We're fixing for Eloy to go to the States, meet some people, you know, get the newspapers interested. And the same guy is helping with getting our message out there to the farmers and workers."

"Who is this guy?"

But Morgan was racing on with the story. "Between us, buddy, okay? You should see it, Ray, see what we're doing, I mean. They're like these little comic books; pictures and stories to counteract the Reds. José Marti, that kind of thing. I know about comic books. That's one thing I do know about. I'm coming up with ideas, and the Embassy guy's putting the money behind it and getting the illustrations and printing organized."

"Bill, listen to me. Who is this guy? Do I know him?"

"Between us, okay? He's the press guy there. John Dempsey."

Morgan saw straight away the look on Ray's face.

"What?"

"Bill, John Dempsey's status as press attaché is a cover. He reports directly to the CIA station chief."

If Ray had caught him with a sucker punch, Morgan didn't show it.

"He's working for us, Ray, we're not working for him. Big difference."

Ray looked incredulous. "You think?"

Neither man spoke for a few seconds.

Morgan's inscrutable smile was back. "You worry too much. Come on, there's a party waiting. Let's get drunk. It's your last night."

"You don't drink, you schmuck," said Ray.

"In your case, I'll make an exception."

*

As things had turned out on that last night in Havana, he hadn't got drunk with Morgan. He'd found the whole prospect of saying his goodbyes too hard to handle, and an hour after their talk—when he'd shaken enough hands and the chance presented itself—Ray slid round the side of the house, just as he'd come in. He walked away through Miramar's empty streets and grand houses. He didn't even say goodbye to María. Especially María.

He'd had every intention of going straight back to the apartment to pack for the early bird flight. But the further he walked, the less sure he'd become of anything. The curfew had been lifted days ago, but with so many of Miramar's rich former residents having fled the country, the streets were deserted—until he reached the downtown area around Thirtieth Street, where suddenly a scene like carnival day opened up before him. Ordinary people, the poorer people of the city, were everywhere, walking, talking, dancing, drinking, celebrating—just out in the warm night air for the hell of it.

It didn't take Ray long to decide the Bodeguita was a better option than the an empty apartment for his last night in Havana.

He was still drinking with Jamie, Amelia and Gordie when the sun came up the next day. They poured him into a cab and Amelia stood shotgun as he blearily gathered his things and muttered under his breath about life, the universe and everything. She walked him out of the building and onto the sidewalk. When the taxi arrived, she pecked him on the cheek and started to walk away, without waiting for Ray to depart.

"Hey!" said Ray, slurring his words. "Where you going?"

"Home," said Amelia.

"Just like that?"

"Yeah, just like that. I'll see you, Ray."

"You're all heart, Amelia."

She gave a little wave and disappeared.

Ray made the flight, but only just. He'd carried on drinking as he waited at José Marti and then Miami airport, and didn't begin to sober up until sleep finally dragged him down into a light coma, somewhere over Kentucky.

45

When the committee concluded for the day, it was already nearly six o'clock in the evening.

Phil had left a message on Ray's phone. He'd managed to trace John Dempsey to a nursing home in DC, not more than a half-hour ride from the Senate. Even better, he'd arranged for Ray to visit the man at six-thirty. It was going to be tight. Ray said hasty goodbyes to María and Capaldi and promised to call in later.

Against all odds, Ray found a cab the moment he stepped out onto First Street. The rush-hour traffic was already at its height. Red lights were everywhere on the short trip to the Arlington Memorial Rest Home, and they were forced to stop and start with monotonous regularity. But as the cab finally crossed Memorial Bridge, Ray began to relax. The Potomac River was gray-green under a darkening sky and the last vestiges of daylight were receding behind unnaturally bright yellow street lamps. Commuters heading for the Metro stations had their collars up against the cold air, in sharp contrast to the cyclists in bright plastic helmets and backpacks and lightweight reflective jackets, always the same whatever the weather. To Ray, they looked like an insect species.

The cab's heater was blowing hot, damp air from the front seats to the back, but still it felt good to be out and above ground. Over what had been a long day, the committee room had stoked Ray's desire to get out as soon as possible.

The care home was a low-rise, courtyarded building set in extensive grounds that were mounded with grassy hummocks and shy trees, either newly planted or very slow growing. Inside, the smell of medication, cleaning fluids and what seemed to Ray to be urine, suffused the warm air. He gave his name at the reception desk. A couple of minutes later a nurse appeared and asked Ray to follow her down the magnolia-painted corridor.

"Mr. Dempsey is in the conservatory," she said over her shoulder as Ray trailed dutifully behind. "Please don't be too long. Strictly speaking, visits are not encouraged out of designated hours."

She opened the door to a glass-framed addition to the building, warmer than the corridor. Ray was squeamish about getting old and hated himself for finding these kinds of homes anathema. He knew such facilities were necessary and, more often than not, both comfortable and caring. He just didn't want to go there himself. Ever.

The regulation armchairs, high-backed and forlorn, were pushed tight to the walls and, for the most part, empty. Two or three residents occupied the remainder, each isolated one from another, presumably by choice. Ray noticed that one of the chairs had been turned to face the large windows. He could just see the top of a head above the chair back. He crossed the floor of the conservatory, an absurd, all-purpose institutional smile on his face designed to hide his embarrassment and reassure the residents that he meant no harm. No one took the slightest notice of him, with or without the smile.

Ray approached the chair turned to the window in a wide circle so as not to startle the occupant. Whoever was sitting there still had a full head of silvery hair spilling out from the middle of a white sports visor, partially obscuring his face.

"John?" Ray said.

"Morgan's telephone number was Veradero 28377," said the old man.

Ray pulled up a chair. John Dempsey may have become physically frail, but his mental faculties were still impressively sharp. Ray had not caught him napping in the chair by the window, far from it. Dempsey had been refreshing his elephantine memory from the pages of his own book, '*The Deadbeats*' which was still open on his lap.

"Let's cut to the chase right away," said Dempsey, "I'm not giving evidence."

Ray was still taking his coat off. He laid the coat on the wide window ledge above the hot air vents and sat down before responding.

"Can I ask why?"

"You can. Because I'm old and I don't give a shit. If that's what you came for, we're done."

Ray pulled up a chair and sat. He had to think so fast that when the words came out of his mouth, he felt he was hearing them for the first time.

"The truth is John, PBS have asked me to front up a documentary. Fifty years on, you know, that kind of thing."

"It's all in the book," Dempsey shot back at him. The old man was drumming the copy on his lap repeatedly. "The book I personally sent you for review. That would have been nineteen sixty-nine. Nothing ever appeared in the *Sun-Times* or anywhere else with your byline, Ray."

So the hostility had a reason and a valid reason at that, impossible to answer honestly without causing further offence. The truth was there would have been very little Ray felt he could have said in praise of a book he recognized had taken the author ten years of his life to write. But he had to come up with something. He opted for a partial version of the truth.

"It was ten years on, John. All I wanted to do was forget Cuba."

"So what are you doing now, mixed up in this thing fifty years later?"

"Time changes things. María asked me to help."

Dempsey fidgeted in his chair, pulling himself more upright and straightening his neck to relieve stiffness.

"Always had the notion there was something between you and her. Was there?"

"No."

"Remember Pam?"

The old guy was trying to wrong foot him. Ray knew that, but still the sharp tone took him by surprise.

"Yes, I remember Pam."

"She asked for the transfer you know? We didn't push her."

"That was then, John."

"I'm serious. She was a talented girl, but then I don't have to tell you that. She did well after Havana, found her niche working honey traps in Eastern Europe. But I think you knew that already."

So that was it. Ray was due a whipping and the old man was intent on giving him forty lashes without leaving his chair. For failing to review the book, for being one of the 'deadbeats' himself—a liberal too blind to see—too enamored with the romance of revolution to smell communism burning in the background, too busy screwing around to take the threat to America, to freedom and democracy, seriously. Earlier in the day, he'd wondered if Dempsey might have changed over the years. He had his answer.

Dempsey reached out and pressed a button on the wall near his chair. In the distance, Ray heard a faint buzz.

"John," said Ray as a nurse came in to the room, pushing the door open with a wheelchair, "just so you know, the PBS guy who's producing? As far as I can make out, he's taking the line that Castro was forced into the arms of the Soviets, by us."

"Bullshit," said Dempsey.

"I know."

Ray stood as the nurse took Dempsey by the arm and eased him forward in the chair. Ray took his other arm and together, they helped him stand and then collapse back into the waiting wheelchair.

"Maybe if I could just get a crew down here, just for an hour or so. I could show him there's an alternative view."

"It's all in the book," said Dempsey, "let's go nurse."

As the nurse began to wheel the old man away, Ray saw he'd left the book behind. He picked it up and caught up with Dempsey.

"Here, John." Ray handed the book to him; it's dust cover showing rips and repairs with Sellotape.

"The book's out of print now, John. Academics only. Think about it. The country's got a right to know the truth."

*

Ray picked up the lobby phone and dialed through to María's room the moment he got back to the hotel.

It was nearly ten o'clock and he feared María might already have given up waiting. When no one answered, he was certain she'd already gone to sleep, but he went through to the bar just to be sure. María was there, sitting alone with a coffee in front of her on the table.

"I thought you might have gone to bed," he said. He sat down beside her.

"No, I said I would wait for you."

A waiter appeared, and Ray ordered a Jack Daniels for himself and another coffee for María.

"He won't do it," said Ray when the waiter left them.

"I understand," said María. "Thank you."

"But I haven't given up. Not yet. He finally agreed to my returning tomorrow morning. And I've done something I'm not proud of, but it was all I could think of. It's a little crazy."

María smiled graciously by way of encouragement, but it was obvious to Ray she was exhausted.

"I'm sorry. You must be so tired after today."

"Yes. But the coffee helps."

"Listen, don't worry about it. If it happens, I won't be at the committee in the morning. I'll come around lunchtime."

The waiter returned with their drinks. Ray took a gulp from the Jack Daniels. María spooned sugar into her coffee.

"You still like it sweet," said Ray.

"I miss Cuban coffee," said María. "There's a store near us in Cleveland where I can buy good beans now. At home, I make it strong."

Her words made Ray pause. He stared at her for a moment and then looked down, twisting his glass round and round on the table, encouraging the ice to melt into the liquor.

"But there's something on your mind?" said María.

"How did you know?"

"Because you're quiet. And you never used to be quiet."

Ray reached into the breast pocket of his jacket and retrieved the photograph he'd found in his den, the one in the glass frame of himself with Morgan and María taken in the mountains of the Escambray fifty years before.

"I found this at home."

María took the photograph from him and studied it.

"My God. We were so young. So very young."

"I want you to keep it. To remember those times. And me, naturally."

"I have never forgotten you, Ray."

He wouldn't meet her look.

"What is it, Ray?" said María.

"I want to understand why," said Ray. "Why you let me believe—why you didn't contact me when you got to the States."

The gracious smile was back.

"That's a hard question, Ray. Maybe too hard for now."

"Maybe it's unfair of me. I've just wondered why, that's all."

"No, not unfair," María said.

Ray took another sip from his drink, and waited.

"I'm just not sure I can explain. And I feel—so ungrateful."

Ray shook his head but said nothing. He knew he was pressing hard, but he needed to understand.

"I know you tried everything when they put me in prison," said María, "I know about the letters you wrote and the politicians you tried to persuade. I know you tried to send money and food."

"I stopped when your sister gave me the news."

"How can I explain? In the beginning, the treatment was worse *because* of the attention, and none of the money or the food ever reached me. I didn't think I could survive, not after what had happened, not without the children. But then, when I found out I'd been reported in America as a suicide, I stopped thinking altogether. It was the hope that hurt so much. I felt dead. I was sure I would die in prison, and when others were no longer fighting for me, I was able to become nothing, just another prisoner—it was easier for me. Can you understand?"

"Of course. I was wrong to ask. I'm sorry."

"No. You are right to ask. It is I who am sorry. Can you forgive me?"

Ray nodded his head but could find no words.

"Then, when I came to America, I was carrying so much rage inside. I thought everything that had happened would eat me alive if I let it. I could not forgive, but I could try to forget. Try to live each day like the first day. Try to think about the children and then the grandchildren. Try to forget the past. I didn't talk to anyone. I just kept it inside. That was my way."

"Of course."

"Dear Ray. And then I come to you after fifty years and ask for your help once more. Like a ghost. But do you see, it has taken me this long to be strong enough?"

Ray reached across the table and took her outstretched hand. "I do. Of course I do." Tears came to him unexpectedly, for the first time in many years. He knew he was a foolish man—foolish and now old to boot. But it didn't seem to matter anymore.

"Okay. Enough of that," he said, "I want you to tell me about George. And the girls!" he said. "And the grandchildren. Everything!"

"Now?"

"Yes, now. Why not?"

"Fifty years, Ray!"

"We could make a start!"

*

They said goodnight at the door to María's room. When Ray got to his own room, he dialed his son Phil straight away. The bleary voice at the other end said it all.

"Do you know what time it is, Dad?"

"I know, son, I'm sorry. I wouldn't do this to you if I had a choice."

"Midnight," Phil said, his tone clipped.

Ray half-expected to hear the click of the receiver, but moments later, his son recovered. "Hold on, let me go down to the extension. Everyone's asleep here."

When Phil picked up the extension, Ray asked about Sally and was told she seemed okay, a little subdued maybe given it was the holidays and the grandchildren were with her, but okay.

"She might like a call," said Phil, "preferably during daylight hours."

"I know, Phil. Listen, I need you to do something for me, and it's a big ask."

"Shoot."

"I need a film crew for tomorrow morning, here in DC."

"No problem."

"Really?"

"No! What are you, *crazy*?"

PART FOUR

46

The next morning, Ray waited outside the hotel, collar up against the freezing air watching the sluggish traffic crawl through DC. He was expecting a film crew, trusting he'd spot them easily enough with so few people about. He was not expecting his son and daughter-in-law, with a friend called Jake who happened to own a camera, a couple of microphones and a bare minimum of lighting equipment.

He squeezed into the cab beside Anni and Jake, giving Anni a little peck on the cheek and holding her hand. It was nine twenty-five a.m.

"What's going on?" Ray said.

Phil turned to his father from the front seat, his expression suggesting a very short fuse.

"Dad, please. Don't say a word, unless it's to express your lifelong debt. Our plane left at six-fifteen this morning. Mom is holding the fort with the kids, Anni and I were up at four and Jake has been up all night packing kit since I called him at one a.m. Okay? I'm not in the mood."

Ray looked from one face to another. Then he settled back in the seat.

"Okay."

"Okay," said Phil, turning away and taking a slurp from his Sprite. "Got an address?"

"The Arlington Rest Home. South Rolfe and Fourteenth, off the Columbia Pike," Ray said to the cabbie.

Ray waited some minutes into the ride before saying anything at all, let alone anything that might be construed as negative.

"Some good news," he said, pausing for a reaction and getting none. "I called a guy I know at WGBH Boston."

Still nothing. Ray elected to soldier on.

"I talked to him a little about this thing. He says with the fifty-year anniversary of the revolution, they might want to do something."

"Uh-huh," said Phil, still on his guard.

"Well, it makes me feel better about today, you know, more comfortable. I don't like to lie. This'll be broadcast standard, right?"

"Dad," said Phil with more than a hint of menace.

"I was just asking," said Ray. He squeezed Anni's hand again.

No one spoke for the rest of the short journey.

*

María was alone at the witness table with her lawyer. After the opening preliminaries, in which Senator Wallace found time to comment on the slow pace of proceedings the previous day, Capaldi opened a file in front of him and consulted the contents carefully.

He stood up to speak. "With the committee's indulgence, I would like to present something of the background to events later dubbed the Trujillo Conspiracy. Events that impacted on William Morgan and are therefore relevant to these proceedings."

Senator Hawkes nodded his approval.

"President Rafael Leónidas Trujillo came to power in the Dominican Republic in 1930, head of a military coup backed by the United States, and by the CIA in particular. His regime was soon notorious for its barbaric methods, ranging from assassination of his political opponents to mass murder. In 1937 for example, his troops massacred twenty thousand unarmed Haitian workers who were living illegally in the mountains of the Republic. The instruments of state repression under this man were both brutal and far-reaching. In another well-documented case, Trujillo had an academic who had written a dissertation unfavorable to the regime, spirited from Columbia University in New York to Santa

Domingo. The academic, whose name was Jesús Galindez Suárez, was dangled above a cauldron of boiling water and lowered down little by little until death occurred. Trujillo was much ridiculed, and to an extent feared, in Cuba. He was known as 'Chapita,' which translates as 'bottle cap,' for his taste in fancy uniforms bearing a myriad of unearned medals and his love of bicorne hats—"

Capaldi glanced up at the committee members to check they understood the reference. He couldn't be sure.

"Those are hats of the type worn by Napoleon and other military men of past ages."

"Thank you, counsel," said Senator Hawkes. "Please proceed, we'd like to cut to the chase here, if possible."

"Certainly, sir," said Capaldi. "The chase, as you put it, is this. On January 20, 1959, just three weeks after the revolution, US State Department records show a meeting called by the revolutionaries in Havana to discuss strategies for the overthrow of Trujillo. Castro's personal hatred of the right-wing dictator, friend to Batista, was an open secret, and often publicly stated in the heat of revolutionary fervor. By April, Castro was actively supporting an invasion by two hundred Dominican exiles, aiming to use the same tactics as the successful Cuban Revolution. The invasion was a disaster."

Again, Capaldi checked on his audience before continuing.

"So much for Cuban antagonism toward Trujillo. The sentiments were entirely mutual, Trujillo fearing the popular revolution would spread to his own country and end his reign with a left-wing, potentially communist, takeover. Thus, just as Castro was acting against the Dominican Republic's regime, President Trujillo was plotting his own invasion of Cuba. And it was William Morgan he had chosen as his instrument.

"Trujillo had many friends in the United States, especially in the corridors of power. In particular, J. Edgar Hoover, head of the FBI, was known to be sympathetic to Trujillo's cause. Around this time, Hoover made the public statement that he personally favored an invasion of Cuba to remove Castro from power, despite official US policy to the contrary.

"There were also several United States representatives in Congress, and Senators, supportive of the Trujillo regime, not least because of its vehement opposition to communism and willingness to export its views to other countries in the region. Amongst the Trujillo apologists were Pennsylvania Representative Francis Walter, Senator James Eastland of Mississippi and Senator George Armstead Smathers of Florida."

Senator Wallace had been shuffling in her seat for some time already. The mention of senatorial involvement in some kind of underhand conspiracy was too much for her.

"Counsel, this really is going too far. You've been specifically requested to stick to the facts and here you are engaging in some kind of smear against members of the Senate without a shred of evidence. I, for one, would propose the striking of this so-called evidence from the record, and I would formally ask the chair to insist upon a return to the business in hand, which in my opinion has already eaten up far too much time."

Senator Hawkes sighed deeply and opted for diplomacy.

"Counsel, it is my fervent hope that you are ready to conclude your introduction to today's proceedings. Is that correct?"

"Absolutely, Senator. I have said all that need be said at this stage."

"I'm delighted to hear it," said Hawkes. "Now let's get on. As it appears only Mrs. Jensen is here present, I assume we will hear from her now?"

"Yes, sir," said Capaldi. He turned to María and gave the merest hint of a satisfied smile. "It's all yours," he said under his breath.

"And just where are we in terms of time now?" said Senator Hawkes in an attempt to deflect further antagonism and bring the committee back to business.

The question was directed at counsel, but it was María who answered, her voice bold and confident. She leaned forward to the microphone.

"July 1959, Senator. It was hot, very hot, that summer. I remember because I was eight months pregnant—"

47

María couldn't wait to get away from Havana.

As she packed a small suitcase with the clothes she would need for the three-day trip, she kept glancing at the much larger suitcase open on the bed, fabulously empty and ready to embrace all the purchases she was planning to make in the Miami stores. Naturally, she would be shopping mostly for baby things; tiny things, things so cute it made María's heart flutter to think of them. But she'd promised herself new clothes too, up-to-date, modish skirts and pants, some of the new-style tops she'd seen in a catalogue, thin-strapped and sexy. Of course, she would have to guess at her size after the baby was born, but she was quite determined to recover her figure, even if she had to stop eating altogether.

There were other reasons she was excited that morning. For one, her sister Betania had arrived at the house late the night before. She had traveled from her home in Santa Clara to make the trip to Miami with them. She, too, was packing in her room right now.

For another, she was sick and tired of the house in Miramar, a house that had come to feel like some kind of public meeting place, a bar or a café, where people came and went as they wished. It wasn't a home, more like a barracks, and María needed a break more than ever. Guards too stupid to open the door for her, even though they could see she was carrying an armful of groceries, had more than once caused her to lose her temper. Then, she would shout and storm around until the brave *barbudos* took refuge in the garden or outside the front door. With Rosa to back her up, they ruled the roost, but for all their admonitions, things quickly reverted to chaos.

At other times, usually in the evenings, the dining room, with its mirrored wall and long glass table, was full to overflowing with shady characters and men in uniform smoking fat cigars or cigarettes, drinking coffee and rum as they pored over maps. They spoke in low, serious tones, jabbing fingers at this objective or that, arguing one with another, until her husband ostentatiously closed the doors against her, sometimes with a wink and a smile that did nothing to improve her mood.

Once, that dreadful man, Father Velazco—the fat priest who drank like a fish and whose lustful eyes followed her everywhere, in spite of her pregnancy; a man who made her flesh creep long after he'd gone and who left behind him a lingering odor of sweat and cheap eau de cologne—had come to the house to talk to William. He was taken to the anteroom behind the walk-in refrigerator, where the radio equipment was kept under lock and key. Happily she had little to do with him, though even the half-hour of polite conversation she'd been forced to engage in when the meeting was over had left her feeling dirty.

Nevertheless, over the months past she had supported her husband totally and she was more than aware of the dangers involved in a conspiracy of this kind. She understood that a word out of place could bring down the whole enterprise, with devastating consequences. But this didn't mean she found the process comfortable or satisfying in any way—quite the contrary. She hated everything about the constant tension and fear this conspiracy had created, and even worried that the atmosphere might, through her, affect the unborn baby in some way.

But the trip to Miami, dangerous and difficult as it might be for William, was also a milestone, signifying the end of this terrible time. There was little she could do to affect the outcome other than her duty in creating a convincing cover for the journey. Of all the jobs she had been asked to do, showing enthusiasm for a couple of days shopping was far and away the most pleasant, and she elected to throw herself completely into the fiction.

"Hey, are you ready yet?" Betania said as she came in. "We're going to be late."

Betania was younger than María by a couple of years and looked up to her older sister as a hero of the revolution in her own right. But they were also very different creatures. And when it came to shopping, especially in Miami, Betania knew it was she who must take the lead in all matters relating to both her older sister's taste in clothes and the baby's needs. She had prepared a list before she even arrived at the house in Miramar, and had gathered a file of photos and illustrations from various catalogues and magazines with what she called 'suggestions.'

"Yes, almost," said María.

"And you have the empty case?"

"There, on the bed."

"Then let's go, okay? William is waiting downstairs, walking up and down, up and down."

María knew she and her husband had made a good decision in keeping the true purpose of the trip between themselves. Knowing more than was necessary could only compromise the twenty year old. If they did run into a problem, Betania's passion for shopping would be utterly convincing. Besides, her sister's total lack of curiosity about the nature of Morgan's planned 'business' meetings in Miami made their actions a sin of omission only.

María had every intention of telling Betania the full story in time. But only when they were safely back in Havana.

48

Special Agent Lehman L. Stafford Junior and Special Agent Thomas H. Errion were waiting airside at Miami International Airport for passengers to disembark the Havana flight.

Both men were smartly turned out as always, but with extra attention to detail that day. The neat creases in their gray suit pants were razor sharp, the collars of their matching button-downs crisp and white, and their thin dark ties were held firmly in place with tiepins. They'd studied copies of Morgan's file and seen photographs, including those taken during his incarcerations in military prison. They also had Morgan's police record from Cleveland and clippings from the local paper, *The Cleveland News*, which had provided some of the up-to-date background on this man's exploits in Cuba. Allowing for journalistic license, it seemed this former hoodlum had miraculously managed to transform himself into something of a celebrity, even a hero of sorts, at least on the island.

They spotted him straight away. Morgan stood out from the crowd by virtue of his height and build, but otherwise he looked like any other returning American tourist. He was wearing white sports slacks, tan loafers and a light blue short-sleeved shirt, over-printed with images of palm trees and cocktails. On first impressions, Morgan was not the slick wheeler-dealer they'd expected. In real life, he looked more like a buffoon. Stafford's raised eyebrow made Errion nod his head in agreement. The two agents made their way through the arriving passengers to intercept their quarry.

"William Morgan?" Stafford said.

Morgan had spotted the agents long before they said a word.

"That's me," he said, and gave María's hand a reassuring squeeze.

Stafford showed his gold shield in its black leather wallet.

"Agent Stafford, FBI. This is Agent Errion. We have some questions for you."

"What questions?" said Morgan.

Betania was looking at María for some kind of explanation and getting nothing in return.

"Questions concerning neutrality matters and internal security. Would you come with us, please, sir?"

"Am I under arrest?"

"No, sir, not at this time. The interview would be best conducted on a voluntary basis. But I would highly recommend your cooperation. To avoid embarrassment."

Morgan looked at each of them in turn. "Okay. Give me a moment, guys."

The two agents backed away a few feet. Morgan turned to María. Her face was pale.

"It's okay," he said to her. "Betania?"

"*Si?*" said María's sister. She looked more ashen than María.

"Don't worry, okay? Can you get the bags and a cab, and get María to the hotel?"

"*Si,*" Betania said.

"Good girl," Morgan said. "I'll join you there. This won't take long." He turned to María again, and this time whispered to her.

"I love you. Don't worry, okay? It's just routine. I knew it would happen, just not this quick. I'll be half an hour behind you, okay?"

María nodded, her lips tightly pressed together.

"Half an hour," said Morgan. He kissed her and smiled. "Go ahead, baby."

He saw María look over her shoulder as she walked away, arm in arm with Betania.

"Mr. Morgan?" said Errion. "This way."

*

The next morning, Morgan, María and Betania had breakfast together on the terrace of the Hotel Montmartre. He'd been rattled by the FBI interview the day before—too many well-informed questions about conspiracies against Fidel—and he was keen to hide the fact from his wife and sister-in-law.

The sky above them was a vibrant blue and they were glad of the shade from the umbrella over their table. Morgan had the works—eggs, hash browns, bacon and waffles with syrup—and took a good deal of stick from the girls for his insatiable appetite and broadening waistline.

"Come on," said Morgan. "Rosa's a fine cook, but she still hasn't got the American breakfast down. I'm making the most of it. You should too."

Betania had a pile of clippings from various magazines and catalogues on the table beside her grapefruit and toast, and she'd picked up a map from reception so they could plan their day; or rather, so *she* could plan the day. María was happy to let her take the lead. She had other things on her mind that morning, like what her husband would be doing while they were trawling the stores.

As Betania twittered on, fussing over where they might have lunch, Morgan winked at María as he always did when he wanted to reassure her, his mouth full with the last morsels of breakfast. Her smile in return was weaker than she'd hoped, but he didn't appear to notice. Someone or something behind her had caught his eye. María turned to see a huge, olive-skinned man in an ill-fitting dark suit, his hair slicked back, lolloping toward their table.

Morgan reached under the table and squeezed María's hand before standing to greet the man.

"Hey, Carl," he said in a voice strange to María, deeper and looser, with a drawl that was new to her. "How's it going?"

"Pretty good, Billy, pretty good," he said, taking Morgan's outstretched hand. "I'm sorry to interrupt your breakfast and all."

The man retreated to a respectful distance.

"Carl, meet my wife María. This here's Carl Longobucco," said Morgan. "We used to work together. Isn't that right, Carl?"

"Them were the days," said Longobucco, "before, you know—long time ago. My pleasure, ma'am," he added, bowing his head but not daring to offer his hand to María.

She felt almost sorry for him.

"Betania here is my sister-in-law," said Morgan.

"Ma'am," said Longobucco, blushing all the way to his thick neck. He turned to Morgan. "You want I should wait outside till you're done?"

"I'm done," said Morgan. "We can go."

"Nice to meet you's," said Longobucco. He turned to go, the relief obvious on his face.

Morgan wiped his mouth on the white cotton napkin and re-tucked his sports shirt into the pants. Then he leaned over and kissed María.

"I'll see you at five," he said. "Then we'll do that thing, okay?"

"Okay," said María. "Be careful."

She watched him go a little way until Betania, shrieking with delight and waving the map about, could no longer be ignored.

"*La Tropicana para la comida. Claro!*" said Betania. Lunch venue decided, she looked her sister up and down, apparently with some distaste. "María, you're going to have to change that dress," she said.

*

The penthouse suite of the Eden Roc had an unrivalled view over Miami. Longobucco went up in the elevator with Morgan, but he and the muscle man who'd driven them waited outside the door when Morgan went in.

Bartone and Nelson were waiting. There was a bar with a studded leather front to it and optics behind. Sliding glass doors leading to a broad terrace were wide open. Bartone was behind the bar, pouring drinks. Nelson was sitting on a barstool, watchful.

"Billy!" said Bartone.

He put down the bottle and came round the corner of the bar to greet Morgan with a bear hug, like they were long-lost friends.

"So, you're here."

"As you see," Morgan said.

Bartone turned to Nelson.

"What'd I tell you? Like clockwork, this guy. Dependable, ain't that right, Billy? Always were. Come on, let's fix you a drink. What'd you have?"

"Just a beer."

"You don't want nothing stronger?"

"I just had breakfast."

"So?" said Bartone. He laughed at his own joke.

Morgan could smell his musk-scented aftershave. Nelson remained stone-faced at the bar, save for the sly smirk at one corner of his mouth that was pretty much a permanent fixture. He didn't rise to shake hands.

"Hey, Frankie," Bartone said over his shoulder, "get the kid a beer." He was still holding Morgan by the arms, nodding genially, but managing to study Morgan closely at the same time.

"Come on, big man. Let's get some air. It's like the old days again, eh?"

Bartone led the way out to the terrace.

"Take a look at that view. The whole city, the beach, the ocean. And ninety miles that way, the future. Just waiting to be grabbed. You know what I'm saying? Come on, sit."

Nelson brought the beer in a bottle and an attaché case and sat with them.

"Frankie, fill us in, why don't you?"

"It's all where it should be," said Nelson. "The Dominicans are almost there with the money. We got three main suppliers with consignments from Georgia, another from here in Miami courtesy of Mister Bartone here, and some bits and pieces from a couple of specialists."

Nelson leaned forward in his chair conspiratorially. "Bazookas, maybe two, maybe more. We're looking to you to finalize a couple of deals in Jacksonville. They want to meet the man."

"If I can shake the Feds."

"What are you talking about?"

"They picked me up at the airport."

"And?"

"Questions. But they knew stuff."

"And?"

"And nothing. But I wonder where they're getting it."

Bartone grinned and put a hand on Morgan's shoulder. "Don't worry."

"I do worry," Morgan said.

"And I'm telling you, don't," said Bartone. He looked at Nelson. "Frankie, tell Billy he ain't got nothing to worry about."

"The Feds—how can I put this? Let's just say they're not working against us."

"That's not how it seems on the receiving end," said Morgan.

"Take my word for it," said Nelson, "the local office is going through the motions. Higher up the tree, we have friends. Those friends are very supportive."

Nelson lifted the case from the floor beside his chair, laid it on the table and flicked open the brass catches.

"A down payment," said Bartone. Nelson swung the case around to show Morgan a dozen neat bundles of used notes. "From the Dominicans. Expenses, a sweetener for our friends in Jacksonville, and a little something for you to show their good faith. If this works out, you're going to be a rich man, Billy boy. Very rich. When the Dominicans come up with the rest of the cash, we go. Until then, nothing moves. So you got a few days with your wife and—who is it?"

"Her sister."

"Yeah, okay, whatever. So stay out of trouble, have a good time, go shopping, buy some things for your family. Frankie?"

"You'll have a guy riding shotgun for the Dominicans when it comes to it," said Nelson, "guy called Betancourt. Just to make sure you don't run away with their investment."

"I don't need passengers on this," Morgan said, looking from one to the other.

"It's been agreed, Billy," said Bartone. "It's a little thing. And you'll need to show yourself to the Dominican ambassador. You'll hear from me when they're ready. What about your end?"

"Everything's in place," said Morgan.

"How can you be sure?" said Nelson.

Morgan was suddenly angry.

"Because I am. I fought with these guys already. They're my people. Who are your people by the way? I keep meaning to ask."

Nelson just grinned. "Yeah? Well, you asked. If I were you, Mr. Morgan—"

Bartone cut Nelson off. "Billy won't let us down. Ain't that right, Billy? Now, the nuts and bolts. You want another beer?"

Morgan was back at the Capri before five in the evening, just as he'd promised, in time to hear the girls giggling and chatting on their way to Betania's room. He opened the room door to see the bellhop struggling down the corridor behind them, weighed down with shopping bags. With everything dumped on Betania's bed, Morgan tipped the boy five dollars and dutifully stood by as the day's haul was held up, item by item, for his approval or wonderment.

Two hours later, María and Morgan had showered, eaten in the hotel restaurant and were in a cab heading south. They left Betania in her room fawning over the purchases with the TV on. Morgan had with him a brown paper bag, the type you get at the grocery store for smaller items like a bottle of liquor. The bag was lying on the seat between them. Leaving it there like that was making María uncomfortable.

"You might forget it," said María.

"I won't forget," replied Morgan.

She almost contradicted him. But she knew this wasn't the time for banter, so she simply picked the bag off the seat and put it on her lap. Still she gripped the paper bag tightly.

When they reached the Hecht Cinema, a few blocks back from the beach hotels and casinos that lined the shore, they bought two tickets for the seven-thirty screening of *The World of Suzie Wong*. Morgan handed over the money and chatted amiably with the young girl in the sidewalk box office. Reflected in the glass booth, he could see the tan Ford that had followed them all the way from the Montmartre. The car had parked up on the far side of the street.

He and María took time to buy popcorn before going into the darkened theatre, already showing a trailer to the lurid feature, *Attack of the Killer Leeches*. As they walked down the side aisle, Morgan was pushing popcorn into his mouth and staring wide-eyed at the screen as some poor sucker in an unconvincing leech costume—probably still hoping to make it big in Hollywood—dragged a screaming blonde down into the swamp.

At the side exit, close to the screen, Morgan took a last handful of corn, put the bucket down on the floor and pushed open the bar handle, letting María go ahead of him. They walked down the alley and, a couple of blocks later, hailed another cab.

*

Thelma was still living in the same crummy apartment under the South Dixie highway, just as her girlfriend, Karen—the same girl who'd come over that day over a year ago to take care of her—had told Morgan by phone. He was glad to find her so easily, but he was also disappointed. He knew how much she hated the place and he'd hoped she might have moved on. It would have eased his conscience.

Thelma answered the door with the baby gurgling in her arms. Her hair was done up in a creased floral scarf. An auburn fringe, cut a little too severe, poked out over her pale forehead. She looked from him to María and back as if irritated or confused.

"What do you want?" she said.

At first, it wasn't clear that she even recognized Morgan under the weak neon of the stair light. However, the impression that Thelma greeted almost any intrusion from the outside world in much the same way was hard to resist.

"Can we come in?" said Morgan. "This is María, my wife."

Thelma looked again at María, quizzically now, and she seemed to take in the swollen belly, barely hidden under María's maternity dress. She stared almost rudely at the bulge and then turned away from the door, letting it swing open behind her.

Inside, the apartment was strewn with baby clothes and diapers in various stages of the wash cycle. The sink was full and the TV was on, showing some kind of situation comedy with canned laughter laid over. With the volume turned down low, the sound was like buzzing insects trapped in the room.

"It's wash day," said Thelma. "I would have tidied if I'd known you were coming."

Morgan and María sat side by side on the sofa, pushing toys to one side in order to make room. Thelma sat opposite, perched on the edge of the chair, the child on her knee like a ventriloquist's dummy.

"How far are you?" she said to María.

"I'm due next month, about the eighteenth of August," María replied. "Who's this?" she said brightly, reaching out to Thelma's baby and doing everything she could think of to keep the conversation going.

"Jacqueline. Jack."

"Will she come to me?" said María. "I need the practice."

"She prefers men, but you can try if you like."

María took the tiny girl and started to walk around the room, rocking the child in her arms until she felt the little body relax. For a while, all eyes were on María and the baby, but then Morgan turned to Thelma and began to talk to her, telling her small, inconsequential things to begin with, like the names they'd thought of for their own baby when it came. Thelma said nothing, but she listened. As the minutes went by, she occasionally replied in short, staccato sentences.

María went over to the kitchen sink and pulled a tissue from the box on the counter to wipe at the dribble on Jack's chin. She heard Thelma say she'd read about Morgan in the papers. She heard her say she'd been seeing someone, but with the baby it was hard. He was, she said, one of the guys from the construction site who'd worked with Jack. His marriage had broken up when his wife had run away with a shoe salesman. When that went wrong, the wife had come home, but only to get a divorce. She was still there.

Then María heard Morgan say how Jack's death had been the end of a lot of things for him too, how it had been the reason he'd gone to Cuba in the first place. María felt for her husband. He was struggling to find the words.

Morgan had scrunched the brown paper bag in the course of talking and it was now tightly sealed, folded over and over on itself.

"This is for you," said Morgan. He handed Thelma the bag. "And little Jack there."

Thelma was hesitant, but after a quick glance at María for reassurance she took the bag from him, perhaps imagining a toy or a pair of booties for Jack, something they'd picked up in the course of the shopping spree they'd mentioned.

"What is it?" she said.

Morgan had his head down like a shy schoolboy. Thelma patiently unrolled the brown paper bag and looked inside. One by one she pulled out the bundles of used twenty-dollar bank notes and put them on her lap. There were five in all, each neatly tied with a blue paper band, amounting to five thousand dollars.

49

There was nothing wrong with María or the pregnancy, but that was the story they'd use to explain why the trip was being cut short.

Truth was, the heat from the Feds was making life all but impossible. All pretence of secret surveillance had been dropped in favor of a very visible presence wherever they went. Whatever about Nelson's claim to friends in high places, it seemed the message was not filtering down to the troops.

Betania was naturally a little peeved to see the trip cut short, albeit only by a couple of days, but as they'd managed to buy so much more than she'd dared hope—already the large suitcase would barely close—she'd kept her feelings to herself.

Getting plane tickets proved remarkably straightforward given it was the height of the season. A call to the airline from Bartone's people had smoothed the process. When Morgan spoke to Bartone himself, they agreed he should definitely skip the airport and instead make his way to the Eden Roc without trying to shake the tail. Once inside the hotel, that would be the last time the Feds would see Morgan.

"I hate that man," María said, when the packing was done.

Morgan followed her out onto the balcony. Three floors below, the streets and avenues, hotels and shops of Miami were all lit up, casting an orange glow that domed over the city like a bubble, completely obliterating the stars in the black sky beyond.

"Come on," he said, putting his arms around her again, this time from behind, letting his hands rest on her round belly. "A week at the outside and I'll be home, and this whole thing is over."

"You said that to me once before, do you remember?"

"What, *chica*?"

"You told me it was over, the fighting was finished, no more killing."

"No one's going to get killed, trust me."

*

The Eden Roc would be both more secure and easier to vacate when the time came. That's what Bartone had said, and with some justification. Owning the hotel's door concession meant he could control the comings and goings, set up an early warning if needed and tell the management exactly what to do.

A clean hire car was waiting in the underground car park with the keys in the ignition. Longobucco would give Morgan the all-clear to use the service exit, and ten minutes later, he'd be on the highway to Tampa. There, he could lie low until the Dominicans came up with the rest of the money and the guns were safely loaded and en route from Georgia. But, for today at least, he would do exactly as Stafford had requested, and stay in regular touch regarding his whereabouts, keeping the FBI office informed of any material changes in his circumstances.

So it was, that at eleven-thirty in the morning, Morgan picked up the phone in his new room at the Eden Roc and rang the FBI's Miami office. He spoke to Special Agent Errion. He said he'd moved hotels and wanted to let them know that María had flown back to Havana following what he called 'medical complications with her pregnancy.' The agent didn't seem happy and told Morgan to make himself available for a second interview that afternoon at the FBI Miami offices. Morgan agreed. He called Errion 'sir.'

The call over, Morgan put his suitcase on the bed and began to unpack. He put a range of shirts, some still bearing price tags from the Eden Roc's menswear shop, on hangers in the wardrobe and left a pair of shoes under the bed. Then he took his wash kit to the bathroom and laid out the razor, toothbrush and hair comb in a way that looked natural.

Returning to the bedroom, Morgan pulled back the pristine coverlet on the bed, before messing the sheets and throwing his pajamas down on top. He picked up the photograph of a yacht called *Lucimi*, given to him by Longobucco, and looked at it closely before putting it on the dresser. It was a fine yacht, he thought. Too bad he wouldn't get to sail in her.

Then he took the Colt 45 from the small of his back where he'd tucked it into the waistband of his pants. Longobucco had passed it under the table in the hotel bar, scarcely seeming to care who might see. But then Carl was none too bright, God love him, which in some ways was just as well, thought Morgan.

He clicked the release and ejected the magazine from the gun's grip. The magazine was full. He used his thumb to free the top round from the clip and held the 9mm shell in his fingers, turning it this way and that to catch the light on the brass casing. Then he put it upright on top of the photograph of the Lucimi like a miniature paperweight, took a last look around the room and went to go.

He opened the door and thought to himself that leaving the shell was a dumb thing to do. Maybe. But where's the harm? Even Stafford and Errion had to have a funny bone between them—surely.

50

Morgan didn't show up for the interview—naturally enough—nor had he been seen entering or leaving the hotel, so later that day, Stafford and Errion went to the Eden Roc to find him.

They arrived mob-handed in two cars, anticipating trouble from whichever heavy was on the door that day, prepared to scoop up Bartone, Longobucco and anyone else who was connected or could be useful in the same net. But it was Morgan who was the prime target and who was now seriously pissing them off.

When the doorman stood in their way, Stafford had him arrested. By the time they hit the lobby, there was a hush to staff and guests. The men in suits strode through, badges held high, hands hovering over their holstered sidearms. The manager, Jean Suits, rushed out from his office behind the reception desk as soon as he realized what was going on. Anxious to assist in any way that might clear his lobby of Federal Agents at the earliest opportunity, he said he'd be happy to personally open up Morgan's room for the agents, search warrant or no search warrant. He rode up in the elevator to the sixth floor with Stafford, Errion and two others, talking incessantly in spite of their stony expressions, and apologizing as best he could for the doorman's actions, telling them what they already knew: the guy was a Teamsters member and as such, there was little Suits could do to get rid of him without what he called 'repercussions.'

Suits was still talking when they hit the sixth-floor corridor. He stopped abruptly when they noticed the door to Morgan's room was open. Stafford and Errion straight away drew their weapons in readiness. Errion crouched, pistol double-gripped as the training manual instructed, and Stafford darted to the other side of the door before calling out.

"FBI. Put your hands where I can see them and don't move."

When nobody responded, they rushed into the room. It was empty.

*

A week later, Morgan was feeling rested from his time in Tampa, driving from Riviera Beach back toward Miami with Ramirito at the wheel of the car. The young man had quietly flown in from Havana to be Morgan's point man for the deals, another pair of eyes and ears, and more mundanely, his driver.

Ramirito had met Morgan in Tampa, then driven him to Jacksonville and on to Riviera Beach. He stood by, nervous and observant, as Morgan shook hands, checked sample weapons and handed over large sums of money to overweight guys with orange suntans. He'd also fixed the fishing boat charter that would take Morgan ten miles off the Miami coast that very night, to rendezvous with the fifty-foot yacht plying its way south from Georgia. The yacht was loaded with half a million dollars worth of small arms, uniforms and heavy weapons, including mortars and a couple of bazookas.

Two days before, they'd slipped into Miami to have lunch with Manuel Benitez, a Batistiano and former head of Cuba's national police force, a man who made Ramirito's blood run cold just to watch him eat his French fries, snapping at forkfuls with his false teeth like an overweight piranha. Rolando Masferrer had joined them. He was a former Senator under Batista and a newspaper publisher, smooth as you like in a silk suit. Then there was Lemus, a banker who was putting up some of the money; he had piggy eyes and round spectacles. He spoke very little, but was watchful. Lemus had come along for a drink after the meal, and Morgan had greeted him like an old friend and cracked jokes with the group, though it was obvious to Ramirito that

Morgan was being studied and assessed by each of his companions.

Despite the scrutiny, Morgan was always at ease, even with people who scared the shit out of Ramirito with their conspicuous money and ruthless eyes.

"Will it be the same guys today?" said Ramirito as they reached the suburbs of Miami.

"And Bartone," said Morgan, "and Betancourt who's riding shotgun. Probably that toad Nelson, too."

"*Madre mía*, I don't like this, boss. In the Escambray, no problem, but here?"

"Just one step at a time, my friend. And it's not like we have the option to let them down, now is it?" said Morgan with a grin. "At least, not yet. Say, what time is it?"

Ramirito checked his watch. "Three-thirty."

A couple of blocks later, they were passing through a shopping street.

"Okay," said Morgan, "when you see a payphone pull over, okay? I need to make a call."

A few minutes later, they found a phone outside a pharmacy.

Morgan rang Ray's office number, as they'd arranged. The secretary put him through.

"Hey, how's it going with the grown ups?" Morgan said.

"Don't ask," replied Ray.

"How does a short vacation sound?"

51

Ramirito stayed with the car when they reached the Dominican Consulate. They parked out of sight of the street behind the tall iron gates guarding the courtyard of the building.

As it turned out, Morgan was the last to arrive in the Consulate's conference room. The Consul, Augusto Ferrando, greeted him with a warm handshake. The others in the room were standing around a conference table laid with drinks and snacks. Benitez had come in his old police uniform. Bartone was wearing a white suit as usual. Even Nelson had brushed up for the occasion, with a blue sports jacket over his Fred Perry tennis shirt.

Morgan had never been in this room before, nor indeed to the Consulate. Previous meetings had taken place in restaurants or hotel rooms. Today was different because, in the eyes of the Dominicans at least, it constituted an official ceremony, a formal send-off. The Generalísimo himself was due to call.

The small talk was painful as they waited for the phone to ring. At least Ferrando had finally elected to have the champagne opened by the waiting staff, having hesitated for twenty minutes. The giant portrait of the dictator—bicorn hat, chin thrown back, in full military dress, gold epaulettes and medals fighting for space on his chest—hung heavily over the fireplace. Everyone was relieved when the phone finally rang. Ferrando picked up, having first of all straightened his ceremonial chain of office.

"*Generalísimo!*" said Ferrando. "We are honored."

The Consul came to attention as he spoke.

"*Si—Si, Momento per favor.*"

Ferrando took the receiver from his ear and cleared his throat.

"Gentlemen, the *Generalísimo* sends his compliments and his best wishes for our enterprise. He has requested to speak to you, Mr. Morgan, in person."

Morgan took the receiver from Ferrando, who looked pleased as punch to have handed the boss on to someone else. He beamed at the others in the room, perhaps expecting congratulations.

"*Generalísimo*," said Morgan, "I salute you."

To Bartone's surprise in particular, Morgan did just as he'd said and, with the receiver in his left hand, gave a sharp salute to the giant portrait above the fireplace, hand quivering at his brow, heels clicking together. So credible was the action that Ferrando followed suit, as did Betancourt and Benitez. Only Bartone and Nelson were left with their hands in their pockets.

"*Si, generalísimo!*" said Morgan, his voice unnaturally loud even in the large conference room. "All preparations are in place. My men are ready to do their duty, and if necessary, to die in the attempt to free Cuba. We thank you for leading us in this glorious crusade."

Morgan listened again for a moment and then said, "When General Pedraza lands with his forces he will find the island cut in half by our men. Cienfuegos, Santa Clara and Trinidad will be in our hands and many communists will be dead. *¡Viva Cuba Libre!*"

Morgan saluted again and handed the receiver to Ferrando. He quickly took a slurp from his champagne glass to hide his relief. He wasn't sure how long he could keep this up.

Ferrando stood up straight, cleared his throat again and spoke into the receiver, but it was clear the Generalísimo had already rung off. To hide his confusion, Ferrando proposed they charge their glasses for the formal toast.

The waiters did a final round before leaving the room. Ferrando's assistant, a young man with pockmarked skin, brought an attaché case and a polished mahogany box to the table and put them in front of the Consul.

"Comandante Morgan," said Ferrando, flicking open the catches on the attaché case and opening the lid. "One hundred and fifty seven thousand dollars. The last installment, courtesy of the people of the Dominican Republic, and our illustrious leader."

Ferrando twisted the case round for Morgan to see. Involuntarily, the others in the room edged a little closer, intrigued to see that much money bundled together. Even Bartone was impressed, not least because a substantial portion was owed to him for the weaponry he'd provided to supplement the Georgia shipment; weaponry that was, at that very moment, being loaded onto a chartered fishing boat tied up in Miami harbor.

Ferrando picked up the mahogany box, the size and shape of a hardback book, and held it in his hands as if it were a sacred offering.

"This," said the Consul with pride, "is for you. It is a personal gift from Generalísimo Trujillo himself. He asked me to give it to you before your departure."

Ferrando opened the lid of the box in a way that suggested he may well have rehearsed this moment. Inside, a gleaming gold-plated Colt 45 nestled in luxurious navy-blue felt.

Morgan was actually impressed. The weapon was his favorite piece and though the gold plating was not what you'd call subtle, it was, to Morgan at least, a thing of great beauty. He reached out and gently freed the Colt from its velvet bed. Holding it in one hand, he ran his fingers over the gold body, tracing the line of the barrel, marveling at the touch.

Finally, Morgan remembered where he was and found some words of thanks, adding as an afterthought that he hoped to kill many communists with the gun.

*

He was still cradling the Colt as the coast of Florida melted into the horizon. Morgan was sitting on the gunwale of the fishing boat, upwind of Betancourt who was throwing up over the stern. The smell of diesel fumes in the warm evening air was probably not helping the guy, he thought.

He might have felt sorrier for Betancourt if he'd known that by the end of the week the man would be dead at the hands of the Generalísimo himself, a victim of the purge of those who had fallen for Morgan's double-cross. But as the sun sank lower and the boat yawed as it ploughed through each successive sea swell, Morgan had other things on his mind.

"That's her!" the boat's captain shouted down from the flying bridge.

Morgan stood, feet astride to steady himself against the swell. He tucked the Colt in the small of his back. Half a mile to the west, he could see a yacht riding head to wind with just the jib up to keep her steady, the white hull pink in the dusk light.

Twenty minutes later, they were alongside and the last of the guns from the fishing boat were being hauled onto the yacht by fish crane. It was clear Betancourt, who was now semi-conscious, would not be able to go on, so Morgan clambered aboard the yacht alone.

At the wheel was a Cuban called Raul. There was another man who said his name was Alfonso. He told Morgan he was Argentinean. It didn't much matter. Both were hired hands and neither was part of the big picture. Besides, with Betancourt out of the way, Morgan was more confident he could persuade them to cooperate when the time came.

As he watched the fishing boat chug away to the west, smoke puffing from the little black stack, Morgan thought how familiar this all was—the boat, the guns, the twelve-hour passage to the Cuban coast—and how strange that sometimes life goes in a big circle and you end up right back where you started.

He thought about María waiting for him at home, no doubt anxious, but with the guys around to reassure her. He thought about Menoyo, who would be making preparations for the meeting at the house in Miramar. He thought about Ray, who right now should be on a flight to Havana. He looked down at the deep ocean and heard the slow rhythm of the boat's engine, and he thought about Jack.

"What's she called?" he said to the Cuban who was helming the boat.

Morgan offered him a cigarette he'd just lit. The Cuban took the cigarette without saying thanks and without shifting his eyes from the darkening horizon.

"She don't got no name."

"Every boat's got a name," Morgan said.

"Yeah?" said the Cuban. He cupped his cigarette against the wind and took a long drag before blowing smoke against the wind. "Well this one don't."

52

The nameless yacht should have made landfall off the coast of Las Villas province. But the heavy load meant that even with the throttle wide open, the thirty horsepower engine was barely adequate for the ninety-mile journey.

Plus, a strengthening headwind was forcing them to burn fuel much faster than anticipated and they were now running dangerously low. It was full night when Morgan took the decision to head for Havana harbor as the only possible option. It would mean customs and the very real possibility that the conspiracy would blow wide open, destroying months of hard work, but there was no choice. He radioed ahead and raised Menoyo at the Miramar house to tell him about the change of plan. Menoyo would arrange some of their men to take care of the cargo without involving the port authorities.

Morgan used the change of plan to justify pulling one of the Thompson submachine guns from a box in the cabin, loading the magazine and holding the weapon ready as they motored into the harbor entrance. Lights from the city beyond made the harbor seem even darker. Green and red navigation buoys flickered weakly. Only the sweep of the lighthouse beam penetrated the shadowy scene, bouncing off the white hulls of moored boats.

A hundred feet off the harbor wall, the Cuban and the Argentinean were beginning to panic. It was too quiet, they said. Morgan made reassuring noises for as long as he could, but as they neared the jetty, he steadied himself against the cabin door, flicked the safety and cocked the weapon, sighting the two men standing together toward the boat's stern.

"Make a move and I'll kill you both, I swear to God."

*

Menoyo, meanwhile, was greeting the last of the conspirators to arrive at the Miramar house. They joined the others seated around the glass table in the dining room, smoking cigars and cigarettes, their numbers bizarrely doubled by the floor-to-ceiling mirror on the wall behind them. There were murmurs of approval and a ripple of applause when Menoyo gave them the news—somewhat doctored—that Morgan had made landfall safely and was at that very moment unloading the weapons with a small force of one hundred men near the city of Santa Clara.

"Gentlemen," said Menoyo, "it has begun."

Upstairs in the bedroom, María and Ray were sitting together on the bed. Cross-legged on the floor, Jamie was casually fiddling with the two Nikon cameras either side of him, as relaxed as if waiting for a bus.

Unlike the photographer, Ray and María were straining to hear anything they could from the room below and not saying a word. There was a handgun on the bed by María—just in case.

Outside the front door, Redondo and Ramirito were on guard duty. They heard a car pull up down the street and then the sound of someone running toward the house. They'd been told everyone who was coming had already arrived, so whoever this was, it was not one of the conspirators.

Both men flicked the safeties on their M-16 rifles and held them at waist level pointing down the drive toward the street beyond. The figure they saw jogging toward them was a large man in uniform with a rifle slung over his shoulder, as if on fatigues. When he was just a few yards from them, he slowed to a walk, breathless and smiling behind his full black beard.

"All right, boys?" said Fidel, catching his breath and wiping at the sweat on his forehead. "Well, shall we go in?"

When the door to the dining room opened and Fidel strode in flanked by Redondo and Ramirito, Menoyo stood up.

"Gentlemen," he said, "a new comandante has joined up."

It was the agreed signal for Carreras, Montiel, Fleites and Artola hiding behind the kitchen door and in the garden to rush into the room, guns at the ready. Only one man even tried to run. He shoved past Redondo to reach the hallway and then, for reasons that would never be clear, elected to run up the grand staircase toward the first floor.

In the bedroom, Ray and María heard the commotion and were on their feet. María picked up the gun and faced the door; even Jamie got up from the floor, readying one of the Nikons as if it too were a weapon.

The man never made it to the bedroom. Redondo aimed at the fleeing figure from the hallway and fired. He hit the man in the arm, pain and surprise making him fall to the floor on the top landing, grasping at his injured hand in disbelief, now dripping with blood. The man started to whimper like a puppy.

Ray was sure his heart stopped beating at the sound of the shot. Even María jumped. But as they listened with all the attention of cornered animals, it was their own men they heard shouting and calling to each other. There was no more gunfire. It seemed a lifetime, but it was only two minutes later that Ramirito knocked at the door and put his head round the jamb.

"You can come down now," he said, grinning from ear to ear.

On instinct, Jamie zoomed, the shutter clicked and a bright flash froze the moment forever.

53

Morgan was waiting for them at Havana's military airbase. He was standing on the tarmac beside a C-47 transport plane as three vehicles—two jeeps and a car—swept around the control tower in a snaking crescent toward him.

The vehicles pulled up around the plane. Menoyo, Ramirito, Redondo, Fleites, Artola, Carreras, Montiel and the others jumped out. Ray and Jamie followed on, Jamie clicking away with one camera, then another. The vehicle lights cast long shadows over the fuselage of the plane. As one of the prop engines fired into life, smoke from the exhausts enveloped the still-celebrating huddle and Menoyo shouted for them to get aboard.

Ducking low to avoid the back draft of the propellers, now spinning too fast to see, the men started to clamber up the metal ladder into the plane. Morgan turned to wait for Ray and put an arm around his shoulders to lead him toward the plane. He was saying something Ray could scarcely catch against the noise of the engines.

"What?" Ray shouted.

"I said—"

Again, the words were blown away. Morgan gestured to Ray to climb aboard. Behind them, a crewmember pulled the ladder up and reached out to close the door. The plane started to judder forward.

They had to brace themselves to avoid falling into the laps of the others already sitting in two long rows either side of the fuselage, paratrooper-style. Morgan clipped in and helped Ray find the other end of his belt. The plane was already turning through ninety degrees at the runway end.

"Take a look at this," said Morgan.

The engines began to throttle up to full revs. Morgan reached behind his back and took out the gold-plated Colt.

"Trujillo," Morgan said loudly, "turns out he's not such a bad guy after all!"

Ray shook his head and said, "You love it, don't you?"

Morgan laughed and called across to Menoyo on the other side of the plane.

"Gallego!" He tossed the gun to Menoyo, whoops of derision coming from the others.

Menoyo passed the gun down the line and gave Morgan a two-fingered horn. Then he pointed to his own head.

"Where's the goddamn general's hat I ordered!"

The plane picked up speed and, slewing from side to side, began to roar down the runway.

*

Just as Morgan had promised, Ray was given a ringside seat for the final act of the conspiracy as it went down. Morgan had said quite clearly the story would not be an exclusive. When the C-47 reached Las Villas and the radio base was set up at Trinidad airport, those words turned out to be something of an understatement.

Over the three days it took to convince the Dominicans that everything was going according to plan, newspaper men, radio reporters, even a couple of television film crews invited to record the denouement—live as it happened—waited alongside the men of the Second Front.

Fidel naturally wanted to make all the capital he could out of the abortive counter-revolution, and it was he who had personally insisted the press was there in force, before flying in himself with Camilio Cienfuegos to witness events first-hand.

Morgan kept up radio contact with the Dominicans, using his agreed codename of Henry, after Henry Morgan, the infamous pirate. It was a private joke the Dominicans didn't get. Like a patient fisherman, he'd reeled in when he could and played out some slack when he couldn't.

At one level, the game was child's play. At a signal from Morgan or Menoyo, the Second Front guys would go off into the distance and begin firing their weapons in the air, shouting to one another and even pulling the pin on the occasional grenade for added realism. With a convincing background in place, Morgan would call through to Johnny Abbes, his contact at the other end of the signal, who happened also to be head of the Dominican military intelligence service.

"3JK—3JK. This is Henry, repeat, this is Henry," Morgan would say, lounging back on two legs of an office chair in the Trinidad airport radio room. "Come in—"

When Abbes responded, Morgan would tell him of their successes and explain the gunfire as pockets of Fidelista resistance that would soon be crushed. He said they'd cut the island in half, but needed the promised reinforcements and weapon drops to arm the people who were rising up to follow the Second Front against the communists.

Still the Dominicans were wary. Reports of arrests, not just in Havana but taking place all over the island, had leaked in the press over the three days and caused much consternation in Cuba, Dominica and the US. Nobody seemed certain of what was really going on, but Morgan told Abbes the reports were lies, propaganda from a regime quaking in fear and trying desperately to keep a lid on what was happening.

Finally, on the night of August 13, 1959, a Dominican C-47 circled the airport looking for the burning beacons they'd been told would mark the runway. To add weight to the charade, all electricity to the Trinidad region had been cut on Fidel's orders. Fires had also been set in oil drums at various points around the city to suggest heavy fighting had taken its toll.

Ray was standing outside the Nissen hut with Ramirito and Redondo, watching the lights of the plane wobble as the pilot corrected his approach. Jamie had positioned himself behind an electricity bunker that would hide him and also support a long lens.

A few moments later, they saw the touchdown and heard the whine of the engines as the pilot slipped the prop blades into reverse attitude. By the light of the long line of beacons, they saw the tail finally bump down halfway up the runway and watched as the plane taxied closer, nose up, the headlights set in each wing becoming more and more dazzling.

In the shadows of a mango tree some distance from the runway, Ray could see two figures he knew to be Fidel and Camilio Cienfuegos, staying out of sight of those in the plane, but with a vantage point on what would happen next.

There was smoke drifting over the runway from the beacons. All around him, the men of the Second Front were beginning to cheer and wave their weapons in the air, and Ray heard cries of "Down with Fidel! Death to the communists!" as the plane ground to a halt and the props began to slow. Ray saw the pilot push back the side window of the cockpit and scan the ground around the plane, clearly checking for anything suspicious. Although the props had slowed, Ray noticed they hadn't stopped turning. The fuselage door opened and the first figure appeared in the open doorway.

Almost at the same moment, someone with a film camera broke loose from the corralled press corps, presumably to get a better angle. The others, sensing the story might go to he who dares, followed suit and in the confusion, camera lights were flicked on. A moment later, a pistol was thrust out of the cockpit window and shots were fired. Ray backed away to the cover of the electricity bunker next to Jamie and a young man in uniform crouching there for cover. The guy was clearly scared out of his wits. He was hugging his rifle and hunkered down low behind the bunker.

The Second Front men returned fire on the cockpit and the figures they could see around the doorway to the plane. Confusion reigned. Stray bullets flew this way and that.

There were shouts to surrender—though who was shouting to who was unclear. Besides, any sense was drowned out by the revving of the airplane engines as the pilot tried to turn the nose. The side door of the plane was still wide open, stairs lolling out and crumpling as they snagged the ground.

Ray looked frantically around to get his bearings. He could see at least one body lying on the grass lit by the planes own headlights. Another couple of men were also on the ground, but still moving, presumably wounded. The backwash from the plane's props was forcing others back to the cover of the tree line. Bizarrely, some of those who had emerged from the plane were being marched toward the nissen hut under guard, apparently unconcerned about the bullets flying around, like a vignette from another scene altogether.

Ray had almost forgotten about the young man beside him who chose that moment to aim his rifle in the direction of the airplane, resting the stock on the bunker top. There was no time even for the young man to pull back on the rifle's bolt and chamber a round before he fell backwards bottom first to the ground, his head and shoulders following on with a thud you couldn't hear, but you could feel.

He lay a couple of feet from Ray. His body was twitching and his eyes were open as Ray crawled towards the boy's head. There was no entry wound to be seen and at first, no blood. The young man's eyes appeared to be focused on the black sky, but as Ray came into his sight line, he turned his head. His lips were pursed together. Ray tried to cradle his head, stupidly nervous and unsure as to exactly what he ought to be doing. He slipped his hand under the young man's neck. It was then he felt the sticky wetness soaking into the ground beneath. The young man opened his lips slightly as if about to speak and Ray saw the mass of broken teeth where the bullet had hit.

Suddenly, Ray turned on his heel and began striding towards the nissen hut.

"Ray!" Jamie called after him. But if he heard, he didn't stop. A ragged victory chant was coming from the crowded hut. A group was gathered outside craning to get a view of the captive counter-revolutionaries. They didn't see Ray coming until he began pushing his way through, trying desperately to get to those in the hut. There was no way he'd ever make it. He stopped trying. He looked at the blood on his hands. Even if the rebels were not in the way, he was suddenly drained and exhausted. The only thing holding him upright was the crowd around him.

54

He had tried to put his personal horror following events at the airport to one side, but the television show, broadcast on August 14, just days after the capture of the conspirators, was even more strangely artificial and sinister. Ray, like the rest of the nation, including no doubt the staff of the American Embassy and the Dominicans, had tuned in to see the program.

What they all saw was Morgan and Menoyo sitting cross-legged on the studio floor, looking pleased as punch with what they'd done, and Castro bounding around accusing the conspirators and cutting across them if they had the temerity to respond. At one point Castro had his arm around Morgan and was telling the audience how the American had fooled Trujillo. He even pointed out the gold-plated Colt, given to Morgan by the Generalísimo for his troubles. The 'show' lasted for nearly three hours, and at the end, Castro said he'd personally authorized the payment of one hundred thousand dollars to Morgan and Menoyo for their parts in foiling the plot.

Castro was very publicly 'paying them off,' in effect, casting Morgan, Menoyo and the whole Second Front as mercenaries, and in the process—at least to Ray's mind—putting an end to Menoyo's political ambitions. As far as he could see, *Il Maximo* knew just what he was doing.

But it was Amelia who would confirm his worst fears. He met her at the Bodeguita, having finally given up trying to write the story.

"It's not just the so-called conspirators," she said, "they're arresting everyone. Anyone who's shown the slightest sign of opposing the regime. Anyone who even hints the communists are undesirable. It's a full-scale purge, and all on the back of Mr. Morgan's little ruse."

"What do you know?" said Ray.

"It's unofficial, but the figure I hear is four thousand arrests. In three days, Ray. Three days. Right now, there's over a hundred people being held in the movie theatre at Camp Libertad. Then there's the air force. Not so much decimated as decapitated. Half the officers are behind bars. You see what I mean? Someone's cleaning house. The question is, who and why?"

"That's two questions," said Ray, sullenly.

"Hey, give me a break. While you're out playing cowboys and Indians with the boy wonder, I'm doing your job for you here. My glass is empty, by the way."

Ray signaled for two more to the bartender.

"So," said Amelia, lighting her cigar and puffing hard to get it going, "the why is pretty clear. You only need an opposition if you're planning on free elections. How about the who?"

"The communists," said Ray, his tone flat, like a schoolboy stating the obvious, "or Fidel."

Amelia blew a cloud of thick smoke skyward and leaned across the table closer to Ray.

"And the difference is?"

*

Ray arrived late for the Second Front's press conference, hosted at Menoyo's newly opened club bar. The place was transformed, and not just by the efforts to redecorate.

For a start, many of the assembled had donned homemade newspaper versions of Trujillo's famous bicorn hat. For another, the drinks were flowing freely and there was a distinct party atmosphere. Morgan was holding court from a hastily erected platform at one end of the bar, with reporters and comrades from the Second Front seated at tables and chairs as if for a cabaret. They weren't disappointed.

Morgan was struggling to control a pet Guenon monkey with objections to wearing his or her own miniature version of the bicorn. The animal was a gift from the guy who ran the pet shop where Morgan bought his aquaria supplies. He should have said no. Now, he wished he had. The monkey was screeching, obviously freaked by the dark, smoky environment of the bar.

"Chapita!" Morgan said. He was struggling to keep a hold of the animal. "*Por favor, ¡calmate, calmate!*"

Morgan turned to the crowd. "I don't think Chapita here likes the hat. The guy in the store told me he was good as gold. Seems I was misinformed."

Morgan was playing the crowd, and he was good at it, thought Ray, even better than he used to be. Maybe a little too good.

Menoyo shouted in order to be heard over the din.

"As I was saying, William here took Trujillo's money and liberated it. The whole lot, and the check presented to us by Fidel tonight, is going to the Agrarian Reform Program!"

A whoop of joy and applause came from the crowd. Even the press guys joined in. A couple of hands went up to ask questions, including Ray's.

"Mr. Halliwell!" said Menoyo. "Welcome! You have a question?"

"That's right, Eloy," Ray shouted back. "I'd like to ask about the arrests!"

Not everyone heard the question, but some did. Those close to Ray turned to look at him and grew quiet. It wasn't clear if Menoyo had heard him.

"There are reports of up to four thousand arrests since the conspiracy broke. Can you tell us, were there four thousand people involved?"

The whole room was catching on. The change in atmosphere was eerie.

Morgan handed the monkey over to Carreras on his left and took the microphone.

"Hey, Ray."

"Bill. I was just asking—"

"Yeah, I heard you. We don't know the exact numbers, Ray."

"No? You think four thousand is accurate?"

"I've not heard that figure. I think you'll find that's not even close to true. Next question?"

"I have another," said Ray.

"Mind if I give someone else a chance here, Ray? Yeah, you."

The event broke up soon after. Morgan made a beeline for Ray at the bar, just as Ray knew he would.

"So, what was that all about?"

"That's what I heard."

"It's bullshit."

"I hope so, Bill, I really do."

"Don't you see what we've achieved here? National television. Eloy up there next to Fidel. The Second Front back in the news. A grateful nation and a very grateful leader."

"Yeah, I saw the check."

"It's all going to the farms, you know that."

"Yeah, but the people don't. Listen, Bill, what they saw was you guys getting paid off for services rendered."

Morgan's face darkened. He was trying hard to control himself.

"Coming from anyone else, Ray, I swear—"

"What? You going to knock me down now?"

At that moment, Carreras appeared with Chapita and dumped him on Morgan's shoulder.

"Hey, *gringo*," said Carreras, "take your goddamn animal."

Ray stood up from the bar.

"Hey!" said Morgan. "Wait up."

"I'll see you, Bill. I've got a deadline."

55

Morgan hadn't the heart to get rid of the big fish.

The fact that it had gobbled up the smaller ones in its rush to get at the crackers when they first arrived was—according to Morgan—a simple case of over-enthusiasm. And though the big fish had since snacked on his tank mates from time to time, Morgan had put the cause down to a peckish incontinence, a function of natural instinct rather than malice aforethought, as it might appear to the untrained eye.

His passion for his fish, and indeed a growing fascination with the bullfrog tadpoles he fed to them, had turned to obsession, not least because Morgan had become a prisoner in his own home. He knew there were good reasons why, but still captivity rankled and he was beginning to feel like a fish in a tank himself.

The five hundred thousand dollar price Trujillo had put on his head after the double-cross was certainly one of them. A few days before, shots had been fired at the house from a speeding car on the road beyond, breaking a window and leaving pockmarks in the white stucco around the front door. It was stupid and amateur. Still, Morgan was so angry he wanted to get in one of the jeeps and give chase straight away. But his new bodyguards talked him out of it. Instead, he took out his frustration by digging at the stucco with a knife until he managed to retrieve a flattened thirty-eight caliber round. Later, he studied the formless lump of lead under a magnifying glass for any clues as to who might have been behind the shooting. The shell was of course mute and meaningless, just as he'd known it would be.

Trujillo's offer of a bounty had led directly to Fidel's offer of bodyguards, with the consolation that if Morgan couldn't get at his assassins, their chances of reaching him were slim. Fidel had even gone so far as to personally insist on allocating eleven trusted men of his own to patrol the immediate Miramar streets, guarding all access routes to the house itself. Eleven men, many who'd seen action in the Sierra, in addition to Ramirito, Redondo and the other Second Front guys who were still staying with them on a regular basis. If the house sometimes felt like a jail, it was also a fortress.

In practice, putting safety first meant virtual house arrest was the only option. Not least because whenever Morgan did appear in public, crowds desperate to get close to their hero surrounded him, making the job of guarding his personal safety nigh on impossible. With the TV exposure, *el Americano* was now the biggest celebrity on the island, at least after Fidel and his inner circle.

Not that the idea of a hit man frightened him. Quite the reverse. Morgan was itching for the chance to take the guy on, *mano a mano*, if only he knew who exactly was hoping to collect. But from all the reports, there was a queue of potential candidates, all of them faceless men, save for one who'd been arrested as he landed on the Cuban coast, having taken a boat from Miami with a sniper's rifle in his luggage. G2, the Cuban intelligence service, would be asking him some leading questions right about now, thought Morgan. He swept his hand-net to catch a small Angel fish.

But there was another, far more positive reason for Morgan's renewed fascination with aquatic life. The Ministry of Agriculture had finally approved his proposal for fish farms and frog farms in Las Villas. Buoyed by the news, he'd bought more fish tanks and used one to isolate the big fish. He put only a little gravel in the bottom of the tank, so he could observe the big fish whenever he wanted. He bought another tank to keep the tadpoles. He fed the tadpoles to the fish, and dried food to the new breeds he'd bought at the aquaria store near the harbor. He'd bought books and devoured their contents, remembering much of what he'd learned as a kid. He spent hours studying the fish in his tanks and comparing their markings and behavior with the official accounts. He separated out the young and learned all he could about breeding.

He was grateful to have a hobby he loved so much and which helped the long hours confined to the house pass more quickly. The fish and the frogs also helped to keep him calm under other pressures. He'd read Ray's piece for the *Chicago Sun-Times* and he was angry. That was the reason he'd left a couple of messages asking Ray to come over. When he'd got no response, he decided to send a car—or rather a jeep—with Redondo and a couple of the bodyguards to track Ray down and persuade him they needed to talk.

Morgan netted five or six tadpoles, tapped the net on the wall of the tank and watched them squirm. Chapita kept reaching forward as if to help, but her only real interest was in whether the little creatures might be edible or fun to play with. The monkey was grabbing at his pants, chattering in the high-pitched *'oo-oo-ee'* that meant she wanted something; in this case to sit on Morgan's shoulder, her favorite vantage point on the world.

He lifted the lid on the newest fish tank of all—the one he'd bought via mail order, along with brackish water species, mostly dull browns and greens like their environment, and a powerful aerator that alone had cost twenty-five bucks—and gently lowered the net into the murky water. He watched the squirming creatures swim free. Morgan was still watching as the doorbell rang and the first of the tadpoles became lunch for an adolescent Guppy.

Naturally, Morgan had been preparing for a fight with Ray, but in his mind, it was a fight he would start and finish. As things turned out, it was Ray who was first out of his corner, and Morgan could hear him shouting in the hallway as he went out to meet him.

"What the hell is this? Get your hand off my frigging chest, you goon!"

Ray was being frisked by two of the bodyguards on door duty, one of them holding him back against the wall. The other ran his hands down each leg and patted down Ray's torso, with Redondo looking on bemused.

"Let him go," said Morgan. "Mr. Halliwell doesn't carry concealed weapons, isn't that right, Ray?"

The bodyguards stood back.

Morgan turned away and put a reluctant Chapita down on the floor. He said over his shoulder, "Come on in."

Ray glared at the men in uniform around him and followed Morgan into the living room, sidestepping the monkey who clearly felt Ray might provide an alternative perch, and was clamoring to be lifted.

"And I'm not happy with you either, Bill," said Ray. He pushed Chapita away. "And you," he said to the monkey, "keep away from me, goddamn it!"

Morgan was at the fish tank again, his back to Ray.

"So," Ray said, "what the hell is this? Sending a jeepload of your boys to pick me up, whether I want to come or not? Maybe you've been spending too much time with Bartone. We're supposed to be friends, Bill."

"I thought so too," said Morgan. "Then I read your article."

"Come on, how well do you know me? I write as I find, you know that. It's my job."

"You made me sound like an asshole."

"I did nothing of the kind."

"A patsy, Ray," said Morgan, "some kind of dumb hick without a clue. I gave you ringside."

"Give me a break, Bill. The world and his brother had ringside, courtesy of Fidel and his insatiable appetite for publicity. And my God, they swallowed it whole. Why in God's name worry about what I write? You're the man, Bill, the big hero, savior of the revolution. All I did was point out the repercussions. Four thousand arrests, Bill. Innocent men and women, anti-communists, legitimate opposition, all caught up in the same net."

"That was never the plan."

"I know that! And I'm not blaming you personally, I'm saying there's ruthless elements in this regime willing to use any excuse, any pretext—"

Morgan swung around to Ray, his eyes fierce and blazing with anger.

"You got it wrong, Ray," he said.

"You always seem to be telling me that, Bill. I think I'm right as it happens."

"I thought you understood the island! You saw things before the revolution. You know the sacrifices that were made. Now you write just like any other goddamn McCarthyite bullshit reporter, shouting 'Reds! Reds!' from the rooftops."

"Not so," said Ray, quietly but firmly.

"You want Batista back? The bad ol' days, Ray? Politicians on the take calling the shots?"

"Don't lecture me, Bill."

"Seems to me you're the one giving the lectures, Ray, without a goddamn idea of what you're talking about."

"That's your opinion! Wake-up time is here."

"Goddamn right that's my opinion! Whose side are you on? Does it even matter to you? Or is it all just a chance to pass judgment and walk away without a scratch?"

"Stop it!" said María. "Stop it, both of you!"

She was leaning on the back of a sofa near the door to the hallway and holding her distended tummy with her other hand.

"You're like children!" she said.

Morgan was still angry. Angrier somehow now María was a witness.

"Time to go, Ray. You're just an asshole tourist here. Get yourself back to Chicago where you belong."

"My plane leaves this afternoon."

"Stop! Stop! Stop!!"

María was shouting. Then she coughed, and coughed again. She was suddenly pale, her eyes unfocused and glassy.

"María," Morgan said. "What is it? What's wrong?"

56

"Tammy was born on August 29, 1959," María said, moving the microphone a little closer to her mouth, just as Senator Hawkes had asked her to do. "It should have been the beginning of a happy time for us, for William and me, and the new baby."

Senator Wallace interrupted. "I'm sorry," she said, "but again, I fail to see the relevance of this to the matter in hand. Senator, I think we're straying yet again."

María was feeling Ray's absence from the committee room keenly. She had only the vaguest idea what he and Everett were hoping to get from John Dempsey, and in the face of Senator Wallace's irritation, she suddenly felt very alone.

"Continue," said Senator Hawkes.

Senator Wallace leaned forward to speak. "I must say—"

"Continue, please, Mrs. Jensen."

Wallace, having been publicly put in her place by her junior, a man she had been placed on the committee to monitor and if necessary control, was clearly seething at the implied rebuke. She threw her pen down in a petulant display of frustration and sat back in her chair, arms tightly folded.

Hawkes ignored her. Her attempts to dictate the proceedings had begun to annoy him on day one, and he'd been looking for an opportunity to stamp his authority. María looked from one senator to another. She was worried the very visible rift was somehow her fault and she tried to think carefully about what she should say next.

"It was the next day we heard that William had been expatriated."

"And how did the news come to you, Mrs. Jensen?" asked Hawkes.

"A letter. But before that, there was something in the newspapers. An interview with a man called Francis Walter. He was a member of the House of Representatives."

Everett Capaldi leaned forward to the microphone and María gave way to him.

"Francis Walter was a close associate of Edgar J. Hoover, and for the record, he was chairman of both the House Committee on Immigration and Naturalization and the House Un-American Activities Committee."

"Thank you, Counsel," said Senator Hawkes. "Go on, please, Mrs. Jensen."

"After that," said María, "the phone never stopped ringing. There were reporters at the door and in the street outside. I remember because it was the day after I had come home from the hospital with Tammy. Outside the hospital, crowds of people had gathered to wish us well and just to see William with the baby. As we drove home together, children were running alongside the car, mothers waving from the windows of their houses and calling my name, too. The very next day, we got the news. William was devastated. He tried not to show it, but I'd never seen him like that before. I thought it would pass in time, but I'm not sure it ever did, not really. Not until the end."

"Mrs. Jensen," said Senator Wallace, "is it not the case that your husband made a statement via a Cuban broadcast in which he specifically renounced his American citizenship?"

"Yes, Senator," said María, "but only because he was so angry and only because he knew the decision would stand, no matter what."

"Whatever about that, Mr. Morgan made such a statement, isn't that right?"

"Yes. He did."

Wallace turned to Hawkes.

"Well, it seems to me, here endeth the lesson, Senator. In fact, I fail to see sustainable grounds for continuing with this hearing at all. As I said before the proceedings began,

Morgan willfully repudiated his American citizenship with a public broadcast."

Capaldi saw his chance and took it instantly.

"Senator, with all due respect, the purpose of this committee is to establish the legitimacy of the United States action against one of its own citizens and the basis on which that decision was taken. Morgan's response is after the fact. I'd like to read you—"

"My remarks were addressed to the chair, Counsel, not you."

"Nevertheless, with Senator Hawkes' permission, I'd like to quote from a recently declassified FBI memorandum of a State Department meeting called to review Morgan's case—"

"Counsel, I for one have heard quite—" Senator Wallace said, trying to silence the lawyer. But Capaldi would not be cowed. He stood up from the desk and at the same time raised his own voice to drown out Senator Wallace.

"I quote, 'The crux of this analysis is that it does not clearly delineate where initiative lies for ruling *on* or *starting* expatriation,' end quote. Senator Hawkes, what this means is there was no legal basis for Morgan's expatriation. It was quite simply a vindictive act of revenge by individuals and whole agencies within the US government—"

"Unfounded! Unsupported and irrelevant!" Wallace cut across him, her voice several decibels higher. "You should know better, Counsel. In all conscience, I must object!"

"Enough!" said Hawkes. "That's quite enough. The dignity of this committee is under attack, and it is my role to defend it and to govern these proceedings in an appropriate manner. Counsel, you will hold your evidence until I, as the chair of this committee, ask for it. Do you understand?"

"Yes, Senator," said Everett Capaldi.

"And, Senator Wallace," said Hawkes, turning to look her in the eye, "I am afraid I have to ask you to consider your position on this committee."

Senator Wallace was stunned. She looked at Hawkes as if she hadn't heard the words at all.

Nobody moved a muscle. Nobody spoke a word.

Senator Wallace gathered her papers. She pushed back her chair, stood up and then, addressing everyone present, though no one in particular, she said, "I will be making a formal complaint to the House Oversight Committee and demanding that any decisions taken here be deemed null and void."

And with that, she left the room through the committee door.

In the awkward silence that followed Senator Wallace's departure—a silence that seemed to go on interminably—it was clear even Hawkes had been badly shaken by the turn of events. He was whispering to Chad Dyer, and presumably getting some reassurance in return that Wallace's threat was unlikely to derail the committee's findings, even if it caused a mountain of trouble for Hawkes personally. Whilst the two men were conferring, the door opened and Ray bowled in, a beaming smile on his face and waving what appeared to be a CD or DVD case in one hand.

Ten steps into the room, Ray stopped, suddenly aware of an atmosphere pregnant with tension. It didn't take him long to notice Senator Wallace's empty seat, but he was at a loss to understand the meaning, and at something of a loss as to what to do next. It was a relief when Capaldi waved him over to the witness table.

"Don't ask," said Capaldi.

Ray took his seat.

"You okay?" Ray whispered to María.

She nodded. Ray turned to Capaldi.

"I've got it," he said. "It's all there. I think—"

Capaldi raised a hand to silence Ray. "Wait."

All eyes were on Hawkes and Dyer, still deep in subdued conversation. The seconds ticked by, but nobody else said a word. Even the stenographer looked embarrassed, shifting uncomfortably in her chair. Finally, they could see Hawkes nodding agreement with whatever Dyer was telling him and Hawkes turned back to the microphone.

"That was unfortunate to say the least. Let me be absolutely clear. Nothing like the events of the past few minutes will occur again, or I will personally see to it that this committee is dissolved instantly. I will also make it my mission to block any further public hearings on this issue. Do I make myself clear?"

"Yes, Senator," said Capaldi quickly, "perfectly clear. Thank you."

"No more theatrics, Counsel. Do we understand each other?"

"Completely, Senator, my apologies. It won't happen again."

"You now require a unanimous verdict from this committee. Do you understand the implications?"

"Yes, sir, I do."

"Proceed," said Hawkes curtly. "Let the record show Senator Wallace has absented herself from these proceedings as a matter of conscience. The committee also notes the renewed presence of Mr. Halliwell. Counsel?"

"Thank you, Senator. We'd like to present some video evidence."

PART FIVE

57

The audiovisual technician who'd set up the screen in the committee room turned off the lights and the rough title Phil had put at the front end of the interview was suddenly legible. It read simply, 'Mr. John Dempsey, former Press Attaché to the United States Embassy in Havana, 1955–1962. Recorded at Arlington Memorial Seniors Residence on December 18, 2007.' There was no mention in the titles that Phil had spent hours cutting down the long interview on Dempsey's time in Cuba to just ten minutes of footage relevant to Morgan.

A moment later, Dempsey was visible, framed against the picture window of the home. He seemed to be signing some kind of form with a woman's help. The woman then held up a vanity mirror and Dempsey checked his appearance.

"Am I okay?" Dempsey said.

Her muffled reply was inaudible, but Ray's disembodied voice could be heard clearly.

"That's great, John. Thank you. Maybe we can start by outlining your role at the Embassy."

"My official job was press attaché," said Dempsey, his voice clear and strong despite his years. "In practice, I reported directly to the CIA head in the Embassy or to the ambassador himself. I was a CIA man. My unofficial job, especially after the summer of 1959, was what I would call psychological warfare."

Ray was nodding on camera in the next shot, presumably covering a cut in the material. Then the camera picked up Dempsey again to hear the next question.

"What was your relationship with William Morgan?"

"Relationship overstates the case. Morgan was a wild card and our paths occasionally crossed. More so as time went by."

"Did Morgan at any time work for the United States government? I'm thinking of the CIA in particular."

"No, never. Never directly, anyhow."

"You're saying he did indirectly?"

"I'm saying he was, on rare occasions, useful to our interests, often without knowing it. For example, the propaganda we distributed in the Escambray. Right around that time I was putting together a TV show, a drama set in Cuba that would show the communists in their true light. It never got off the ground. Ambassador Bonsal and the State Department were too nervous. Getting the message out there via comic books was some compensation. That was his idea and we backed it."

"But more than that?"

"No. Like I said, Morgan was a wild card. He could have been very useful to us, but as an asset he was totally unreliable. When he first went to the mountains to join the Second Front of the Escambray, we considered cultivating him, but it was quickly apparent the guy was a loose cannon."

"Meaning?"

"Meaning a chequered background. Meaning his loyalty to his country took second place to his loyalty to his comrades. Morgan was a high-risk investment, as he proved with the Trujillo conspiracy."

"You met with him around that time?"

"I did. And regretted it. We very nearly got sucked in and I personally took plenty of flak. Ambassador Bonsal hauled me into the penthouse and showed me the FBI report on Morgan's time in Miami."

"So Ambassador Bonsal took the threat seriously?"

"Very seriously indeed. In fact, he rang the Cuban foreign secretary, Raúl Roa García, and told him Morgan's intentions included a possible attempt on Castro's life. As far as Bonsal was concerned, Morgan was a threat not just to Castro, but to US–Cuban relations in general. He had a point. An American assassin? How would that look? But the Trujillo thing finally proved Morgan was not one of us and never would be. From then on, all we did was monitor."

"How?"

"Army Intelligence had an asset in place within Morgan's circle."

"Gerry Hemming?"

"Yes, I believe so."

"What about Lee Evans?"

"No idea. Not one of ours."

Dempsey shifted uncomfortably in his seat and reached for a glass of water. He was no longer looking at Ray.

"Can you say how you first came to be aware of the expatriation of William Morgan?" came the off-camera question.

"A memo," said Dempsey crisply. "An FBI memo requesting we expedite action against Morgan and, if possible, recover his passport."

"And did you?"

"No. At least not immediately. Dan Braddock, Chargé d'Affaires at the time, argued against on the grounds that any such move would be seen as punitive and even provocative given Morgan's popularity on the island, and especially given his high profile after the conspiracy. Dan went back to State and the FBI and told them so. They went ahead anyway."

"Despite the Embassy's objections?"

"There was no in-principle objection. We just didn't want to go public at that time. All Dan did was point up the potential fallout."

"Can you elaborate?"

"Morgan was a celebrity. A national hero. Being seen to attack him would just rebound; that was Dan's view, and I agreed. We take away the guy's citizenship and it looks like we're pissed, right? Which in turn means we had an interest in the success of the conspiracy, which in turn means Fidel's accusations of imperialist aggression gain substance. Obvious, really. But as I say, State and the FBI weren't listening."

"Did you have an interest in the conspiracy?"

"Not directly, no."

"Indirectly?"

"No. It was Trujillo's idea. With a little help from his friends."

"Who were his friends?"

"Not us. Not the agency."

"FBI?"

"Yes."

There was another pause. This time Dempsey kept his guard up and waited.

"Why do you think," said Ray, this time on camera, "your advice was ignored?"

"Why? Because State and FBI had other priorities."

"Like what?"

"Like removing an element from the mix that was simply stirring up the waters and making everything muddy."

"That element being Morgan?"

"Exactly."

"How would expatriation remove Morgan from the mix, as you put it?"

"There were two goals to the action. The first was to send a clear signal to American citizens, not just in Cuba but in a variety of Latin American countries and elsewhere, that involving themselves in 'local politics' was not a good idea and would carry consequences. Joining revolutions of the left wing variety was especially to be discouraged. Morgan's activities had hit the headlines in the US and could only shake things up at home too, with young men anxious to make a name for themselves following in his footsteps. This was the late fifties and early sixties—youthful rebellion was fine for the movies, but we didn't want it on the college campus. We needed to keep the lines between American and un-American activities absolutely clear. Morgan was over the line. The conspiracy put the spotlight right on him, lit him up like a Christmas tree."

"That's the second reason you mentioned? The expatriation was intended to put out the lights, so to speak?"

"I wouldn't put it that way."

"How would you put it?"

Dempsey took a deep breath.

"Hoover knew that without the protection and potential for retribution implied in being a United States citizen, somebody, sooner or later, would try to collect Trujillo's reward. Of course, he knew. He even encouraged some freelance interest in the contract stateside. He certainly did nothing to put obstacles in the way. That's not for broadcast on TV, okay?"

"Okay. No broadcast. But this was about eliminating Morgan? Assassination?"

"Hoover didn't pull the trigger."

"But he knew someone would? In effect, it was open season on Morgan," said Ray.

Dempsey hesitated, but only for a second.

"Expatriation was a neat way of dealing with the problem by proxy, requiring only a certain patience. The right event, or series of events, you might say. But the agency was not in control of the show. Nor was Hoover. When it happened, how it happened and who got to him first was no longer the direct concern of the United States government or its agencies. It was all about how the cards fell."

As the lights were flicked back on in the committee room, the image of John Dempsey on the screen faded to a ghostly watermark of washed-out pastels.

The sudden intrusion of stark neon brightness made the room feel clinical and dead, not least because for some time nobody spoke and only the soft tapping of the stenographer finishing her transcription filled the void.

58

Mario Marin was only a boy—just nineteen. But he hero-worshipped Morgan and would do anything for the man who was now one of the most famous figures in all Cuba; a man who had rescued him from a poor, dull existence helping his father farm coffee in the Escambray and turned him into a trusted aide and personal driver.

The tiny strip farm Mario and his father worked happened to be on the boundary of the biggest of the new fish farm sites. There'd been a little disruption with the bulldozers coming and going, not much, but enough that Morgan got to know both father and son in talking to them about compensation of some kind. It was Mario's father who asked quietly, not for money, but for Mario to be given a chance to escape the drudgery of scraping a living from the hard land. Morgan had told him things would get better for the farmers now, but Mario's father had smiled an old and distant smile and said only, "Perhaps so."

Mario was waiting outside the house for him with Camilio, who would ride shotgun. Camilio was one of Fidel's allotted bodyguards. A few years older than Mario, he had taken the younger man under his wing over the months they'd been working together. The two of them seemed to get along well, which had the advantage of making them a good team.

The meeting would officially dissolve the Second Front of the Escambray and Morgan was not looking forward to the event. But it could no longer be put off. There had been pressure from Castro himself and there was no reason for the Second Front to have any kind of independent identity in the new Cuba. Such a thing would be seen as a direct challenge to the regime and everyone, from Menoyo down, recognized that the time had come. Although the meeting was merely a formality, nevertheless it was a sad affair for all, just as it was for Morgan. Something would be lost forever.

When they arrived outside the club half an hour later, Mario and Camilio waited with the jeep. In the upstairs bar, the atmosphere was solemn, like a wake, because everyone knew that's exactly what it was. Over the next ten minutes, the last of the comrades arrived, all except Edel Montiel. When Menoyo asked about him, it was Jesús Carreras who spoke.

"Edel has gone to the Escambray," he said. He didn't elaborate.

"But he knew about the meeting?" said Menoyo.

"Yes."

"Then why is he not here?"

Menoyo knew the answer, as did everyone else in the room, but Carreras told them anyway.

"Because he says the time for talking is over. Edel has gone to prepare for the fight to come."

It was late when Morgan got back to the Miramar house. Mario and Camilio dropped him at the door where two more of the bodyguards detailed by Fidel were standing sentry.

"All quiet?" Morgan said in Spanish to the guards. He was watching the tail lights of the jeep vanish, deep in thought.

"*Si, boss, tranquilos,*" said the taller of the two men.

They had been with Morgan for several weeks, but with so much on his mind, he was struggling to remember their names.

"Santiago?"

"*Si,*" said the tall man.

"And—don't tell me; Alvaro?"

"*Adelmo, Señor Morgan,*" said the other. What did it matter if he got a name wrong? It didn't. So why worry he thought to himself. And yet he did worry. Or maybe he was just tired.

"Damn. Okay. *Buenas noches, mis amigos, y gracias,*" said Morgan. He opened the door and went inside the quiet house.

"*Buenas noches, comandante.*"

Closing the door, he looked up the grand staircase toward the bedroom where María and Tammy were no doubt sleeping, and felt a desperate desire to hold them both close.

María was sleeping peacefully on her side with just a sheet covering her. The fan was spinning above her. Tammy was silent, but when Morgan looked into her cot, her big eyes were wide open and staring straight back at him as if she'd been waiting for his return. Her tiny hands were clenched and held to either side of her head, and as Morgan gave her his index finger to cling to, Tammy began to gurgle and wriggle with excitement.

Concerned to leave María asleep, Morgan picked Tammy from the cot and wrapped the cotton sheet around her like a shawl. He held her sitting in the crook of his arm, one hand pressed lightly against her chest to keep her steady. He walked her out of the bedroom and down the stairs toward the living room.

He didn't put the main lights on, but flicked the two switches controlling the lights in the big wall aquarium and the smaller tanks on stands to either side. He went to the refrigerator to look for the bottle Rosa or María would have prepared for the nighttime feed. He put a pan of water on the stove and, still holding Tammy, walked back to the fish tanks to wait for the water to heat.

The wooden barstool he'd commandeered months before to feed the fish and watch them close up was between the tanks as always. Morgan perched there, turning Tammy for a better view of the purple and green lights of the tanks, lurid and luminous in the darkened room.

"So," Morgan said quietly to his daughter, "let's see who's awake, shall we?"

Tammy was making little noises, sitting on Morgan's lap apparently transfixed by the lights in front of her.

"There we go," said Morgan. "Now that little fella, he's called a Kissing Gourami. See his lips, like he's ready for a big kiss? That's how he fights the other fish, using his mouth. And this guy. He's a Rainbow. See the colors, reds and greens and orange and purple. He's a nice guy, unlike my little terror here, the Convict fish. See the stripes? Sometimes he's called a Zebra fish. He's small but he's mean, you've got to keep an eye on him—"

Morgan didn't hear María on the stairs. Nor did he notice her come into the room until she was almost upon him.

"Hey," she said. She stood behind him and put her hands on his shoulders.

"Hey, chica," said Morgan. "I wanted you to sleep. I put some water on to heat the bottle."

"Okay, I'll see to it."

"Go back to bed. Baby and I are just checking out the tanks. We'll get to it."

María caught a sharp tone right at the end of Morgan's words that would never normally be there. She almost didn't want to know.

"Should I ask how it went?" she said.

"Edel didn't come."

"Edel? Why not?"

59

A week after the meeting, Morgan was still brooding on the outcome. So many thoughts and feelings were revolving around in his head that he'd hardly spoken to Hemming or Mario in the course of the three-hour drive to the provincial city of Trinidad, en route to the mountains of the Escambray to check progress on the farm sites.

The public notice of the dissolution of the Second Front had been reported in all the newspapers, and no one would notice Edel's sudden departure. But in going like that, without a word, he'd been rash and stupid, thought Morgan, and might well have endangered his comrades by association.

Back in the Escambray, they'd been close. Morgan commanded the Tigers but Edel was his *capitán*, his right-hand man, his eyes and ears, and sometimes, when there were tough decisions to make, his conscience.

But the Trujillo thing had changed all that. The change was subtle at first. Edel had been upset because he felt 'excluded,' as he saw it, from his comandante's plans. Morgan went so far as to mention the Bartone connection— relying on Edel as a trusted friend to tell no one—to try to explain why he had to act alone.

They'd argued and Morgan too had got angry. Lately though, even he was beginning to wonder if there was some sense to Edel's words. Perhaps he'd overplayed his hand, tried too hard to show Fidel who his real friends were. The thought was eating at him.

But what was done was done and Edel should have come to him first. Whatever their differences. That was the chain of command. That would have been the act of a friend.

They were in the blue Oldsmobile, cruising into the city with the top down. People called out and waved as they always did, but Morgan paid much less attention to them than usual. His ebullience, his ready smile and easy laugh, were conspicuous by their absence. Being so preoccupied, he didn't see the police car parked awkwardly on the sidewalk until they were almost upon it. Nor did he notice the policeman with his arm raised to flag them down until Mario said, "Boss? Up ahead."

The officer was pointing to a parking spot behind the police car, instructing Mario to pull over.

"Do what he says," said Morgan. He turned to Hemming and Castro, just a glance, but they knew what he meant: I'll handle this, but be ready anyway.

Mario pulled over and the policeman walked over to Morgan's side of the car. He had a broad grin on his face.

"Comandante!" he said. "Welcome to Trinidad."

It took a moment for Morgan to recognize Menoyo's former secretary and translator in the Escambray.

"*Hija de puta!*" said Morgan. "Miguel! What in God's name are you doing dressed up like that?"

"Earning a living, *americano*, just like you."

There was a coffee stand near the parking spot. The tin roof and block walls, painted bright yellow, had in front a wooden plank serving as a rough bar where customers could lean or put their coffees down. Empty paper cups and napkins from pastry snacks littered the sidewalk.

Mario waited with the car. Hemming and Camilio went along with Morgan and Miguel, still toting their Thompsons but slung casually over the shoulder. They stood apart from Morgan to give him a chance to talk with his friend. Miguel seemed nervous and keen not to be overheard.

"So," said Miguel, "how goes it?"

"Okay, okay," said Morgan. "You know I'm a father too, yes?"

"*Sí, sí*, congratulations, my friend. It's a wonderful thing."

Miguel asked about the baby and María, and they caught up on the gossip about old friends. He kept his voice low as he said, "Some of the boys are back in the mountains, you know?"

"Yeah," said Morgan, "yeah, I know."

"Sinesio Walsh? He was Tigers."

"Sinesio?"

"Near El Nicho," said Miguel, almost in a whisper. "And Plinio Prieto. He's got a radio. He's making broadcasts. Anti-communist."

Morgan offered Miguel a cigarette and noticed a tremble in his friend's hand as he took one.

"What about you?" said Morgan.

Miguel shook his head and blew smoke.

"Me? No. No way. I have a family now, a job, not a great job but a job, you know?"

"Sure."

"My fighting days are over. I don't say everything is right, but I have to look out for my kids now."

There was a silence between them and then Miguel took another look around to make sure what he said next was just between them.

"I was waiting for you today. I knew you were coming to town, driving from Havana."

Morgan was clearly surprised.

"It's okay. I spoke to Gallego. He told me to talk to you and he told me you would come today."

Miguel checked around again before speaking.

"William, I can't get involved, you know that?"

"You said. I understand that, it's no crime."

"But I have a message for you. That's why I'm here. Edel Montiel asks to meet with you."

"Edel? Where is he?"

"In the mountains. But he will come down if you agree. Tomorrow evening. There's a cemetery, south of the city. I can show you."

Morgan said nothing. Hemming was ten yards away but Camilio was just walking back from giving Mario a coffee.

Miguel waited until he passed. He took another drag on his cigarette.

"What shall I tell him, William?"

Gerry Hemming and Camilio were not happy about Morgan going out alone. He told them he was going to see Miguel in his home, but both men argued against the idea and wanted to go along. Morgan said no, and when they saw he was adamant, they had little choice but to give in, whether they liked it or not.

The sun was low when Morgan parked the fisheries jeep outside the honey-colored archway leading to the cemetery. The jeep was a compromise with his bodyguards; less conspicuous than the Oldsmobile, less of a target.

The working day was over, people were already in their homes and no one saw Morgan arrive and walk into the cemetery amongst the eight-foot-high mausoleums and crypts. Cicadas were pulsing a steady rhythm in the humid air and seemed to have fallen into time with each other.

Morgan reached a point where two paths crossed and was about to go on when he heard Edel's voice, low and close by.

"William—"

Edel was half hidden in the gap between two crypts. The two men embraced and held each other by the arms.

"If they find you here you're a dead man, Edel."

"I know."

"Goddamn you. I ought to shoot you myself."

"Maybe, William."

"You should have come to me. You should have talked to me first."

Montiel shook his head and let go of Morgan's arms.

"You weren't listening. None of you were. In the meetings—"

"You should have come to me! Forget the goddamn meetings. Me!"

"So you could talk me out of it?"

"No! Yes! So I could get you to see sense. You can't achieve anything like this; you can't take on the army and the militias alone."

"I'm not alone, William. There are many others."

"Not enough! Not enough. Except to get yourselves hunted down and killed."

"There were twelve in the beginning. You remember?"

"That's different."

"No. No difference, except maybe we know what we are doing now. We know how to fight a mountain war. You were our teacher, remember?"

"That's all past, that whole time. It's another world."

"Yes, now of course, this is a brave *new* world, where men are free to speak their minds. To elect their own leaders, live their lives without fear. To own their own land, decide their own futures."

Morgan shook his head, but said nothing.

"Am I right, William?"

"We're comrades, Edel. Friends. From the old days."

"*El Gordo*," said Montiel with a smile. "You remember? Big fat Yankee, white suit torn and stained from the climb into the Escambray, all puffing and red from the sun. You weren't fat for long, William."

Morgan smiled. "There was nothing to eat."

"There was *jutia*!"

"Rat meat. It's a goddamn rat."

"I had some last night. You don't know what you're missing."

"Oh, yes I do. Believe me, I don't miss the rat meat, or the goddamn berries or mushy rice or any of that. Not even a little."

Morgan turned back to face Montiel. He said the words slowly and deliberately.

"You should have come to me, Edel."

"That's the thing, William," Montiel said. He kicked at the dirt path. He looked Morgan in the eye. "I'm coming to you now."

60

Morgan called Menoyo's father, Carlos, at ten o'clock at night and asked to visit their home in the next hour or so. Carlos had had no hesitation in saying yes, despite the hour, only adding that Morgan should come round to the back of the house and let himself in by the alley door. But as Carlos put the phone down, he knew this visit, without Eloy and so late in the evening, was not a social call.

"Who was that?" Jacinta had called out from the kitchen.

"William," Carlos replied. "He's coming over."

"Now?" said Jacinta, appearing at the door and still drying her hands on a dishcloth. "With Eloy?"

"No."

Carlos was shuffling the dominoes, sweeping them around and around the patio table top with both hands as Morgan pushed open the alley door to the garden.

"William?"

"*Si*, Carlos, it's me," said Morgan. "I'm sorry about the hour."

"It is not yet my bedtime. Sit. You will have some rum?"

Carlos poured another glass for his guest without waiting for a reply from Morgan.

"You know," said Carlos, "I love to play dominoes, but making up a four is not so easy these days, unless I go and play in the cafés, and that means I drink coffee and leave Jacinta alone in the house, so I don't go so much. But you can play with two, did you know that?"

"That's how it's done in the States," said Morgan, lighting a cigarette.

"Okay, so we play. Twenty-eight pieces, seven for you, seven for me, the rest in the bank. Go ahead."

Carlos pulled his seven *fichas* toward him. He put each one on its edge, faces hidden from Morgan, as he spoke.

"You know where the name comes from? Dominoes?"

"No, but I'm guessing you do," said Morgan, grinning. He took his own pieces and laid them out in two short walls, their faces hidden from Carlos.

"The word *Domini* is the name of the masks worn in the Venice Carnival. These masks were white with black spots and they were named in turn from the winter hoods of French priests that were black on the outside and white on the inside. So, already you learn something this evening. Show me your highest double."

Morgan turned over a double four.

"Ha!" said Carlos as he slapped a double five down in the centre of the table. "But Cuba is not a black-and-white world. Everything here is gray, eh, William?"

Morgan put a five and one on the table crossways to the double.

"Yeah, something like that," he said.

Carlos followed on with a five and a six.

"So tell me."

"I have a decision to make, Carlos. But it's a decision that means I have to let people down, no matter what."

"Go on."

"I made María a promise. I told her I was done with fighting. I told her she and the baby would come first and I'd never do anything to put them at risk."

"That sounds like a good promise, especially with another child on the way. You are a father now. It's your turn."

Morgan put a one and a two on the table.

"Two days ago, in Trinidad, I met with Edel Montiel."

"I see," said Carlos, his tone solemn. "And Edel is asking for your help?"

"Yeah."

"Can you help?"

"Yeah. If I choose to, I can. He wanted me to go to the US and try for weapons or financial support, but I said no. There are three weapons caches left over from the Trujillo thing. No one knows about them, but they could be discovered any day."

"I see." Carlos laid a *ficha* of one and six and looked up at Morgan. "Your turn again. Why did you keep these weapons?"

"I don't know, Carlos. I just did."

Morgan studied the line of *fichas* on the table, both ends requiring a *ficha* with one pip, and realized he couldn't go.

"*Yo pasa*," said Morgan.

"Ah ha," said Carlos, "in the traditional blocking game, yes. But we are playing the drawing game. You can pick up another *ficha* when you pass."

Morgan took a tile from those face down on the table, a one and a four, and laid it down.

"Good," said Carlos. "Different rules make for a different outcome, and we should think about this thing with Edel in the same way. Do you believe in what he is doing?"

"I don't know. I want to trust Fidel. But the signs aren't good."

"I have to agree with you," said Carlos. He laid another tile. "And so the choice appears to be to fight or not to fight."

"I guess. Already, as you know, many of our former comrades have gone back to the Escambray."

"And if you fight, you break your promise to María. But if you don't, your loyalty to your friend is in question. A friend whose cause you have sympathy for? Your go."

Morgan picked up again from the bone yard of face-down tiles, but didn't lay down.

"Yeah."

"I see."

Carlos made his play with a double three and reached over for the stub of cigar. Morgan held out his lighter, flipped the lid and sparked the flame into life. Carlos leaned forward and puffed several times to get the damp stub going. Then he sat back in his chair and took a sip of rum.

"You know, when you get older you're supposed to get wiser so young people can come to you for advice. Like now. But the trouble is, age does not necessarily bring wisdom. Aches and pains, yes. Bad teeth, yes. But wisdom? I don't know. Have you talked to Eloy?"

"We talk all the time, you know that, but I wanted to think about the Edel thing before I go to Eloy with it."

"I see," said Carlos, letting a cloud of smoke snake from his nostrils. "Perhaps because Eloy too, believes the time has come to fight?"

"We've talked about it."

"William, I will tell you what I see, but in the end, you must decide for yourself. I am an old man who knows less with every passing year. In my heart, I have hope. In my head, not so much. I believe Castro is a communist, plain and simple. The regime is communist, plain and simple. This may not be a bad thing, but it is not the social democracy we've talked about so often or the social democracy you and Eloy and the others fought for. For the moment, it is hidden, here one minute, gone the next. It is my opinion that the fight for freedom in this country is not yet over. But that does not mean it is your fight. Perhaps another generation should take the burden now. Perhaps you and Eloy have done enough."

"We're the only ones who can pull together a big enough force to fight effectively against army and militias. Edel and the other small groups out there can't do it alone. Sinesio Walsh has his own group, but no more than eight or ten. Plinio Prieto is up there. There's plenty of my boys itching to go and I'm doing nothing but talking them out of it."

"I see," said Carlos, laying his *ficha*, a three–five. He began to tap the last remaining tile on the table, not noisily in the Cuban style, but with a soft, almost inaudible rhythm.

"You know, when we talked about the capitalists and the communists, right and left, this dogma and that dogma, we always talked about a third way, a middle road. Can you see a middle road here?"

"Between letting María down and letting Edel go hang? Not really."

"No man should have to choose between family and friends. They are the same thing, in different ways perhaps, but in the end, the same. This is how we express our deepest values and beliefs. You know, sometimes a decision appears impossible for a very good reason. Because it is. You understand? In such cases, it is right not to decide. Our only duty is to not let others make the decision for us."

"How?"

"You say the weapons might soon be discovered?"

"Where they are, maybe."

"Then get them to a safe place, but keep yourself out of the fighting and wait. Wait and see. This is a way to be prepared for the worst whilst hoping for the best. A way of keeping your promise to María. A way also of supporting Edel and the others. If, and only if, the time is right, you have the means to act. Keep your choices open until you are ready to know the right way, William. But be careful who you trust. Especially an old man like me. *"Vale, mi hijo?"*

Carlos slapped his last *ficha* on the table.

"Domino!"

61

Morgan was knee-deep in water and digging with a shovel like his life depended on it. In the same ditch a line of ten or so others were digging alongside. The humidity was sky-high. The temperature was in the nineties.

The Hanabanilla fish farm—unlike the sites in the Escambray, this one was situated in a swampy lowland area north of Trinidad bordering the huge Lake Hanabanilla — now had almost six hundred workers and several of the larger ponds were already fully stocked. The drainage ditches linking them together served a dual purpose; keeping water levels even and providing a home for the bullfrogs. Already, the noise of their throaty calls filled the air, but with the earth so friable, the only way to keep the water flowing freely was to dig and then dig some more. Whenever Morgan was on site, he led by example.

Single-storey, long wooden huts—the cladding still new and smelling of creosote—were arranged in a line, barrack style, close to the entrance of the complex. Every day, trucks arrived with feed, new equipment, fresh stock or whatever else had been ordered up from the city. The place had the feel of a military camp, and in some ways, that's exactly what it was.

The farms had been Morgan's idea and had become Morgan's personal fiefdom. He may have been an undisciplined maverick as a young man in the US army, but now, in charge of his own business, with a cannery turning out tins of frog's legs for export and a factory drying and stitching the skins to make products like handbags and shoes, he ran things with exemplary military efficiency.

There were many old faces amongst the workers. Comrades from the Second Front played lead roles in the organization. Others, like Menoyo and Fleites, Ramirito and the rest of the guys, were regular visitors. Lee Evans used the farm as a base when scouting for cotton growing sites and Gerry Hemming had special duties now that the threat from Trujillo's bounty hunters was beginning to recede. But the bulk of the workforce had been recruited from local people, farmers and their families for instance, those who could benefit most from regular work and regular pay.

Time magazine had sent a reporter to meet with Morgan on the farm and they'd printed an article referring to Morgan as 'Frogman'. He was happy with that. He was asked about communists and went on record saying there were no communists working the farm as far as he knew, and that was the way it would stay. He said to the reporter, "The reds tried to hold a meeting here and I threw them out. Fidel knows that. So does Raul."

For the first few months, María had come with him on the trips up to the farms, but now she was pregnant again, she stayed home in Havana anxious to avoid the heat and the long journey. The roads were pretty bad all the way, and the last ten miles or so was nothing more than dirt track. In the rains, digging out the big two-and-a-deuce GMC trucks stuck up to their axles got to be a regular chore. Some of the heavier shipments carried a special consignment that only Morgan or Hemming knew about and few others were allowed to handle. The crates were marked 'hazardous waste' and the contents were discreetly transferred to oil drums at the farm, then sealed and buried.

Morgan was holding a bullfrog in each hand. He'd been about to cut into the wet bank of the ditch but just before the blade cut one or other of them in two, he noticed the renegades lurking there. He was checking them for size and any sign of ill health when he heard the bell clangs coming from the compound. Chow time wasn't for another hour so he figured it must be the guys arriving. He handed the frogs over to the foreman and clambered out of the ditch, his boots squelching and filled with muddy water.

They'd eaten well. Morgan had cooked fish on a barbeque made from one of the fifty-gallon drums. Menoyo, Fleites, Artola and Carreras had brought beer. It was almost midnight and the camp was quiet, except for the workshop where the last of the drums were being sealed. There would be no further shipments and it was a relief to know that the job was almost done. Checkpoints en route had become more assiduous and more curious with every passing week, but so far, so good.

Every few seconds, a flash of blue light lit up the dark windows and from their table under the stars, they could hear the crackle and fizz of the welding torch. Night was the allotted time for the work because the camp was deserted with few prying eyes to wonder what was going on. But the mood was serious, even somber as they leaned with their elbows on the table under the stars, pushing beer cans this way and that, smoking cigarettes or cigars. So many meetings in so many different places and times had seen these same faces assembled that there was no need for a formal agenda. They spoke to one another in words that were almost a code. Had someone overheard, there would have been little in the way of solid information to be gleaned. Nevertheless, they kept their voices low.

"Then we are agreed," said Menoyo.

"It's not now," Morgan replied, "but it may be soon."

"I still don't like it," said Carreras. "There is not one thing to say go. It is everything. Why wait?"

"To be sure, to be certain," said Artola, "this is no small thing."

"You think I don't understand that?" Carreras spoke quickly, adding a shrug of the shoulders and opening his palms, Italian style as if to say, *'Come on, it's me you're talking to.'*

"And now?" Fleites yawned and scratched at his chest.

"Everything as usual. The same routines for all of us. Nothing out of the ordinary," said Menoyo.

"Well, my routine is to sleep and that's what I'm going to do," said Artola. He stood and clapped his hands on Carreras' shoulders. "You too, my friend."

As the meeting broke up, Morgan became aware of a figure standing a little way off. He was suspicious until he recognized Mario.

"I'll catch you up," he said to the others as he stood and stretched. "Leave the clearing for the morning."

He signaled Mario to join him as the others went their own ways to the dormitory beds.

"Mario? What is it?"

"I need to talk to you, boss."

"Now? Can't it wait till morning?"

"Maybe now."

The young man looked shy, a little awkward. Something was troubling him.

"Okay," said Morgan. "What's on your mind?"

"I want to fight. I've thought about it. I want to go to the mountains—with Edel."

62

Morgan found Lee Evans lying on a sun lounger by the now empty pool, cleaned out but still awaiting water, a luxury the revolution had yet to prioritize.

"Let's go, Lee," Morgan shouted from the patio doors. He'd been staying with them for a couple of weeks now since coming back from the States where he'd gone to negotiate a cotton seed deal.

Morgan went back inside to take a last sip from his coffee. He was tired and irritable. The new baby, born only six weeks before, had kept both he and María awake, and the Mario thing had put him out of sorts. He'd done his best to talk the boy out of his plan, but it was clear the kid had been harboring the idea for quite a while. Morgan wanted to tell him to bide his time, but he couldn't do that without bringing Mario into the loop and that was a security risk he couldn't take, not without consulting the others and not without putting Mario in danger if anything happened. They'd been close and Mario must have seen or heard something of what was going on, but not the whole story. In the end, Morgan had let the boy go and whilst he admired Mario's conviction, he wondered if he'd made the right decision.

He drained the rest of his coffee. There was still no sign of Evans so Morgan went out again. This time, there was no mistaking his tone.

"Hey! Come on! Shift!"

Evans sat up a little and shaded his eyes to see Morgan.

"I'm sick, boss," he called back.

"What do you mean, sick?"

Evans had been fine the day before, and the day before that. He'd driven in to the INRA every day with Morgan to talk about cotton with some committee or other on the sixteenth floor.

"Come on, last day of the week."

"I got a temperature, boss. Really."

Morgan was increasingly impatient with the young man from Ohio. He'd seemed so keen when he first arrived, but since then he'd dragged his heels over pretty much everything except drinking with the boys and hearing war stories.

"Get your sorry ass into the jeep. I don't have time for this."

Having pried the kid from the lounger—and what Morgan saw as a simple case of bad attitude—the drive to town was businesslike. When they got to the INRA building, they went their separate ways with only a few words, arranging to meet at five for the drive back to Miramar.

People had started to call the INRA, 'the government within the government' because it had so much power over land policy—and so, people's lives. All of which meant Morgan was forced to spend a good deal of time in their offices talking about the frog farms and the whole aquaculture business.

It was three-ten in the afternoon when the first explosion rocked the INRA building. To those inside, especially those on the side of the building facing the harbor, it seemed a miracle the windows remained intact. At three-thirteen, a second, larger explosion thudded into the walls, sending shockwaves through the air that made the INRA people gasp and hold onto the furniture. Two or three windows on Morgan's floor cracked at the corners and one shattered spectacularly just a few feet from where his meeting was taking place.

Everyone rushed to look out over the city, wondering where the blasts had come from. Somewhere near the harbor, a massive plume of dense, black smoke—black like only the smoke of burning gasoline or oil can produce—was bubbling over the skyline like ink in water. In whatever vehicles they could muster, Morgan and others in the INRA building, raced to the harbor to find a scene of terror and devastation awaiting them.

The Le Coubre, a transport ship carrying seventy-six tons of munitions, cases of Czechoslovakian-made rifles and machine guns, hand grenades, ammunition, flame throwers and the highly inflammable liquid used in them, and a huge quantity of napalm—jellied gasoline—was a tangled wreck of twisted metal.

As Morgan arrived at the harbor, the first of the dead and injured were being brought from the ship to the harbor-side wharf and laid on the concrete by dockworkers, fire fighters and ambulance crews. Those that could still benefit were receiving emergency medical treatment where they lay; others were being carried to the overcrowded ambulances. All around, the thick black smoke from the still burning ship made seeing anything clearly—even breathing—extremely difficult.

Morgan, along with many others, did what he could to help the injured. The ferocity of the blast and the overwhelming human cost was shocking. Injuries were horrific, especially the burns. Later, the body count would list seventy-five dead and over a hundred wounded.

Morgan saw another stretcher emerge from the smoke— two running dockworkers carrying a man who was calling for his wife or mother and clutching at his charred face.

Shading his eyes and coughing, Morgan was making his way through toward the ship's gangway when a figure emerged and then vanished in the smoke in front of him. He wondered if he were mistaken. But as the smoke cleared again, he saw Guevara only a few feet away. A moment later, Guevara turned and saw Morgan, and the two men were face-to-face, isolated from everything around them by the smoke.

In the two or three seconds that elapsed before they moved on, a world of meaning passed between them. It was as if, amidst the vision of hell created by the pitiful cries, the sirens and the black smoke, each man had found a focus for his hatred.

Morgan had hurried to the docks without waiting for Lee Evans.

Which perhaps was just as well. Evans had hidden himself in a toilet on the sixteenth floor immediately after the explosions.

When he thought it safe, he left the toilet, avoided the elevator and went down the stairs of the INRA building to the street. Despite the confusion caused by the explosion, he found a cab to take him back to the Miramar house.

María was there, and Evans, who was clearly in a hurry, told her he'd come for his things. He packed a bag and, on his way out to the waiting cab, asked María to tell Morgan he'd been called away on business—apparently he had some horses to buy that couldn't wait—and would return in a week.

The cab drove Evans to José Martí Airport, where he took the next available flight to Miami.

63

The day after the destruction of the Le Coubre, a mass rally in Havana honored the victims and presented a massive demonstration of national unity in the face of the tragedy.

The coffins of the dead were carried in a procession headed by the leaders of the regime, including Fidel, Guevara and Osvaldo Dorticós, who had replaced Urrutia as President of Cuba. Menoyo and Morgan were with them in the front line of the marchers. The men walked abreast of one another with their arms linked.

The March skies were gloomy and gray and threatening rain as the leaders, including Menoyo and Morgan, stood on the public platform around Fidel for the speeches. *Il Maximo* was at his most passionate and moving. He acknowledged the Le Coubre as an act of sabotage, but denied the explosives had been set in Cuba and claimed the ship was booby-trapped elsewhere by 'those who do not want our country in a position to defend itself,' international interests that 'wished to bring the Cuban people to their knees.' He made no bones about singling out the United States government as the chief culprit in the many acts of aggression the people of Cuba had suffered in recent months, including the 'illegal flights and bombing raids' emanating from the US. He was referring to a number of over flights into Cuban airspace by light aircraft intent on dropping 'bombs' and, more specifically, setting fire to sugar cane fields. There was a chill in the air that was nothing to do with the weather, and the somber expressions on the faces of those on the platform and the gathered crowds was depressing to witness.

Amongst the news reporters and photographers in front of the platform, a young man called Alexander Korda took a shot of Guevara from a low angle, head and shoulders outlined against the flat skies; an image that would become an icon reproduced on T-shirts and posters for generations to come.

When Morgan arrived home after the rally, María was on the phone. He was exhausted and barely registered that his wife was speaking in English to whoever was on the other end of the line.

He poured a shot of Jack Daniels and busied himself with netting tadpoles for the fish in the aquaria to lunch on, when María covered the mouthpiece with her hand and said to him, "It's Ray. He wants to speak to you."

They hadn't spoken since Ray left the island.

"Bill?" she said gently. "Please? He says it's important. He's calling from Chicago."

Morgan took a gulp from his drink and let the net fall into the water. He watched as the tadpoles began to swim free. María brought the phone as close as the lead would allow.

"He's coming, Ray," she said, "and thank you. I will send of photo of Tammy. Take care."

She covered the mouthpiece again.

"William?"

Morgan put his glass down and took the phone from her. He was lighting a cigarette for himself.

"Hi," he said.

"Hey, Bill," said Ray, "It's been a long time. I hear congratulations are in order—again."

"That's right."

"Well, congratulations."

"Yeah, thanks."

There was a pause.

"Bill," said Ray, drawing a breath, "there's something I think you should know. That's why I'm calling."

"What's that?"

"Look, I'm just telling you this as it's come to me, as a friend. I don't know what to make of it. There's a guy on the Miami Herald, guy called Jones. We know each other and he knows about our connection. He's doing a story, but they're holding it back while they check out the source."

"And?"

"The source is a certain Jack Lee Evans, twenty-three years old, originally from Oklahoma."

"He disappeared from here yesterday without a word."

Ray sighed deeply. "Well, he's talking now and he's talking about you, Bill. From what I understand, he's going on record to say he and you were on-board the Le Coubre in the morning prior to the explosion."

"That's bullshit! The kid has to be crazy saying a thing like that," said Morgan.

"He's saying more than that, Bill. He's saying he saw six sticks of dynamite and he saw the fuse being tested at what he describes as 'an oceanfront house.' He's saying a dockworker planted the bomb, but he knew about the plot a couple of days ahead. He's saying he got out of Cuba fast and that he plans to disappear in the mid-west where nobody can find him."

"And he's saying I'm somehow involved?"

"Not exactly. He's saying you probably didn't know, but note the probably. I just thought you should know."

"They're going to print this?"

"I think they will. The editors were clearly suspicious of Evans, and they've been making efforts to check out his background, but I think in the end they will, yes. I'm sorry, Bill. I'm sorry I had to break this. I know you think I'm—"

"I think you're a good friend, Ray. We just had a difference of opinion, that's all."

"I'm glad. What will you do?"

"Fight fire with fire, I guess. What else can I do? Besides, it's total bullshit. There's not a shred of truth and I've got witnesses. I just don't understand why."

"I could try to check him out if you like, see if he's tied to anyone."

"Like who?"

"Bill, I don't know, anyone. The Mob, the Agency, maybe even Trujillo."

"Nah, I'd have known. The kid's crazy, that's all. He got spooked, maybe with some reason—you know what I mean?"

"How are things down there?"

"Interesting."

They talked a little while longer and when they were done, Morgan replaced the receiver and stood still, staring into space. Chapita saw his chance and took it. He made a leap from a chair back and clawed a grip on Morgan's back to save sliding to the floor.

"Goddamn it, Chapita!" said Morgan. "Get off me!"

Morgan grabbed Chapita by the nape of his neck and tore the monkey off his back. The monkey was letting out little screams. Morgan threw the animal to the sofa. Chapita landed easily on all fours, but scrabbled to hug a cushion as if to defend itself.

"William?" María said. "What's the matter? What did Ray say?"

64

On the morning of October twenty-first, 1960, Morgan was preparing to drive to Army Headquarters in Havana to deliver a wedding gift to his friend Juan Almeida Bosque, a General of the Revolutionary Armed Forces of Cuba. The gift he took with him that morning was a frogskin handbag.

The last months had seen escalating tensions between Cuba and the United States reach crisis point. As Morgan said goodbye to María, to his daughter Tammy and to the new baby, Angelina—just six months old on that day—he was not unaware of the preparations for war going on all around him. Far from it.

In the United States on that same day, October twenty-first, more than sixty million people were preparing to tune in to the fourth and final televised debate between Presidential hopefuls Richard Nixon and John F. Kennedy. The candidates made their opening statements on the topic of US relations with Cuba. Kennedy, the liberal, was going in hard and not above securing vital votes with rabble rousing. He argued strongly for a denunciation of Castro as a dangerous communist and blamed the Eisenhower administration for failing to intervene. It was left to Nixon to point out that the Charter of the United Nations specifically prohibits the interference of one country in the internal affairs of another. A hard line on Cuba had become the touchstone for any aspiring president.

From the Cuban perspective, open discussions of intervention on US national television could have left little doubt as to the intentions of the capitalist monolith to the north. The signs were lit up in bright neon; the training and arming of dissident groups in the United States and Mexico, most of them loyal to the former dictator, Fulgencio Batista; the recent recall of Ambassador Bonsal and the severing of meaningful diplomatic relations between Havana and

Washington; not to mention the economic sanctions, beginning with halving the vital sugar quota, followed by a full embargo on trade. Mr. Nixon said in his opening remarks for the televised debate that the intention was, quote: to 'quarantine this regime so that the people of Cuba themselves will take care of Mr. Castro.' End quote.

If the situation internationally was, to say the least, unstable, conditions on the island had become little short of chaotic over the hot summer. Castro's rhetoric against the United States had intensified with every passing week and the wholesale appropriation of US business interests had effectively entrenched the battle lines between the two countries. People's militias all over the island were preparing for the full-scale invasion their leader claimed was imminent. Acts of sabotage in the cities were blamed on the imperialists across the water and ruthless suppression of internal opposition had become the order of the day.

But on that cloudless morning as Morgan drove through the streets of Havana toward Army HQ and his appointment with General Juan Almeida, he felt no threat to his person or to the preparations he and his comrades had put in place. They had been careful. They had hidden the weapons without being discovered. And they were ready, if and when the time came. The Le Coubre thing and the mad claims Evans had made had gone nowhere and as far as Morgan was concerned, the whole thing had been forgotten.

As always, even months after the Trujillo conspiracy, people on the streets shouted and waved as he passed by in the electric-blue Oldsmobile.

Morgan was driving roof down. Never one to hide his light, he had no intention of skulking around or trying to be inconspicuous. The gold-plated 45 holstered, as always in recent times, at his hip. A Thompson submachine gun was conspicuous in the hands of Gerry Hemming who was sitting beside Morgan. Two or three hand grenades were stowed in the glove compartment. The radio telephones were turned on, tested and working, and Camilio was in the back seat, his own submachine gun resting on his knees, dark glasses obscuring his eyes and a bush cap pulled low on his head. It was as if Morgan were challenging the regime to try it if they dared.

Only a few months before, Morgan had been tortured by decisions over what he should or shouldn't do. Not any more. By October twenty-first, the die was cast, and Morgan was doing exactly as Carlos had suggested—preparing for the worst whilst hoping for the best. And as the people called out "*el Maranero*"—the trickster, his new moniker since the Trujillo affair—Morgan waved back to them, confident and content that he'd found the elusive 'third way.'

There was one more passenger that day, much to Gerry Hemming's irritation—Chapita, Morgan's pet monkey, who insisted on crawling over the seat backs and gripping onto shoulders or hair with each curve in the road.

65

Gerry Hemming had business of his own and was only going part way with Morgan, just as far as the Hotel Nacional, at the junction of Alvenida Twenty-three and Paseo.

It was as Hemming got out of the Oldsmobile—fighting off Chapita's attempts to go with him—that he had a chance to study the drab olive sedan idling a hundred yards back with three, or possibly four men inside. He'd noticed the sedan a couple of blocks back, but it wasn't until the vehicle pulled over in tandem with the Oldsmobile that he was sure the car was tailing them. Hemming put the Thompson down on the seat next to Morgan.

"Boss," he said as he leaned over, "we got company. And get hold of the chimp, will you?"

Morgan wrestled Chapita down onto the front seat next to him and studied the rearview mirror to check out the sedan.

The dusty matt-green of the car signified a government vehicle, and even if the individual occupants were impossible to identify at a distance, the clumsy technique tended to confirm the hypothesis.

"G2." Morgan relaxed. It would be a clever assassin who would use the cover of incompetent internal security operatives in order to get a shot at their target.

"We've got nothing to hide. They want to drive with us to Army HQ, let them."

"You want I should stay?"

"Not a chance. Pick you up here at three?"

"Yeah, I'll be done by then. Keep an eye, okay?"

Morgan rejoined the lines of traffic. Hemming waved him off and then turned to face the sedan as it too pulled away.

As the car came alongside, Hemming was standing with his hands on his hips, his obvious scrutiny of those inside the vehicle intended to be both a challenge and a warning.

The nervous faces of four young men in uniform, who collectively looked far more like the hunted than the hunter, scarcely registered Hemming's presence, so intent were they on offering advice with gestures and hand signals to the driver on keeping up with the Oldsmobile. As Hemming would later say himself, a carload of wannabe G2 agents on a watching brief hardly comprised a threat and was certainly not unusual in the torrid atmosphere of the times.

Hemming had told Morgan he was going to his bank to arrange a transfer of funds from the US. In actual fact, Hemming was on his way to a meeting with his US Army Intelligence handler, a thin, wiry man he knew only as Todd. Hemming would be taking yet another positive message on the progress of the reformed Second Front's plans and his personal assessment that Morgan's commitment to fight could, and indeed should, be relied upon. But he also wanted to ask about Evans. If it turned out Evans was a stoolie for the agency or any other US interest, Hemming was ready to quit there and then.

He'd also decided he would argue in the strongest terms that the US and the agency should get over the Trujillo thing now and throw Morgan a lifeline if they wanted to see Castro gone. Citizenship restored and visas for Morgan's family would do it. The rumors of an invasion were everywhere on the street and had certainly never been convincingly denied by Todd in previous conversations. Hemming would tell them that if they wanted Morgan in the mountains as one of the leaders of a diversionary internal insurrection, they better act fast. It was common knowledge that anything less than full-scale invasion had little chance of success without the diversion of a force in the mountains.

Although he would never tell Todd or anyone else, Hemming had every intention of going with Morgan to the Escambray when the time came.

*

As Hemming was sitting down to a beer in the bar of the Nacional, Morgan was turning off Avenida de los Presidentes just a little way down from where Alejandro and his companion had cack-handedly been caught in the process of placing a car bomb two years before.

The drab olive sedan was still with him and Morgan was driving slowly in order to bring them closer, until they were directly behind. When the traffic halted at a stoplight, Morgan turned and waved to the men in the car.

"Say hi to our friends," Morgan said quietly to Camilio, as Chapita jumped into the back seat and scrambled onto the collapsed hood. "And grab Chapita, will you? I don't know what's got into him today."

The young men in the sedan looked startled, but recovered sufficiently to return the wave. Morgan took hold of Chapita and put him in his lap where he could hold onto the monkey with one hand and steer with the other. For the next six blocks, until they passed the Hotel Capri, the sedan stayed with the Oldsmobile. And as Morgan showed their papers and passed through the checkpoint of Army Headquarters, he saw the sedan park in the street outside the gates.

Morgan had Chapita on his shoulder. He went up the stairs to Almeida's offices with Camilio following behind. He said 'hi' to Almeida's secretary, a woman called Marisa who was usually bubbly and full of smiles but who seemed subdued and edgy that day, and asked if the big man was in.

"You can go straight in," said Marisa, busying herself with a file of papers on her desk.

"Thanks, Marisa. Look, Chapita's waving to you," said Morgan.

She nodded but said nothing.

Morgan wanted to ask her if she was okay, but decided he'd chat to her on the way out. He knocked on the frosted glass of the door and pushed it open. Almeida was sitting at his desk. He stood up to greet Morgan, but instead of walking around the desk and giving his friend a bear hug, he lingered, fiddling with his pen and saying nothing.

"*Juan! ¿Qué tal amigo?*" said Morgan. He went toward the desk, holding the bag out for Almeida. Chapita started screeching and holding tight to Morgan's face, almost covering his eyes.

"Chapita! Stop it!' said Morgan, reaching up to grab the monkey and lift it from his shoulder and over his head like he was taking off a sweater. It was in the course of manhandling Chapita that from the corner of his eye, Morgan became suddenly aware of the two men who'd been behind the door and partly obscured by a tall gray filing cabinet, pointing submachine guns directly at him.

The sight of the men simply made no sense and Morgan swung round to Juan Almeida as if willing him to laugh at the joke. But Almeida was not laughing. His expression was blank, like a man in shock.

The two men with the guns were jabbering but hadn't moved from their places by the wall. One of them was gesturing toward Morgan's sidearm and shouting repeatedly, "*¡Apártese las manos!*" but the idea of drawing his weapon amongst friends, despite everything going on around him, seemed to Morgan, madness.

He heard the heavy footsteps of several men rushing into Marisa's office and looked toward the door he'd just come through to see Camilio stand aside. The young men who had been following in the sedan pushed past him. And as Chapita screamed and screeched, two of the men restrained Morgan's arms while the third grappled at his holster to retrieve the gold-plated Colt.

Morgan was still staring at Camilio. His trusted bodyguard kept his eyes fixed on the floor directly in front of his feet.

66

It was Ramirito who brought the news of Morgan's arrest to Menoyo.

The young man was breathless. He tumbled down the stairs of the below-ground café on F Street and Linea, where Menoyo was sitting drinking coffee with Max Lesnik and Roger Redondo.

He kept gabbling about Juan Almeida, about Jesús Carreras being pulled from one of the frog farm trucks on its way to the Escambray, spitting out the words and hardly drawing breath, leaving the men at the table with more questions than answers. Menoyo pulled the younger man down onto one of the chairs and held him by the shoulder.

"*¡Ramirito!*" said Menoyo. "*¡Despacio! ¿Qué dice usted?*" *What are you saying?*

There were tears of anger running down Ramirito's cheeks. He tried to explain what he knew, and while the men listened carefully, their minds were already working overtime on the implications and on what to do next.

*

In the Miramar house, Rosa was preparing hamburgers for the evening meal, on Morgan's request. More often recently, he'd asked for what Rosa dismissively referred to as *'la comida americano'*. As she worked, she became aware of the phone ringing and ringing in the living room. No-one was picking up.

Finally, she could bear it no more. She washed the meat juices from her hands, cursing the layabouts in uniform, the so-called bodyguards and the hangers-on who were forever under her feet, but quite incapable of making themselves useful in any way. She despaired at the American's tolerance for these men, who could not even pick up a phone, despite the fact that María and the new baby were trying to sleep upstairs.

"*¡Por Dios!*" she said out loud. She irritably shut off the tap and picked up a dishcloth to dry her hands.

She was still drying her hands and muttering under her breath as she walked brusquely into the living room to find María holding Angelina in her arms and staring down at the receiver, as if she hadn't a clue what to do about the constant ringing.

"*¿María?*" said Rosa. "*¿Qué pasa?*"

When María turned her head, Rosa could see her face was pale with fear.

"*Él es tres horas tarde. Él es nunca tarde. Nunca.*" He's never late. Never.

Rosa knew María was right. Morgan would never keep them waiting without sending word, but she was also certain María was overreacting. This would be her husband on the phone explaining why he was not yet home.

Rosa picked up the receiver. "*Hola?*"

She was smiling reassurance at María, but there was nothing she could do to hide the change in her expression as Menoyo spoke, quickly and succinctly. When Rosa put the receiver down less than twenty seconds later, María was already shaking and drawing quick, short breaths, her mouth wide open and her eyes fixed on the front door.

It was then Rosa heard the gunning of engines from the drive, the squeal of brakes and the sound of men's voices raised in anger and confusion in front of the house.

*

Ray Halliwell was wrapping up the daily briefing for his foreign news team in the Chicago offices of the *Sun-Times* newspaper when his secretary knocked at the glass door to the conference room. He scowled at her and carried on talking.

"I want more on the advisors. Over a thousand Americans are known to be in-country—as I hear the phrase goes—and almost all are Special Forces. Let's get comments from the new administration and give them a push on Dulles' Domino theory. What happens to Cambodia and Laos if the Viet Cong keep making ground? Okay, that's it, guys."

As the news staff filed out of the room, Ray's secretary hovered sheepishly, knowing she was probably in for a rocket. Interruptions to the daily briefing were almost unheard of. The golden hour, as it was called in the newsroom, would set the priorities for the day, and just a week after the closest ever Presidential election that saw Kennedy take the White House by a margin of 0.01 percent of the vote, there was plenty to talk about. Aside from the failed coup against Vietnam's dictator Ngo Dinh Diem, the passing of the landmark Civil Rights Bill at home and trouble in the Belgian Congo, a report had surfaced in the Guatemalan paper *La Hora* of advanced plans for a full-scale invasion of Cuba. It was all on the morning's agenda, leaving little space for interruption.

"Cindy," Mr. Halliwell said as he gathered his papers and stood up to go, "tell me what matters more than the start of the next world war?"

"There's a woman to see you. She's waiting in your office and she says it's a matter of life and death."

"It always is. Name?"

"Miss Blanquita Peres. She said to tell you she's here about William Morgan."

"Where's María?" Ray asked Blanquita when they were alone.

"At home. Under house arrest, with the children."

"How is she?"

Blanquita shrugged but said nothing.

"Who else have they arrested? Menoyo?"

She shook her head. "Only Jesús Carreras. And Morgan. No one else, not yet."

"And you? You're going back?"

Blanquita looked at the floor, then directly at Ray.

"I can never go back. My home is here now. In America."

Half an hour later, Ray was standing in Jim Sturry's office. He had his coat on.

"Yeah, I hear what you're saying, Ray. What I don't get is what you're planning to do about it."

"Come on, Jim."

"Don't even think about it. What can you possibly achieve acting the crazy man?"

"Jim, there's no choice about it."

"I'm telling you this can't happen. You'll get yourself arrested and that'll help no-one. And you can't just walk out on this job. I can't help you if you do this."

Ray said nothing and for the briefest moment, Sturry seemed to relax, sure he'd won the case. Ray turned and went to the glass door of Sturry's office. He turned back and said, "I'll see you, Jim."

And with that he walked out. Ray was half way through the newsroom when he heard Sturry's voice calling after him.

"Don't do this, Ray!"

67

The Cubana Airlines flight Ray took from Miami International Airport to José Martí Airport outside Havana was eerily empty.

Gone were the tourist families in their starched casuals, the shady gamblers, the 'good ol' boys' with drinks in hand, heading down for golf or fishing trips, and the Cubans laden with shopping bags and luxury goods from the Florida stores. In their place, a motley smattering of isolated men in suits, sharp-featured and serious, or military types in ill-fitting olive-green uniforms, sat isolated amongst the swathes of vacant seats. He'd taken this flight so many times before. But never had it felt like the plane was heading into a war zone. Now it did. There was not even a drink in sight, as if cabin service had been suspended for the duration.

Before leaving, Ray had gone to his apartment to pack after leaving the paper and only then thought he should calm down and perhaps approach the situation with a little science. He put in a call to Cindy in the office, who for some reason whispered as she agreed to locate a number for Morgan's parents, Tammy and Alexander Morgan. Ray had spoken to Tammy on the phone, but it was clear Morgan's mother was too upset to talk. She managed to tell him that the Democratic Representative for Cleveland, a man by the name of Thomas Ashley, was working on Morgan's behalf. With her voice cracking and breaking into sobs, Ray promised to do what he could and put the phone down.

A call to Thomas Ashley's office confirmed the Representative's interest in the case. Ashley had made approaches to the State Department in order to secure legal representation for Morgan. He had received the vague response that, although supplying a list of Cuban attorneys was a possibility, no confirmation that such action had been taken could be given to the Representative. Ashley's assistant added that the official he'd dealt with made it clear that as Morgan was no longer a United States citizen, there were no grounds for the Department to actively intervene in his case. Ashley also said that Mrs. Tammy Morgan had subsequently asked the Representative to halt any action by the Department for fear it might 'add to her son's predicament,' as she put it.

José Martí Airport, by contrast to the plane and its passengers, was teeming. People formed queues everywhere and unruly crowds blocked corridors and exits. All were hopeful their exit visas would pass the scrutiny of the armed soldiers and immigration officers, checking papers and relieving the departing passengers of their valuables; wallets, jewelry, watches and anything else that might raise money for the regime or line the pockets of individuals.

Amidst the mayhem and panic of the crowds clamoring to get away, Ray was pushing his way out of the building to find a cab when he heard his name being called. Amelia Frankenheim was just arriving at the airport to catch her flight out of the country.

"Do I have to ask what you're doing here?" she said.

She'd reported on Morgan's arrest for her own paper, *The Baltimore Sun.*

"They wouldn't let me near him and I sure they won't let you either," she said.

"I can try."

"The G2 are picking up journalists, especially American journalists, on charges of spying and counter-revolution whenever they need evidence of imperialist sabotage. The gloves are off, Ray."

"I'll talk to the Embassy."

"They're shutting-up shop. You know that. They won't listen."

"They have to listen."

Amelia studied him.

"This *is* personal for you, isn't it, Ray?"

"I guess it is."

"What do you know? Why, I'm almost proud of you."

She rummaged in her handbag and pulled out a laminate card.

"Here. It may not do any good, but you never know. There's no photograph and they never look at them too closely."

"What is it?"

"We call it the 'get out of jail free' card. The revolutionary council issues them only to approved journos."

"You were approved?"

"I guess I'm losing my touch. Getting soft in my old age."

"Amelia Frankenheim? Never. Not you."

Amelia tried to smile, but couldn't muster anything convincing.

"That's why I'm going, Ray. I'm not proud of it, but there it is. Battle fatigue, I guess. You're a sweet kid. Watch yourself, okay? For me."

She kissed him on the cheek.

Ray said, "You getting sentimental on me?"

"Maybe I am."

*

John Dempsey was surrounded by cardboard boxes and piles of paper destined to go straight into one of the wheeled canvas post bins, now employed to ship documents to the overflowing incinerator in the basement of the Embassy building.

Many of the top-secret documents that might prove embarrassing if they fell into the wrong hands had already been shipped out. But it was always possible sensitive material had been overlooked, or worse still stashed away by local Embassy staff sympathetic to the regime. Dempsey had volunteered to be among the last to leave the island in order to be sure the house was clean, so to speak.

He was making a final check on his desk drawers when he looked up to see Ray standing at the door to his office.

"Well, well," said Dempsey. "Ray. I'd offer you coffee or a drink, but as you can see, we're a little short-staffed and I'm kind of busy. What can I do for you?"

"Morgan," said Ray, stepping over the littered piles on the floor.

"Yes," said Dempsey, pausing for a moment before throwing more paper into the bin. "Morgan. Pity, he could have been useful."

"What are you guys doing about it, John?"

Dempsey gave a hollow laugh.

"Us? Tell me, what do you see around you, Ray? The annual Embassy spring clean? The United States government in its wisdom has severed all diplomatic relations with the Cuban government and we're shipping out. Oh, and then there's the small point that Morgan is not a US citizen. Out of our hands."

"Come on, John—"

"No, *you* come on, Ray! Where've you been anyway? Has the desk job addled your brain? We're at war. Undeclared, but that's just a formality. Morgan's a statistic now, one of thousands behind bars, and there's not a goddamn thing I even want to do about it. The 'big man' in the blue Oldsmobile just got wise the hard way."

"You're paid to protect American interests! That means Americans, John. That means Morgan."

"You're not listening, Ray, but then listening was never a strong point of yours, was it? Mogan's no more a citizen of our great country than Fidel himself. Not anymore."

The punch, when it came, caught Dempsey full square on the jaw, sending him sprawling amongst the papers on the floor. Leaning back on his elbows, Dempsey looked more surprised than hurt, almost as surprised as Ray, who'd last employed physical violence in seventh grade. Both men were glaring at each other and breathing hard.

"Stupid, Ray," said Dempsey, "very stupid."

*

Ray picked Jamie up at the old apartment and together they took a cab to the Miramar house.

As soon as they arrived, Jamie jumped from the back seat and began taking shots of the house and the guards at the front door. Ray flashed the laminate card and, with all the authority he could muster, told the two men he was here, as arranged, to interview the woman of the house about her counter-revolutionary activities.

The guards were confused. Nobody had told them to expect a journalist and photographer, but because Ray and Jamie were Americans and also because Ray threatened to take this up with Guevara himself, the guards allowed them in rather than face the wrath of their superiors.

It was Rosa that Ray found first, with the baby in her arms. She was preparing something in the kitchen. While Jamie studied the fish tanks and whistled his appreciation of the world within, Ray went to the hallway to find María running down the grand stairs toward him.

As they embraced, María kept repeating the words, "Oh God, Ray, Oh God—"

*

Ray did not go to his hotel room at the Capri when he left María, but to the old apartment. Jamie made coffee while Ray made calls. "What have you got?" said Jamie. Ray slowly put the phone down.

"A meeting. Menoyo and the others from the Second Front. At his club, tonight. After they close."

"But what can they do? Aren't they next in line?"

"I suppose, Jamie. I don't know."

Jamie handed him the hot coffee.

"Here."

"Thanks."

"Maybe you should get some sleep. Use the bed."

Ray was rubbing his eyes with one hand. He didn't touch the coffee.

"No. I can't sleep now."

"Ray?" said Jamie.

"What?"

"How long have we worked together?"

"I don't know."

"Three years now. And every time we do a story I get you what you want, don't I? You know how?"

Ray didn't reply. Jamie took the coffee cup from Ray's hand.

"I listen. You talk and I listen. Do me a favor? Listen to me for once. Get your head down, the better to do what you got to do, okay?"

Ray slept for an hour, maybe an hour and a half. It was two in the morning by the time he was paying off the cab outside Menoyo's club. He went down the side alley as agreed and knocked at the metal door. Ramirito opened it.

"You're here," Ramirito said, like he'd been waiting a lifetime.

"As you see, Ram."

"Come, come. We all wait for you."

Menoyo, Fleites, Artola, Lesnik, Redondo, Ramirito and the others at the meeting completely understood the gravity of the situation. But still they struggled to believe the regime would dare to bring the full weight of its power to bear on either Morgan's case or that of Carreras. Both men were former comandantes and both were heroes of the revolution in the eyes of the people. For better or for worse, Morgan's celebrity status especially was thought of as some kind of defense against incontinent action by Castro and his security services.

But, as the weeks dragged by and the expectations of early release faded, Menoyo and his comrades began to doubt their initial judgments. There was the example of Huber Matos and many other former heroes of the revolution who were now serving long prison sentences for criticizing the regime's communist leanings. And as it became apparent that Morgan and Carreras might pay a similar price, they knew they had to act.

Menoyo had quietly secured a promise from the Brazilians of asylum for three men from the Second Front to join the many others desperately attempting to escape the reach of a regime now lashing out in all directions. The Argentinean ambassador to Cuba, Julió Amoedo, had agreed to take three more.

But there were twelve men in the Second Front's inner circle who would not be safe in the new Cuba, and none would accept the offer of asylum without provision for all. They knew they would have to come up with another plan and they were still talking about what to do when Ray joined them.

The handshakes and hugs were perfunctory, and they were soon down to business. Menoyo told Ray about the Foreign Embassy's offers and explained why taking up those offers was not an option.

"But for María," he said. "It could work. She too will face trial."

"She's under house arrest," Ray said. "They're not just going to let her walk."

"No," said Menoyo. He reached into his pocket and pulled out a small plastic bag folded over on itself, containing a white powder. He pushed the bag across the table toward Ray.

"What is it?"

"Pills, for sleeping. Broken into—" He struggled for the word and finally found it. "Powder. For the guards."

Ray stared at the bag, unsure if Menoyo was serious.

"You think it will work?"

"We can try. *You* can try. You can visit her, as an American. A journalist."

"Isn't there another way?"

Menoyo shrugged as if to say, *what do you suggest?*

Ray picked up the bag. He nodded agreement.

Menoyo ran through the plan. Once the guards were drugged, Ray should call. There would be a car waiting for María and the children. They'd try to make it to the Brazilian Embassy in daylight in order to avoid raising suspicions by driving at night. He had false papers prepared for María in case they were stopped, but using two other cars ahead of them, they'd radio back any unexpected roadblocks they might encounter, and as far as possible, the car with María and the children would take an alternative route.

As they waited together for Ram to bring a car round to drive Ray back to the apartment, Menoyo took his Colt from its holster and put it on the table.

"Take this."

"No," said Ray. "I don't even know how to use it."

"But if the plan goes wrong, you may need this to defend yourself and to defend María and the children."

Ray stared hard at the gun. He looked back at Menoyo.

"I don't even know how to use it."

"I will show you," said Menoyo.

68

When it came to it, the whole thing proved absurdly easy.

Ray showed up at the house in Miramar with an armful of groceries, including fresh coffee beans, baby milk, cold beers and hamburger meat. The guards were the same two guys he'd met before, so he had no trouble convincing them he was just saying goodbye and doing the lady a favor before flying back to the States.

He showed them one of Jamie's photos taken outside the house and featuring them standing to attention in the middle of the shot. He'd brought two copies, and the men were delighted when Ray told them they could keep the photographs and that they should look out for their pictures in the *Chicago Sun-Times* soon.

Rosa cooked up the meat and prepared a meal of homemade fries and burgers in buns, sufficient for the guards and themselves. Stomachs full with traditional American fare, the two men turned down the offer of beer, but accepted hot strong coffees when María brought them out to the front step. Ray, meanwhile, phoned through to Menoyo's club.

"Just wanted to say goodbye," he said.

"Good luck, Ray," said Menoyo. "What time is your flight?"

"Not till later, but I'm planning a siesta. A couple of hours."

Then he rang off and turned to María.

"OK, now we wait."

They were in the front room. The children were upstairs with Rosa. María had already packed a couple of small bags with bare essentials and some money. Her passport had been taken from her long before. Ray sat beside her. They were facing the fish tanks and the view to the back garden.

"There's time to rest," said Ray, "you could take a nap, upstairs, a little—"

"I couldn't sleep now," María replied quickly, cutting him off. "Sorry," she added, appropros of nothing in particular.

"No, of course."

There was so much, and so little, to say. For a long time, they were quiet.

"Ray?" María said, catching him unawares.

"What?"

"After? When this is done, it's going to be difficult for you."

"Me?"

"Yes. You."

"You're crazy."

"Am I?"

"You should be thinking about yourself."

"I am. You see, I am. I have to decide what to do."

Ray turned to look at her.

"What do you mean?"

María didn't speak straight away, but he was sure he knew what she was thinking.

"We'll get Bill out, one way or another, sooner or later."

"Yes, of course."

Again, they were silent for a minute or more. It was Ray who spoke first.

"I would care for you," he said, "in America. I'd be there, María. For you and for the children. You know that?"

She put her hand on his and smiled.

"Yes."

"But you'd never do that, would you?" Ray said.

"The choice is not mine, Ray."

"You said you have to decide. That's the same."

"No, it's not the same. I have to decide for others, for the children, for Bill. What is best for them."

"And you? What's best for you?"

"To do my duty, to preserve those I love—"

"Then let me get you out of this country María. I can help. It may take a while, but I know people."

"I can't!" María was suddenly angry, her voice raised. "Don't you see? Don't you see you can't just start and stop this thing! We are caught, Ray. Trapped. We couldn't walk away even if we wanted to. Even if they would let us. Too much would be left behind. It's too late, Ray."

"No. I won't accept that. There must be something."

María put her hand to his face.

"You must. All along, that is how it has been. We do what we must. There are no free choices. I wish it was another way."

"It doesn't have to be—"

She put her hand to his mouth to quiet him.

"Hold me?" María said. "Just for a little while. Just till its time."

Two hours after Ray's call to Menoyo, it was full night and both guards were unconscious, slumped in the portico. Ray made another call, let the phone ring three times and then put the receiver down without waiting for anyone to pick up. A radio message had the car outside the house in less than five minutes. Ramirito was driving, Menoyo in the front passenger seat. They parked on the road—not wanting to take the chance the guards might wake—and María, Ray and the two children hurried down the drive to meet them. Ray put Tammy on the back seat as Menoyo loaded the bags in the trunk. And suddenly, in a way Ray hadn't anticipated, there was no time to say goodbye. The decision had already been taken that Ray should not go with them for fear of drawing attention, but to go like this—

María was holding the baby and about to get into the car.

"Listen," Ray said, "I'll come to the Embassy soon. We're going to get you out of the country, okay? It may take a little—"

"Ray," she said interrupting him, "thank you. Thank you for everything."

Menoyo was next to them. "We must go."

She got into the car and they drove away, leaving Ray on the sidewalk.

*

María was allocated a cot for the children in the overcrowded garage of the Brazilian Embassy.

Designed to hold five or six vehicles with room to spare, the garage had been hastily converted to a dormitory for the two hundred refugees fortunate enough to be allowed asylum. Many hundreds more were still waiting hopefully outside the gates guarded by police and militia, who had no compunction about shooting anyone who attempted to scale the fences or rush the sentries. One desperate man had even tried to drive his car through the crowds in the hope of crashing through the gates. He was already dead by the time the car smashed into the low brick wall around the Embassy grounds.

Others who had managed to gain access to the Embassy were forced to sleep outside in makeshift tents, and much the same story was true at the Peruvian Embassy and at the Embassy of Argentina.

As best she could, María nursed the children and tried to calm them with songs and stories. She missed Rosa, who had gone to Santa Clara to tell María's mother and sister what had happened, and she missed her husband and worried about him constantly. Refugees together, the people housed in the Embassy garage supported one another and helped with taking care of the children when they cried, shared some of their own meager food rations when they could and exchanged stories about how they came to be there. And like all refugees, many were scared and anxious, and silly rows over nothing would sometimes puncture the subdued atmosphere with raised voices and tears that left everyone sullen and depressed.

At night time, María lay in the cot with her daughters and thought about her husband and her family in Santa Clara, her mother and her sister, who must by now have heard the news from Rosa. She felt desperately alone. She knew she could not stay in the Embassy for long, not just because of the conditions but because others needed help, and with the space already full to overflowing, the Embassy officials, who had been kind and attentive, were already beginning to push her toward leaving the country when arrangements could be made.

But María didn't want to leave Cuba. How could she find any peace of mind if she were to leave her husband to rot in jail? Naturally, she had to protect the children, and to do that she must make them and herself safe from the regime's reach. But leaving the island? Leaving William to his fate? These were not options she could easily contemplate.

She thought carefully about what to do all night. The next morning, she went to the Embassy office and asked to use the phone. She rang her mother and her sister, Betania, speaking only in oblique terms about an upcoming birthday and the chance of a visit, for fear of being overheard somewhere down the line.

69

Early in January 1961, twelve men, including Eloy Menoyo, met at their favorite spot—the below ground café at F Street and Linea—to decide their futures in the light of all that had happened.

With Morgan and Carreras in prison and the ruthless suppression of the nascent rebel groups in the Escambray in full flood, with more than seventy thousand militia and army soldiers dedicated to the eradication of all opposition, the twelve knew they had left it too late to go to the mountains. Some, those who had been keener than others to begin the fight against the regime, were angry. But it didn't matter anymore. That door was closed.

The chances of asylum in one of the Latin embassies in Havana had already been discounted and it fell to Menoyo to propose a radical alternative.

"I have arranged a boat to take us to America," he told the men. "It will leave from Alamar. Everyone here is invited to come."

A long debate followed. To be prepared to give your life for a cause you believe in, only to be forced to run in order to save yourself, stuck in the craws of some of those listening to Menoyo. Others worried about leaving loved ones to face the consequences of their actions. Others still, saw the simple rationale that they would be no good to their families or to the fight against communism if they ended up behind bars like their comrades.

Emotions ran high as the talk veered from grief to anger and back again, but in the end, the chance to regroup and return stronger, the better to carry on the fight, convinced all but one man to give up family and homeland and go with Menoyo to the United States.

Ramirito, with a wife and a new baby and a modest life in the rural town of Camajuani, north of Santa Clara and within sight of the Escambray Mountains, made the hardest decision of his life and decided to stay in Cuba.

As the men stood up to go, many would afterwards remember the crisp salute Ramirito offered his commanding officer. The young man stood to attention, tears tumbling down his cheeks as he said farewell to his comrades.

*

María's mother and her sister Betania queued with the other visiting relatives at the Brazilian Embassy that day. Papers were carefully checked and a head count made on the way in. They explained that they had come to take the children out for the day to give them a break from the dreary routine inside the compound walls. So it was, that when María's mother, sister and two children walked back through security, no eyebrows were raised and no questions asked. Betania would wait for a couple of hours before she left the Embassy by the same route to join them at the bus station.

Ray arrived at the Embassy at lunchtime. He negotiated security with the laminated press pass Amelia had given him and made his way to the garage. Amongst the hundred or so people there, it took him a while to ask about the woman called María Morgan with her two small children. Some just shook their heads, but others knew who he was talking about and pointed out her cot. But when he got there, a woman he didn't recognize was sitting alone.

"Hi," said Ray. "I'm looking for María?"

Betania stood up and came close to him before speaking.

"Are you Ray?"

"Yeah."

"María asked me to tell you not to worry. She has made her decision."

"What do you mean?"

"María has gone."

*

In his hotel room at the Capri, Ray had let dusk come without turning on the lights in the room.

Not knowing what else to do, he'd spent all afternoon on the telephone, ringing whoever he could think might be able to influence Morgan's fate. He'd spoken again with Alexander, Morgan's father. He'd managed to track Representative Ashley down at the Senate in Washington and been reassured that all that could be done with the State Department was being done. He'd spoken again to the Swiss Embassy Chargé d'Affaires, as the Swiss were now handling American interests in Cuba since the US Embassy had finally closed its doors. And he'd tried for anyone in the regime who would listen. He'd got no further than Guevara's secretary. Then he'd gone to work on Amelia's press card, bending it this way and that until the laminate cracked at the edge. He peeled back the plastic as carefully as he could to get to the handwritten line with her name. Using a razorblade, he scratched at the paper until her first name was almost erased. He worked less on her surname, confident he could turn Frankenheim into Halliwell more easily.

As he worked, Ray's throat was sandpaper-dry and grungy from the constant stream of cigarettes he'd smoked that day. The room smelt stale, so he opened the window and looked out on the view over the city. María was out there somewhere. But where, he could only guess. Even if he could have found her, he knew he'd just be leading the authorities straight to her. He tried to imagine her on a bus, or hiding in a basement like the basement at Pilar's. He thought of her walking up the trail in the Escambray ahead of him. He saw her in the garden at Miramar with the smoke from the oil drum drifting around her and the summer dress she'd worn that day. He thought of her kissing him goodbye and wondered if that was the last time he'd ever see her.

He'd been standing there for over an hour by the time he came back to reality. The sun had sunk quickly, as it always does close to the Equator, and it was almost full night by the time he went to the bathroom and rummaged through his wash kit for the roll of sticking plaster he'd bought from the hotel store earlier in the day. He examined the roll and then caught sight of himself in the mirror. The man he could see still looked uncertain, even nervous. If once upon a time, he'd been content to observe, to report, to be simply a witness to events, what he was about to do would push him over the line forever.

He took the roll of plaster to the room and put it on the dresser next to the Colt. He sat on the bed, staring at the gun.

70

The weather was cold that day, with a north wind bringing rain and a chill to the air, quite foreign to the island. As Ray stepped out of the taxi, the stone walls of La Cabana appeared more grey and forbidding than ever.

He joined the queue of hopefuls waiting for access to their loved ones held inside. Some had baskets of food. Others were holding documents like they were precious possessions, letters of permission, letters from lawyers or from friends and family, letters that offered hope. The attention of the prison guards mainly concentrated on what people had in their bags or in their pockets, with only a rudimentary body search. Still, Ray had to consciously control his breathing and occasionally wipe the sweat from his brow as his turn came closer. The cold weight of the Colt strapped to his ankle with the roll of plaster filled him with dread and if he could have gone back on the plan, he would have gladly done so at that moment.

A man and his wife in their forties were in front of him. Their basket of food was laid out on the search table with the contents unwrapped, being prodded by another guard, when suddenly, the searching stopped dead. At a shout from somewhere behind Ray, all the guards stood to attention.

Ray turned to see Guevara. His heart sank. As the comandante strode past the queue with three or four soldiers at his heel, Ray did what he could to hide himself in the line of people. Guevara was chewing on a cigar. He waited for the inner door to be unlocked. The guards were still at attention as the door opened and he disappeared into the corridor beyond. Ray breathed again and tried to control the thump, thump of his heart, pounding hard in his chest.

One of the guards motioned Ray forward to the table. He was told to empty his pockets and put everything on the table. Another guard studied the laminate press card and compared it to Ray's passport. The man's brow furrowed. Then something distracted him and he seemed to lose interest. He handed the card and passport back to the guard checking bags. Ray was through. He joined a line of relatives waiting by the barred entrance to the prison's *galleras* and the visitors' room.

Ten minutes later, Ray was sitting at a table set out in a line with many others like a school classroom. One by one the prisoners with a visitor were being brought up from the *galleras*, their hands clamped in front of them with handcuffs. Ray had his back to the door and had to keep craning around to see if Morgan was one of them. Then he would go back to tapping on the table nervously, wondering exactly what he would say to Morgan that would make any sense. The fact that María and the children were safe—wherever she was now Ray had to assume it was better than being here and maybe even trapped in the embassy—was the main thing. The Colt strapped to his ankle was another story. Ray was relying on Morgan to fix a plan for that. He even had hopes Morgan might refuse to take it. And still his heart was pounding.

He glanced around again. Another prisoner was being led in, searched at the door and then taken by the arm to one of the tables. But it was not Morgan. The man looked weak and sick and he stumbled as he walked, held up by the guard. His legs, it seemed, did not have the strength to carry him. An older man and a woman with a bundle clutched to her chest were waiting. Both were weeping.

Ray was watching the group when he became aware of someone moving behind him. He turned to see a glimpse of uniform and assumed it was a guard leading Morgan to the table, but before he could register his mistake, Guevara sat heavily in the chair opposite Ray. The shock was total.

"Mister Halliwell."

Ray could find no words.

"I heard you were here," Guevara said in Spanish. He was scratching at his chest and the cigar stump was still clamped between his teeth.

"*Qué tiene?*" Ray said, trying and failing to hide his complete surprise.

"I might ask you the same question," said the second most important man in Cuba, the head of the national bank and now an international figurehead recognized the world over, feted, loved and loathed, but never ignored.

Again, Ray chose to say nothing.

"To see Morgan, yes? No. Communist coup, a revolution betrayed. You remember? You write like all reactionaries, Mister Halliwell. Threatened, you scratch back like rats."

"And you?" said Ray, finally finding his voice. "What exactly is this place for if not to scratch back?"

"Me? You mean us, the revolution? We have very little reason to justify our actions, especially not to you Mister Halliwell. We act from historical necessity. We are the new world order, nothing less. Your government will come to recognize that, one way or another. Welcome to the future, a future that will not include Mister Morgan, I fear."

"And what becomes of a revolution that uses the methods of a dictatorship, *Mister* Guevara? What difference is there in the end?"

"A great difference. As you will see." Guevara paused and sat back on two legs of the chair. "So?"

Ray waited.

"What should we do?" Guevara said. As he spoke, he motioned to the guards by the door and Ray was aware they would soon be at the table.

"Listen to me," Ray said, leaning forward, "your new world order will cost lives, many lives. Things were rotten before, we all know that. You have a chance to make things better. Why throw it away with this. Look at it. Look at them!"

Ray was angry now, pointing to the group nearby, clawing at each other as the guards tried to prise the woman's hands away from the prisoner and lead him back to the cells. Ray was abruptly lifted by his arms from the chair.

"Before it's too late, before your own people learn to hate the revolution—"

"Enough!" shouted Guevara, suddenly angry too. "Get him out! Out of the country! Get him out, now!"

"Innocent people will pay for your brave new world!" Ray shouted as they led him away. He struggled against the guards, but never took his eyes from Guevara. "Innocent people!"

*

Two hours later, Ray was at José Martí Airport under close guard right up to the moment he was bundled aboard the next Cubana Airlines flight to Miami.

With the flight full to overflowing, Ray was allocated a jump seat designed for crew only. The guards stayed with him until the doors were closed. The stewardess next to him stared straight ahead, unsure of the stone-faced American next to her. Ray sat rigid, aware of his own breath coming and going, aware of the volcano of feelings in his chest, staring a fixed, unblinking stare, unable to think a coherent thought, unable to think about Morgan or María, unable to conceive of a future for any of them that made sense.

He left Cuba for the last time with the Colt still strapped to his ankle and with his back to America. He was looking down the length of the plane at more than a hundred blank faces, most of them Cuban, all flying to an unknown future.

*

Saying goodbye to her children as they boarded the bus was the hardest thing María had ever had to do. She kept things light, kissed them all and waved them off before melting into the crowds and making her way to Menoyo's club, where he was ready for her with all she required for her own journey.

Traveling alone and at night, María made her way to a safe house in Santa Clara. Dressed in the olive-green uniform of the revolutionary army and with false papers supplied by Menoyo, citing her as an INRA employee on secondment from Havana, María prayed the separation from her children would not be for long. It would fall to her mother and sister to take care of the baby and her two-year-old sister for the time being, and María knew the children would be in safe hands, but still she worried.

Leaving the Embassy to go into hiding alone was an impossible decision she would have never dreamed she could make only a few months before. Now, it seemed the only sensible course of action. If it meant leaving the city of Havana, her children and her imprisoned husband behind, it also meant the chance to go on fighting for all she believed.

She knew she would be tried in absentia by the same court as her husband. It made her desolate that he would face the judges alone, without her by his side. Dr. Jorge Luís Carro—Morgan's court-appointed lawyer—had sent word to expect prison sentences of up to nine years in the event they were found guilty of the charges against them, namely 'aiding and abetting counter-revolutionary forces at the direction of foreign interests.'

But María knew the statutes bore no relation to the sentences handed down and anything could happen in the current climate. Those days spent waiting and worrying in the safe house were the worst. Only the decision to fight on, for William, for the children, and for her country, sustained her resolve.

*

A week later, several men, many with small cases holding only the barest essentials, were making their separate ways a few miles to the east of Havana and the harbor of Cojimar.

Some were making the journey by bus, some by cab or car and some by foot. Each man had already taken leave of families, friends and loved ones, and there was very little left to say as they gathered in a crowded harbor-side café. They were watchful and subdued, sitting in groups of no more than three or four in order to avoid attracting attention to themselves, waiting patiently for night to fall.

Cojimar Harbor was little more than a fishing village. It was here that Ernest Hemingway kept his boat, *The Pilar*, captained by Gregorio Fuentes who was the inspiration for Hemingway's short novel *The Old Man and the Sea*, the book that had won him the Nobel Prize for Literature in 1952. Hemingway was still living in his *finca* outside Havana as the men drank their coffees or beers, smoked cigarettes, sitting still, mostly silent, brooding on the journey ahead and all they were leaving behind. But the great writer would follow them in a few months, never to return to the island or his home.

Menoyo was the first to go aboard the boat. He stowed his small case of clothes below and then went back to the deck. The engines were already running, diesel fumes and the spitting of the bilge water from the exhaust accompanying the others as they walked up the gangplank, careless now of attracting attention, knowing that in less than ten minutes they would throw off the lines holding the boat to the harbor wall and head for the open sea.

With the last glimpse of the sun vanishing over the horizon, the fishing boat chugged clear of Morro Castle guarding the entrance to Cojimar Harbor. Menoyo was standing on the port side of the boat with Roger Redondo. They were both smoking cigarettes.

As they stared at the land, the silhouette of La Cabana fortress, backlit by the city of Havana beyond, was thrown into stark relief, perched high on its rocky promontory. And the revolving beam of the lighthouse at the very apex of the fortress, where tall cliffs fell steeply away to the water below, swept over the sea and over the fishing boat and the men on-board, like the hand of a clock.

FINALE

71

Senator Hawkes checked his watch against the wall clock in the committee room and conferred with Chad Dyer. To Ray, María and Capaldi, sitting together at the witness table looking toward the bench, Senator Wallace's empty seat was still strangely conspicuous by her absence.

Capaldi held the pages of the concluding statement, prepared many months before, and waited for the Senator to signal readiness. After a brief conference with Chad Dyer, Hawkes leaned forward to the microphone.

"Okay, Counsel, thank you. Please proceed."

"Thank you, Senator."

Capaldi cleared his throat and laid the statement on the table in front of him. He glanced at María and Ray, before picking up the first sheet of paper and starting to read.

"A small article of only a couple of lines had appeared in the daily paper, *Revolución*, reporting Morgan's arrest, but no one on the island really believed the story. Rumors circulated throughout the city that Morgan had gone to the mountains to begin the fight against the communists, and that the regime was simply lying in order to hide an embarrassing truth from the people.

He was held first at the new headquarters of G2, the revolutionary government's secret police service, located in a sprawling mansion in Miramar, at the end of Fifth Avenue where the road to Jaimanitas Beach begins. The Directorate, as the building was then called, had cells and interrogation rooms, and around thirty full-time staff under the leadership of Ramiro Valdés, a close associate of Che Guevara.

For several weeks, Morgan was held incommunicado and subject to regular interrogations. Conducted largely without significant physical intimidation—Morgan was considered a hard man better tackled with the carrot than the stick—the interrogations were aimed at persuading him to incriminate other members of the Second Front in a counter-revolutionary movement that was, for the most part, a concocted scenario. He was told his wife was under house arrest with his children and that Jesús Carreras had also been arrested, but otherwise he knew nothing about what might be happening in the outside world. His interrogators also told him they had witnesses to the preparations for counter-revolution, in particular the movement of weapons and ammunition to the Hanabanilla farm complex and that two caches had been discovered there.

Morgan stonewalled. He knew he had to buy time and he just had to hope Menoyo and the others would use it well. Despite threats and even promises that he and María and the children would be allowed to leave the country if he named names, he gave nothing away.

He and Carreras were eventually transferred to the dreaded La Cabaña prison, the old fortress guarding the entrance to Havana Harbor, completed by the Spanish in 1744. It was the biggest fortress of its kind in all the Americas. The two men had been brought there to await trial.

Along with hundreds of others incarcerated by the regime—some critics of communism, some Batistianos, some former fighters from the Escambray and the Sierra, many of whom had fought alongside Castro only to fall foul of him later, students, common criminals and many who were innocent of any wrongdoing—Morgan and Carreras were now just numbers amongst a thousand or so others whose fates hung in the balance.

The prisoners were held in the cavernous *galeras* of La Cabaña. The former storerooms for ammunition magazines or barrack facilities were double-height tunnel spaces, with barrel-shaped roofs made of the same gray stone as the fortress walls but green with mould and lichens. The outward end of each of the twenty or so *galeras* faced the moat of La Cabaña and was open to the elements, save for two rows of thick metal bars spaced about a yard apart. At the inner end, also secured with thick black bars, two masonry watchtowers called *garitas* dominated the prison yard and could train their machine guns on anyone in the yard or the surrounding *galeras*.

Conditions were primitive. The men were crowded into spaces that might be adequate for two hundred, but were far too small to hold them all. A single latrine—no more than a hole in the floor—would cater for up to fifty men. One bucket of water a week was allocated to each man for washing. The floors of the *galeras* were filthy and stinking, and a breeding ground for diseases like the dysentery that afflicted many prisoners.

The bunks, stacked four high in the *galeras*, were mean and hard, but nevertheless, with too few beds or blankets to go round in the horribly overcrowded prison, bunk space was coveted and jealously guarded. Many had to sleep on the stone floors and do whatever they could to combat the rats and cockroaches that owned the prison's *galeras* by night and crawled over their faces and hands as they tried to steal a few hours sleep. The regime inside La Cabana was brutal. The early morning 'inspections,' often carried out in the middle of the night straight after the executions, were designed to instill terror in the inmates.

And every night—night after night—every prisoner in La Cabana could not help but hear the executions of men who had only a few hours before shared their *galeras*, and talked of their hopes and fears before being summoned to kangaroo trials, never to return. Executions were carried out in the early hours before dawn in accordance with Che Guevara's belief that the victims would be more compliant and easier to kill at such times.

But the inmates of La Cabana knew the real purpose of the nighttime executions was twofold and oddly contradictory—to obscure the deed from daylight scrutiny, while generating maximum psychological terror for the inmates of the prison awaiting their own trials.

In many ways, the nighttime executions reflected the dark and confused purposes of a revolution hijacked by fear. Some fears were real, very real. Not least, the revenge of the American government, frightened out of its wits by the threat of communists at home and abroad, capable of extreme prejudice against the red menace, without concern for the consequences. The new leaders of Cuba knew this and were convinced an invasion was imminent. Within just a few months, and only weeks after Morgan's trial, they would be proved right with the now infamous Bay of Pigs disaster. But many 'enemies' of the new Cuba were innocent men and women caught up in the hallucinations of a regime that saw shadowy threats everywhere.

William Morgan met the harsh reality of life in La Cabana with an extraordinary display of rigorous discipline and an apparently unbowed spirit.

In contrast to his friend and comrade Jesús Carreras, who went deep inside himself and tended to stay at the back of *galera* Seven, morose and silent, Morgan comported himself with military efficiency and a very public display of defiance.

Every morning, he would make his bed, ensuring the hospital corners were exactly forty-five degrees and that all wrinkles were smoothed out of the stained cotton.

He never hurried through the daily 'inspections,' where prisoners were forced to run the gauntlet of guards with sticks ready to beat them as they passed. Something in his demeanor and his reputation as a fearsome fighter allowed him to pass unharmed through the rows of guards, many of whom were either too afraid or too in awe of *el Americano* to dare strike him. Other prisoners stayed close to Morgan in the hope of coming under his protection.

In the prison yard, Morgan would perform his morning calisthenics as prescribed by the United States Army training manual. By the beginning of February 1961, he was in the best shape he'd been since the Escambray, and with the help of the appalling food in the prison, he'd dropped twenty pounds.

Squat thrusts, side benders, press-ups and sit-ups were the core of his twelve-exercise routine followed with unyielding vigor every day. With the exercises complete, Morgan would then engage in long periods of drill, loudly barking orders or reciting a 'Jody'—the traditional call and response work song of the army—most often taking both parts himself, though he welcomed any of the inmates who wanted to join in.

Morgan's calls of, "Right—turn!" "About—face" or "Platoon—halt!" echoed around the stone walls of the yard, and served their purpose in keeping his own spirits and those of the other prisoners up, whilst letting the guards and prison officials know he was there in a way they could not ignore."

Capaldi lifted his eyes to the committee to check he had their full attention. He did.

"William Morgan was called to trial with no prior warning at four o'clock on the afternoon of March 9, 1961. He marched in military fashion to meet his accusers, singing aloud *'As the Caissons Go Rolling Along'* to the cheers of the other inmates of La Cabana.

Morgan was the first to arrive in the makeshift courtroom, a former soldier's mess in the fortress, followed by his co-defendant Jesús Carreras and ten others facing charges of counter-revolutionary activities. His wife was to be tried in absentia as part of the same proceedings.

Before the trial began, the presiding officer of the court, *Capitán* George Robraño Marieges, gave the defendants and their counsels half an hour to talk over their defense. Dr. Jorge Luís Carro—Morgan's lawyer—was representing five defendants that day, including a young man who had been captured in the mountains of the Escambray on February third, just a month before the trial. The young man's name was Mario Marin.

The trial opened with a statement by the Assistant District Attorney of the Supreme Court, Dr. Fernando Flores Luís Ibarra, nicknamed *'charco de sangre'* or *'pool of blood.'* He called upon the tribunal of hastily assembled, unqualified jurors to hand down sentences of thirty years in prison for all the conspirators arraigned before them, except Morgan and Carreras. For the former comandantes of the Second Front of the Escambray, Dr. Ibarra demanded the death sentence.

Amongst the thirteen witnesses called to give evidence against Morgan and Carreras, many admitted under cross-examination by Dr. Carro they'd never met the defendants in person before that day. But the star witness for the prosecution knew both Morgan and Carreras personally.

Mario Marin had surrendered to the militia men he was fighting when he ran out of ammunition. He knew the penalty for taking up arms against the regime was death. In turning state's evidence and becoming the only defendant to plead guilty to the charges, Marin hoped he would earn a commuted sentence.

He testified that on two occasions to his knowledge, guns and ammunition were transported with Morgan's approval to the farm at Hanabanilla. He said that Carreras was a frequent visitor to Morgan's home, and was involved in planning and coordinating military action by rebel forces in Las Villas province. And he spoke of Morgan's contacts with Edel Montiel and other rebel groups.

Dr. Luís Carro, when he heard Marin's testimony, refused to represent the young man any further.

Morgan denied all the charges against him and said, 'I stand here innocent, and I guarantee this court that if I am found guilty I will walk to the execution wall with no escort, with moral strength and with a clear conscience. I have defended this revolution because I believe in it.'

Within an hour, the five-man tribunal returned their verdicts on the twelve defendants in the courtroom and on María Morgan. Three were acquitted. Seven were found guilty and sentenced to various terms in prison of up to thirty years. Mario Marin was sentenced to fifteen years. Mrs. Jensen, here beside me, was sentenced to thirty years in absentia.

William Morgan and Jesús Carreras were found guilty on all charges and sentenced to death. Morgan and Carreras were taken from the courtroom and locked in one of La Cabana's *capillas*, the tiny chapels that were once used for prayer by the soldiers of the Spanish garrison. Now, they were used to keep prisoners awaiting their executions.

At around eleven o'clock the same evening, Morgan was taken from the *capilla* to the prison office, where, according to fellow prisoner John Martino, who later wrote a book detailing his experiences and his acquaintance with William

Morgan, a woman, thought to be Morgan's sister-in-law Betania, brought two young children to see him. Morgan was allowed to spend half an hour in the office with his children before being returned to the *capilla*."

Capaldi looked up at the committee bench and then glanced at María and Ray sitting beside him. He knew how painful this was for her, even after so many years. He'd talked with her about what he would say and she'd agreed. But still, he wondered if he'd made the right call in reliving all this in front of his client. It was then that María reached over and put her hand on his arm as if to grant permission. Capaldi cleared his throat and went on.

"There is no record of the last few hours Morgan and Carreras spent together locked in the tiny chapel. We know a priest was present, a Father Dario Casado, and we know he took a letter from Morgan and smuggled it out of the prison. The letter was addressed to Morgan's wife.

At approximately two-thirty in the morning, guards came to the *capilla* and took Jesús Carreras away. He was led through the *galeras* and down the narrow stone steps leading to La Cabana's dry moat and *el Paredón. The wall.*

The prisoners of La Cabana were awake as they always were on execution nights. And they did not have long to wait for the familiar shouts of the officer in charge calling his men to aim and fire.

The ragged volley of rifle shots rang out an instant later. Then came the terrible pause when no one, prisoner and guard alike, could speak or move a muscle or even breathe with any ease; interminable seconds that made men want to cry out, to scream and protest the injustice of another man's fate they might very well share in the nights to come.

The awful relief of the coup de grâce was brutal and perfunctory, but almost welcome. The single shot splintered the air, reverberating around the walls and *galeras* of the stone fortress as it always did, leaving behind a silence so deep and so profound that the hammering of coffin nails seemed like jumbled, long-delayed echoes.

William Morgan would have heard the firing squad volley, the coup de grâce and the silence that followed. Five minutes after, he would have heard the boots of the guards on the stone floor coming toward the *capilla* and the sound of keys unlocking the door.

By all reports, he was calm as the officer in charge of the execution detail read the formalities from a paper in his hand. I quote, in translation from the original: 'William Alexander Morgan, you have been found guilty of treason and sentenced to death. You had three requests. To see your wife. Request denied. To speak with *Il Maximo*, Fidel Castro. Request denied. To have your sentence carried out immediately. Request granted.'

The officer took a smart step backwards, leaving the doorway clear for Morgan to leave the *capilla*. Morgan gave the officer a crisp salute and went out to take his place between the four waiting guards.

Either side of the poorly lit, broad tunnel, the inner openings of the *galeras* were crowded with the pale faces of the other prisoners pressed against the black metal bars. And yet not one of them made a sound. Morgan stood to attention. All that could be heard was the clank of the *capilla* door and the jangling of keys as the officer locked the empty chapel and took his place at the head of the detail.

Someone—nobody would ever be sure who the man was—began to whistle slowly and deliberately the tune of Morgan's favorite marching song, '*As the Caissons Go Rolling Along.*' The first two bars were solo, but as the officer called '*¡Avance!*' and the detail moved forward, others joined in, and then others still, until the whistling of almost a thousand men filled the gloomy tunnel like a choir in a cathedral.

As Morgan and the detail of guards approached the end of the tunnel, the prisoners began to beat a steady rhythm on the bars and bunks of the *galeras* using boots, metal cups, anything that would make a noise, and a low chant began to grow in intensity and drown out the whistling.

'*Morgan! Morgan! Morgan!*'

Stepping out from the dark tunnel into the sultry night air, Morgan had to squint and cover his eyes at the blinding arc lights strategically placed behind the firing squad and trained on *el Paredón*. He noticed Father Dario Casado waiting for him in his long black cassock and white stole at the bottom of the stone steps. He could not hear the distant sounds of the penultimate night of Havana's annual carnival still pulsing on the streets of Havana and floating across the narrow neck of water to La Cabana.

Nor would he have been aware of the Swiss Chargé d'Affaires' attempts to secure clemency for him. With the American Embassy in Havana now closed and diplomatic relations severed, it was hardly surprising that no representations on Morgan's behalf were made by any United States agency.

A personal appeal from Morgan's mother was addressed to President Osvaldo Dorticos and delivered by hand to the regime's Foreign Ministry immediately after the verdict was returned. No response was ever received.

With the chanting of the prisoners rebounding around the walls of the moat and the prison *galeras*, Morgan took the last step to the dusty ground of the moat and stopped to make the sign of the cross in front of Father Dario Casado. In return, he received a blessing from the young priest who had given him the last rites in the *capilla* just an hour before.

Beside Father Casado, Morgan's lawyer, Dr. Jorge Luís Carro, was waiting. Morgan thanked Carro for all he'd done and embraced him, saying, 'I am a believing Catholic and not afraid. Now I'll find what's on the other side.'

As the chants from the *galeras* began to die down, a soldier holding a length of rope ready to tie Morgan's hands was waiting by the wooden killing post, just a few yards away from Dr. Carro. The earth around the base of the post was wet with the blood still soaking into the ground. If Morgan thought about his friend Carreras who'd died in that spot just minutes before, he didn't show it. Instead, he looked directly at the young soldier, smiled and said, '*Momento por favor.*'

Morgan walked boldly toward the line of soldiers, and when he reached the first of them he stopped dead in front of the young man and saluted.

'*Estáte tranquillo. Te perdono.*' *Be calm. I forgive you.*

The soldier was so surprised, he did no more than blink rapidly and stand a little stiffer at attention.

Morgan moved to the next man and said the same words and gave the same salute. One by one, he traversed the line until he reached the officer in charge. But before he could speak, an impatient voice barked out an order from behind the line of the firing squad.

Morgan looked to see who had spoken. But with the blinding arc lights shining directly into his eyes, it would have been impossible to identify the three or four silhouetted figures standing in the shadows. And yet he may well have recognized the voice.

Morgan turned back to the officer and saluted, telling him to have courage.

'*Que tenga coraje.*'

Then he made a sharp about-turn and marched the fifteen yards to the sandbagged el Paredõn where the soldier with the rope was still waiting.

'*Estáte tranquillo. Te perdono,*' he said to the soldier. The soldier did not meet his gaze, but continued to tie his hands behind his back.

Morgan stood up straight in front of the killing post. The soldier backed away.

The same voice he'd heard a few moments before shouted to him to kneel and beg for his life.

'*¡Arrodíllese y suplique perdón!*'

'*¡No me arrodillo para ningún hombre,*' Morgan shouted in response. *I kneel for no man!*

Before any order was given, a single shot from a high-powered Belgian sniper's rifle rang out. The bullet struck

Morgan's right knee, shattering the patella and almost causing him to fall to the ground.

Somehow, he found the strength to remain on his feet despite the agonizing pain. He spat out in defiance and forced himself to stand up straight once more. Seconds later, a second shot hit him in the left leg and this time he crumpled, his face hitting hard on the blood-soaked ground, his mouth gritty with dust. Though his breathing was coming fast, Morgan made no sound at the excruciating pain he must have felt, and no cry for quarter.

'¡Ya ve!' the same voice shouted. '¡Le hicimos arrodillarse después de todo!' We made you kneel after all.

The bolt action on the Belgian rifle could be clearly heard as the sharpshooter reloaded.

When it came, the third round hit Morgan in the left shoulder where he lay, sending him flying backwards onto his roped hands. The fourth, a moment later, caught him in the right shoulder, smashing the collarbone and spinning him in the opposite direction.

And still, Morgan did not cry out.

An officer, none could later identify, walked toward him carrying a Thompson submachine gun. The officer stood a few yards away, aimed from the hip and emptied the entire magazine into Morgan's chest.

Morgan was no longer moving and was surely already dead when a second officer—another of the men who had been standing in the shadows—walked through the firing squad that had not fired a shot and went to the body on the ground.

Taking out his sidearm, this man fired five shots into Morgan's head.

There were eyewitnesses to Morgan's death, but none were able to recall who the men in the shadows were or whose voice it was that ordered Morgan to kneel, nor could they identify with any certainty those responsible for the obscene travesty that finally ended his life.

We will probably never know the truth.

William Morgan's body, encased in a rough pine coffin, was handed over to his sister-in-law Betania, and he was buried alongside his friend and comrade Jesús Carreras at noon the next day in the Carreras family crypt.

Neither man had taken up arms against the regime, a crime that would merit the death sentence under the laws of the revolutionary regime. For aiding and abetting rebel forces and secreting arms that might be used against the regime's forces, a maximum of nine years in prison was the appropriate punishment.

So why did these men die? Why were they murdered in front of a firing squad assembled that night only to provide the semblance of an official sanction?

Again, we may never find a definitive answer. For Morgan in particular, there is some circumstantial evidence of a conspiracy to eliminate him. A short while after Morgan's execution, Capitan Delio Gómez Ochoa, the man who led the abortive invasion of the Dominican Republic and a close personal friend of Castro, was suddenly released without any explanation from a life sentence in the Dominican Republic. Around the same time, Trujillo and Castro—mortal enemies at a personal level and opposites in their politics—concluded a deal that meant a beleaguered Cuba could buy rice from the Republic at a quarter of the going rate.

But whatever the truth of those rumors, there's no need for a complicated conspiracy to explain William Morgan's death. A perfect storm of malevolent forces had been gathering around him for some time.

The dictator Trujillo, the man who had put a five hundred thousand dollar reward on his head, wanted Morgan dead. The Castro regime hated his popularity with the people and feared his capacity to organize against them, and wanted him eliminated as a threat. And the United States government, in denying him his right to citizenship, gave tacit approval for the extremists of both the right and left to conspire together and finally crush him.

William Morgan was not a CIA agent, nor was he a communist. But in those difficult days and troubled times, taking the center ground, finding a third way, was enough to get you killed.

William Morgan was his own man, a maverick yes, a man searching for a cause, for something to believe in, to live and die for, a man who found that cause in fighting for the freedom of the people of Cuba and, at the same time, found his own place in the world. He also found the love of his life. In combining a belief in individual liberty with social justice, Morgan was a rebel, but to his core, an American rebel.

In conclusion, Senator, and with your permission," said Capaldi, "I'd like to enter in the record William Morgan's last letter to his wife, written in 1961."

Capaldi reached into the file on his desk and took out a fragile, yellowed piece of paper with ragged tears at the edges of the folds. He glanced at María.

"I have in my hands the original document, sir," said Capaldi. "Facing certain death, William Morgan was content to leave history to decide his guilt or innocence. He declared his love for his wife and said he did not want revenge or bitterness or anger in response to his execution. He asked for only one thing. That one day, the truth be told."

Capaldi put the fragile paper down on the table in front of him and looked up at Senator Hawkes.

"I'd like to thank this committee for granting William Morgan's last request."

72

After two long days in the subterranean committee room, Ray and María stood side by side on the Capitol's steps and breathed in the cool afternoon air, as if surfacing after a long, deep dive. Around them, shoals of uncertain tourists were vying for position in posing photographs of their friends and loved ones against the fleeting backdrop of Washington in winter.

"Excuse me, please?" said a portly man in his forties with a European accent that was hard to place. Holland maybe, or Germany. "Would you take the photo for us?"

He held out a silver-colored compact camera and made a kind of half bow to Ray.

"Just here, press here. Thank you."

The portly man retreated to stand with a plump woman wearing a hat with earflaps, a sensible backpack and white trainers. She was holding what was probably a city guide in her hand. The man stood stiffly beside her, but then relaxed and smiled and put his arm around the woman.

"Okay?" said Ray.

"Okay!" said the man.

Ray took the shot and handed the camera back.

"Thank you so much," said the man. "I can do the same for you, perhaps?" he said.

"That's okay, thank you," said Ray.

The man gave another little bow before he and his partner melted back into the crowd and were gone.

Ray turned back to stand alongside María. As they looked west down the mile-long National Mall, they could see the orange disc of the setting sun, punctured just a few degrees off-centre by the austere geometry of the Washington Monument. Without taking her eyes from the view, she took his arm. And with the red and yellow of winter leaves aflame, still clinging to the shiny black branches of the trees lining the avenue, they talked about hope, though neither of them said a single word.

AFTERWORD

William Morgan's widow won her long battle for the reinstatement of his citizenship in 2007.

At the time of writing, she continues to lobby both United States agencies and the Cuban authorities to assist her in having Morgan's remains repatriated to America for burial in his hometown. Naturally, the ongoing freeze in diplomatic relations between the two countries hampers her case.

William Morgan and his widow are the heroes of this story and I humbly dedicate this partial version of history to them both. They would be the first to acknowledge the many unsung heroes of the revolution, men and women who suffered under Batista's tyranny, who made extraordinary sacrifices in the cause of freedom and sometimes paid with their lives. History does not record their names but this book is also dedicated to their memory.

Of those cited by history as heroes, people like Huber Matos and Camilio Cienfuegos, one man stands out for me personally, not least because of his commitment to the cause of freedom and reconciliation more than fifty years after the revolution.

His name is Eloy Gutierrez Menoyo. He is a true hero in the original sense of the word, the Greek sense of 'a man who, in the face of danger and adversity or from a position of weakness, displays courage and the will for self-sacrifice, for the greater good of humanity.'

He returned to Cuba and to the Escambray mountains in 1962 with a small band of men in order to take up arms against the Castro regime. He was betrayed and spent 22 years in prison. Menoyo was finally released on December 20th 1986 following representations by the Spanish Prime Minister Felipe González Márquez.

He spent some time in Spain before returning to America where he founded Cambio Cubano, an organization dedicated to peaceful transition towards democracy and pluralism. In the complex and often tense, sometimes violent world of Cuban-American politics, Menoyo advocates a simple philosophy, namely that all sides should reconcile with the past in order to embrace a better future.

After visiting Cuba and meeting Fidel Castro—for which action Menoyo encountered much criticism, particularly amongst Cuban interest groups in America—he decided to base himself in Havana, though it meant leaving his wife and children who live in America, in order to facilitate dialogue with the regime. As if that were not enough, at one time, the US Government threatened to fine him $250,000 for violating travel restrictions between the two countries. To date, the regime in Cuba has not responded to his initiative.

Nevertheless, Menoyo continues to wait and hope. His father was a social democrat and Menoyo, like Morgan, who learned at his side, believes passionately in a third way between the extremes of left and right. Extremism is the easy way out. The middle way, far from being easy, is the hardest road of all. It is also the best way.

Neither Fidel Castro nor his brother Raul, head of state as I write this in 2012, has been prepared to talk to Menoyo. But perhaps with a younger generation emerging, with new ways to talk directly to others via the internet, to tell their stories and to bear witness, Menoyo's hope for a brighter future is becoming slowly more infectious, more irresistible, and above all, more possible. Perhaps a new generation might just be able to create a bridgehead between rich and poor, north and south, left and right.

Now is certainly the time for the government of the United States to end 'el bloqueo', the fifty-year embargo against Cuba. Far from encouraging greater democracy and respect for human rights, the blockade serves only to create a scapegoat for the entrenched attitudes of the regime. Now is certainly the time for the Cuban regime to put an end, once and for all time, to the persecution of their political opponents.

How to begin? America must acknowledge the often baleful influence of its extraordinary power to threaten the island's independence. From the intervention of 1898 and the Platt amendment, to The Bay of Pigs and Helms-Burton, to gangsters and businesses that behaved like gangsters, perhaps the moral imperative lies with America to redeem the past and take the lead on change. For every action, there's a reaction and maybe, just maybe, that reaction might be towards internal reform in Cuba.

Mistakes have been made on all sides for half a century or more, but surely, there is a middle road for the leaders of both nations to explore. Surely, there is room for the people of Cuba to begin to hope for a better future. Surely, the time has come to redeem the past and to begin to live in the present, 'for life, liberty and the pursuit of happiness' to become more than words on paper, for the leaders of both nations to unclench the fist and to offer instead, the hand of peace.

AUTHOR'S NOTE

American Rebel harks back to an old tradition in narrative, one that has fallen out of fashion over time, where the real and the imaginary, truth and myth, fact and fiction, are blended to create a story that is the sum of all these elements combined.

Many of the characters in this book lived, or indeed are still living, full independent lives of their own. Many of the events you have witnessed actually happened. Others are the product of imagination alone. But some events did not happen as described in this book, just as some characters had no independent existence outside the world of *American Rebel*. A few are amalgams, composites or facets of real people documented in newspapers or books; others are pure invention, conjured to meet the demands of a good story. Whether or not this is a legitimate method of dealing with history, I leave to you, the reader, to decide.

So how to find your bearings? What can you rely on as truth and what must be seen as fiction? I could of course argue that the distinction is not so important, but that would be disingenuous. Instead, let me offer concrete clues to the overall balance of truth and fiction in the stories of the main characters; enough, I hope, to satisfy natural curiosity, but also to encourage the reader to look further into the written history.

Morgan really did lose a buddy called Jack Turner. Some accounts have Turner's body showing up in the Havana harbor, the victim of Batista's secret police. Others tell a different story, claiming Turner died in a prison cell under interrogation. Others still, claim Jack Turner had nothing to do with Morgan's decision to go to Cuba. I have chosen to present an imaginary scene to begin the story that might well have happened and that is not contradicted by any of the available documentary evidence.

Morgan was a gunrunner and mobster before joining the rebels and he did make regular trips from Miami to the Cuban coast with guns. He really did love comic books, something that inspired the wonderful illustrations by Jeremy Jones. I have tried to write a book that Morgan himself might enjoy reading.

He really did shoot at planes with only a submachine gun and he inspired the men he fought with in a way his US Army record would never suggest. He really did marry in the mountains, start fish farms and die with extraordinary valor. His wife really did drug the guards and make her escape to an embassy and she really did serve twelve years behind bars in appalling conditions, having been found guilty of treason. She arrived in America in a small boat with nothing, exactly as depicted in these pages.

Ray Halliwell, in contrast, did not have an independent life outside of this book. More's the pity, because he will figure prominently in forthcoming works. American Rebel is the first in a series of books set in various locations around the world with Ray as a lead character. The next, yet to be titled is set in Eastern Europe.

The battle to restore Morgan's citizenship happened and did take almost fifty years to come to pass and to reach a conclusion. I have shown that event happening in front of a Senatorial Committee comprised of imaginary characters, which I hope may serve to represent, in crude terms at least, something like the spectrum of American political conviction.

I have changed names. Not so much in Cuba, but more so in America. I have done this primarily to protect Morgan's widow and her children from unwanted intrusions by press or interested persons, though always conscious that her story has been covered in national press, expecially since the fight to clear Morgan's name and recover his citizenship. However, I have changed names and places in order that I do not intrude more than necessary and so that privacy is preserved as far as I am able. Otherwise, the essential facts remain substantially true to life.

In fact, the key to *American Rebel* might almost be drawn along these lines: All that surrounds Ray is fictional—Pam, for instance, and Ray's life in Chicago—but, I trust, representative of the character and the times. All that surrounds Morgan—bar Ray, naturally, and the name changes I've mentioned—tends to be based on fact, as supported by a variety of independent sources.

ABOUT THE AUTHOR

Joss Gibson studied English and American Literature at the University of Kent at Canterbury before becoming a journalist.

From local papers and radio, he moved to television current affairs as a director and then film drama, initially as a location manager and first assistant director, and later as a producer, winning an Emmy Award. At various times he has also worked as a scriptwriter and teacher of creative writing, psychology and media.

Joss Gibson lives in the south of England and in France.

6813046R00233

Printed in Great Britain
by Amazon.co.uk, Ltd.,
Marston Gate.